Prodigal
Summer

By the Same Author

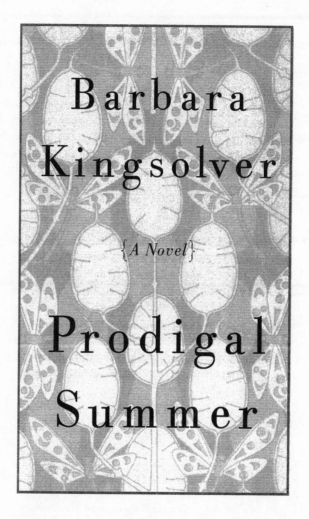

Barbara Kingsolver

{*A Novel*}

Prodigal Summer

HarperCollins*Publishers*

HarperCollins books may be purchased for educational, business, or sales promotional use. For information, please write: Special Markets Department, HarperCollins Publishers Inc., 10 East 53rd Street, New York, NY 10022.

Information about the poetry, translations, and literary criticism of Aaron Kramer (published 1938–1998) is available on the website www.aaronkramer. com. Aaron Kramer's personal papers are archived at the Special Collections Library of the University of Michigan.

FIRST EDITION

Original artwork by Paul Mirocha

Designed by Nicola Ferguson

Library of Congress Cataloging-in-Publication Data is available upon request.

ISBN 0-06-019965-2

00 01 02 03 04 RRD 10 9 8 7 6 5 4 3 2 1

—for Steven, Camille, and Lily,
and for wildness, where it lives

Acknowledgments

This novel grew from soil richly blessed by my Virginia friends and neighbors. I'm especially grateful to Neta Findley for a friendship that has brought me home, and to her late husband, Bill, and their son Joe, whose stories and humor have enriched my life and this book. A tithe of my future apple crop goes to Fred Hebard of the American Chestnut Foundation for all kinds of help and an education in trees; the foundation's chestnut breeding program—a far more systematic project than the one invented for this tale—will someday return the American chestnut to American woodlands. Thanks also to Dayle, Paige, and Kyla, our family's family. I'm grateful to Jim and Pam Watson for carriage rides, good humor, and good will; Miss Amy for peace of mind; Randy Lowe for good advice; and the Cooperative Extension Service for answering perhaps the strangest questions they've ever been asked. Bill Kittrell of the Nature Conservancy provided valuable insights, as did Braven Beaty, Kristy Clark, Steve Lindeman, and Claiborne Woodall. Finally, I'm forever indebted to Felicia Mitchell for laundrymat friendship and the poetry of yard sales, and for taking me to the farm that first evening when I almost didn't go.

In the wider world I'm beholden to a network of friends and colleagues larger than I can ever thank by name, though some rise to the top: blessed thanks to Emma Hardesty for years of our lives; to Terry Karten for believing in literature in spite of everything; to Jane Beirn for graciously connecting the private me with the public world; to Walter Thabit for Arabic curses; to Frances Goldin for recipes, Yiddish syntax, infallible instincts, unconditional love, and, basically, everything—for more than you, who could ask. I'm grateful to the family of Aaron Kramer for their generosity in allowing me to use his exquisite poem "Prothalamium," from *The Thunder of the Grass* (International Publishers, New York); in discovering the beauty and breadth of his life's work as a writer of passion and social conscience, I feel I am finding a kindred spirit. I thank Chris Cokinos for his wonderful book *Hope Is the Thing with Feathers*; Carrie Newcomer for invisible threads; W. D. Hamilton (in memoriam) for boldness and brilliance; Edward O. Wilson for those things and also devotion. Dan Papaj brought to my attention many wonderful lepidopteran mysteries, and solved others. Robert Pyle also helped answer butterfly and moth questions. Mike Finkel's article "The Ultimate Survivor" (*Audubon*, May–June 1999) introduced me to a new way of looking at coyotes. Paul Mirocha turned my spare suggestions for the endpapers into a work of art.

For their comments on various drafts of the manuscript I thank Steven Hopp, Emma Hardesty, Frances Goldin, Sydelle Kramer, Terry Karten, Fenton Johnson, Arthur Blaustein, Jim Malusa, Sonya Norman, Rob Kingsolver, Fred Hebard, Felicia Mitchell, and the enthusiastic chorus at HarperCollins; all of it helped. Any errors of fact that have persisted in the face of all this expertise are supremely my own.

I'm pretty sure I owe my particular way of looking at the world, colored heavily in greens, to my parents' choosing to rear me in the wrinkle on the map that lies between farms and wildness, and to my brother, Rob, mentor and coconspirator in snake catching and paw-paw hunting. My sister, Ann, has expanded her soul for my support in ways that sometimes resemble wings. My daughters, Camille and Lily, are such experts in grace and wonder that they deliver me a world baked fresh daily. And for Steven, whose perfect ear and steady hand were beside me through this book as they are through life altogether, I offer up my thanks to the fates of mate choice and can't believe my luck.

Prothalamium

Come, all you who are not satisfied
as ruler in a lone, wallpapered room
full of mute birds, and flowers that falsely bloom,
and closets choked with dreams that long ago died!

Come, let us sweep the old streets—like a bride:
sweep out dead leaves with a relentless broom;
prepare for Spring, as though he were our groom
for whose light footstep eagerly we bide.

We'll sweep out shadows, where the rats long fed;
sweep out our shame—and in its place we'll make
a bower for love, a splendid marriage-bed
fragrant with flowers aquiver for the Spring.
And when he comes, our murdered dreams shall wake;
and when he comes, all the mute birds shall sing.

—Aaron Kramer

Prodigal
Summer

{ I }

Predators

er body moved with the frankness that comes from solitary habits. But solitude is only a human presumption. Every quiet step is thunder to beetle life underfoot; every choice is a world made new for the chosen. All secrets are witnessed.

If someone in this forest had been watching her—a man with a gun, for instance, hiding inside a copse of leafy beech trees—he would have noticed how quickly she moved up the path and how direly she scowled at the ground ahead of her feet. He would have judged her an angry woman on the trail of something hateful.

He would have been wrong. She was frustrated, it's true, to be following tracks in the mud she couldn't identify. She was used to being sure. But if she'd troubled to inspect her own mind on this humid, sunlit morning, she would have declared herself happy. She loved the air after a hard rain, and the way a forest of dripping leaves fills itself with a sibilant percussion that empties your head of words. Her body was free to follow its own rules: a long-legged gait too fast for companionship, unself-conscious squats in the path where she needed to touch broken foliage, a braid of hair nearly as thick as her forearm falling over her shoulder to sweep the ground whenever she bent down. Her limbs rejoiced to be outdoors again, out of her tiny cabin whose log walls had grown furry and over-bearing during the long spring rains. The frown was pure concentration, nothing more. Two years alone had given her a blind person's indifference to the look on her own face.

All morning the animal trail had led her uphill, ascending the mountain, skirting a rhododendron slick, and now climbing into an old-growth forest whose steepness had spared it from ever being logged. But even here, where a good oak-hickory canopy sheltered the ridge top, last night's rain had pounded through hard enough to obscure the tracks. She knew the animal's size from the path it had left through the glossy undergrowth of mayapples, and that was enough to speed up her heart. It could be what she'd been looking for these two years and more. This lifetime. But to know for sure she needed details, especially the faint claw mark beyond the toe pad that distinguishes canid from feline. That would be the first thing to vanish in a hard rain, so it wasn't going to appear to her now, however hard she looked. Now it would take more than tracks, and on this sweet, damp morning at the beginning of the world, that was fine with her. She could be a patient tracker. Eventually the animal would give itself away with a mound of scat (which might have dissolved in the rain, too) or something else, some sign particular to its species. A bear will leave claw marks on trees and even bite the bark sometimes, though this was no bear. It was the size of a German shepherd, but no house pet, either. The dog that had laid this trail, if dog it was, would have to be a wild and hungry one to be out in such a rain.

She found a spot where it had circled a chestnut stump, probably for scent marking. She studied the stump: an old giant, raggedly rotting its way backward into the ground since its death by ax or blight.

Toadstools dotted the humus at its base, tiny ones, brilliant orange, with delicately ridged caps like open parasols. The downpour would have obliterated such fragile things; these must have popped up in the few hours since the rain stopped—after the animal was here, then. Inspired by its ammonia. She studied the ground for a long time, unconscious of the elegant length of her nose and chin in profile, unaware of her left hand moving near her face to disperse a cloud of gnats and push stray hair out of her eyes. She squatted, steadied herself by placing her fingertips in the moss at the foot of the stump, and pressed her face to the musky old wood. Inhaled.

"Cat," she said softly, to nobody. Not what she'd hoped for, but a good surprise to find evidence of a territorial bobcat on this ridge. The mix of forests and wetlands in these mountains could be excellent core habitat for cats, but she knew they mostly kept to the limestone river cliffs along the Virginia-Kentucky border. And yet here one was. It explained the cries she'd heard two nights ago, icy shrieks in the rain, like a woman's screaming. She'd been sure it was a bobcat but still lost sleep over it. No human could fail to be moved by such human-sounding anguish. Remembering it now gave her a shiver as she balanced her weight on her toes and pushed herself back upright to her feet.

And there he stood, looking straight at her. He was dressed in boots and camouflage and carried a pack larger than hers. His rifle was no joke—a thirty-thirty, it looked like. Surprise must have stormed all over her face before she thought to arrange it for human inspection. It happened, that she ran into hunters up here. But she always saw them first. This one had stolen her advantage—he'd seen inside her.

"Eddie Bondo," is what he'd said, touching his hat brim, though it took her a moment to work this out.

"What?"

"That's my name."

"Good Lord," she said, able to breathe out finally. "I didn't ask your name."

"You needed to know it, though."

Cocky, she thought. Or cocked, rather. Like a rifle, ready to go off. "What would I need your name for? You fixing to give me a story I'll want to tell later?" she asked quietly. It was a tactic learned from her father, and the way of mountain people in general—to be quiet when most agitated.

"That I can't say. But I won't bite." He grinned—apologetically, it seemed. He was very much younger than she. His left hand reached up to his shoulder, fingertips just brushing the barrel of the rifle strapped to his shoulder. "And I don't shoot girls."

"Well. Wonderful news."

Bite, he'd said, with the northerner's clipped *i.* An outsider, intruding on this place like kudzu vines. He was not very tall but deeply muscular in the way that shows up through a man's clothing, in his wrists and neck and posture: a build so accustomed to work that it seems tensed even when at ease. He said, "You sniff stumps, I see."

"I do."

"You got a good reason for that?"

"Yep."

"You going to tell me what it is?"

"Nope."

Another pause. She watched his hands, but what pulled on her was the dark green glint of his eyes. He observed her acutely, seeming to evaluate her hill-inflected vowels for the secrets behind her "yep" and "nope." His grin turned down on the corners instead of up, asking a curved parenthetical question above his right-angled chin. She could not remember a more compelling combination of features on any man she'd ever seen.

"You're not much of a talker," he said. "Most girls I know, they'll yap half the day about something they haven't done yet and might not get around to."

"Well, then. I'm not most girls you know."

She wondered if she was antagonizing him. She didn't have a

gun, and he did, though he'd promised not to shoot. Or bite, for that matter. They stood without speaking. She measured the silence by the cloud that crossed the sun, and by the two full wood-thrush songs that rang suddenly through the leaves and hung in the air between herself and this man, her—prey? No, her trespasser. *Predator* was a strong presumption.

"All right if I just follow you for a while?" he asked politely.

"No," she snapped. "That wouldn't suit me."

Man or boy, what was he? His grin dissolved, and he seemed suddenly wounded by her curtness, like a scolded son. She wondered about the proper tone, how to do that. She knew how to run off a hunter who'd forgotten when deer season ended—that was her job. But usually by this point in the conversation, it was over. And manners had not been her long suit to begin with, even a lifetime ago when she lived in a brick house, neatly pressed between a husband and neighbors. She pushed four fingers into her hair, the long brown bolt of it threaded with silver, and ran them backward from her hairline to tuck the unraveled threads back into the braid at her nape.

"I'm tracking," she said quietly. "Two people make more than double the noise of one. If you're a hunter I expect you'd know that already."

"I don't see your gun."

"I don't believe I'm carrying one. I believe we're on National Forest land, inside of a game-protection area where there's no hunting."

"Well, then," said Eddie Bondo. "That would explain it."

"Yes, it would."

He stood his ground, looking her up and down for the longest while. Long enough for her to understand suddenly that Eddie Bondo—man, not child—had taken off all her layers and put them back on again in the right order. The dark-green nylon and Gore-Tex were regulation Forest Service, the cotton flannel was hers, likewise the silk thermal long johns, and what a man might find of

5

interest underneath all that she had no idea. No one had been there in quite a while.

Then he was gone. Birdsong clattered in the space between trees, hollow air that seemed vast now and suddenly empty. He had ducked headfirst into the rhododendrons, leaving behind no reason to think he'd ever been there at all.

A hot blush was what he left her, burning on the skin of her neck.

~

She went to bed with Eddie Bondo all over her mind and got up with a government-issue pistol tucked in her belt. The pistol was something she was supposed to carry for bear, for self-defense, and she told herself that was half right.

For two days she saw him everywhere—ahead of her on the path at dusk; in her cabin with the moonlit window behind him. In dreams. On the first evening she tried to distract or deceive her mind with books, and on the second she carefully bathed with her teakettle and cloth and the soap she normally eschewed because it assaulted the noses of deer and other animals with the only human smell they knew, that of hunters—the scent of a predator. Both nights she awoke in a sweat, disturbed by the fierce, muffled sounds of bats mating in the shadows under her porch eaves, aggressive copulations that seemed to be collisions of strangers.

And now, here, in the flesh in broad daylight beside this chestnut stump. For when he showed up again, it was in the same spot. This time he carried his pack but no rifle. Her pistol was inside her jacket, loaded, with the safety on.

Once again she'd been squatting by the stump looking for sign, very sure this time that she was on the trail of what she wanted. No question, these tracks were canine: the female, probably, whose den she'd located fourteen days ago. Male or female, it had paused by this stump to notice the bobcat's mark, which might have intrigued or offended or maybe meant nothing at all to it. Hard for a human ever to know that mind.

And once again—as if her rising up from that stump had conjured Eddie Bondo, as if he had derived from the rush of blood from her head—he stood smiling at her.

"There you are," he said. "Not most girls I know."

Her heart beat hard enough to dim her hearing in pulses.

"I'm the *only* one you know, looks like, if you'd be hanging around the Zebulon National Forest. Which you seem to be."

He was hatless this time, black-haired and just a little shaggy like a crow in the misty rain. His hair had the thick, glossy texture she envied slightly, for it was perfectly straight and easy and never would tangle. He spread his hands. "Look, ranger lady. No gun. Behold a decent man abiding by the law."

"So I see."

"More than I can say for you," he added. "Sniffing stumps."

"No, I couldn't lay any claim on being decent. Or a man."

His grin grew a shade darker. "That I can see."

I have a gun. He can't hurt me, but she knew as she thought these words that some other tables had turned. He'd come back. She had willed him back to this spot. And she would wait him out this time. He didn't speak for a minute or more. Then gave in. "I'm sorry," he said.

"For what?"

"For pestering you. But I'm determined to follow you up this trail today, for just a little while. If you don't mind."

"What is it you're so determined to find out?"

"What a nice girl like you is sniffing for in this big old woods. It's been keeping me up nights."

He'd thought of her, then. At night.

"I'm not Little Red Riding Hood, if that's what's worrying you. I'm twice as old as you are." *Twiced as old,* she'd said, a long-extinguished hillbilly habit tunneling into her unpracticed talk.

"I doubt that sincerely," he said.

She waited for more, and he offered this: "I'll keep a little distance, if you like."

What she didn't like was the idea of his being behind her. "My preference would be for you to walk on ahead, and please take care not to step on the trail of this animal I'm tracking. If you can see to keep off of it." She pointed to the three-day-old cat tracks, not the fresher trail in the leaf mold on the down side of the trail.

"Yes ma'am, I believe I can do that." He bowed slightly, turned, and walked ahead, his feet keeping an expert's distance from the tracks and hardly turning the leaf mold, either. He was good. She let him almost disappear into the foliage ahead, then she took up the trail of the two males walking side by side, cat and man. She wanted to watch him walk, to watch his body without his knowing it.

It was late afternoon, already something close to dark on the north side of the mountain, where rhododendrons huddled in the cleft of every hollow. In their dense shade the ground was bare and slick. A month from now the rhododendrons would be covered with their big spheres of pink blossoms like bridesmaids' bouquets, almost too show-off fancy for a wildwood flower on this lonely mountain. But for now their buds still slept. Now it was only the damp earth that blossomed in fits and throes: trout lilies, spring beauties, all the understory wildflowers that had to hurry through a whole life cycle between May's first warmth—while sunlight still reached through the bare limbs—and the shaded darkness of a June forest floor. Way down around the foot of this mountain in the valley farmland, springtime would already be winding down by the first week of May, but the tide of wildflowers that swept up the mountainsides had only just arrived up here at four thousand feet. On this path the hopeful flower heads were so thick they got crushed underfoot. In a few more weeks the trees would finish leafing out here, the canopy would close, and this bloom would pass on. Spring would move higher up to awaken the bears and finally go out like a flame, absorbed into the dark spruce forest on the scalp of Zebulon Mountain. But here and now, spring heaved in its randy moment. Everywhere you looked, something was fighting for time, for light, the kiss of pollen, a connection of sperm and egg and another chance.

He paused twice on the trail ahead of her, once beside a flame azalea so covered with flowers it resembled a burning bush, and once for no reason she could see. But he never turned around. He must be listening for her step, she thought. At least that, or maybe not. It really didn't matter.

They reached the point where the old bobcat trail went straight up the slope, and she let him go. She waited until he was out of sight, and then turned downhill instead, stepping sideways down the steep slope until her feet found familiar purchase on one of the Forest Service trails. She maintained miles of these trails, a hundred or more over the course of months, but this one never got overgrown because it ran between her cabin and an overlook she loved. The fresher tracks had diverged from the bobcat trail and here they were again, leading exactly where she thought they'd go: downhill, in the direction of her recent discovery. Today she would bypass that trail. She'd already forced herself to stay away for two weeks— fourteen long days, counted like seasons or years. This was the eighth of May, the day she'd meant to allow herself to go back there, sneaking up on her secret to convince herself it was real. But now, no; of course not now. She would let Eddie Bondo catch up to her somewhere else, if he was looking.

She'd dropped down from the ridge into a limestone-banked hollow where maidenhair ferns cascaded from outcroppings of stone. The weeping limestone was streaked dark with wet-weather springs, which were bursting out everywhere now from a mountain too long beset with an excess of rains. She was near the head of the creek, coming into the oldest hemlock grove on the whole of this range. Patches of pale, dry needles, perfectly circular, lay like Christmas-tree skirts beneath the huge conifers. She paused there with her feet in the dry duff, listened. *"Nyaa nyaa nyaa,"* spat the chickadees, her familiars. Then, a crackle. He'd doubled back, was tracking her now. She waited until he emerged at the edge of the dark grove.

"Lose the bobcat?" she asked him.

"No, lost you. For a while."

"Not for long, I see."

He was wearing his hat again, with the brim pulled low. She found it harder to read his eyes. "You weren't after that cat today," he accused. "That trail's a few days old."

"That's right."

"I'd like to know what it is you're tracking."

"You're a man that can't hold his horses, aren't you?"

He smiled. Tantalizing. "What's your game, lady?"

"Coyotes."

His eyes widened, for only a second and a half. She could swear his pupils dilated. She bit her lower lip, having meant to give away nothing. She'd forgotten how to talk with people, it seemed—how to sidestep a question and hide what was necessary.

"And bobcats, and bear, and fox," she piled on quickly, to bury the coyotes. "Everything that's here. But especially the carnivores."

She shifted, waiting, feeling her toes inside her boots. Wasn't he supposed to say something after she finished? When he didn't, she suggested, "I guess you were looking for deer the other day?"

He gave a small shrug. Deer season was many months over and gone. He wasn't going to be trapped by a lady wildlife ranger with a badge. "Why the carnivores, especially?" he asked.

"No reason."

"I see. You're just partial. There's birdwatchers, and butterfly collectors, and there's gals like you that like to watch meat eaters."

He might have known this one thing could draw her talk to the surface: an outsider's condescension. "They're the top of the food chain, that's the reason," she said coldly. "If they're good, then their prey is good, and *its* food is good. If not, then something's missing from the chain."

"Oh yeah?"

"Yeah. Keeping tabs on the predators tells you what you need to know about the herbivores, like deer, and the vegetation, the detritovores, the insect populations, small predators like shrews and voles. All of it."

He studied her with a confusion she recognized. She was well accustomed to watching Yankee brains grind their gears, attempting to reconcile a hillbilly accent with signs of a serious education. He asked, finally, "And what you need to know about the shrews and voles would be what, exactly?"

"Voles matter more than you think. Beetles, worms. I guess to hunters these woods seem like a zoo, but who feeds the animals and cleans up the cage, do you think? Without worms and termites you'd be up to your hat brim in dead tree branches looking for a clear shot."

He took off his hat, daunted by her sudden willingness to speak up. "I *worship* worms and termites."

She stared at him. "Are you trying to make me mad? Because I don't talk to people all that often. I've kind of forgotten how to read the signs."

"Right there I was being what you call a pain in the ass." He folded his cloth hunter's hat in half and stuck it through a loop in his pack. "And before that I was being nosy. I apologize."

She shrugged. "It's no big secret, you can ask. It's my job; the government pays me to do this, if you can believe it. It doesn't pay *much,* but I'm not complaining."

"To do what, run off troublemakers like me?"

She smiled. "Yeah, a fair share of that. And trail maintenance, and in August if it gets bad dry they make me sit in a fire tower, but mostly I'm here watching the woods. That's the main thing I do."

He glanced up into the hemlock. "Keeping an eye on paradise. Tough life."

"Yep. Somebody's got to do it."

He nailed her then, aimed his smile straight into her. All his previous grins had just been warming up for this one. "You must have some kind of a brain, lady. To get yourself hired in this place of business."

"Well. Brain, I don't know. It takes a certain kind of person. You've got to appreciate the company."

"You don't get a lot a visitors?"

"Not human ones. I did have a bear in my cabin back in February."

"He stay with you the whole month?"

She laughed, and the sound of it surprised her. How long since she'd laughed aloud? "No. Long enough to raid my kitchen, though. We had an early false thaw and I think he woke up real hungry. Fortunately I was out at the time."

"So that's it, just you and the bears? What do you live on, nuts and berries?"

"The Forest Service sends up a guy with a jeepload of canned food and kerosene once a month. Mainly to see if I'm still alive and on the job, I think. If I was dead, see, they could stop putting my checks in the bank."

"I get it. One of those once-a-month-boyfriend deals."

She grimaced. "Lord, no. They send up some kid. Half the time when he comes I'm not at the cabin, I'll be out someplace. I lose track and forget when to expect him, so he just leaves the stuff in the cabin. I think he's a little scared of me, truth to tell."

"I don't think you're a bit scary," said Eddie Bondo. "Truth to tell."

She held his eye for as long as she could stand it. Under the sandpaper grain of a two-day beard he had a jaw she knew the feel of against her skin, just from looking at it. Thinking about that gave her an unexpected ache. When they resumed walking the trail, she kept him five or six steps ahead of her. He was quiet, not somebody who had to fill up a space between two people with talk, which was good. She could hear the birds. After a while she stopped to listen and was surprised when he did, too, instantly, that well attuned to her step behind his. He turned toward her with his head down and stood still, listening as she was.

"What?" he asked after a bit.

"Nothing. Just a bird."

"Which one?"

She waited, then nodded at the sound of a high, buzzing trill. "That one there. Magnolia warbler. That's really something."

"Why's that?"

"Well, see, because they've not been nesting up on this ridge since the thirties, when these mountains got all logged out. Now the big woods are growing back and they're starting to breed up here again."

"How do you know it's breeding?"

"Well, I couldn't prove it. They put their nests way up where you'd have to be God to find them. But it's just the male that sings, and he does it to drum up business, so he's probably got some."

"Amazing," said Eddie Bondo.

"Oh, it's not. Every single thing you hear in the woods right now is just nothing but that. Males drumming up business."

"I mean that you could tell all that from a little buzz I could just barely hear."

"It's not that hard." She blushed and was glad he'd turned and was walking ahead of her again so he didn't see. How long since she'd blushed? she wondered. Years, probably. And now twice, in these two visitations. Blushing, laughing, were those things that occured only between people? Forms of communication?

"So you do watch birds," he accused. "Not just the predators."

"You think that little guy's not a predator? Consider the world from a caterpillar's point of view."

"I'll try to do that."

"But no, he's not the top of the food chain. Not the big bad wolf."

"I thought the big bad wolf was your game, ranger lady."

"Now *there'd* be a real boring game, in this day and age."

"I guess so. Who shot the last wolf out of these parts, Daniel Boone?"

"Probably. The last gray wolf, that's right, just around then."

"There's another kind?"

"Yep. The gray everybody knows about, the storybook wolf. But there used to be another one here. A little one called the red wolf. They shot all those even before they got rid of the big guys."

"A little wolf? I never heard of that."

"You wouldn't. It's gone from the planet, is why."

"Extinct?"

She hesitated. "Well. Depends on how you call it. There's one place way back in a Louisiana swamp where people claim to see one now and again. But the ones they've caught out of there are all interbred with coyotes."

They kept their voices low. She spoke quietly to his back, happy to keep him ahead of her on the trail. He was a surprisingly silent walker, which she appreciated. And surprisingly fast. In her lifetime she'd met very few men who could keep up with her natural gait. *Like you're always leaving the scene of a crime,* that was how her husband had put it. *Can't you just stroll like other women do?* But no, she couldn't, and it was one more thing he could use against her in the end. "Feminine" was a test like some witch trial she was preordained to fail.

"But you did say you've seen coyotes up here," Eddie Bondo charged softly.

Coyotes: small golden ghosts of the vanished red wolf, returning. She wished for a look at his face. "Did I say that?"

"Almost but not quite."

"I said I look for them," she said. The skill of equivocation seemed to be coming to her now. Talking too much, saying not enough. "If they *were* here, I'd be real curious to see how they affected the other populations up here. Because they're something new."

"New to you, maybe. Not to me. I've seen more of them than a dog has ticks."

"Really?" From the back of his shoulders she couldn't tell how he felt about that, or whether it was even true. "New to this place, is what I meant. They weren't even here back in Daniel Boone's day, or in Indian times."

"No?"

"Nope. There's no real record of their ever living here. And then they just up and decided to extend their range into southern Appalachia a few years ago. Nobody knows why."

"But I'll bet a smart lady like you could make an educated guess."

Could, she thought. *Won't.* She suspected he already knew much of what she was telling him. Which was nothing; she was keeping her real secret to herself.

"It's not just here, either," she added, hating the gabby sound of herself evading the issue. *Not most girls you know, but just watch me now.* "Coyotes have turned up in every one of the continental United States in the last few years. In New York City, even. Somebody got a picture of one running between two taxicabs."

"What was it doing, trying to catch the subway?"

"Trying to catch a rat, more likely."

She would be quiet now, she decided, and she felt the familiar satisfaction of that choice, its small internal tug like the strings pulled tight on a cloth purse. She'd keep her secret in the bag, keep her eyes on the trail, try to listen. Try, also, to keep her eyes away from the glossy animal movement of his dark hair and the shape of the muscles in the seat of his jeans. But the man was just one long muscle, anywhere you looked on him.

She set her eyes into the trees, where a fresh hatch of lacewings seemed to be filling up the air between branches. Probably they'd molted out after the rain. They were everywhere suddenly, dancing on sunbeams in the upper story, trembling with the brief, grave duty of their adulthood: to live for a day on sunlight and coitus. Emerged from their slow, patient lives as carnivorous larvae, they had split down their backs and shed the husks of those predatory leaf-crawling shapes, left them lying in the mud with empty legs askew while their new, winged silhouettes rose up like carnal fairies to the urgent search for mates, egg laying, and eternal life.

The trail ended abruptly at the overlook. It never failed to take her breath away: a cliff face where the forest simply opened and the mountain dropped away at your feet, down hundreds of feet of limestone wall that would be a tough scramble even for a squirrel. The first time she'd come this way she was running, not just her usual fast walk but *jogging* along—what on earth was she thinking? And had nearly gone right over. Moving too fast was how she'd spent her first months in this job, it seemed, as if she and her long, unfeminine stride really *were* trying to leave the scene of a crime. That was two summers ago, and since that day her mind had returned a thousand times to the awful instant when she'd had to pull up hard, skinning her leg and face in the fall and yanking a sapling sourwood nearly out of the ground. So easily her life could have ended right here, without a blink or a witness. She replayed it too often, terrified by the frailty of that link like a weak trailer hitch connecting the front end of her life to all the rest. To *this*. Here was one more day she almost hadn't gotten, the feel of this blessed sun on her face and another look at this view of God's green earth laid out below them like a long green rumpled rug, the stitched-together fields and pastures of Zebulon Valley.

"That your hometown?" he asked.

She nodded, surprised he'd guessed it. They hadn't spoken for an hour or more as they'd climbed through the lacewinged afternoon toward this place, this view she now studied. There was the silver thread of Egg Creek; and there, where it came together like a thumb and four fingers with Bitter, Goose, Walker, and Black, was the town of Egg Fork, a loose arrangement of tiny squares that looked from this distance like a box of mints tossed on the ground. Her heart contained other perspectives on it, though: Oda Black's store, where Eskimo Pies lay under brittle blankets of frost in the cooler box; Little Brothers' Hardware with its jar of free lollipops on the dusty counter—a whole childhood in the palm of one valley. Right now she could see a livestock truck crawling slowly up Highway 6, halfway between Nannie Rawley's orchard and the farm that used to be hers and her dad's. The house wasn't visible from here, in any light, however she squinted.

"It's not *your* hometown, that's for sure," she said.

"How do you know?"

She laughed. "The way you talk, for one. And for two, there's not any Bondos in Zebulon County."

"You know every single soul in the county?"

"Every soul," she replied, "and his dog."

A red-tailed hawk rose high on an air current, calling out shrill, sequential rasps of raptor joy. She scanned the sky for another one. Usually when they spoke like that, they were mating. Once she'd seen a pair of them coupling on the wing, grappling and clutching each other and tumbling curve-winged through the air in hundred-foot death dives that made her gasp, though always they uncoupled and sailed outward and up again just before they were bashed to death in senseless passion.

"What's the name of that place?"

She shrugged. "Just the valley. Zebulon Valley, after this mountain." He would laugh at Egg Fork if she declared its name, so she didn't.

"You never felt like leaving?" he asked.

"Do you see me down there?"

He put a hand above his eyes like a storybook Indian and pretended to search the valley. "No."

"Well, then."

"I mean leaving this country. These mountains."

"I did leave. And came back. Not all that long ago."

"Like the mag-no-lia warblers."

"Like them."

He nodded. "Boy, I can see why."

Why she'd left, or why she'd come back—which could he see? She wondered how this place would seem to his outsider's eye. She knew what it *sounded* like; she'd learned in the presence of city people never to name her hometown out loud. But how did it look, was it possible that it wasn't beautiful? At the bottom of things, it was only a long row of little farms squeezed between this mountain range and the next one over, old Clinch Peak with his forests rumpled up darkly along his long, crooked spine. Between that ridge top and this one, nothing but a wall of thin blue air and a single hawk.

"Sheep farms down there," Eddie Bondo noted.

"Some, yeah. Tobacco. Some dairy cattle."

She kept to her own thoughts then, touching them like smooth stones deep in a pocket as she squinted across at Clinch, the lay of his land and the density of his forests. Last spring a dairy farmer had found a coyote den over there in the woods above his pasture. A mother, a father, and six nursing pups, according to local gossip all dead now, thanks to the farmer's marksmanship. She didn't believe it. She knew how Zebulon men liked to talk, and she knew a coyote family to be a nearly immortal creation. "Mother and father" was a farmer's appraisal of something beyond his ken; a coyote family was mostly females, sisters led by an alpha female, all bent on one member's reproduction.

Fourteen days ago, when she found the den over here on her own mountain, she'd felt like standing up here and crowing. It was the same pack, it had to be. The same family starting over. They'd chosen a cavern under the root mass of a huge fallen oak near Bitter Creek, halfway down the mountain. She'd found the den by accident one morning when she was only out looking for some sign of spring, headed downmountain with a sandwich stuck in her pocket. She'd hiked about two miles down the hollow before she found Virginia bluebells blooming along the creek, and was sitting among them, eating her sandwich one-handed while watching a towhee through her binoculars, when she saw movement in the cavern. The surprise was unbelievable, after two years of searching. She'd spent the rest of the day lying on a bed of wintergreen and holding her breath like a crush-stricken schoolgirl, waiting for a glimpse. She got to see one female enter the den, a golden flank moving into darkness, and she heard or sensed two others hanging around. She didn't dare go close enough to see the pups. Disturb these astute ladies and they'd be gone again. But the one she saw had a nursing mother's heavy teats. The others would be her sisters, helping to feed the young. The less those Zebulon Valley farmers knew about this family, the better.

Eddie Bondo clobbered her thoughts. The nylon of his sleeve was touching hers, whispering secrets. She was called back hard into her body, where the muscles of her face felt suddenly large and dumb as she stared at the valley but tried to find his profile in her peripheral vision. Did he know that the touch of his sleeve was so wildly distracting to her that it might as well have been his naked skin on hers? How had she come to this, a body that had lost all memory of human touch—was that what she'd wanted? The divorce hadn't been her choice, unless it was true what he said, that her skills and preference for the outdoors were choices a man had to leave. An older husband facing his own age badly and suddenly critical of a wife past forty, that was nothing she could have helped. But this assignment way up on Zebulon, where she'd lived in perfect isolation for twenty-five months—yes. That was her doing. Her proof, in case anyone was watching, that she'd never needed the marriage to begin with.

"Sweet," he said.

And she wondered, what? She glanced at his face.

He glanced back. "Did you ever see a prettier sight than that right there?"

"Never," she agreed. Her home ground.

Eddie Bondo's fingertips curled under the tips of hers, and he was holding her hand, just like that. Touching her as if it were the only possible response to this beauty lying at their feet. A pulse of electricity ran up the insides of her thighs like lightning ripping up two trees at once, leaving her to smolder or maybe burst into flames.

"Eddie Bondo," she tried out loud, carefully looking away from him, out at the sky-blue nothing ahead. "I don't know you from Adam. But you could stay one night in my cabin if you didn't want to sleep in the woods."

He didn't turn loose of her fingers after that.

Together they took the trail back into the woods with this new thing between them, their clasped hands, alive with nerve endings like some fresh animal born with its own volition, pulling them forward. She felt as if all her senses had been doubled as she watched this other person, and watched what he saw. He ducked under low branches and held them with his free hand so they wouldn't snap back in her face. They were moving close together, suddenly seeing for the first time today the miracle that two months of rain and two days of spring heat could perform on a forest floor. It had burst out in mushrooms: yellow, red, brown, pink, deadly white, minuscule, enormous, delicate, and garish, they painted the ground and ran up the sides of trees with their sudden, gilled flesh. Their bulbous heads pushed up through the leaf mold, announcing the eroticism of a fecund woods at the height of spring, the beginning of the world. She knelt down in the leaf mold to show him adder's tongue, tiny yellow lilies with bashful back-curved petals and leaves mottled like a copperhead's back. He reached down beside her knees to touch another flower she'd overlooked and nearly crushed. "Look at this," he said.

"Oh, *look* at that," she echoed almost in a whisper. "A lady's slipper." The little pink orchid was growing here where she knew it ought to be, where the soil was sweetened by pines. She moved aside to spare it and saw more like it, dozens of delicately wrinkled oval pouches held erect on stems, all the way up the ridge. She pressed her lips together, inclined to avert her eyes from so many pink scrota.

"Who named it *that?*" he asked, and laughed—they both did—at whoever had been the first to pretend this flower looked like a lady's slipper and not a man's testicles. But they both touched the orchid's veined flesh, gingerly, surprised by its cool vegetable texture.

"The bee must go in here," she said, touching the opening below the crown of narrow petals where the pollinator would enter the pouch. He leaned close to look, barely brushing her forehead with the dark corona of his hair. She was surprised by his interest in the flower, and by her own acute physical response to his body held so offhandedly close to hers. She could smell the washed-wool scent of his damp hair and the skin above his collar. This dry ache she felt was deeper than hunger—more like thirst. Her heart beat hard and she wondered, had she offered him a dry place to sleep, was that what he thought? Was that really all she had meant? She was not sure she could bear all the hours of an evening and a night spent close to him in her tiny cabin, wanting, not touching. Could not survive being discarded again as she had been by her husband at the end, with his looking through her in the bedroom for his glasses or his keys, even when she was naked, her body a mere obstruction, like a stranger in a theater blocking his view of the movie. She was too old, about to make a fool of herself, surely. This Eddie Bondo up close was a boy, ferociously beautiful and not completely out of his twenties.

He sat back and looked at her, thinking. Surprised her again with what he said. "There's something up north like this, grows in the peat bogs."

She felt unsettled by each new presence of him, the modulations of his voice, the look of his fingers as they touched this flower, his knowledge of peat bogs she had never seen. She couldn't take her eyes from the close white crescents of his nails at the tips of his fingers, the fine lines in his weathered hands. She had to force herself to speak.

"Lady's slippers up there? Where, in Canada?"

"It's not this same flower, but it traps bugs. The bee smells something sweet and goes inside and then he's trapped in there unless he can find the one door out. So he'll spread the pollen over the place where the flower wants it. Just like this, look here."

She bent to see, aware of her own breathing as she touched the small, raised knob where this orchid would force its pollinator to drag his abdomen before allowing him to flee for his life. She felt a sympathetic ache in the ridge of her pubic bone.

How could she want this stranger? How was it reasonable to do anything now but stand up and walk away from him? But when he bent his face sideways toward hers she couldn't stop herself from laying a hand on his jaw, and that was enough. The pressure of his face against hers moved her slowly backward until they lay together on the ground, finally yielding to earthly gravity. Crushing orchids under their bodies, she thought vaguely, but then she forgot them for it seemed she could feel every layer of cloth and flesh and bone between his body and her thumping heart, the individual follicles of his skin against her face, even the ridges and cracks in his lips when they touched her. She closed her eyes against the overwhelming sensations, but that only made them more intense, in the same way closed eyes make dizziness more acute. She opened her eyes then, to make this real and possible, that they were kissing and lying down in the cold leaves, falling together like a pair of hawks, not plummeting through thin air but rolling gradually downhill over adder's tongues and poisonous *Amanitas*. At the bottom of the hill they came to rest, his body above hers. He looked down into her eyes as if there were something behind them, deep in the ground, and he pulled brown beech leaves from her hair.

"What about that. Look at you."

"I can't." She laughed. "Not for years. I don't have a mirror in my cabin."

He pulled her to her feet and they walked for several minutes in stunned silence.

"The head of the jeep road's here," she pointed out when they came to it. "My cabin's just up ahead, but that road runs straight downhill to the little town down there. If that's what you were looking for, the way out."

He stood looking downhill, briefly, then turned her shoulders gently to face him and took her braid in his hand. "I was thinking I'd found what I was looking for."

Her eyes moved to the side, to unbelief, and back. But she let herself smile when his hands moved to her chest and began to part the layers of clothing that all seemed to open from that one place above her heart. He peeled back her nylon jacket, slipped it off her shoulders down to her bent elbows.

"Finding's not the same as looking," she said, but there was the scent of his hair again and his collar as he laid his mouth against her jawbone. That wool intoxication made her think once again of thirst, if she could name it something, but a thirst of eons that no one living could keep from reaching to slake, once water was at hand. She worked her elbows free of her jacket and let it drop into the mud, raised her hands to the zipper of his parka, and rolled the nylon back from him like a shed skin. Helping this new thing emerge, whatever it was going to be. They moved awkwardly the last hundred yards toward her cabin, refusing to come apart, trailing their packs and half their nylon layers.

She let go of him then and sat down on the planks at the un-sheltered edge of her porch to pull off her boots.

"This where you live?"

"Yep," she said, wondering what else needed to be said. "Me and the bears."

He sat next to her and brought his finger to her lips. No more talking about this, he seemed to be saying—but they had never talked about *this,* she was still not sure it was real. He guided her shoulders to the floor and lay next to her, stroking her face, unbuttoning her undershirt and touching her under her clothes, moving down, finding her, until it was only his mouth on hers that stopped her from crying out. She arched her back and slid her weapon gently out and away across the floorboards. This was all much too fast, her pelvis arched itself up again and she did cry out then, just a woman's small moan, and she had to pull away to keep from losing herself to him completely. She opened her eyes and caught sight of her pistol at the edge of the porch, aiming mutely down the valley with its safety on. The last shed appendage of her fear.

Carefully she took both his hands off of her, raised them above his shoulders, and rolled over him and pinned him like a wrestler. Straddling his thighs this way, looking down on his face, she felt stunned to her core by this human presence so close to her. He smiled, that odd parenthetic grin she already knew to look for. *It's that simple, then,* she thought. *It's that possible.* She bent down to him, tasting the salt skin of his chest with the sensitive tip of her tongue, and then exploring the tight drum of his abdomen. He shuddered at the touch of her warm breath on his skin, giving her to know that she could take and own Eddie Bondo. It was the body's decision, a body with no more choice of its natural history than an orchid has, or the bee it needs, and so they would both get lost here, she would let him in, anywhere he wanted to go. In the last full hour of daylight, while lacewings sought solace for their brief lives in the forest's bright upper air, and the husk of her empty nylon parka lay tangled with his in the mud, their two soft-skinned bodies completed their introductions on the floor of her porch. A breeze shook rain out of new leaves onto their hair, but in their pursuit of eternity they never noticed the chill.

It seemed to take forever, afterward in the thickening twilight, to recover her resting heartbeat. He lay looking past her into the darkened woods, apparently untroubled by his own heart. Thrushes were singing, it was that late. A wind kicked up, shaking more raindrops out of the trees to ring like buckshot on the cabin's tin roof and scald the naked parts of their bodies with cold. She studied a drop of water that hung from his earlobe, caught in the narrowest possible sliver of a gold ring that penetrated his left ear. Could he possibly be as beautiful as he seemed to her? Or was he just any man, a bone thrown to her starvation?

With his left hand he worked out some of the tangles his handiwork had put into her hair. But he was still looking away; the hand moved by itself, without his attention. She wondered if he worked with animals or something.

Coming back from someplace he'd been, he moved his eyes to her face. "Hey, pretty girl. Do you have a name?"

"Deanna."

He waited. "Deanna and that's all?"

"Deanna and I'm not sure of the rest."

"Now that's different: the girl with no last name just yet."

"I've got one, but it's my husband's—*was* my husband's. Or it *is,* but *he* was." She sat up and shivered, watching him stand to pull his jeans on. "You wouldn't know, but it leaves you in a quandary. That name is nothing to me now, but it's still yet stuck all over my life, on my driver's license and everything."

"'Still yet,'" he mocked, smiling at her, considering her words. "That's the male animal for you. Scent marking."

She had a good laugh at that. "That's it. Put his territorial mark on everything I owned, and then walked away."

Amazingly, Eddie Bondo walked to the end of her porch and peed over the edge. She didn't realize it until she heard the small, sudden spatter hitting the leaves of the mayapples and Christmas fern. "Oh, good Lord," she said.

He turned to look at her over his shoulder, surprised. "What? Sorry." His arc declined and dribbled out, and he tucked himself away.

She said quietly, "You're still in my territory."

~

Deanna had been chaste through her teens, too shy for the rituals of altered appearance that boys seemed to require and, lacking a mother, too far outside the game to learn. When she went away to college she found herself taken in and mentored by much older men—professors, mainly—until she married one. Her farm-bred worldliness, her height, her seriousness—*something*—had caused her to skip a generation ahead. She'd never before known what men in their late twenties had to offer. Eddie Bondo knew what he was doing and had the energy to pursue the practice of making perfect. They didn't get any sleep between dusk and dawn.

It was first light before she recovered the calm or belated contrition to wonder what she might have lost here—other than, momentarily, her mind. She knew that most men her age and most other animals had done this. The collision of strangers. Or not strangers, exactly, for they'd had their peculiar courtship: the display, the withdrawal, the dance of a three-day obsession. But the sight of him now asleep in her bed made her feel both euphoric and deeply unsettled. Her own nakedness startled her, even; she normally slept in several layers. Awake in the early light with the wood thrushes, feeling the texture of the cool sheet against her skin, she felt as jarred and disjunct as a butterfly molted extravagantly from a dun-colored larva and with no clue now where to fly.

From the look of his pack she guessed he was a homeless sort, out for the long tramp, and she wondered miserably if she'd coupled herself with someone notorious. By late morning, though, she'd gathered otherwise. He rose calm and unhurried and began carefully removing items from his pack and stacking them in organized piles on the floor as he searched out clean clothes and a razor.

A criminal wouldn't take the time to shave, she decided. His pack appeared to be a respectable little home: medicine cabinet, pantry, kitchen. He had a lot of food in there, even a small coffeepot. He found a place to prop his small shaving mirror at an angle on of one of the logs in the wall while he scraped the planes of his face one square inch at a time. She tried not to watch. Afterward he moved around her cabin with the confidence of an invited guest, whistling, going quiet only when he studied the titles of her books. *Theory of Population Genetics and Evolutionary Ecology:* that kind of thing seemed to set him back a notch, if only briefly.

His presence filled her tiny cabin so, she felt distracted trying to cook breakfast. Slamming cupboards, looking for things in the wrong places, she wasn't used to company here. She had only a single ladderback chair, plus the old bedraggled armchair out on the porch with holes in its arms from which phoebes pulled white shreds of stuffing to line their nests. That was all. She pulled the ladderback chair away from the table, set its tall back against the logs of the opposite wall, and asked him to sit, just to get a little space around her as she stood at the propane stove scrambling powdered eggs and boiling water for the grits. Off to his right stood her iron-framed cot with its wildly disheveled mattress, the night table piled with her books and field journals, and the kerosene lantern they'd nearly knocked over last night in some mad haste to burn them-selves down.

At some point they'd also let the fire in the wood stove go out, and the morning was cold. It would be July before mornings broke warm, up here at this elevation. When she brought over two plates of eggs, he stood to give her the chair, and she huddled there with her knees tucked into her flannel gown, shivering, watching him through the steam above her coffee cup. He moved to the window and stood looking out while he ate. He was five foot six, maybe. Not only younger but half a head shorter than she.

"No offense," she observed, "but guys of your height usually get away from me as fast as humanly possible."

"Oh, yeah?"

"Yeah. They kindly like to *glare* at me from the far side of the room. It's like being tall is this insult I arranged for them personally."

He paused his fork to look at her. "No offense, Miss Deanna, but you've been consorting with too many worms and voles." She laughed, and he angled a grin at her, a trout fisherman casting his fly. "You're what we western boys call a long drink of water."

He seemed to mean it. Her long thighs and feet and forearms—all her dimensions, in fact—seemed to be things he couldn't get enough of. That was amazing. That, she appreciated. It was his youth that made her edgy. She suppressed the urge to ask if his mother knew where he was. The most she allowed herself was the question of his origins. "Wyoming" was his answer. A sheep rancher, son of three generations of sheep ranchers. She did not ask what might bring a Wyoming sheep rancher to the southern Appalachians at this time of year. She had a bad feeling she knew.

So she looked past his lure, through the window to the woods outside and the bright golden Io moth hanging torpid on the window screen. The creature had finished its night of moth foraging or moth love and now, moved by the first warmth of morning, would look for a place to fold its wings and wait out the useless daylight hours. She watched it crawl slowly up the screen on furry yellow legs. It suddenly twitched, opening its wings to reveal the dark eyes on its underwings meant to startle predators, and then it flew off to some safer hideout. Deanna felt the same impulse to bolt—to flee this risky mate gleaned from her forest.

A sheep rancher. She knew the hatred of western ranchers toward coyotes; it was famous, maybe the fiercest human-animal vendetta there was. It was bad enough even here on the tamer side of the Mississippi. The farmers she'd grown up among would sooner kill a coyote than learn to pronounce its name. It was a dread built into humans via centuries of fairy tales: give man the run of a place, and he will clear it of wolves and bears. Europeans had killed theirs centuries ago in all but the wildest mountains, and maybe even those holdouts were just legend by now. Since the third grade, when Deanna Wolfe learned to recite the Pledge and to look up "wolf" in the *World Book Encyclopedia,* she'd loved America because it was still young enough that its people hadn't wiped out all its large predators. But they were working on that, for all they were worth.

"You had a rifle," she said. "The other day. A thirty-thirty, it looked like. Where is it now?"

"I stashed it," he said, simple as that. He was clean-shaven, bare-chested, and cheerful, ready to eat up powdered eggs and whatever else she offered. His gun was hiding somewhere nearby while his beautiful, high-arched feet moved around her cabin floor with pure naked grace. It occurred to Deanna that she was in deep.

What might bring a Wyoming sheep rancher to the southern Appalachians at this time of year was the Mountain Empire Bounty Hunt, organized for the first time this year. It'd been held recently, she knew, around the first day of May—the time of birthing and nursing, a suitable hunting season for nothing in this world unless the goal was willful extermination. It had drawn hunters from everywhere for the celebrated purpose of killing coyotes.

Moth Love

usa was alone, curled in an armchair and reading furtively—the only way a farmer's wife may read, it turns out—when the power of a fragrance stopped all her thoughts. In the eleventh hour of the ninth day of May, for one single indelible instant that would change everything, she was lifted out of her life.

She closed her eyes, turning her face to the open window and breathing deeply. Honeysuckle. Lusa shut the book on her index finger. Charles Darwin on moths, that was what she'd been lost in: a description of a virgin *Saturnia carpini* whose scent males flocked to till they covered her cage, with several dozen even crawling down Mr. Darwin's chimney to find her. Piles of Lusa's books on the floor were shoved halfway out of sight behind this old over-stuffed chair, the only spot in the house she had claimed as her own. When she first moved in she'd dragged this chair, a strange thing upholstered in antique green brocade, across the big bedroom to the tall, south-facing window, for the light. Now she leaned forward in her seat and moved her head a little to see out through the dusty screen. Far away at the opposite edge of the hayfield her eye caught on Cole's white T-shirt and then made out the rest of him there, the forward-arching line of his body. He was leaning out from the tractor seat, breaking off a branch of honeysuckle that had climbed into the cedary fencerow high enough to overhang the edge of the field. Maybe that plume of honeysuckle was just in his way. Or maybe he was breaking it off to bring back to Lusa. She liked to have a fresh spray in a jar above the kitchen sink. Survival here would be possible if only she could fill the air with scent and dispatch the stern female ghosts in that kitchen with the sweetness of an unabashed, blooming weed.

Cole was nearly a quarter of a mile away across the bottom field, tilling the ground where they'd soon set tobacco. It seemed unbelievable that his disturbance of the branch could release a burst of scent that would reach her here at the house, but the breeze was gentle and coming from exactly the right direction. People in Appalachia insisted that the mountains breathed, and it was true: the steep hollow behind the farmhouse took up one long, slow inhalation every morning and let it back down through their open windows and across the fields throughout evening—just one full, deep breath each day. When Lusa first visited Cole here she'd listened to talk of mountains breathing with a tolerant smile. She had some respect for the poetry of country people's language, if not for the veracity of their perceptions: mountains breathe, and a snake won't die till the sun goes down, even if you chop off its head. If a snapping turtle gets hold of you, he won't let go till it thunders. But when she married Cole and moved her life into this house, the inhalations of Zebulon Mountain touched her face all morning, and finally she understood. She learned to tell time with her skin, as morning turned to afternoon and the mountain's breath began to bear gently on the back of her neck. By early evening it was insistent as a lover's sigh, sweetened by the damp woods, cooling her nape and shoulders whenever she paused her work in the kitchen to lift her sweat-damp curls off her neck. She had come to think of Zebulon as another man in her life, larger and steadier than any other companion she had known.

But now there was her husband across the field, breaking off the honeysuckle branch to bring back to her. She was sure of it, for he'd tucked it between his thigh and the padded seat of the Kubota. Its cloud of white flowers trembled as he bounced across the plowed field, steering the tractor with both hands. His work on the lower side was nearly done. When he returned to the house for his late-morning coffee and "dinner," as she was learning to call the midday meal, she would put the honeysuckle branch in water. Maybe they could talk then; maybe she would put soup and bread on the table and eat her bitter words from earlier this morning. They argued nearly every day, but today had already been one of their worst. This morning at breakfast she'd nearly made up her mind to leave. This morning, he had wanted her to. They had used all the worst words they knew. She closed her eyes now and inhaled. She could have just let him laugh, instead, at her fondness for this weedy vine that farmers hated to see in their fencerows.

This week's gardening column in the paper was devoted to the elimination of honeysuckle. That had been the jumping-off point for their argument:

"'Be vigilant! The project will require repeated applications of a stout chemical defoliant,'" she'd read aloud in her version of a stupid, exaggerated mountain burr that she knew would annoy Cole. But how could she help herself? It was the county Extension agent who wrote this awful column called "Gardening in Eden," whose main concern, week after week, was with murdering things. It stirred up her impatience with these people who seemed determined to exterminate every living thing in sight. Grubbing out wild roses, shooting blue jays out of cherry trees, knocking phoebe nests out of the porch eaves to keep the fledglings from messing on the stairs: these were the pastimes of Zebulon County, reliable as the rituals of spring cleaning.

And he had said, "If you're making fun of Zebulon County, you're making fun of me, Lusa."

"*This* I need to be told?" she'd snapped. As if, sitting in this kitchen where she felt the disapproving presence of his dead mother, she could forget where he'd grown up. Cole was the youngest of six children, with five sisters who'd traveled no farther than the bottom of the hollow, where Dad Widener had deeded each daughter an acre on which to build a house when she married, meanwhile saving back the remainder of the sixty-acre farm for his only son, Cole. The family cemetery was up behind the orchard. The Wideners' destiny was to occupy this same plot of land for their lives and eternity, evidently. To them the word *town* meant Egg Fork, a nearby hamlet of a few thousand souls, nine churches, and a Kroger's. Whereas Lusa was a dire outsider from the other side of the mountains, from *Lexington*—a place in the preposterous distance. And now she was marooned behind five sisters-in-law who flanked her gravel right-of-way to the mailbox.

Silently then, after snapping at him, she'd watched Cole eat his breakfast for a while before slapping down the offending newspaper and getting up to face her work, stepping out the kitchen door to retrieve yesterday's milk from the cool back porch. She was still in her slippers and seersucker nightshirt at that point; they hadn't been out of bed for an hour yet, and the fog was still lifting above the creek. An Io moth rested on the screen, her second-favorite moth, whose surprising underwings were the same pinkish gold as her hair. (Her favorite would always be *Actias luna,* ethereal green ghost of the upper forests.) "Worn out from your big night of love," she scolded, "that's what you get"—but of course he'd had no choice. All the giant silkworm family, the Ios and lunas she admired, did their eating as caterpillars and as adult moths had no mouths. What mute, romantic extravagance, Lusa thought: a starving creature racing with death to scour the night for his mate.

She picked up the milk and handled it carefully, noting that it was nicely set, ready to separate. There wasn't but a gallon. They kept only one milk cow for the homemade butter and cream Cole liked, and milked her only in the evenings now. Lusa had shocked everyone with her proposal of eliminating the inconvenient four A.M. milking by putting up the cow with her calf in the barn overnight. She could even pasture mother and calf together and skip milking altogether if she needed to drive to Lexington for a weekend (did it take a scientist to think of this?). On days when Lusa wanted to milk, they simply pushed the calf into a pasture separate from his mother so her udder would be full by evening. Cole's sisters disapproved of this easy arrangement, but Lusa felt smug. If they'd spent their girlhoods as slaves to the twice-daily milkings, that was not Lusa's problem. She had her own ways of doing a thing. She'd neatly mastered the domestic side of farming in less than a year, and Cole loved her cooking more than he'd loved his mother's. Now, as she stood at the sink dipping the skimmer and watching the cream flow smoothly over the rim in a stream so thin it was nearly green, she had an inspiration: fat bouquets of savoy spinach stood ready for picking in her backdoor garden. Sautéed in butter with sliced mushrooms, a bay leaf, and this cream, they'd make for a fragrant, sensuous soup Cole would love. She could have it ready by noon when he came in for his dinner. She would concentrate on soup, then, and try to let this argument go by.

But Cole wouldn't do it. "Why don't *you* write the garden column for the newspaper, Lusa?" he'd goaded her from the breakfast table. "Think of all you could teach us sorry-ass bumpkins."

"Cole, I have to concentrate on what I'm doing here. Do we have to fight?"

"No, dear. I'm just *sorry*," he said, not sorry at all, "that I'm not from someplace fancy where people keep their dogs in the house and their gardens in window boxes."

"Will you ever let it go? Lexington's not *fancy*. People there just have more to read and write about than killing the honeysuckle in their hedgerows."

"They needn't to bother. They don't have hedgerows. Every city yard I ever saw ended in the flat killing mulch of a sidewalk."

In many species of moths, Darwin had observed, *the males prefer to inhabit more open territory, while the females cling under cover.* She and Cole were a biological cliché, was that it? A male and female following their separate natures? She glanced up from her waterfall of cream, wondering how to gentle down this thing between them.

"A city person is only part of who I am," she said quietly. The lines they drew in argument were always wrong; he put her in a camp she hadn't chosen. How could he understand that she'd spent her whole sunburnt, freckled childhood trapped on lawn but longing for pasture? Spent it catching butterflies and moths, looking them up in her color-keyed book and touching all the pictures, coveting those that hid in wilder places?

He cracked his knuckles and locked his hands behind his head. "Lusa, honey, you can take the girl out of the city, but you can't take the city out of the girl."

"Shit," she said aloud, giving in to pure irritation. Did he actually think he was clever? She'd mishandled the skimmer and dropped it too low, right at the end, giving up most of the cream she'd just skimmed. Now it would take another half day to separate again. She tossed the skimmer into the sink. "For this I spent twenty years of my life in school." She turned to face him. "I'm *sorry* my education didn't prepare me to live here where the two classes of animals are food and target practice."

"You forgot 'bait,'" he drawled.

"It's not funny, Cole. I'm so alone here. You have no idea."

He picked up the paper and folded it back to the beef prices. So that would be that. Her loneliness was her own problem, and she knew it. The only people she ever talked to, besides Cole, were all in Lexington. When he suggested that she make friends *here,* she could picture only the doe-eyed, aggressively coiffed women she saw in Kroger's, and then she'd run to the phone to snipe about small-town life with Arlie and Hal, her former lab mates. But lately their support had run out on Lusa, to the tune of embarrassing phone bills: *What's the problem, exactly? You're not happy, so walk away, you've got feet. Get back here while you can still recover your grant money.*

She set herself to the task of sterilizing the milk utensils, trying to forget Arlie and Hal. Her former and present lives were so different that she couldn't even hold one in her mind as she lived the other. It embarrassed her to try. Instead she soothed herself with an ancient litany: *Actias luna, Hyalophora cecropia, Automeris io,* luna, cecropia, Io, the giant saturniid moths, silken creatures that bore the names of gods into Zebulon's deep hollows and mountain slopes. Most people never knew what wings beat at their darkened windows while they slept.

It was just one more thing she couldn't talk about—her education, which far outstripped her husband's. Cole's standard joke: "I loved education so much, I repeated every grade I could." And Lusa had never, ever believed his self-deprecation. From the day they'd first met at the University of Kentucky she'd recognized him as a scholar of his own kind. Cole was there for a workshop on integrated pest management. A group of farmers in this county had raised the tuition and sent him to Lexington knowing Cole would ignore the claptrap and bring back to them anything worth knowing. Their confidence was justified. He'd not been automatically impressed with Lusa's status as a postdoctoral assistant, but had pressed her with questions when he saw how well she knew the gelechid moths, denizens of a grain crop in storage. His eyes, the blue of a rainless summer sky, had begun to follow her in a way that either alarmed or flattered her, she couldn't say which. She'd showed him her lab and her father's larger one in the same building, where he studied the pheromones of codling moths, notorious pests of apple trees. The laboratory moths lived scrutinized lives in glass boxes where scientists learned to fool the males into mating with scent-baited traps so their virgin brides might vainly cover the world's apples with empty, harmless eggs.

Later on (but not much), Lusa and Cole had slept together in her apartment on Euclid Street. Cole made love like a farmer, which is not to say he was coarse. On the contrary, he had a fine intelligence for the physical that drove him toward her earthy scents, seeking out with his furred mouth her soft, damp places, turning her like fresh earth toward the glory of new growth. Her body, which she'd always considered too short and hourglass-curved to be taken seriously, became something new in the embrace of a man who judged breeding animals with his hands. He gave her to know what she'd never before understood: she was voluptuous.

She told him about the scent cues animals use to find and identify their mates. Pheromones. That delighted him. "So it's all about sex. All you people in that laboratory, all the livelong day. And getting paid for it."

"Guilty," she confessed. "I study moth love."

He was interested in moth love. More interested still when she explained to him that even humans seem to rely on certain pheromonal cues, though most have little inclination to know the details. Cole would, she thought. Cole, the man who buried his face in every fold of her skin to inhale her scent. He could only love sex more if he had antennae the shape of feathers, like a moth, for combing the air around her, and elaborately branched coremata he could evert from his abdomen for the purpose of calling back to her with his own scent.

He'd asked, "When you fall in love with somebody for no apparent reason you can think of, then, is that what's going on? The pheromones?"

"Maybe," she'd answered. "Probably."

He'd rolled onto his back then and locked his fingers behind his head, providing her with an opportunity to study him from close range. He was astonishingly large. His shoulders, his hands, the plane of his broad, flat stomach and chest—all of him made her feel tiny and delicate. Here was a happy giant, naked in her bed.

"Tell me this, then," he said. "How come a woman will do everything humanly possible to cover up what she really smells like?"

"I have no idea." Lusa had wondered this before, of course. Even shaving armpits defeats the purpose. The whole point of pubic hair is to increase the surface area for scent molecules, and she told him so.

"Damn if this isn't another thing entirely, sleeping with a lady scientist," he'd declared, smiling at her with a face she'd already begun to think about missing. Damn if *he* wasn't another thing entirely. And soon he would be gone, the happy, earnest enormity of him, his closely trimmed beard that marked lines on his jaw and up the center of his chin to his wonderful mouth. His beard made her think of the nectar guides on the throats of flowers that show bees the path to the sweet place where nectar resides.

Her Euclid apartment had seemed to suit him so well that he delayed his departure for two days after the seminar's end. They hardly left her bed, in fact, and she had to call her lab to claim sudden illness. She was on the verge of asking him—not out of guile, but just for curiosity—whether he habitually slept with women he'd just met, when he proposed marriage. Lusa was speechless. For the next year he courted her with an intensity that caused her to ovulate during his visits. She began taking real care, lest a pregnancy too close to their wedding provide his relatives with the goods on Lusa they seemed to want. Her mother's language had an expression for people like Cole's sisters: "Born with ten fingers so they can count to nine."

Cole had finished his breakfast now and glanced up at Lusa as he lit a cigarette. He seemed startled to find her staring at him. "What?" he asked.

"I was just remembering how much we used to like each other."

"Oh, I forgot to tell you. Herb will be up later this morning to borrow the pressure sprayer. Don't be surprised to see him digging in the storeroom."

She glared. This was typical Cole, to answer an appeal to his emotional core by appearing not to have one. "I don't want Herb in our storeroom," she replied flatly. "So. I guess I'll have to go down to the barn and dig it out myself."

"What for? Herb knows what a pressure sprayer looks like. Hell, he's the one talked me into buying it, and now he uses it more than I do."

"And on his way to finding it he'll be handling my collecting funnels and insect nets, storing up tales for Mary Edna to whisper to Hannie-Mavis by way of Lois and Emaline. No thank you."

Cole leaned back in his chair, smiling. "The three most efficient means of communication: telegraph, telephone, tell a Widener woman."

"I used to think that was funny. Before their favorite subject was me."

"They don't mean any harm."

"Do you really believe that?" She shook her head, turning her back on him. They *did* mean her harm. They had from the beginning. Since she'd become mistress of their family home last June, they'd had little to say to her and everything to say *about* her. Before Lusa herself ever set foot in the Kroger's or the hardware store, she was already known as a Lexington girl who got down on all fours to name the insects in the parlor rather than squashing them.

"My sisters have more to do than to sit around hating you," Cole insisted.

"Your sisters haven't learned my name yet."

"Lusa, come on."

"You ask them. I'll give you ten dollars if one of them gets it right—the whole thing, Lusa Maluf Landowski. They make a show of not being able to remember it. You think I'm kidding? Lois evidently told Oda Black my maiden name was Zucchini."

"Now, that can't be."

"Oda was clucking that she could see why I'd rushed you to the altar to be rid of *that*." She watched his face, trying to see if he even understood this humiliation. Lusa had kept her own name when they married, but it hadn't mattered: everyone called her Mrs. Widener, as if there were no Lusa at all.

"Well, in spite of despising you with all her heart," he said patiently, "Lois invited us down for a big supper Memorial Day. She wants us all to go out to the cemetery in the afternoon to decorate Mommy's and Dad's graves."

Lusa cocked her head, curious. "When did she call?"

"Last night."

"The whole family's invited? How can Lois do that? Her kitchen's the size of a phone booth."

"It was much bigger before the ruffles and plastic ducks prevailed."

Lusa had to smile.

He gestured. "*Here's* the kitchen. Why don't you ever invite everybody up here?"

Lusa stared at him, slack-jawed.

"Well, what?"

She shook her head. "How can you possibly be so dumb? How can you sit there in the middle of this hurricane of hateful women and act like it's a nice, sunny day out?"

"*What?*"

She marched to the corner cabinet in the dining room and returned with a particular china plate, which she held up like a flash card. "This means nothing to you?"

"It's your wedding china."

Her wedding china, true—it had been her family's, a pattern from England with delicately tinted botanical paintings of flowers and their pollinators. But did they have to scorn everything she loved? "You don't recall what happened at the dinner I had here last July, a month after we married? The birthday party for you that I spent about two weeks cooking, without help, in my first failed attempt to impress your family?"

"No."

"Let me help you out. Picture your eldest sister. Picture her sitting in that chair, blue hair and all, forgive me, wearing a face that would curdle milk. Picture me serving her dinner on this plate, right here."

He laughed. "I recall Mary Edna took a bite of potatoes and saw a black widow or something underneath and screamed."

"It was the wing of a sphinx moth. A *painting* of a sphinx moth. I would not have china with black widows on it. And she didn't scream, she laid down her fork and crossed her hands like a corpse and has refused my invitations ever since. Even *Thanksgiving,* Cole, for God's sake. In your family home, where you and your sisters have eaten every Thanksgiving dinner of your lives, prior to the mortal offense committed by your wife against Her Majesty Mary Edna."

"Let the rest of them come without Mary Edna, then. She's always made too much of herself for being the oldest."

"They won't come without Mary Edna."

He shrugged. "Well, then, maybe they're just country folks that don't understand plates with bugs and fancy Latin words printed on them. Maybe they're scared they'll use the wrong fork."

"*Damn* you, Cole. Damn your whole family, if all you can do is ridicule me." She grew hot in the face and felt like smashing the plate for effect, but the gesture would be all wrong. The plate seemed more valuable than the marriage.

"Oh, Lord," he clucked. "They warned me about marrying a redhead."

"*Shuchach!*" she muttered, sinking her teeth into the harsh Arabic consonants as she stomped into the dining room to put the plate away. Lusa was embarrassed by her tears, shamed that the spurned invitations still stung. Too many times in this past year she had hung up the phone and walked around in circles on the braided rug in the parlor, a grown, married woman with a degree in entomology, sobbing like a child. How could she care so much what they thought of her? Any girl who pursued the study of insects had learned to ignore public opinion. But what she couldn't bear, then or now, was the implied belief that she was a curiosity, a nonsense of a woman. Lusa feared in retrospect that she'd judged her own father the same way, pitied him for being such a bitter, unworldly man, for devoting himself to agriculture in disinfected laboratories smelling of ether. Both her parents had come from farming lineages, but they had no more acquaintance with actual farm work than could be gleaned on a Sunday drive through the racehorse pastures east of Fayette County.

Lusa had wanted to be different. She'd craved to shock people with her love of crawling things and her sweat. She could still feel the childhood desire in her body, a girl bending close to breathe on the mirror when hard play on summer days dampened her strawberry hair into dark-brown tendrils against her face. As a woman, she'd jumped at an unexpected chance: to be a farmer's partner.

She'd never expected the strange, effete legacy that followed her here to Zebulon, where her new relatives considered her old ones to be a family of fools who kept insect pests alive in glass boxes, on purpose.

She returned to the kitchen without looking at him. If he could act like this wasn't tearing him apart, she could do the same. "Check," she said. "Do not serve anything to a Widener on bug plates. I'll remember that. And check, open the door to Herb the great and glorious varmint killer when he comes to rifle through my storeroom for the pressure sprayer." Herb and Mary Edna were a perfect marriage, in Lusa's opinion: the one was exactly as superior and tactless as the other.

"What in the world does that mean?" Cole asked.

"Do you know what Hannie-Mavis told me yesterday? She said

one time Herb found a den of coyotes up in the woods above his fence line, a mother and a litter of nursing babies. She said he put a bullet in every one of their heads, right in their den."

Cole gave her a blank look.

"Is that true?" she demanded. "Did you know about it?"

"Why bring up the subject?"

"When was it? Recently?"

"No-oh. It was way last spring, I think. Around the time your mother got sick. Before the wedding, anyway. That's why you didn't know about it."

"Oh, back that long ago. So it doesn't matter now."

He sighed. "Lusa, they were meat-eating animals setting up camp on a dairy farm. What do you think Herb's going to do, give his profits away to the wolves?"

"Not wolves, coyotes."

"Same thing."

"*Not* the same thing. Did it occur to anybody to be *interested* in the idea of coyotes being here, two thousand miles or something from the Grand Canyon?"

"I expect he was interested in what they eat. Such as a newborn calf."

"If that's even what they were—coyotes—which I doubt, knowing Herb's eyesight. I also doubt if he shot them, to tell you the truth. I bet he missed. I *hope* he missed."

"Herb Goins with a rifle is a frightening proposition, I will not argue with that. But if you care to know my end of it, Lusa, I hope he got them."

"You and everybody else in the county. I know. If Herb didn't get them, somebody else will." She wished she were dressed. She felt vulnerable and unconvincing in her nightshirt. She went back out to the porch, letting the screen door slam behind her. She set the milk back into the cooler to reseparate and noticed that the Io moth was still hanging on the porch screen. She reached up and gently slapped the screen where it clung. "Better fly on out of here," she said. "No insect is safe around here." She watched the moth flare open, showing its watermelon-colored underwings with their startling pair of black pupils. An owl's eyes, she thought, a perfect likeness. Pity the little bird that opens its mouth for a bite of moth and gets stared in the face by *that*. Jolly old life, full of surprises.

She returned to the kitchen with a jar of last summer's tomatoes in each hand; instead of the soup she would make *imam bayildi*, her mother's stuffed-vegetable recipe, which Lusa herself much preferred to anything milky. Cole wasn't crazy about *imam bayildi*. He was even skeptical of spaghetti, which he called an "Eye-talian" dish. But it was his fault she'd lost the cream, so fine, then, let him eat foreign food. *I've stooped to this,* she thought. *The former National Science Foundation scholar with the most coveted postgraduate fellowship in her department now wields her influence on the world through acts of vengeful cooking.*

His whole big exasperating person was still there at the table, smoking cigarettes. Arcs of pale ash stretched like starry nebulae across the dark tabletop between his left hand and the ugly tin ashtray balanced halfway off the table. The whole scene looked like something she'd like to wad up and throw away. It wasn't like Cole to be this slow getting out to his cattle and his tractor. It was a full hour past dawn now; the sun was well up. Was he that determined to vex her?

"What does Herb want with our pressure sprayer, anyway?" she asked.

"I don't know. No, I do know. He said they're exterminating at the church. They've got some kind of bees moved into the walls, Mary Edna said."

"Oh, that's perfect. Exterminating God's creatures down at the church. It's a good thing God didn't leave Herb and Mary Edna in charge of Noah's ark. They'd fumigate it first, and then they'd sink it."

He refused to laugh. "Lusa, honey, where you come from

44

maybe they think it'd be nice to have a church full of bees. People get sentimental in a place where nature's already been dead for fifty years, so they can all get to mourning it like some relative they never knew. But out here he's alive and kicking and still on his bender."

"My husband, the poet. Nature is an uncle with a drinking problem."

He shook his head. "That's how it is. You have to persuade it two steps back every day or it will move in and take you over." Cole could fend off her condescension with astonishing ease. He had his own I-can-put-up-with-this tone of voice that made Lusa want to scream her red head off.

"Take over what?" she said, trembling to hold back a rage. "You're nature, I'm nature. We shit, we piss, we have babies, we make messes. The world will not end if you let the honeysuckle have the side of your barn."

We have babies? I didn't notice, his look seemed to say. But he asked her instead, "Why tolerate a weed when you can nip it in the bud?"

Every word they said to each other was wrong, every truth underneath it unsayable, unfindable. Their kindnesses had grown stale, and their jokes were all old chestnuts, too worn out for use. Lusa threw down the dish towel, feeling suffocated in clichés. "You have a nice day out there in the big woolly jungle. I'm going to go do your laundry. Your damn cigarettes are stinking up the kitchen."

"While you're cursing tobacco, you might consider it was last year's crop that bought your new washer and dryer."

"Yil'an deenuk!" she shouted from the hallway.

"If my Ay-rab mama had taught me to swear, I wouldn't be proud of it," he called back.

Ay-rab mama, Polack daddy—he held this against her too, apparently, along with the rest of his family. But hadn't she ridiculed *his* accent, his background? And yet neither of them, truly, was that kind of person. Layers of contempt crouched camouflaged beneath one another until it was too much to sort out—if she and Cole were married a hundred years they'd still be fighting without knowing why. She felt sick and defeated, stomping from room to room to collect cast-off shirts or socks they'd shed in the downstairs rooms (some were hers). There was nothing to say, but still they said it, the honeysuckle and the tobacco. In less than a year of marriage they'd already learned to move from one argument to the next, just like the creek that ran down the mountain into this hollow, flowing out of its banks into the ruts of their driveway, then back again into its creek bed at the bottom of the valley. Arguments could fill a marriage like water, running through everything, always, with no taste or color but lots of noise.

Bitter Creek, that stream was named, and the hollow running up the back of their farm into the National Forest, people called Bitter Hollow. Perfect. *I am too young to feel this way,* she thought, trudging upstairs to collect the rest of the laundry while he headed out to till the bottom field. How would it be in ten years? Had she really wanted so badly all her life to live on a farm? A bird in the hand loses its mystery in no time flat. Now she felt like a frontier mail-order bride, hardly past her wedding and already wondering how she could have left her city and beloved career for the narrow place a rural county holds open for a farmer's wife.

It was only four hours later, in the eleventh hour of the ninth of May, as the dryer clicked and droned downstairs and she sat beside her bedroom window reading, that Lusa's life turned over on this one simple thing: a potent rise of scent as her young husband reached out his muscled arm for a branch of flowers. Here was what she'd forgotten about, the full, straight truth of their attachment. Her heart emptied of words, for once, and filled with a new species of feeling. Even if he never reached the house, if his trip across the field was disastrously interrupted by the kind of tractor accident that felled farmers in this steep county, she would still have had a burst of fragrance reaching across a distance to explain Cole's position in the simplest terms conceivable.

Lusa sat still and marveled: This is how moths speak to each other. They tell their love across the fields by scent. There is no mouth, the wrong words are impossible, either a mate is there or he's not, and if so the pair will find each other in the dark.

For several more minutes her hands lay motionless on her book while she considered a language that could carry nothing but love and simple truth.

Ten days later the marriage would reach its end. When it came, Lusa would look back to that moment at the window and feel the chill of its prescience.

No one would have called it a premonition, exactly; Cole's tractor did not overturn. And it wasn't tobacco that killed him, or at least not smoking. She could have allowed him the pleasure of two packs a day, it would have made no difference in the long run, since there was to be no long run. Tobacco's failure was partly to blame, though—the drop in price supports that had pressed him to take part-time work driving grain deliveries for Southern States. Lusa knew this outside job shamed him as a farmer, even though there was hardly a family in the whole valley that got by solely on farm profits. For Cole the failure was not simply one of money, but of attachment. He hated being away from the farm for even one night when he had to make a run over the Blue Ridge and down into North Carolina. She had told him they could find the money elsewhere—maybe by borrowing against next year's cattle, though he mistrusted debt, and the new tractor had already put them in deep. Or she could teach at the community college in Franklin. (Would that also shame him? She wasn't sure.) She was thinking of that, picturing herself with a class of nursing students in a biology lab, just before the sheriff drove up to inform the next of kin.

It was very early, a damp dawn that had committed itself to nothing yet, still perfectly windless and scentless. May nineteenth, still a nothing of a day, though the date would never again pass unnoticed, after this. She was standing at the same upstairs window watching fog drift up the edges of the fields, uphill along the hedgerows, like the ghost of some ancient river whose tributaries no longer heeded gravity. There was a strange quality to these mornings when Cole was away and she woke up here alone; she was free. As free and disembodied as a ghost. She focused her eyes out in the middle distance of the yard, where she could see the frenzied movement of nocturnal insects in the shadows, noctuid moths looping crazily through the last minutes of this night's search for a mate.

When she saw Tim Boyer's sedan with its seal on the side, she understood. If he were just hurt, in a hospital, that was something Tim could have stopped down below to tell. He could have given the news to Lois or Mary Edna first. This was a different mission—requiring notice to the wife. She knew why. Did not know the details—would never know some of them, in fact. The damage to the body was of the kind that sisters and brothers-in-law discuss at length but wives are never told about. But she knew enough.

Now, she thought, her body going cold, as the long white car moved so slowly up the driveway that she could hear the individual pops as the gravel shifted beneath the tires. *Right now, from here on everything changes.*

But that would not be true. Her decision and all the rest of her days would turn not on the moment when she understood that Cole was dead, but on an earlier time at that same window when she'd received his wordless message by scent across a field.

{3}

Old Chestnuts

ight years a widower, Garnett still sometimes awoke disoriented and lost to the day. It was because of the large empty bed, he felt; a woman was an anchor. Lacking a wife, he had turned to his God for solace, but sometimes a man also needed the view out his window.

Garnett sat up slowly and bent toward the light, seeing as much with his memory as with his eyes. There was the gray fog of dawn in this wet hollow, lifted with imperious slowness like the skirt of an old woman stepping over a puddle. There were the barn and slat-sided grain house, built by his father and grandfather in another time. The grass-covered root cellar still bulged from the hillside, the two windows in its fieldstone face staring out of the hill like eyes in the head of a man. Every morning of his life, Garnett had saluted that old man in the hillside with the ivy beard crawling out of his chin and the forelock of fescue hanging over his brow. As a boy, Garnett had never dreamed of being an old man himself, still looking at these sights and needing them as badly as a boy needs the smooth lucky chestnut in his pocket, the talisman he rubs all day just to make sure it's still there.

The birds were starting up their morning chorus. They were in full form now, this far into the spring. What was it now, the nineteenth of May? Full form and feather. He listened. The prothalamion, he had named this in his mind years ago: a song raised up to connubial union. There were meadowlarks and chats, field sparrows, indigo buntings, all with their heads raised to the dawn and their hearts pressed into clear liquid song for their mates. Garnett held his face in his hands for just a moment. As a boy he had never dreamed of an age when there was no song left, but still some heart.

{4}

Predators

She sat cross-legged on the floor of the porch, brushing out her hair and listening to the opening chorus of this day. A black-and-white warbler had started it long before dawn, breaking into her sleep with his high-pitched "Sweet *sweet!*" Deanna could picture him out there, circling the trunk of a poplar, tilting his tiny little zebra-striped head toward the first hints of light, tearing yesterday off the calendar and opening the summer of love with his outsized voice. She'd rushed out to the porch in her nightgown and bare feet, the hairbrush mostly an afterthought lying on her lap. She needed to listen to this: prodigal summer, the season of extravagant procreation. It could wear out everything in its path with its passionate excesses, but nothing alive with wings or a heart or a seed curled into itself in the ground could resist welcoming it back when it came.

The other warblers woke up soon after the black-and-white: first she heard the syncopated phrase of the hooded warbler with its upbeat ending like a good joke, then the Kentucky with his more solemn, rolling trill. By now a faint gray light was seeping up the edge of the sky, or what she could see of the sky through the black-armed trees. This hollow was a mean divide, with mountains rising steeply on both sides and the trees towering higher still. The cabin was no place to be if you craved long days and sunlight, but there was no better dawn chorus anywhere on earth. In the high season of courtship and mating, this music was like the earth itself opening its mouth to sing. Its crescendo crept forward slowly as the daylight roused one bird and then another: the black-capped and Carolina chickadees came next, first cousins who whistled their notes on separate pitches, close together, distinguishable to any chickadee but to very few humans, especially among this choir of other voices. Deanna smiled to hear the first veery, whose song sounded like a thumb run down the tines of a comb. It had been the first birdcall to capture her fascination in childhood—not the calls of the meadowlarks and sparrows that sang outside her windows on the farm every morning, but the song of the veery, a high-elevation migrant that she encountered only up here, on fishing expeditions with her dad. Maybe she'd just never really listened before those trips, which yielded few trout and less conversation but so much silent waiting in the woods. "Now, 'at's a comb bird," her dad had improvised, smiling, when she asked, and she'd dutifully pictured the bird as a comb-shaped creature, bright pink. She was disappointed, years later, when she discovered its brown, ordinary birdness in the Peterson field guide.

The dawn chorus was a whistling roar by now, the sound of a thousand males calling out love to a thousand silent females ready to choose and make the world new. It was nothing but heady cacophony unless you paid attention to the individual entries: a rose-breasted grosbeak with his sweet, complicated little sonnet; a vireo with his repetitious bursts of eighth notes and triplets. And then came the wood thrush, with his tone poem of a birdsong. The wood thrush defined these woods for Deanna, providing background music for her thoughts and naming her place in the forest. The dawn chorus would subside in another hour, but the wood thrush would persist for a long time into the morning, then pick up again in early evening or even at midday if it was cloudy. Nannie had asked her once in a letter how she could live up here alone with all the quiet, and that was Deanna's answer: when human conversation stopped, the world was anything but *quiet*. She lived with wood thrushes for company.

Deanna smiled a little to think of Nannie down there in the valley. Nannie lived for neighborly chat, staking out her independent old-lady life but still snatching conversation wherever possible, the way a dieter will keep after the cookies tucked in a cupboard. No wonder she worried for Deanna.

The sky had a solid white cast by now, mottled like an old porcelain plate, and the voices began to back off or drop out one by one. Soon she'd be left with only the thrush song and the rest of her day. A few titmice and chickadees were congregating at the spot underneath a chokecherry, a dozen yards from her cabin, where she always scattered birdseed on top of a flat boulder. She'd chosen a spot she could watch from her window and had put out seed there all winter—ordered birdseed by the fifty-pound bag, in fact, along with her monthly grocery requisition. The Forest Service never questioned it. It wasn't exactly policy to feed chickadees and cardinals, but apparently the government was willing to do whatever it took to keep a wildlife monitor sane through the winter, and in Deanna's case it was birdseed. Sitting at the table beside the window with her coffee on snowy February mornings, she could lose hours watching the colorful crowd that gathered outside, envying the birds their freedom in the intense cold. Envying, even, their self-important fuss and bustle. A bird never doubts its place at the center of the universe.

Now that it was the third week of May, buds were emerging and leaf-eating insects of every kind would soon be hanging thick on the trees, and these little Napoleons could find plenty to eat elsewhere, but they'd probably gotten addicted to her handouts. She was addicted to their presence, too. Lately she'd been thinking about dusting off her Smokey the Bear hat (she'd been issued both Park Service and Forest Service uniforms, as a glitch of this hybrid job) and putting it out there on the boulder every morning with seed on the brim so the birds would get used to landing on it. Eventually she'd be able to put it on and walk around with a gaggle of chickadees on her head, for no purpose other than her own foolish amusement.

She'd finished brushing out her hair. It cascaded down her back and shoulders and folded onto the porch floor where she sat, rippling all around her like a dark, tea-colored waterfall glittering with silver reflections. More silver each year, and less tea. She'd told her husband (*ex-* already by then), when he asked her why, that she was moving up onto the mountain so she wouldn't have to cut her hair. Apparently it was a rule for women in their forties: the short, perky haircut. He probably hadn't understood the joke, thinking it was some embryonic vanity on Deanna's part, but it wasn't. She rarely noticed her hair except to let it out of its braid for a run once a week or so, like a neglected hound. She just hadn't liked the rule, hadn't wanted to look her age, or *any* age. And who could be bothered with haircuts, weekly or monthly or whatever they had to be? Deanna actually didn't know. She'd managed to live her life apart from this and most other mysteries owned by women. Eyeliner, for instance: what was the instrument of its application, did it hurt, and what on earth was the point? She'd never quite had a real haircut. Her dad had known better than to take a girl child to his barber, and if he'd meant to think of some other option, he didn't get around to it before her wild mane grew down to the backs of her knees. The most she'd done in the way of coiffure was to untangle it from tree branches and trim the ends with the scissors on her Swiss Army knife. That was the only kind of woman she had ever known how to be, in Zebulon County and later on as a schoolteacher and attempted wife in Knoxville. Up here in the woods, finally, she could be the only kind of woman there was.

The kind without a man. Eddie Bondo was gone, and that had to be for the best.

He'd said he'd be back, but she did not believe it. He'd taken everything with him when he went—"everything" being his pack, which admittedly wasn't much. If what he said was true, that he intended only to hike over to Clinch Peak for a day or two and then come back to see her again, he would need his pack. So she couldn't judge his leaving by what he'd taken or left. It wasn't that.

He'd called her hair a miracle. He'd said it was like rolling himself up in a silkworm's cocoon.

She turned her face to the sky and listened to the blessed woods—that was what he'd left behind. A chance to listen to the dawn chorus and brush her hair without being watched. Eddie Bondo had left her this hard, fine gem of her very own, this diamond solitaire of a life.

She stretched her legs straight in front of her while she rebraided her hair into its familiar rope, an exercise her hands could do without mirror or attention. When she'd snapped the rubber band back onto it from her wrist, she bent her forehead to her knees, giving her hamstrings a good, painful stretch. Then she lay straight back, flat on her back like a girl, mouth and eyes open wide to the tree branches overhead. She gasped, dizzy, falling up, straight up into the treetops. Thought about the first time he'd laid her down on this porch. She wondered how she would look to him now, lying here like this.

She cursed aloud and sat up. Damned thing, self-consciousness, like a pitiful stray dog tagging you down the road—so hard to shake off. So easy to get back.

No man had ever spoken to her so freely of her body, or compared it to such strange and natural things. Not only a silkworm. Also ivory, for instance, which he claimed was unnaturally smooth.

He'd lived in Canada last summer into fall, he said—had gone up there to make money on the salmon run and stayed on hunting caribou around the Hudson Bay, and somewhere in the process had learned to work walrus ivory into knife handles. She listened to his stories, imagining the possibility of touching nature's other faces. She'd known no other but this one. She asked him what birds were there, and he seemed to know but couldn't name any except the game birds people shot for food. She had been listening too hard, she realized now, for the things he left out—what he meant or believed. To have her bare stomach compared to walrus ivory, was this strange compliment hers alone? She had no idea how to take him but had taken him nearly as hard as possible. It still ran a shock of physical weakness all the way through her to think of certain things: his body against hers, the scent of his skin. The look of awestruck joy on his face when he entered her.

She jumped up, shuddered from the cold and nonsense, and went inside to get dressed and find her day. She walked a circle around the room, stepping into jeans and boots without slowing down much. While she buttoned her shirt with one hand, she banged open the cupboard with the other and reached into the Dutch oven to grab some of yesterday's cornbread. She took a bite and stuffed the rest into her jacket pocket to eat on the trail, or later on, while she waited in the blind she was going to build. She'd wasted too much of this morning already. She'd stayed away from the den for such a long time, the first two weeks on purpose and the last ten days of necessity. She hadn't dared to go. Even if she'd gone out alone, or lied, he could have followed her.

She took the Bitter Creek trail down the mountain as fast as she could without breaking into a run, which would be pointless. If they were there, they would still be there in ten minutes. Or they might not be there at all. They were wary creatures, almost beyond a human's conception of wariness—and the day she'd discovered them, they surely had seen her first. It wasn't reasonable to think she could have outwitted or outsensed them. They could only assume she was an enemy, like every other human whose stink they'd ever caught wind of. If this was the same family that had lost half its members in one day over in the Zebulon Valley, the survivors would be cautious.

She was sure it was that family, or else some other refugees of human damage. Why else would they have ventured so high up the mountain into this forest, so far from the fencerows and field margins that are a coyote's usual domain? When they came over here to whelp their pups, they'd have dug themselves multiple dens. Backup plans were their trademark, the famous coyote wiles. Everything that was possible to know about them, though, Deanna knew. That only the alpha female would bear young, for instance; the other adults in the pack would forgo reproduction. They'd support the alpha instead, gathering food, guarding the den, playing with the pups, training them to forage and hunt after they emerged with their eyes open. If their parents got killed, the pups would hardly suffer for their absence—that was the nature of a coyote family. That was the point of it. And if Deanna's discovery of this burrow had disturbed the pack, its members would have moved those pups already to another place, in the middle of the night. Any predator that needs to sleep at night has already lost the game, with a coyote.

She slowed to a walk and then stopped a quarter mile from where she recalled the den as being, to consider building her blind. She'd have to be near enough to see, but downwind, of course, and the wind direction would change between morning and afternoon. She could build only one blind, since she wanted to create as little disturbance as possible and leave few clues in case anyone else should be poking around here. Mornings, then, it would be. She'd build the blind uphill and come to it only in the mornings, when the sun had warmed the fields down below and the air was still rising up the hollows toward the mountaintop.

She'd forgotten how far down the mountain she'd come that first time, to find this den by accident. Now as she searched it out she couldn't even be sure whether she was still on National Forest land or on the farm below that bordered it—there wasn't a fence here. But it was in deep woods, and higher than you'd expect. There wasn't enough known about coyotes in Appalachia to say what was really normal. They surely couldn't like the mountaintops; they'd prefer lowland fields because of field mice, among other things. But this family had its own history. It'd been shoved to the wall. So it had come up high, to stage its raids from safe hiding, like Geronimo.

She began to move forward again slowly, breaking and collecting low branches from sourwood trees. She left the path, protecting her eyes as she pushed her way through a thick clump of rhododendrons. Her intention was to circle wide around the den to where she could look at it from across the creek. The rhododendrons were almost impossibly dense, but that was fine: no one would find her trail. She wondered briefly about whoever farmed the land below here, and whether he liked to hunt. Probably he wouldn't come here. Most local farmers never set foot in the woods except in deer season, and then only with their friend Jack Daniel's for company. The real trouble, the bear poachers and that ilk, generally came from other places. Those men specialized and so had to range widely.

She sidestepped slowly downhill until she could see across the creek to the tangle of roots at the base of the giant fallen tree. She raised her binoculars to the slice of darkness beneath the roots, held her breath, and focused. Nothing. She sat down on a damp mattress of last autumn's leaves and prepared to wait. No point building a blind until she knew they were still here.

~

Deanna knew exactly when the morning ended. She never wore a watch, and for this she didn't need one. She knew when the air grew still enough that she could hear caterpillars overhead, newly hatched, eating through thousands of leaves on their way to becoming Io and luna moths. In the next hour the breeze would shift.

No sense taking a chance; it was time to leave, and she'd still seen nothing—no movement, no sign. No little dogs, foxlike and wolflike and cousin to both, so familiar from her studies that they sometimes ran through her dreams. Awake, she'd had good long looks at only one single animal, a pathetic captive that she'd rather forget, in the Tinker's Mountain Zoo outside of Knoxville. She'd pleaded with the curator to change the exhibit, explaining that coyotes were social, and that displaying a single animal was therefore not just cruel but also inaccurate. She had offered him her services: a graduate student in wildlife biology, finishing up a thesis on the coyote range extension in the twentieth century. The curator had politely suggested that if she wanted to see coyotes in groups she should take a trip out west, where the animals were so common that people got acquainted with them as roadkill. The conversation had given her a stomachache. So she'd written a grant proposal instead, invented this job, and put herself in it as soon as she'd completed and defended her thesis. She'd had to fight some skeptics, wrangling a rare agreement between the Park Service, the Forest Service, and the Department of Game and Inland Fisheries, so that there were almost more words on her paycheck than dollars. But it was working out fine, they all seemed to think now. Two years after her arrival, one of the most heavily poached ranges of southern Appalachia was becoming an intact ecosystem again. All of that was the point, but to her mind only partly so.

She breathed out now, resigned. One day she'd lay eyes on wily *Canis latrans* in the wild, right here in her own home range, on an animal path cross-stitched by other trails to the paths she'd walked in her childhood. It would happen. But it wouldn't be this day.

On her way back up the mountain she consciously slowed her step. She heard another magnolia warbler—a sign and a wonder, it seemed to her, like something risen from the dead. So many others never would rise again: Bachman's warbler, passenger pigeon, Carolina parakeet, Flint's stonefly, Apamea moth—so many extinct creatures moved through the leaves just outside her peripheral vision, for Deanna knew enough to realize that she lived among ghosts. She deferred to the extinct as she would to the spirits of deceased relatives, paying her quiet respects in the places where they might once have been. Little red wolves stood as silent shadows at the edges of clearings, while the Carolina parakeets would have chattered loudly, moving along the riverbanks in huge flocks of dazzling green and orange. The early human settlers migrating into this region had loved them and promptly killed them. Now most people would call you crazy if you told them that something as exotic as a parrot had once been at home in these homely southern counties.

She stopped and stared at her feet. Here were tracks, fresh, and she paused to study them out: front and hind foot alternating single-file in a long, sinuous line, the front foot a little bigger than the hind; this was a canid, all right. The claw marks were there, too, clear as could be. Where the tracks crossed a broad patch of clear mud she knelt down to take a close look, measuring a cleanly outlined print with the knuckle of her index finger. Two and three quarters inches front to back. *You learn what he is by knowing what he isn't,* her dad used to say. This was not a gray fox, and not a red fox. Coyote. A big one, probably male. Alpha's mate.

A little farther on, where the trail crossed a clearing and, most likely, other animal trails, she found his scat. One single turd with an up-curled point on its end like one of Ali Baba's shoes—this was coyote for certain, and who but a big male would make such a show out of his excrement? She squatted down and poked it apart with a twig. A coyote could eat nearly anything: mice, voles, grasshoppers, frogs. Human garbage, a house cat. The farmers down below were right to believe a coyote could take a lamb; working together, a pack might even bring down a full-grown cow. But that would take a huge pack, two dozen animals maybe, more adult coyotes than existed in this county and probably this end of the state. And why on earth would they go to the trouble when there was so much else on the slopes of this mountain for a coyote to eat, with greater safety and ease? Hardly a creature on earth could thrive more capably on junk that was useless to humans. During her thesis research she'd found the notes of a biologist named Murie who'd spent the early decades of his century dissecting coyote scat and recording its splendidly varied contents. He'd cataloged hundreds of different items in his journal. Her favorites were "shreds of woolen clothing" and "watermelon, poached."

From the crumbling consistency of this scat Deanna expected pine nuts and berry seeds, a predictable diet for the locale. She was surprised by the hard, dark glint of an apple seed. Then several more. *Apple seeds* at this time of year, late May? Apples were just barely past blossom-drop stage down in the valley. Wild apples still hanging on to the trees down there in the wilding fields would be a long shot. More likely this fellow had crept into an orchard where someone grew old-fashioned leathercoats that stayed on the tree all the way through winter into spring. Or he might have nipped into someone's root cellar and rolled the last sweet Arkansas blacks out of a bushel basket. Deanna was sympathetic. She'd stolen apples, too, in her time. Her dad's tobacco farm had been short on pleasures from a child's point of view, but when the two of them discovered Nannie Rawley and her orchard, respectively, Deanna found seventh heaven. Nannie was a generous woman who did not count her Arkansas blacks after the guests left.

Deanna's legs ached but she squatted a little longer, taking the time to flatten and dissect the scat completely with her twig. Something else here surprised her: millet seed, both red and white. No millet grew on this mountainside, or on any farm down below, as far as she knew. Certainly not red and white millet together; that was a combination unlikely to be found on any farm. Mostly it showed up in the commercial seed mixes people put out for their birds. Probably this was the birdseed she had put out herself. She stood up blinking, peered downhill through the tree trunks, and thought about it. Who else around here was likely to be feeding chickadees?

"You rascal," she said aloud, laughing. "You magnificent son of a bitch. *You've* been spying on *me.*"

⌒

She spent the afternoon in an edgy distraction, curled into the dilapidated green brocade armchair that sat on her porch against the outside wall, sheltered under the eave. With her field notebook on her knee she cataloged the contents of the scat and the size and location of the tracks and the location of the magnolia warbler she'd heard today. Then she reached back in her memory to the first magnolia warbler and quite a few other things she should have recorded before now. She had ignored her notebooks completely for the full nine days of his visit. Even now she felt abnormally jumpy, in need of something to eat, or to look up, or to check on, and had to scold herself like a child to sit still and focus. She stared at the blank, numbered pages ending with today's date, May 19, and felt coldly disgusted by her laziness and poor concentration. Anything could have happened in those days, life or death, and she would have missed it.

What she had here on this mountain was a chance that would never come again, for anybody: the return of a significant canid predator and the reordering of species it might bring about. Especially significant if the coyote turned out to be what R. T. Paine called a keystone predator. She'd carefully read and reread Paine's famous experiments from the 1960s, in which he'd removed all the starfish from his tidepools and watched the diversity of species drop from many to very few. The starfish preyed on mussels. Without starfish, the mussels boomed and either ate nearly everything else or crowded it out. No one had known, before that, how crucial a single carnivore could be to things so far removed from carnivory. Of course, the experiment had been replicated endlessly by accident: removing mountain lions from the Grand Canyon, for example, had rendered it a monoculture of prolific, starving deer that outbred all other herbivores and gnawed the landscape down to granite. Plenty of people had watched and recorded the disaster of eliminating a predator from a system. They were watching it here in her own beloved mountains, where North America's richest biological home was losing its richness to one extinction after another, of plants and birds, fish, mammals, moths and stoneflies, and especially the river creatures whose names she collected like beads: sugarspoon, forkshell, acornshell, leafshell. Sixty-five kinds of mussels, twenty now gone for good. There were hundreds of reasons for each death—pesticide runoff, silt from tilling, cattle in the creek—but for Deanna each one was also a piece in the puzzle she'd spent years working out. The main predator of the endangered shellfish was the muskrat, which had overpopulated to pestilence along the riverbanks over the last fifty years. What had kept muskrats in check, historically, was the mink (now mostly coats), the river otter (also nearly gone), and, surely, the red wolf. There was no telling how the return of a large, hungry dog might work to restore stability, even after an absence of two hundred years. Rare things, endangered things, not just river life but overgrazed plants and their insect pollinators, might begin to recover.

Or maybe coyotes would turn out to be pests, as newly introduced species nearly always are. Maybe the farmers were right to shoot them—she had to concede it was possible. But she didn't think so. She believed coyotes were succeeding here for a single reason: they were sliding quietly into the niche vacated two hundred years ago by the red wolf. The two predators were hardly distinct: the red wolf may have been a genetic cross between the gray wolf and the coyote. Like the coyote, it was a scent hunter that could track in the dead of night, unlike the big cats that hunt by sight. It was like a coyote in its reproductive rate, and close in size. In fact, judging from the tracks she'd seen, the coyotes here were nearly red wolf–sized, and probably getting larger with each generation—insinuating themselves into the ragged hole in this land that needed them to fill it. The ghost of a creature long extinct was coming in on silent footprints, returning to the place it had once held in the complex anatomy of this forest like a beating heart returned to its body. This was what she believed she would see, if she watched, at this magical juncture: a restoration. If she was not too lazy or careless. And if she did not lead a killer to their lair.

She frowned and conjured notes, remembering the red and white millet and wondering how else she might be influencing the experiment. She bit her pen, trying to concentrate. The longer she worked, the more surely her body's cravings grew from a nudge to a frank distraction. She wanted something to eat, warm and particular. She would not let herself name this craving what it was, so she named it food, a thing that normally didn't merit a second thought in her life here—she ate when she was hungry, and anything would do. But for this whole day her body had been speaking to her of its presence: an ache in the thigh, a need in the gut.

Maybe navy bean soup would do it, she decided, jumping up and going inside. Navy beans steaming in an enamel bowl, smothering the rest of the leftover cornbread. He'd made a bright yellow pone of it in her Dutch oven yesterday morning before he left—to take with him, she'd assumed, but instead he'd left most of it for her. She would bring it back out here to the porch chair and sit facing west, with her back carefully turned on Clinch Peak. Watch the sky turn to flame behind the trees.

She went inside, lit the kerosene lamp, and first went without thinking to the big metal canister where she stored her ten-pound bags of beans, but then paused there, feeling foolish. It was too late to soak them and cook them from scratch as she normally did, making enough at one time for half a week's distracted consumption. But she was pretty sure she had a can of precooked white beans in the back of the cupboard. She flung back doors and raked aside jars of spaghetti sauce, Campbell's soup, ravioli, things she'd forgotten were here—she rarely bothered with much beyond beans and rice. She shoved aside the Dutch oven to look behind it and was dismayed to see the heavy iron lid sitting ajar. Darn it! She must have left it that way this morning in her rush to get out the door, and the army of mice in this cabin didn't need an invitation. She looked inside knowing exactly what she'd see: the crisp round edge nibbled ragged, the scattering of black droppings over the golden surface. Tears sprang to her eyes as she stared into the heavy pot.

"Too much of a fool-headed hurry, Deanna," she said out loud.

It was only food, and she had plenty more, but what she'd wanted was this. She slammed down the lid, swung the heavy pot down from the shelf, and headed outside. She *had* left the lid ajar, no "must have" about it. Living alone leaves you no one to curse but yourself when the toilet paper grins its empty cardboard jeer at you in the outhouse, or when the cornbread is peppered with poop. She could blame the mice if she wanted to, little devils. But they were only doing their job, which was the same as everybody else's: surviving.

All right, then; fascinated by animal scat though she was (the last straw for her ex-husband, *that* part of her thesis), she was not about to eat it, nor eat after a mouse, either. She walked to the end of the porch in her heavy wool socks and continued out to the boulder under the wild cherry. She shook the hunks of yellow cornbread and crumbs onto the ground, adding her loss to the nebulae of birdseed glittering there. Then, dispirited utterly, she went back inside, sat at her table, and ate cold ravioli out of a can while she finished recording her notes. To hell with the body's cravings.

Before sunset she rose from the table and stretched because she was cramped, then walked out to the porch for no good reason, just in time to catch the unusual sight of a luna moth flying in the daytime. The surprising ascent, like a pair of pale hickory leaves caught in an updraft, arrested her there in the doorway. She watched it flutter upward gradually by increments: up, down, then a little higher up, as if it were climbing a staircase in the air. Deanna didn't realize she was holding her breath, even when she released it finally as the creature reached the upper leaves of the chokecherry, landed there, and held on. Luna moths were common enough up here but still never failed to move her because of their size and those pale-green, ethereal wings tipped with long, graceful tails. As if they were already ghosts, mourning their future extinction. This one was out of its element, awake in broad daylight. A busy chipmunk might have rousted it from a lower resting place. Or it was possible she was witnessing the fatal, final disorientation that overcomes a creature as it reaches the end of its life. Once, as a child, waiting with her dad in a gas station, she'd found a luna moth in that condition: confused and dying on the pavement in front of their truck. For the time it took him to pump the gas she'd held it in her hand and watched it struggle against its end. Up close it was a frightening beast, writhing and beating against her hand until wisps of pale-green fur slipped off its body and stuck to her fingers. Her horror had made her want to throw it down, and it was only her preconceived affection for the luna that made her hold on. When these creatures danced above their yard at night, she and her dad called them ballerinas. But this was no ballerina. Its body was a fat, furry cone flattened on one end into a ferocious face like a tiny, angry owl's. It glared at Deanna, seeming to know too much for an insect and, worse, seeming disdainful. She hadn't given up her love for luna after that, but she'd never forgotten, either, how a mystery caught in the hand could lose its grace.

It was later, long past dark, after she'd pinched out the lamp and was nearly asleep in her cot but not quite, when she heard him outside. Those were footsteps, she felt sure, though it wasn't the crackle of a step that she'd heard. It wasn't anything, really. She sat up in bed hugging herself under the blanket, holding her braid in her mouth to keep herself still. It was nothing, but *nothing* isn't an absence, it's a presence. A quieting of the insect noise, a change in the quality of night that means something is there, or someone. Or was it less than nothing, just a raccoon waddling through his endless rounds, come to scavenge the cornbread she'd thrown out?

Finally she heard something definite: the crackle of a step. She groped for the flashlight she kept under the cot, slipped her bare feet into her boots, and got to the door, where she stood quiet, looking out. Should she speak? Why didn't he come?

Out in the darkness beyond the end of the porch where she scattered the seed—that was where he was. She could actually see movement. She put the butt end of the flashlight against her forehead, just above the space between her eyebrows. It was something she'd learned long ago about seeing at night. A light shined from there would reveal nothing of herself to a trespasser, and from that spot on her forehead a beam would go straight to his retinas and return to her own eyes the characteristic color of the trespasser's eyeshine. If it *had* eyes, of course, and if they were looking at her directly.

She waited a little longer, heard nothing. Clicked on her light: only darkness at first. Then suddenly two small lights appeared, bright retinal glints—not the fierce red of a human eye, but greenish gold. Not human, not raccoon. Coyote.

{5}

Moth Love

he spiraling flights of moths appear haphazard only because the mechanisms of olfactory tracking are so different from our own. Using binocular vision, we judge the location of an object by comparing the images from two eyes and tracking directly toward the stimulus. But for species relying on the sense of smell, the organism compares points in space, moves in the direction of the greater concentration, then compares two more points successively, moving in zigzags toward the source. Using olfactory navigation the moth detects currents of scent in the air and, by small increments, discovers how to move upstream.

It was Lusa's nephews running a zigzag course through the metal folding chairs that had set her to ruminating on that passage she'd read on moth navigation, and then roused her suddenly to wonder: When was that, a hundred years ago? Day before yesterday? Reading in bed secretly, hurrying to finish a page or a chapter before Cole got back: there would be no more of that. Now she could read wherever she pleased, read until she finished the book if that was what she felt like. Lusa tried to make this strange dream feel true but couldn't quite connect herself with the person she found herself sitting inside of here, a woman in a borrowed black dress that hung loose in the bosom. This funeral parlor was a place she'd never seen on the inside or even imagined, especially not for the occasion of her husband's wake. The rooms were painted a stale toothpaste green, and the fancy, dark-painted molding around the doors was actually molded plastic, textured with artificial grain to look like wood. What an odd thing, Lusa thought, to buy and install plastic woodwork in this town surrounded on every side by forests.

Beyond the doorway she could hear the people who waited in line, filling the long, narrow hallway like a glass pipette or medicine dropper that kept dispensing solemn visitors into the room, one stricken face at a time. Visitors just now arriving for the viewing would have to wait in line for an hour or more, Mary Edna had just announced (seeming pleased) after going out for reconnaissance. The line was out the door now that it was evening and people were getting off work. Most came in their work clothes, the clean jeans they'd worn underneath their milking overalls if need be; suits and ties would be saved for the funeral tomorrow. Tonight was a friendlier business, their chance to look at Cole and say their private good-byes. There was hardly a soul in the valley who had not turned out, it seemed. Cole was very well loved—Lusa had known this, of course. And also there was the handiwork of the undertaker to be admired, given the accident.

Lusa hadn't had to wait in the line. She was the end of the line, sitting near the head of the casket where people could come over and pay their respects if they wanted to, though most of them knew her only by name and hearsay and couldn't manage much more than a stiff little nod. She knew they were sorry, though. To the rest of Cole's family they were pouring out such a stream of condolences that Lusa feared she might drown in the backwash. She sat on a metal chair flanked by sisters-in-law—Hannie-Mavis and Mary Edna at the moment. When Mary Edna went out front to hold court she was replaced by Jewel or Lois or Emaline, interchangeable blocks in a solid, black-clad wall. Maybe not precisely interchangeable. She felt a little breathing room when it was Jewel, who was less overbearing than Mary Edna of the tree-trunk physique or Lois with her deep smoker's croak. Or Hannie-Mavis with eyeliner à la Cleopatra, even for this somber occasion. In the beginning, when Lusa needed a secret mnemonic to learn their names, Mary Edna had been Menacing Eldest; Hannie-Mavis kept Makeup Handy; Long-faced Lois was Long-haired and Loud; Emaline was Emotional. But Jewel was just Jewel, an empty vessel with two kids and mournful eyes the exact color of Cole's. Lusa couldn't remember ever having had a conversation with Jewel, or having watched her do anything beyond handing Popsicles to the children out in the yard at family gatherings and, once, walking up the drive to ask Lusa if she'd seen their missing bobtail cat.

Jewel's and Hannie-Mavis's five-year-olds were running under-foot, literally: one of the two had just climbed underneath Lusa's legs and the strange black stockings someone had given her to put on. The persistent, spiraling path of these boys through their uncle's wake made her ponder moth navigation: were the children sampling the air for grief in different parts of the room? If so, what would they find in the air around Lusa? She found it impossible to feel anything. Somehow her numbness seemed connected with the great din of noise. As the evening wore on and on, the noise seemed to rise like a tide. So many conversations at once added up to a kind of quacking racket that she could not begin to sort through. She found herself considering, instead, the sounds of non-sensical phrases that bounced into her ears. Mountain speech, even without its words, was a whole different language from city speech: the vowels were a little harsher, but the whole cadence was some-how softer. *'At'en up 'air,* she heard again and again: "That one up there."

Hit's not for sale. Them cows come over on Lawrence again. Wet'sit is, won't be no more tobacco setting this week, Law, no. Hit's a line fence. Why sure, I wouldn't care to. Widener boy, old Widener place, Law, yes, I been up 'air.

Why yeah, fishing, when I's a kid. 'Air's a pond up 'at holler. Bitter Holler.

No, no bid'ness of hers. That's Widener land and everybody knows it, you-all's family place, what does she have to do with it?

No, she won't stay on it. Don't hardly see how she could.

This last, she realized with a start, was Mary Edna. Over near the door, speaking of *her*, Lusa. How could this have been decided already? But it was only natural, even a kindness, Lusa supposed, for them to release her so easily. What else could they expect but for Lusa to pack up her butterfly nets and her foreign name and go back to Lexington now? "Where she belongs," was the end of the sentence she didn't hear spoken aloud.

She felt a strange lightness: Yes! She could walk away from Zebulon County. She'd been granted more than just the freedom to read in bed all she wanted, which would still mean hiding from sisters-in-law who disapproved of reading and probably the whole idea of being in bed. No, it was that she could leave this place, be anybody she wanted, anywhere at all. She put her hands to her face and felt a joyful urge to tell Cole: they could leave now! Oh, God, Cole. She ground her knuckles into her eye sockets and vaguely grasped how far gone she must be. Shock, two nights without sleep, and two days of people eating ham sandwiches in her kitchen had caused her to lose her mind. Her body, as if it belonged to someone else, began to shake with a dry, sharp rack she was helpless to stop, a strange weeping from her throat that sounded almost like laughter. Hannie-Mavis put an arm around Lusa's convulsing shoulders and whispered, "Honey, I don't know what we'll do without him. We're all just as lost as you are."

Lusa looked at Hannie-Mavis. Behind the fiercely curled and blue-mascaraed lashes, her eyes did seem helpless, truly as lost as she claimed. What was she trying to say? That Lusa had no prerogative to the greatest grief? First as mistress of their house, and now as Cole's widow, Lusa was occupying a place she didn't deserve?

"You'll be all right," Lusa told her without feeling. *As soon as I'm gone.*

The evening had the sensation of a dream she would not remember in the morning. Trapped in the endless repetition, she shook the callused palms of men who still milked cows by hand, and accepted the scented, too-soft cheeks of their wives against her own.

"He was a good man. Only the Lord knows why his time came so soon."

"Called home. He's with the Savior now."

"He looks real natural."

She hadn't looked at the body and couldn't contemplate it. She could not really think it was in there, not his *body*, the great perfect table of his stomach on which she could lay down her head like a sleepy schoolchild; that energy of his that she had learned to crave and move to like an old tune inside her that she'd never known how to sing before Cole. His hands on her bare back, his mouth that drew her in like a nectar guide on a flower—these things of Cole's she would never have again in her life. She opened her eyes for fear she would fall into the darkness. A tiny old woman was there, kneeling in front of her, startling Lusa by putting both hands very firmly on her knees.

"You don't know me," she whispered, almost fiercely. "I have an orchard a mile up the road from your farm. I've known Cole Widener since he was a little boy. He used to come play with my daughter. I'd let him steal apples."

"Oh," Lusa said. "Thank you."

The woman looked upward and blinked as if she were listening for a moment. Her eyes were very deep brown, surrounded by pale lashes, and she wore her gray hair in a crown of braids wrapped around her head, like someone from another country or another time. "I lost a child," she said, meeting Lusa's eyes directly. "I thought I wouldn't live through it. But you do. You learn to love the place somebody leaves behind for you."

She released Lusa's knees and grasped her hands instead, holding them tightly for a few seconds before ducking away. Her grip had felt so cool and strong on Lusa's listless fingers, and so fleeting. As the woman went out the door Lusa caught sight of her calico skirt swinging to the side, like a curtain closing.

Sometime after nine o'clock, Mary Edna began to insist that Lusa go home. Herb could take her, she suggested, and then come back to wait out the evening with the rest of the family. Or someone else could do it—there was a volunteer, a Widener cousin, who would stay with her so she wouldn't have to be alone in the house until the others got there.

"But why should I go home if you're all still staying?" Lusa asked, as muddled as a child. And then, like a muddled child who senses she's being wronged, she pushed her faltering will into a dogged single-mindedness. She told Mary Edna she would stay here till the end, until the last person had said good-bye to Cole and left this room. She would see the back of Herb Goins's bald head and the hind ends of Mary Edna, Lois, Jewel, Emaline, and Hannie-Mavis pass through that door, and then she would kiss her husband good-bye. She didn't think about Cole's body or anything else as she declared her intention to stay. She just repeated it, more angrily each time, until she made it come true.

Two days and two nights after the wake, Lusa still hadn't slept. She couldn't understand how her mind could fail to collapse over her body's exhaustion. But it was the opposite: the more tired she felt, the more adamantly her mind seemed to want to keep vigil. Over what? Nobody's going to steal the silver, she mused, not that she would give a hoot if somebody did—and well somebody might, the house was so jammed with visitors. On Friday afternoon, right after the funeral, she had dozed off for just a minute on the parlor couch in a room full of people dressed in their Sunday clothes. She could swear it was the quiet that woke her, the fact that their talk of crops and rain and beef prices and rheumatism suddenly ceased when they realized she was sleeping. Lusa had opened her eyes onto their sorrowful, silent stares, as if she herself were the occasion of a wake, and she'd felt the possibility of sleep frozen away from her ever since.

Things at least quieted down after dark, when all the reasonable hours for eating or visiting were past. Even that nudnick the minister wouldn't show up now. But nights were the worst for Lusa. She had to prowl the upper rooms, avoiding the bedroom where she and Cole had slept but effectively being trapped upstairs since Jewel and Hannie-Mavis still held the downstairs, for the fifth night in a row. Apparently they had moved in. It was Saturday now—Sunday morning, rather, could that be right? Didn't they need to go home to their husbands and children? Lusa lay on top of the coverlet on the daybed in the spare room (her sisters-in-law called it the girls' room), listening to the toneless mutter of their conversation. She wished for deafness—she had already overheard too much, too many suppositions about her fragility, her plans, her lack of religious faith or even her own kin to lean on. Mary Edna had said to the minister, sotto voce, "Now, you *know*, the wife isn't Christian." As though that explained, in part, her impossible bad fortune. All of them, sisters and neighbors, intimated to one another the mysteries of her father's long-lost parentage ("that Jewish business, in the war") and her mother's more recent poor health ("back in the spring, sad—no, not all that old"), without understanding how life had left Lusa with two speechless parents. Ever since the stroke, her mother's frantic eyes searched so desperately for words that Lusa could hardly bear to see it, while her father resigned himself to the silence as if it were his own death and he'd been waiting for it. When she called to tell him her awful news, his son-in-law dead, her father seemed slow to grasp how this new tragedy was connected with him. They hadn't even discussed his coming for the funeral.

Hannie-Mavis and Jewel were down there in the kitchen now, mousy, downcast Jewel playing foil to the more dramatic Handy-Makeup, whose tears invoked constant facial repair (though the emotive Emaline had outdone her earlier by letting out loud wails in front of Cole's baby picture). Things seemed to calm down a lot when the visitors left, but Lusa could still hear them talking and handling food. Everything in the kitchen remained exactly as their mother had organized it. When Lusa had tried to rearrange the cupboards, they'd all treated it as a mistake to be repaired and forgiven. She could picture the two of them now, their hands uncrinkling and reusing squares of aluminum foil to cover the casseroles. The incessant opening and closing of the refrigerator—a whine and a hiss—had become the theme music to Lusa's misery.

If only she could sleep, only leave this place for a little while. When the Regulator clock downstairs chimed one o'clock, she gave up. Sleep would not come to her tonight. There were ghosts everywhere, even here in the neutral guest bedroom where Lusa had hardly spent an hour of her life before this. The bed had no memories in it, but there was Cole's big bass fiddle standing up in the corner, spooking her with its presence as badly as if it were a man standing there in the shadows. She kept thinking of Cole's hands on its neck sliding fluidly up and down, as if there were still some parts of him that hadn't yet conceded to die. One more piece of the bottomless unfairness of this death: she'd never really taken the time to listen to him play. He'd let the music go in recent years, though she knew back in high school he'd been good enough to travel around the area with a bluegrass band. Out of the Blue, it was called. She wondered who the other members were—the fiddle, the guitar, the mandolin, all played by hands that probably had shaken hers in the last few days, though no one had mentioned it. Now Cole was permanently missing from their number, like a tooth knocked out, and his upright bass stood waiting in its corner.

She stared at its dark, glossy curves, realizing that the instrument was old, probably older even than this hundred-year-old house. Other dead men had surely played it before Cole. She'd never asked him where it came from. How strange that you could share the objects of your life with whole communities of the dead and never give them a single thought until one of your own crossed over. Lusa had come only lately to this truth: she was living among ghosts.

She sighed and got up. She would go back to her own bedroom and read Nabokov or something to shut off her mind. Sleep wouldn't be possible in that bed, either—least of all there—but the bedroom at least had a reading light. A book would make morning come sooner. She thought of how Cole used to rise at five A.M., even earlier in the summer, and how she used to dread the break of day with its tangle of work and choices. That dread was nothing, now, compared to the unbounded misery of a sleepless night. At this moment she would give her soul for daybreak.

She found her slippers and skated over the creaky floorboards, heading downstairs to look for the book she thought she'd left in the parlor. In her present state of mind, who knew? She could just as easily have left it in the refrigerator. Earlier today she'd poured the minister a glass of iced tea, stirred in the sugar, placed the sugar-bowl lid on the glass and set it back in the cupboard, then served Brother Leonard the sugar bowl. She hadn't even noticed anything was amiss until Jewel silently got up to reverse the mistake.

She couldn't face any of them after that. Only now, finally, did it seem safe to go down and look for her book. The kitchen had been quiet for a while. Her sisters-in-law must be asleep at their posts on the parlor and living-room couches.

But a fluttering white ascent startled her on the stairs: Jewel or Hannie-Mavis, one of the two, flying upstairs in her nightgown.

"I was coming to check on you. I heard you moving around." Jewel, it was.

"Oh. I was just coming down to get a book."

"You can't be reading now, honey. You need to sleep."

Lusa's shoulders fell helplessly in the darkness. *Tell Lazarus he needs to get up.*

"I can't," she said. "I've tried and tried, but I can't."

"I know. I brought you something to take. I got these from Dr. Gibben when Shel went away. I had the same thing."

Went away. Jewel's husband had left her three or four years ago, a fact so fully undeclared by the family that Lusa had fully forgotten it. And so, take what—poison? Lusa felt for Jewel's hands, heard the clicking rattle of the little plastic bottle. Racked her useless brain for meaning. "Oh, a sleeping pill?"

"Yeah."

"I don't think I could."

"They won't hurt you any."

"I hardly ever take anything, though. Not even aspirin for a headache. I'm kind of scared of pills. I almost feel like I'm scared of falling asleep right now, too. Does that seem silly?"

Jewel's white nightgown hung from the peaks of its ruffled shoulders, suspended in the air like a moth or a ghost. Her voice came from the darkness above it. "I know. You want to just close your eyes on all of it, but at the same time you're thinking there's something you need to see, and you'll miss it."

"That's right." Lusa leaned forward in the darkness, amazed, wanting to touch the face she couldn't see to make sure it was really Jewel. She couldn't reconcile this wise compassion with the woman she knew. The empty vessel, as she had called her.

"After a while, you . . . I don't know how to say it." The voice paused, growing shy, and then Lusa could see in her mind's eye that this was Jewel. "After a while you stop missing a man, you know, in a physical way. The Lord helps you forget."

"Oh, God." Lusa let out a whimper, recalling a body so heavy to her touch, so much like congealed fluid, that she had recoiled from it, just grazing the forehead with her lips before running away.

She sank onto the carpeted stair and began to sob. She couldn't even feel embarrassed, didn't have the energy. The white-winged apparition above her lowered itself down and hugged her tightly.

After a minute they let go of each other. "What am I saying?" Jewel cried softly. "You're so young and pretty. You'll marry again. I know you can't even think of it now, but you will."

Lusa felt emptied out. "You're young, too, Jewel. The same as me."

"No," she said. "Not the same. For me it's done."

"Why?"

"Shhh." She put her hand gently across Lusa's mouth and then stroked her hair. "You need to sleep. You have to give in sometime. You get to a point to where you just start wishing you wasn't living, and that's worse than being scared."

Lusa put out her hand and felt for Jewel's, felt it open the bottle and place one weightless dot on her palm. If she looked just off to the side of it she could see it there, like a distant, guiding star.

"You go up and take that right now. Drink you a glass of water with it and go lay down. Sometimes you just need a little help."

She lay on her side watching the red numbers on the digital clock on Cole's side of the bed. First she feared to feel the effects of the pill in her limbs, and then, slowly, she arrived at the much more dreadful understanding that there would be no effect. When the clock downstairs chimed twice, Lusa felt pure, bleak despair. Jewel was right: this body of hers was crushed with the waiting. Her mind was longing for death.

And then it was over.

Sleep took Lusa away to a wide, steep pasture cleared out of the forest. A man spoke to her by name:

"Lusa."

He was a stranger to her, no one she thought she knew. She could hear his voice but couldn't see him. She was lying in the dewy grass, on her side, wrapped up completely in a dark blanket that even covered her head.

"How did you know it was me?" she asked him through the blanket, because suddenly she understood there were women lying all over this field, also wrapped in dark-colored blankets.

He answered, "I know you. I know the shape of your body."

"You've been looking at me closely, then."

"I have."

She felt an acute, erotic awareness of her small waist and short thigh bones, the particular roundness of her hip—things that might distinguish her from all the other women lying under blankets. The unbearable, exquisite pleasure of being chosen.

"You knew me well enough to find me here?"

His voice was soft, reaching across the distance to explain his position in the most uncomplicated terms conceivable. "I've always known you that well."

His scent burst onto her brain like a rain of lights, causing her to know him perfectly. *This is how moths speak to each other. The wrong words are impossible when there are no words.*

She rolled toward him and opened her blanket.

He was covered in fur, not a man at all but a mountain with the silky, pale-green extremities and maroon shoulders of a luna moth. He wrapped her in his softness, touched her face with what seemed to be the movement of trees. His odor was of water over stones and the musk of decaying leaves, a wild, sweet aura that drove her to a madness of pure want. She pushed herself down against the whole length of him, rubbing his stippled body like a forest between her legs, craving to dissolve her need inside the confidence of his embrace. It was those things exactly, his solid strength and immensity, that comforted her as he shuddered and came into her.

She woke in a sweat, her back arched with simultaneous desire and release. She touched her body quickly—her breasts, her face—reassuring herself of her own shape. It seemed impossible, but here she was after everything that had happened, still herself, Lusa.

It was daybreak. She curled onto her side and stared for a long time out the open window at the solemn poplars standing on either side of the hollow, guarding the mouth of the mountain that still breathed gently into her window. Above the trees stood a pale white sky where the waxing moon must have hung just a little while ago: morning, with its tangle of work and choices. A day of her own, faintly scented with honeysuckle. What he'd reached out to tell her that morning, as she sat near the window, was that words were not the whole truth. What she'd loved was here, and still might be, if she could find her way to it.

She pulled up the sheet and closed her eyes, accepting solitude in the bed that was hers, if she chose it.

{6}

Old Chestnuts

arnett could still remember, from when he was a boy, a giant hollow log way back up in the woods on Zebulon Mountain. It was of such a size that he and the other youngsters could run through it single-file without even bending their heads. The thought made him smile. They had reckoned it to be theirs, for a ten-year-old boy will happily presume ownership of a miracle of nature, and then carve on it with his knife. They'd called it by some kind of name—what was it? Something Indian. The Indian Tunnel.

A surprising fact occurred to Garnett then, for the first time in his nearly eighty years: the unfortunate fellow who'd chopped down that tree, miscalculating its size and then having to leave it, must have been his grandfather. How many times before had Garnett stood right here at the edge of his seedling field staring up at that mountainside, ruminating on the Indian Tunnel? But he'd never put the two facts together. That tree must have come down near a hundred years ago, when his grandfather owned the whole southern slope of Zebulon Mountain. It was his grandfather, the first Garnett Walker, who'd named it, modestly choosing Zebulon from the Bible, even though some still did call it Walker's Mountain. Who else could have felled that tree? He and his sons would have spent a whole day and more with their shoulders against the cross-cut saw to bring down that giant for lumber. They'd have been mad as hornets, then, to find after all their work that the old chestnut was too huge to be dragged down off the mountain. Probably they took away tree-sized branches to be milled into barn siding, but that trunk was just too big of an old monster and had to be left where it lay. Left to hollow itself out from the inside till nothing was left of it but a game for the useless mischief of boys.

Mules, they had to use in those days for any kind of work that got done: mules or men. A tractor was a thing still yet undreamed of. A mule could be coaxed into many a steep and narrow place where a tractor would not go, it was true. But! Some things could be wrought with horsepower that were beyond the power of horse-flesh. That was the lesson he was meant to draw here, God's purpose for these paired recollections of Grandfather Walker and the Indian Tunnel. If they'd had a logging sledge or a good John Deere, that tree would not have gone to waste as boy-tunnel and bear den. Yes, sometimes horsepower can do what horseflesh cannot.

That was just it, the very thing he had been trying to tell the Rawley woman for years. "Miss Rawley," he'd explained until he was blue in the face as she traipsed through her primitive shenanigans, "however fondly we might recall the simple times of old, they had their limits. People keep the customs of their own day and time for good reason."

Nannie Land Rawley was Garnett's nearest neighbor and the bane of his life.

Miss Rawley it was and ever would be, not *Missus,* even though she had once borne a child and it was well known in Zebulon County that she'd never married the father. And that had been some thirty years ago or more, a far cry before the days when young girls began to wear rings in their noses and bells on their toes as they did now, and turn out illegitimate children as a matter of course. In those days, a girl went away for a decent interval to visit a so-called relative and came back sadder but wiser. But not Miss Rawley. She never appeared the least bit sad, and the woman was unwise on principle. She'd carried the child right here in front of God and everybody, christened the poor thing with a ridiculous name, and acted like she had every right to parade a bastard child through a God-fearing community.

And every one of them has forgiven her by now, he reflected bitterly, peering up the rise through the trunks of her lower orchard toward her house, which sat much too close to his own on the crest of a small, flat knoll just before the land rose steeply up the mountainside. Of course there was the tragic business with the child to win them over, but even so, Nannie was the sort, she could get away with anything. *Every one of them just as pleasant as the day is long when they meet her out here in the lane, Nannie all rosy-cheeked amongst her daisies with her long calico skirt and braids wrapped around her head like some storybook Gretel.* They might gossip some, for how could such an odd bird fail to attract the occasional sharp arrow let loose from Oda Black down at the Black Store? But even the vociferous Oda would put a hand beside her mouth to cut short a remark about Nannie, letting the suggestion of it hang but packaging it with deep regret. Nannie bribed Oda with apple pies; that was one of her methods. People thought she was comical and intriguing but for the most part excessively kind. They didn't suspect her little figure of harboring the devil, as Garnett Walker did. He suspected Nannie Rawley had been put on this earth to try his soul and tempt his faith into doubt.

Why else, with all the good orchard land stretching north from here to the Adirondacks, would that woman have ended up as his neighbor?

Her sign alone was enough to give him hives. For two months

now, ever since she'd first crept over on his side to put up that sign, he'd lain awake nearly every night, letting it get on his nerves: Heaven knows it's one thing when a Hereford jumps a fence and gets over onto a neighbor, *that* a body can forgive and forget, but a three-foot plywood sign does not get up and walk. Last night he'd fretted till nearly the crack of dawn, and after breakfast he'd made up his mind to walk out through his front seedling field to check the road frontage. Looking for "signs and wonders," as the Bible said, though Nannie's sign was known only for bad behavior.

He could see it now through the weeds, the back side of it, poking up out of the bank above Highway 6. He squinted to make sure; his eyesight had reached the point where it required some effort. Yes, the lettered side was facing the road, but he knew what it said, the whole hand-painted foolishness of it commanding the roadside—*his* roadside, two hundred feet over his property line—to be a "NO SPRAY ZONE." As if all a person had to do to rule the world was concoct a fool set of opinions and paint them on a three-by-three square of plywood. That in a nutshell was Nannie Rawley.

His plan for today was to hoist that sign with a mighty heave back over her fence into the ditch, where it would be consumed by the swamp of weeds that had sprung up in the wake of her ban on herbicide spraying; then justice would prevail in his small corner of God's green earth. He hoped she was watching.

Garnett waded carefully down the embankment through the tall weeds and yanked up the sign, with enough difficulty that he changed his mind and hoped she *wasn't* watching. He had to grasp it with both hands and wobble the stake for quite a long time to loosen it out of its hole. The woman must have swung a four-pound mallet to drive it in; he was lucky she hadn't dug a posthole with her antique tractor and set it in cement. He could picture it. She had no respect for property, for her elders in general, or for Garnett in particular. No use for men at all, he suspected darkly—and just as well. No love lost there on either side.

He began wading toward the property line, swishing and hacking a path through the weeds ahead of him with the sign. He felt like one of the knights of old, fighting his way through an army of foes with his wooden sword. The bank and road cut were in a hateful condition, just one long tangle of poke, cockleburs, and multiflora briars nearly as high as his chest. He had to stop every few yards to untangle his shirtsleeves from the stickerbushes. This was all Nannie's doing, his cross to bear. Everywhere else in Zebulon County—everywhere but here—the county road workers kept the road cuts mowed or, if the banks were too steep for mowing, like this one that fronted his farm, at least kept them sprayed. It took only one good dose of Two-Four-D herbicide every month to shrivel these leafy weeds to a nice, withered stand of rustybrown stalks, easily raked down afterward to show the world a tidy frontage. But instead he had this, now—this tangle of briars harboring vermin of every kind known to man, breeding in here and getting set to invade his F1 chestnut seedling field. It would take him days to cut through all this with a weed-eater or a mowing scythe, and he wasn't sure his heart could take it. In three short months Garnett's farm—whose fields he kept as neat as pickle, once you got up past the road cut—had come to look like a disgrace to passersby. Probably it was all they talked about down at Black Store, that Garnett Walker was a lazy old man(!), when it was really none other than Nannie Land Rawley, their dear darling friend, working in her unseen ways to ruin him.

It had started back in April when he left this steep weed patch to the county's boys for spraying, since it was a county right-of-way. The first of May he'd done the same again. Both times she'd snuck out here in the middle of the night before road-spraying day, working in darkness like the witch she was, to move her sign over onto Garnett. Now it was the second of June, and the spray truck must be due again soon. How could she always know when it was coming? Was that witchcraft, too? Most people around here couldn't even predict when their own cows were going to calve, let alone prophesy the work habits of a bunch of county-employed teenage hoodlums wearing earplugs, jewelry, and oversized trousers.

In previous years, he had talked to her. He'd had the patience of Job, informing her it was her duty to keep her NO SPRAY ZONE, if she insisted on having such a thing, inside of her own legal property boundaries. He had pointed dramatically at their line fence and stated (for Garnett was a reader), "Miss Rawley, as the poet said, 'Good fences make good neighbors.'"

She would reply, "Oh, people just adore fences, but Nature doesn't give a hoot." She claimed the wind caused the weed killer on his side to drift over into her orchards.

He'd explained it to her scientifically. "One application of herbicide on my bank will not cause your apple trees or anybody else's to drop off all their leaves."

"Not to drop their leaves, no," she'd admitted. "But what if some inspector came tomorrow to spot-check for chemicals on my apples? I'd lose my certification."

(Garnett paused, again, to untangle the sleeve of his work shirt from a briar. His heart was pounding from the effort of bushwhacking through this godforsaken mess.)

Her certification! Nannie Rawley was proud to tell the world she'd been the first organic grower to be certified in Zebulon County, and she was still the loudest one. Fifteen years ago he'd assumed it was a nonsense that would pass, along with rock music and hydroponic tobacco. But that was not to be. Nannie Rawley had declared war not only on the county's Two-Four-D but also on the Sevin dust and other insecticides Garnett was bound and obligated to put on his own seedling trees to keep them from being swallowed whole by the army of Japanese beetles camped out on Nannie Rawley's unsprayed pastures. There was no end to her ignorance or her zeal. She was the sworn friend and protector of all creatures great and small, right down to the ticks, fleas, and corn maggots, evidently. (All but goats, which she hated and feared due to a childhood "incident.") But could she really be such a fool as to fear the certification men, coming around to spot-check her apples? That would be along the lines of the Catholics coming to check up on the morals of their pope. The organic-certification men probably called up Nannie Rawley for advice.

He paused again to catch his breath. In spite of the cool day he felt dark sweat spreading down his shirt from the armpits like a pair of a fish's gills. His arms ached from thrashing the sign, and he felt a queer heaviness in his left leg. He couldn't see his feet but could feel that his trousers were soaked up to the knees from all the dampness down in the weeds. It was practically a swamp. The briars had become almost impossible to get through, and he still had twenty yards to go to reach the line fence. Garnett felt purely miserable and almost lost heart: well, he could backtrack, walk back up to his mowed field, and throw the sign over into her nicely mowed orchard. There was a gate in the fence put in by Garnett's father and Nannie Rawley's, who'd been the best of friends.

But no, he wanted to cross over down here below the fence line and throw the cursed sign into her weeds, where it belonged. He decided to push on, twenty more yards.

If only his poisons *would* drift over onto her trees. He knew very well, and had told her so, that without his constant spraying to keep them down, the Japanese beetles would overrun her orchards completely. She'd be standing out there in her calico skirt under leafless trees, wringing her hands, wondering what'd gone wrong in her little paradise. Success without chemicals was impossible. Nannie Rawley was a deluded old harpy in pigtails.

He could see the fence now—the posts, at least. (His eyesight had clouded to cataracts so slowly that his mind had learned how to fill in details like fence wire, tree leaves, and the more subtle features of a face.) But as he moved toward the property line, the sensation of heaviness in his left leg grew so unbearable, he could hardly drag it. He imagined what he looked like, thrashing and staggering forward like Frankenstein's monster, and embarrassment washed over him but then was replaced, suddenly, by a terrifying thought: he was having a stroke. Wasn't that a symptom? Heaviness in the left leg? He stopped to mop the sweat off his face. His skin felt clammy, and a sick ache gnawed at his stomach. Dear Lord! He could fall down into these weeds and who would find him here? After how many days, or weeks? His obituary would read, "The decayed body of Garnett Walker was discovered Wednesday after the first frost brought down the weeds along his frontage on Highway 6."

His chest felt constricted, like a bulging tree trunk wrapped too tightly in barbed wire. Oh, sweet Jesus! Through his ragged breathing he cried out in spite of himself:

"Help!"

And there she came, down the embankment. Of all God's creatures he had summoned to his aid Nannie Rawley, wearing a pair of dungarees and a red bandanna around her head like that woman on the syrup, Aunt Jemima. She came tearing out of nowhere, sliding down toward him, still carrying something in her hand from whatever home remedy she'd been out messing with—Nannie with her traps to catch codling moths, as if that would settle everything. It looked like a yellow paper box with the bottom cut out. Here I am, thought Garnett, at the end of my allotted days, staring at a yellow paper box with the bottom cut out. My last view of this earthly life: a bug trap.

Dear Lord my God, he prayed silently. I confess I may have sinned in my heart, but I obeyed thy fifth commandment. I didn't kill her.

She had already grabbed him under his soggy armpits and was struggling him up the bank toward the flat ground of her front orchard. He had never felt her touch or her grip before and was shocked by this little woman's strength. He tried to help with his useless legs, but he felt as if he were participating in the sport of alligator wrestling and knew, with a sinking heart, that he was the alligator.

Then at last he was lying on his back on the grass underneath her winesaps. She knelt over him, peering down with concern, and he gasped at the sight of her red-bandanna-crowned head reeling wildly through space. He quickly turned his head to the side; this wasn't the stroke—it always made him dizzy to lie flat on his back looking up.

"Miss Rawley," he said weakly once the spinning of the world had ceased, "I don't like to trouble you. You go on with your business, but maybe if you get a chance directly you could call up the ambulance. I think I've had a stroke." He closed his eyes.

When she didn't answer, he opened his eyes and saw that she was staring down at his left leg, in apparent horror. He felt confused—would there be blood, with a stroke? Or some kind of deformity? Surely not, but he couldn't make himself look.

"Mr. Walker," she said, "you haven't had any stroke."

"What?"

"You haven't gotten a stroke. You've gotten a turtle."

"What?" He struggled to sit up. Suddenly his chest felt better and his head was perfectly clear.

"Look! You've got a snapping turtle hanging on to the side of your boot. I'll bet that thing weighs fifteen pounds."

Garnett was embarrassed beyond speech. He stared down at the monster in its dark, humped shell, a slime-green creature that had sprung from some other part of God's mind, certainly, than most. It had gotten hold of the edge of his leather sole with the vise grip the snapping turtle is famous for, and true to its fame, it appeared to have no plans on letting go until Zebulon County got thunder. Although it did seem to Garnett that its dark little beady eyes were looking up at him fairly sheepishly. Poor thing, thought Garnett, to have to commit yourself so hard to one moment of poor judgment.

In a springtime as rainy as this one, snapping turtles strayed from their home ponds into wet ditches, looking for new places to find their hideous mates and breed their hideous children. *Of course* there would be one waiting for him in that weedy ditch under all those briars—that swamp that had been created by Nannie Rawley—and if he happened to have a turtle on his foot now, it was entirely her fault.

"Well I knew *that*," he said, waving offhandedly at the giant turtle. "I just wasn't feeling well, of a sudden. But I'm better now. I'll just go home by the road, I think."

She screwed up her face, shaking her head. "Not till I get that dinosaur off your heel. Let me go get a stick and whack it to make it turn loose of you."

"No, really. You don't have to."

"Oh, Mr. Walker, don't be ridiculous."

"Well, Miss Rawley," he snipped, "I can't feature it. Knowing what a soft spot you have in your heart for pests and vermin."

"You don't know the half of it. I've had a grudge against snapping turtles ever since that big monster in my pond ate the feet off one of my ducks. There's nothing I'd rather do than bang this old bastard's brains out." She peered down at Garnett, who winced, both at her foul language and at her manner. "But you'd better take off your boot," she added. "I couldn't be held responsible."

"No!" he cried, gaining control of the situation. Her hands had felt so strong, guiding him up the bank like the grip of destiny itself. Like the claws of a she-bear! Having those hands on him once was enough for today. He wasn't going to undress for her. "No, now," he told her sternly, "there isn't any call to take out your grudges on this old fellow. He and I will just head back home now."

"You will," she said.

"Yes. Thank you for your help."

Garnett got to his feet as gracefully as possible, considering, and limped down Nannie Rawley's gravel drive toward the road. The lopsided scrape of his walk sounded like a car with a flat tire. Now he would have to hike one hundred yards up the road to get to his own driveway, and pray to the Lord no one came driving along at that moment to see Garnett Walker transporting fifteen pounds of turtle up Highway 6 in a previously unheard-of fashion.

He turned sideways to cast a glance back. She just stood there in her bandanna and rolled-up dungarees, frowning, with her pale, skinny little arms crossed tightly against her blouse. She was quite put out with him, it seemed, or else she was making her mind up that he was crazy as a loon—one of the two. It made no difference either way to Garnett Walker.

"Oh!" he said suddenly, for he'd nearly forgotten the whole business. He turned back toward her again, tilting his head a little to the side. "I'm afraid your No Spray sign landed somewhere down there in the weeds at the bottom of the road cut."

Her glare dissolved to a happy beam he could see plainly, for it lit up her face like sunshine on Groundhog Day. "Don't you worry, Mr. Walker. The spray truck went by at seven o'clock this morning."

{7}

Predators

ey there," he said, as if Eddie Bondo himself standing in the trail were no more unexpected a find on this warm afternoon than the cluster of puffball mushrooms she'd paused just a minute before to admire.

"Hey yourself," she answered quietly. As if her heart were not pounding at its cage like a sudden captive. "How'd you find me up here?"

"I sniffed you out, girl. You're a sweet, easy trail for a man to follow."

Her abdominal muscles tensed. He might have thought he was joking, but she knew some truths about human scent. She'd walked down city streets in Knoxville and turned men's heads, one after another, on the middle day of her cycle. They didn't know why, knew only that they wanted her. That was how pheromones seemed to work, in humans at least—nobody liked to talk about it. Maybe excepting Eddie Bondo. "I'm fertile, that's what got to you," she said frankly, testing him out, but he didn't flinch. "Just so you know, this is the day." She laughed. "That's what called you down from Clinch Peak."

Eddie Bondo laughed, too, shining that high-beam smile at her through the late-morning drizzle. Could she pretend not to rejoice? How could she not want him back?

"How can you know a thing like that?" he asked.

"What, that my body's talking to yours?" She stomped her boot down on the puffballs, releasing a cloud of spores that rose and curled like golden brown smoke, glittering in the sunlit air between them. Sex cells, they were, a mushroom's bliss, its attempt to fill the world with its mushroom progeny. "Or how can I know about my timing? Which do you mean?"

He stomped the puffballs, too, squashing the leathery white skins like empty baseballs, releasing more puffs. The supply seemed endless. Deanna wondered if these tiny particles would cling to their damp skin or enter their bodies on an inhaled breath.

"Both, I guess," he said finally.

She shrugged. Was he serious? A woman knew both those things if she was paying attention. Deanna turned and headed up-mountain, confident he would follow. "I sleep outside a lot," she said. "I'm on the same schedule as the moon."

He laughed. "What are you, a were-lady?"

She stopped and turned to look at him. It amazed her, the obvious animal facts people refused to know about their kind. "Any woman will ovulate with the full moon if she's exposed to enough moonlight. It's the pituitary gland does it, I guess. It takes a while to get there, but then you stay."

Eddie Bondo seemed amused by this information. "So back in the old days, when they slept on the ground around the fire, wrapped up in skins or however they did, then what? You're saying all the women in the world came into heat at the same time?"

She shrugged again, not really wanting to talk about it if he thought it was funny. It felt like betraying a secret. "Convenient, if you think about it. Full moon, plenty of light."

"Damn," he said. "No wonder that sucker drives men crazy."

"Yep." She turned uphill again, feeling his eyes on every muscle in her long, rain-slick thighs and calves, her gluteus maximus, and the small of her back as she mounted the slope. She was wearing cutoff jeans, a thin cotton shirt, and no bra. She'd had no thoughts of Eddie Bondo when she dressed that morning, only a rush of spring fever and, evidently, a body that wanted to be seen.

"Where you going?" he asked.

"Out for a walk in the rain."

"It's just about let up," he contended. "Finally."

"Don't get used to it. We're in for more."

"Don't tell me that. How can you tell?"

How? About six different ways: first, a wind just strong enough to make the leaves show their white undersides. "I don't know," she said aloud, shutting that door out of habit. Although it occurred to her that this might be the one man she'd met since her father died who would be interested to hear all six.

"You hillbillies around here must have gills like fish. Last few weeks I've been thinking I was going to melt."

"You didn't, I see."

"Turns out I'm not made of sugar."

"Turns out." She smiled to herself.

"So. Where you going?"

"Nowhere—a place I like to go."

He laughed. "That sounds mighty unambitious."

"No, I mean, nowhere important. From a wildlife-management point of view." From anybody's point of view, probably.

"Well now, pretty lady. Does that mean you're off duty?"

She caught her breath, wondering at his power to manipulate her desire. She wanted to stop and tear him apart on the trail, swallow him alive, suck his juices, and lick him from her fingers. "It's just a place I like," she said evenly. "More a thing than a place. It's right up here at the top of these switchbacks."

The trail was extremely steep from this point on to where it lay, the great old friendly hollowed-out shelter she was headed for, a hundred more feet up the mountain. She could hear his footsteps and breathing right behind her, synchronized with hers.

"Animal, vegetable, or mineral?" he asked.

"Vegetable. Dead vegetable. Since way before we were born."

"Is it . . . a big old hollow tree?"

She froze but didn't turn around.

"About ten feet long and yea tall, so you just have to duck your head when you walk into it? Nope, never seen it."

She wheeled to face him, her braid flying. "That's my place!"

"Don't you think a few other people might have run across it? It's been lying there about a hundred years."

"No! Nobody else ever comes up here." She broke into a run, but he overtook her from behind, a little faster than she was at an uphill sprint. With his hands on her hips he pulled but mostly pushed her, and before she could dodge him they had reached the tunnel tree, there was no turning back from it now. There it was, and lodged in the shadows inside of it, stashed neatly away from the rain, were his things: his pack, his tin cup and coffeepot, his whole Eddie Bondo life.

"I can't believe you've been here," she said, still denying it to herself.

"Lots of critters been here, don't you think?"

"No," she said, and nothing more because his mouth was on hers and his body was pushing her inside. He moved his pack aside, moved her backward into the delicate darkness toward the tunnel's very center, the safest place.

"It's mine," she whispered.

"Who cut it down, then?"

She could see nothing but his face, feel nothing but the exquisite grain of his skin against her cheek and his hands on her buttons. "Nobody. It's a chestnut. Blight killed all the chestnuts fifty years ago."

"Nobody chopped it down?"

She knew it was possible. Her dad had told her how people had watched the chestnuts mysteriously dying and rushed to take what was left standing since they needed the lumber so badly. But no, if somebody had gone to that trouble he'd have taken the wood, not left it lying here for dead. She started to say this, "No," but found she couldn't form the word against Eddie Bondo's lips. It became nonsensical beside the fact of her naked back pressed against the soft black crumbling curved inside wall of this womb she had never shared with any twin. He held her breasts in his two hands, looking down at her. She couldn't bear how much she loved that gaze and that touch, those palms on her nipples and those fingertips tracing her ribs and enclosing her sides, pulling her against him as if she were something small and manageable. He kissed her neck, then her collarbones. Stopped briefly then and stood up on his knees to fish for the crinkling packet in his jeans pocket, that premeditation. Of course, he knew she was fertile. He'd be careful.

She sat curled with her back to the wall and her chin on her knees. The tunnel was wide enough that he could kneel in front of her, facing her, to untie her boots and slide off her shorts and his own clothes. It was warm enough for nakedness, a rich, dark warmth full of the scent of sweet old wood. He pressed his face against her knees.

"The full moon?" he asked, against her skin. "That's the secret of everything?"

She didn't say yes or no.

His hands climbed her like a tree, from ankles to knees to waist to shoulders until he cupped her face and looked into her eyes like a Gypsy trying to read the future in tea leaves. He seemed so happy, so earnest. "For that, men write stupid poems and howl and hold up liquor stores? When all they really want is every woman in the world, all at the same time?"

She held his eyes but couldn't speak to tell him how far she'd left all that behind her, so far that even her obedient ovaries sometimes failed to be moved by the moon these days, these years in her middle forties. Some months, no heads turned. She'd been so sure that was what she wanted. How could this be, Eddie Bondo looking in her eyes, taking hold of her braid, and wrapping it around and around his wrist until he had her cheek pinned to his forearm and turned gently away from him? She lay facedown with her head on her hands and the full length of his body against her, his penis gently pressing her solar plexus and his lips touching her temple. Between the skin of her back and his chest she could feel small, prickly islands of chestnut dust. "Deanna," he said in her ear, "I wanted you all the way from West Virginia. I was going to want you from here to Wyoming if I didn't come back."

He breathed on the skin beneath her earlobe and her back arched like a reflex, like a moth drawn helpless to a flame. She had no words, but her body answered his perfectly as he slid himself down and took the nape of her neck in his teeth like a lion on a lioness in heat: a gentle, sure bite, by mutual agreement impossible to escape.

By late morning the rain had stopped completely, setting free a moment of afternoon sun. It stretched into the tunnel's mouth to lap at their naked feet and ankles as they lay side by side. The sensation roused Deanna from where she had been drifting, someplace near sleep but not quite in its full embrace. It was late, she realized with a start. She opened her eyes. This day was going. Was gone already, she might as well say it: to *him,* her time and all the choices she thought she'd made for good. Her gut clenched as distant thunder rumbled and echoed up the hollow, threatening more rain.

She stared at the man who lay flat on his back beside her, sleeping the untroubled sleep of a landlord. Flecks of soft wood and crumbled leaves, shreds of her forest, clung to his body, freckling his cheek and shoulder and even his limp penis. She filled up with loathing for his talkative cockiness, those placid eyelids and the dead careless arm slung across her, heavy as lead. She threw it off of her and rolled away from him, but he moved from sleep to partial wakefulness and reached to draw her back to him.

"No," she said, shoving him, hard. "Just *no,* get off me!"

His eyes flew open, but Deanna couldn't stop her fists from lashing out hard at his chest and shoulders. A bile rose up in her gut, a rush of physical rage that might have branded him black and blue if her arms had found the strength for it before he gathered back his hunter's wits. She nearly spit in his face when he restrained her with a grip like handcuffs on her forearms. This fury had taken her like a storm and left her trembling.

"God, Deanna."

"Let me go."

"Not if you're going to kill me. *God,* woman!" He held her forearms upright on either side of her face and studied her like a bad mistake. Like some mountain lion he'd accidentally caught in a leghold trap for squirrel.

"Just let me go," she said. "I want to get my clothes on."

Carefully he opened one hand, then the other, watching her arms as she moved away from him. "What?" he asked.

"Why did you come back?" She spat the words.

"You seemed pretty happy about it an hour ago."

She shook her head slowly, breathed out through her nose, pressed her lips together so hard they turned white.

He persisted. "You didn't want me to come back?"

She hated that, too, his not knowing. She couldn't look at him.

"Christ almighty, Deanna, *what?*"

"I didn't need you here."

"I know that."

"You don't know anything. You never saw me alone."

"I did, though." There was a hint of that grin in his voice.

She turned to face him with an animal glare. "Is that it? You were watching me like some damn predator and you think you *have* me now?"

He didn't answer this. She turned her back on him again. "I was just fine here before you showed up. For two years, while you were doing whatever you did all that time, I was right here. Not missing people or all the chitchat about the stuff they think they need to have or wear or make happen. For sure not pining for a boyfriend."

He didn't respond. A scarlet tanager broke the silence with his song. She thought of the bird hidden in leaves somewhere, unseen by any human eye but nevertheless brilliant red. Nevertheless beautiful.

"And then one day you're here, Eddie Bondo. And then one day you're not. What's that supposed to mean?"

He spoke slowly: "It's not supposed to mean anything."

"Damn straight it's not."

"I'm gone, then, no problem. Is that what you're saying you want?"

She grabbed her shirt and put it on, dusting damp sawdust from her skin and feeling angry and pathetic. The shirt was inside out, she realized when she tried to button it, so she tied the tails in a knot instead and quickly pulled on her shorts. She hoped to God he wasn't looking at her. She tried to slow down her breathing and remember what she used to be. She crawled to the end of the tunnel and sat there at the edge, facing out, right on the margin where old chestnut wood dissolved into leafy forest floor.

"Deanna. I *said,* do you want me to go?"

"No. And I'll tell you straight, I despise you for it."

"For what?"

She still didn't turn around to look at him, didn't need to see that face. Spoke to the woods instead. "For *shit.* For me wanting you to come back."

When this day started, she'd been content. Finally, after fifteen days of heart-race and butterfly-stomach over any crackle in the woods that might have been his footstep, she'd stopped listening. She was sure of it. She could recall the even-keeled pleasure of hiking up the trail alone, thinking of nothing but this log, trying to picture how the forest had looked back when chestnuts were the dominant tree of the eastern forests. It was something she could see in her mind's eye. This giant would have been the tallest, most immortal thing on its mountain—until the day a fungal blight stepped off a ship in some harbor, grinned at America, and took down every chestnut tree from New York to Alabama. A whole landscape could change, just like that.

She sat still, ignoring her own body and the one that breathed behind her. Out in the light she could almost see the calm air beginning to gather itself for the afternoon, the oxygen burgeoning between the damp leaves. These trees were the lungs of her mountain—not her mountain, *nobody's* damn mountain, this mountain that belonged to scarlet tanagers, puffballs, luna moths, and coyotes. This shadowy, spirited world she lived in was preparing to exhale. It would be afternoon, and then it would be evening and then night. It would pour down rain. He would share her bed.

She wiped tears from the side of her face with the back of her wrist and reached out with her other hand to press her fingertips into the soft, crumbling wood. She touched her fingers to her upper lip, breathing that earthy smell, tasting the wood with her tongue. She had loved this old log fiercely. It embarrassed her to admit it. Only a child was allowed to love an inanimate thing so desperately or possess it so confidently. But it had been hers. Now the spell was gone, the magic of this place that had been hers alone, unknown to any man.

8

Moth Love

usa stood on the front porch, watching rain pour over the front eave in long silver strings. The gabled roof of the farmhouse—her farmhouse—was made of grooved tin that shunted the water into channels running down its steep sides. Some of the trickles poured over as clear filaments, like fishing line, while others looked beaded, like strings of pearls. She'd put buckets on the wide steps under some of the trickles and discovered that each string of droplets tapped out its own distinctive rhythm in its bucket. All morning, the rhythm of each stream never changed—it only grew softer as the bucket filled, then returned to its hollow *rat-tat-a-rat-tat-tat!* after she emptied the bucket.

She'd set out the buckets to collect a drink for the potted ferns on the porch, which were out of the rain's reach and turning brown, even in this soggy weather, as brittle and desolate as her internal grief. She'd meant to return to her work, but the rhythms arrested her. It was a relief to stand still for a minute, listening, without anyone giving her pitying looks and ordering her to go lie down. Hannie-Mavis and Jewel had gone home finally, though they still came up several times a day to "check" on her, which mostly meant telling her to eat, even *what* to eat, as if she were a child. But then they'd go away afterward. Lusa could stand on her own porch in a pair of jeans and Cole's work shirt and watch the rain and let her mind go numb if she felt like it. If she hadn't had a gallon of cherries to pit and pack into canning jars she could have amused herself all morning out here, setting a bucket under each down-spout and making up a song to go with it. Her grandfather Landowski's game: he used to tap out unexpected rhythms with his fingertips on her bony knees, inventing mysterious Balkan melodies that he'd hum against the beat.

"Your zayda, the last landowner in our line," her father used to declare sarcastically, because his father had had a sugar-beet farm on the Ner River north of Lodz, and he'd lost it in the war, fleeing Poland in possession of nothing but his life, a young son and wife, and a clarinet. "Your great zayda who made a name for himself in New York as a klezmer musician, before leaving his wife and child for an American girl he met in a nightclub." Lusa knew, though it wasn't discussed, that with his young mistress the old man had even sired a second family, all of whom perished in a tenement fire—her zayda included. It was hard to say which part of the story Lusa's father held against him—most of it, she supposed. When they flew to New York to witness the burial of the charred remains, Lusa was still too young to understand her father's feelings and all the ironies of the loss. Zayda Landowski hadn't visited her mind for many years. And now here he was, in a syncopated string of water drops on a farmhouse porch in Zebulon County. He'd started out as a farmer before bending the rest of his life around loss. What would he have made of a rainy day in this hollow, with its rich smells of decomposition and sweet new growth?

Lusa smoothed her shirttail and composed herself to look busy and well nourished, for here came Herb and Mary Edna's green truck bouncing up the drive. But it was not the Menacing Eldest behind the wheel this time. It was her husband, Herb, Lusa saw as he pulled up in front of the house, and Lois's husband, Big Rickie, who got out on the passenger's side. Both men tucked their heads down and held the bills of their caps with their right hands as they jogged toward her through the rain. They ducked through the beaded curtain of drips, carefully avoiding her buckets on the steps, and stomped their boots several times on the porch floorboards before taking off their caps. The scents rising from their work overalls put Cole right there with them: dust, motor oil, barn hay. She breathed in, drawing from strange men's clothes these molecules of her husband.

"He needs a gutter put on this porch," Rickie told Herb, as if they also agreed to the fact of Cole's presence here—and Lusa's absence. What mission required this delegation of husbands? Were they going to order her to leave now, or what? Would she put up a fight or go peacefully?

"Rickie, Herb," she said, squaring her shoulders. "Nice to see you."

Both men nodded at her, then glanced back out at the rain, the absent gutter, and the waterlogged fields where they seemed eager to return to work. She eyed the green cockleburs planted like tiny land mines on the cuffs of their khaki trousers.

"Another good hard rain," Herb observed. "Too bad we need it like a hole in the head. One more week of this, the frogs'll drown."

"Supposed to clear up by Saturday, though," said Rickie.

"'At's right," Herb agreed. "Otherwise we wouldn't have bothered you, but it's supposed to clear up."

"To tell me it's supposed to stop raining, you came up here?" Lusa asked, looking from one sun-toughened face to the other for some clue. It was always like this, anytime she got wedged into a conversation with her brothers-in-law. This sense of having wandered into a country where they spoke English but all the words meant something different.

"Yep," said Herb. Rickie nodded to corroborate. They looked like a comedy team: stout, bald Herb was the front man, while tall, gangling Rickie stood mostly silent with his cap in hand and his wild black hair molded to the shape of the cap. He had an Adam's apple like a round oak gall on the stalk of his long neck. People called him Big Rickie even though his son Little Rickie had, at seventeen, surpassed him in many ways. Lusa felt some sympathy with Little Rickie's fate. Life in Zebulon: the minute you're born you're trapped like a bug, somebody's son or wife, a place too small to fit into.

"So," Herb interjected into the silence. "We'll be needing to set Cole's tobacco."

"Oh," Lusa said, surprised. "It's time for that, isn't it."

"I'll tell you the truth, it's past time. All this rain's been keeping everybody's fields mucked up, and now here it is June, perty near too late."

"Well, it's only, what, the fifth or something? June fifth?"

"'At's right. Blue mold will be setting in here come July, if the plants aren't up big enough by then."

"You can spray for blue mold if you have to," Lusa said. Tobacco pathology was not exactly her department, but she'd heard Cole speak of it. She felt desperate to know something in front of these men.

"Can," they agreed, with limited enthusiasm.

"Have you both got your own tobacco plants in? You should go ahead and do your own first."

Herb nodded. "I leased out my allotment this year, since them durn cows are keeping me too busy to mess with it. Me and him got Big Rickie's in on Monday morning, when we had that break in the weather. That puts Cole next."

And what about Jewel? Lusa wondered. Are they also running *her* life, since her husband ran off with a waitress from Cracker Barrel? "So what you're saying is," she interpreted cautiously, her heart pounding in her ears, "on Saturday you and your boys will be coming up here to set the tobacco."

"'At's right. If it dries out for a day first."

"And what about me? Do I get a say?"

Both men glanced at her with the exact same eye: surprised, fearful, put out. But wasn't it her farm? She looked away from them, inhaling the rich scents of mud and honeysuckle and listening to her childish project, her bucket on the step: *Tat-tat-a-tat-tat-a-tat-tat-tat!* She heard a song against the beat, distinctly, the trilling clarinet rising like laughter and the mandolin as insistent as clapping hands. Klezmer music.

"It's my farm now," she said aloud. Her voice quavered, and her fingers felt hot.

"Yep," Herb agreed. "But we don't mind helping Cole out like any other year. Tobacco's a lot of work, takes a whole family. 'At's how people around here do it, anyways."

"I was here last year," she said tersely. "I brought hot coffee out to you and Cole and Little Rickie and that other boy, that cousin from Tazewell. If you recall."

Big Rickie smiled. "I recall you trying your hand at riding behind the tractor and setting a row of plants. Some of them ended up with their roots a-dangling up in the air and their leaves planted in the ground."

"Cole drove too fast on purpose! We were just newlyweds. He was teasing me in front of you guys." Lusa flushed pink up to the hairline, remembering her ride on the little platform attached to the rear of the tractor, grabbing the floppy young tobacco plants from the box beside her. Their disintegrating texture was like that of tissue paper; trying to plunge them into the chunky clay of the furrow as it passed beneath her seemed impossible. They had been married only two days. "It was my first time behind a tractor," she contended.

"It was," Big Rickie conceded. "And most of them plants was roots-down."

Herb steered back to the business at hand. "We got no sets of our own left, but Big Rickie got up a good price on a batch from Jackie Doddard."

"I appreciate that. But what if I don't want to plant tobacco this year?"

"You don't have to do a thing. You can stay in the house if you want to."

"No, I mean, what if I don't want tobacco planted on my farm?"

Now they did not glance at Lusa sideways; they stared.

"Well," she said, "why plant more tobacco when everybody's trying to quit smoking? Or should be trying to, if they're not already. The government's officially down on it, now that word's finally out that cancer's killing people. And everybody's blaming *us*."

Both men turned their eyes out toward the rain and the fields, where it was clear they suddenly wished they could be, rain or no rain. She could see them working hard not to finger the packs of Marlboros in their shirt pockets.

"What would you be wanting to plant, then?" Herb asked at last.

"Well, I hadn't really thought. What about corn?"

Herb and Big Rickie exchanged a smile, passing the joke between them. "About three dollar a bushel, that's how about it," Herb replied. "Unless you mean feed corn, that's more like fifty cents a bushel around here. But a-course you'd be talking about sweet corn."

"Of course," Lusa said.

"Well, let's see. Cole's got a five-acre tobacco bottom, so put it in sweet corn, that'd get you about five hundred bushels, maybe six in a good year, not that we ever have one of those around here." Herb rolled his eyes up, counting on his fingers. "About fifteen hundred dollar. Minus your diesel for your tractor, your seed, and a whole bunch of fertilizer, because corn's a heavy feeder. And some luck getting it sold on the right day. You might end up making near about . . . eight hundred dollars. On your corn crop."

"Oh, I see." Lusa blushed deeper. "We usually clear around twelve or thirteen thousand for the tobacco."

"Yep," said Big Rickie. "That'd be about right. Thirty-seven hundred an acre, minus your tractor costs, your sets, and your chemicals."

"It's what we live on."

She'd said it softly, but the words *we* and *live* hung heavily in the air. She felt them pressing on her shoulders like the hands of a disapproving matron trying to get the message across to a selfish child: "Sit down, your turn is over."

Tat-tat-a-tat-tat-a-tat-tat-tat. Grandfather Landowski's rhythm section was fading out. She needed to empty the buckets and start them over again. She wished these men would go away. Just leave her to muddle through in her own way, however mistaken. She wished she could ask someone for advice without feeling skinned alive and laughed at.

"What else can people grow around here, on little scraps of land at the bottom of a hollow? What can earn you enough to live on, besides tobacco?"

Big Rickie warmed to the subject of bad news. "Turner Blevins up 'air tried tomatoes. They told him he could get ten thousand dollar an acre. What they didn't tell him was if two other guys in the county try the same thing, they've done flooded the market. Blevins fed thirty-five hundred pound of tomatoes to his hogs and dished the rest under."

"What about the other two guys?" Lusa asked.

"Same. They all three lost money. One of them was so sold on tomatoes, he'd put him in a ten-thousand-dollar irrigation system to water 'em with, is what I heard. Now he's back in tobacco, and just hoping for a real dry year so he can turn on his fancy spanking hoses."

"But that doesn't make sense, that they'd all lose money. People need lots of tomatoes."

"Not all on the same day they don't, and that's how tomatoes comes in. If you can't get them suckers all into somebody's grocery cart in five days or less, then you've got you some expensive hog food. And out here in the boondocks, no shipper's going to touch you before he's sure he can make his cut."

Lusa crossed her arms, despairing of the depth of her ignorance.

"Your tobacco, you see, now," Rickie continued, "you hang it in the barn to cure, and then it can just go on hanging there as long as it needs to, till the time's good to sell. Everybody in the county can grow tobacco, but every leaf of it might get lit and smoked on a different day of the year, in a different country of the world."

"Imagine that," Lusa said, sounding sarcastic, though she was actually a little astonished. She'd never thought through these basic lessons before. Tobacco's value, largely, lay in the fact that it kept forever and traveled well.

They stood silent for a while, all three of them staring out into the yard. The rain fell on the big leaves of the catalpa tree, popping them down like the keys on a typewriter.

Lusa said, "There's got to be something else I can make decent money on. The barn's got to have a new roof this year."

Herb smirked. "Mary-jay-wanna. I hear that brings in about the same price per acre as tomatoes, and the market's solid."

"I see," Lusa said. "You're making fun of me. Well, I appreciate your offer to set this weekend, but I'd like to think about the tobacco. Can you still get the sets from Jackie if I let you know tomorrow or the next day?"

"I expect so. Jackie's got that hydroponic setup. It didn't work out too good last year, but this year he's done growed more'n he knows what to do with."

"Well, good. I'll let you know, then, before Saturday. I'll decide what to do."

"*If* it stops raining," Herb said, lest Lusa think she was in charge.

"Right. And if it doesn't, then we're all sunk together, right? I'll make the same nothing off the tobacco I *didn't* grow as you will off the crop you tried to get put in. And think of the time and money I'll save!"

Herb stared at her. Big Rickie smiled out toward the garage. "That's a smart lady, Herb," he said. "I believe she's got the right attitude for farming."

"Well," Lusa said, slapping her hands together. "I've got a gallon of cherries in there that are going to rot if I don't get them canned today. So I'll call you Friday."

Herb leaned out toward the edge of the porch, looking up the mountainside toward the orchard. She was controlling her breathing, counting the seconds until these two got into the truck and lit their cigarettes and drove away and she could sob on the porch swing. Standing up to them took almost more guts than she had.

"I'm surprised you got cherry one off them trees this year," Herb pronounced. "As many durn jaybirds as we've had. Last spring I come over here and shot the birds all out of there for Cole, but I never got around to it this year. So you got you enough for a pie or two anyways, did you?"

Lusa managed to grimace a smile, wide-eyed and fierce. "Miracles happen, Herb."

❧

That would be Jewel at the door, Lusa thought. Jewel thumping her umbrella out in the front hallway (they'd always come in without knocking, all of them, even when Lusa and Cole were newlyweds stealing sex in the afternoons), Jewel's tired voice telling the kids to wipe their feet and hang up their raincoats on the pegs. Then they poured through the kitchen doorway, the older child carrying a box of canning jars on his head, balancing it with both hands. Lusa had called Jewel when she ran out of canning jars.

"Come on in," she said. "You can set the box right down there on the counter."

"Lord, call the police," Jewel cried. "They's been a murder in here!"

Lusa laughed. "Looks like it, doesn't it?" Her apron and the countertops were smeared garishly with the blood of hundreds of cherries. The hand-cranked pitter was clamped to the counter, a mass of dark pits glistening in the bucket underneath like something from a slaughterhouse. She'd been relieved when Jewel offered over the phone to come up and help her finish the canning. Lusa could recognize objectively, without really feeling it, that she needed company or she'd go crazy.

Yet here was her sister-in-law with her hand to her mouth already, mortified by her slip, a joke about death. Lusa had hoped for a sturdier kind of company than this.

"It's OK, Jewel. I know Cole's dead."

"Well, I didn't . . . stupid me. Didn't think." She looked anguished.

Lusa shrugged. "It's not like you're going to remind me of something I've forgotten about."

Jewel stood a minute longer with her hand to her mouth and tears welling, staring at Lusa, while her ten-year-old slowly circumnavigated the kitchen island, balancing the cardboard box of jars one-handed. The younger child, Lowell, reached up to steal a handful of cherries off the butcher block. Jewel gently swatted his hand away. "Aren't people awful?" she asked Lusa, finally. "I *know* what you're saying. When Shel—" But she stopped herself to shoo out the kids. "Go play outside."

"Mo-om, it's pouring down rain!"

"It's pouring down rain, Jewel. They can play on the back porch."

"OK, the back porch, then, but don't bust *anything.*"

"Hey, wait a sec, Chris, here." Lusa scooped a pile of cherries into a plastic bowl and handed it to the older boy. "If you run out of stuff to do, there's a broom and a dustpan out there."

"To sweep with?"

"To play hockey with, you're asking? *Yes,* to sweep with."

Jewel waited for the door to close behind them before she spoke. "When Shel left me, everybody just stopped saying his name or word one about him, like I'd never even been married. But we *were,* for some of those years—I mean, *married.* Even while we were still just dating, if you know what I mean. We ran off to Cumberland Falls two months before the wedding and called it our test-drive honeymoon." For just a few seconds she stared at her hands with a faraway satisfaction, the most womanly expression Lusa had ever seen on Jewel. But then it vanished.

"I swear it's sad," she finished, matter-of-factly. "Pretending that part of my life never happened." She began to unscrew the clamp that held the antique steel cherry pitter to the counter. Lusa had spent half an hour solving the puzzle of that clamp, but of course the pitter had been their mother's. Jewel would know it with her eyes closed.

"This family's intimidating, no doubt about it," Lusa said. She wished she could say how hard it really was—how it felt to live among people who'd been using her kitchen appliances since before she was born. How they attacked her in unison if she tried to re-arrange the furniture or hang her own family pictures. How even old Mrs. Widener haunted this kitchen, disapproving of Lusa's recipes and jealous of her soups.

"Oh, it's not just the family," Jewel said. "It's *everybody;* it's this town. Four years it's been, and I still see people at Kroger's go into a different checkout line so they won't have to stand there and *not* say something to me about Shel."

Lusa mopped red juice from the counter with a sponge. "You'd think in four years they could come up with a new subject."

"You'd think. Not that it's the same, Shel's running off and Cole's being . . ."

"Dead," Lusa said. "It's the same. Around here, people act like losing your husband was contagious." Lusa had been amazed at how quickly her status had changed: being single made her either invisible or dangerous. Or both, like a germ. She'd noticed it even at the funeral, especially among the younger ones, wives her own age who needed to believe marriage was a safe and final outcome.

"Well, at least everybody knows you didn't do anything to run your husband off."

Lusa took a pinafore apron out of the drawer and put the neck strap over Jewel's head, then turned her around to tie the back. "What, and you did? God knows hand-to-mouth farming is a life anybody would run from. I considered leaving Cole a hundred times. Not because of him. Just because of everything."

"Lord, I know, it's a misery," Jewel said, though just then they were both gazing out the kitchen window at a drenched, billowy mock orange in full bloom in the backyard—and it was beautiful.

Lusa took up her sponge again. "Don't you dare tell your sisters I thought about leaving Cole. They'd chop me up and hide the pieces in canning jars."

Jewel laughed. "You make us sound so mean, honey." She donned an oven mitt and lifted the huge, flat lid of the water-bath canner, holding it high in the air like a cymbal. "You want me to put the jars in to sterilize?"

"Go ahead. What do you think I've got here, about eight quarts?"

Jewel appraised the mound of pitted cherries on the stained cutting board, doing some form of math in her head, Lusa realized. She understood with some chagrin that she'd accepted the family's judgment of Jewel as a child and not a woman, simply because she was manless.

"Are you doing preserves, honey, or pie filling?"

"Preserves, I guess, if I don't run out of sugar. I already made eighteen pints."

"Of *preserves?*"

Lusa felt foolish. "It's a lot, I know. When I was up the ladder out there in the tree I was proud of myself for filling up buckets. But now I'm stuck with them."

"Oh no, you'll be glad to have that jam. They're the sweet cher-

ries, aren't they, off that double-trunked tree above the apple orchard? Boy, those are the best cherries. Daddy must have planted
that tree before him and Mommy married. It was already big when
we were kids."

"Really?" Lusa took in her gut the familiar pang of guilt for
owning this tree that Jewel had grown up loving.

"Yeah. They always said it got hit by lightning the winter Cole
was born. That's how it got split in two that way—lightning."

A lightning strike and a jackknifed truck, two unexpected events
circumscribing a life—Lusa knew how far down that road her mind
could go, so she made herself stop. She wondered instead how old
Jewel had been that winter of his birth, whether she'd grown up as
Cole's playmate or his keeper. She'd never asked him these things
about each of his sisters. She'd expected to have years to untangle
those threads.

Jewel must have sensed her gloom, because she spoke up
brightly. "Eighteen pints is enough preserves. Let's can the rest for
pie filling."

"I can't see myself making pies anymore, for just me. Since nobody seems to want to come here for dinner."

"Mary Edna was a stinker to you over that. There wasn't any
reason for her to get so high and mighty. Emaline thinks so, too; she
told me. We both wish we still could have Thanksgiving up here at
the house."

Lusa's head swam with this news. She'd never suspected she had
allies at all, much less the support of a faction. How had she gotten
here, stranded in this family without rhyme or reason? Suddenly she
felt so exhausted by grief that she had to sink into a chair and put
her head down on the table. Jewel let her be. Lusa could hear the
jars clinking gently together, settling into the boiling water bath.
Finally Jewel whispered, "I think you've got about six quarts to go,
no more."

"That's still a lot of preserves."

"Let's make pie cherries, then. And if there's any left over we'll make some pies today. You make the best pie crust of anybody. Better than Mommy's, I hate to say it."

"God, don't say it out loud. Your mother haunts this kitchen. She used to stand in here stirring up fights between Cole and me."

Jewel gasped in mock dismay. "Now why would Mommy do that?"

"The usual thing. Territorial jealousy."

The boys banged in through the screen door, preceded by their empty bowl like a pair of cooperative beggars. The minute Lusa re-filled it, though, want ceded to possession, and they started to slap and fight. "Ow, Chris won't share!" Lowell howled.

"Goodness, we've got no shortage of cherries in this kitchen. Here, I'll get you your own bowl." Lusa was careful to find another one the same size and to fill them both equally. When they retreated again to the back porch she felt a flush of pride at having satisfied them, however briefly. Children were not Lusa's element. That was how she'd always put it to Cole, that babies made her nervous. Since moving here, though, she'd had glimpses of how the indulgence of adult despair could yield to children's needs.

"Five and a half quarts, like I was saying." Jewel laughed. "Excuse me for having pigs instead of children."

"I think I can bear the loss." Lusa sat down at the table again, facing the army of jars she'd already put up this day, little glass soldiers stuffed with their bright-red organs. Who would eat all this? When she left, would she take her preserves back to Lexington in a U-Haul? "What am I doing this for?" she asked suddenly in a dull, hard voice.

Jewel was behind her at once, rubbing her shoulders. "For later," she said simply.

"I should live so long."

"What on earth do you mean by that?"

"Nothing," Lusa said. "I just can't picture *later*. Spending my nothing of a life in this kitchen cooking for nobody."

"I wish you'd make a pie for my kids once in a while. When I get home from work I'm so tired, I practically feed them hog slop on a bun."

Lusa wondered whether this was a real request or an attempt at redeeming her empty life. "I could make a pie and bring it down sometime."

Jewel sat down, brushing a strand of mouse-colored hair out of her eyes. "That's not what I was asking for. I don't know if this is, well, polite to ask. But could they come up here and eat dinner with you sometimes?"

Lusa studied her sister-in-law's face. She seemed so tired. The request was genuine. "Well, sure. You could, too, Jewel, if you didn't feel like cooking. I could use the company."

"But I mean, if I wasn't here?"

"What, like if you had to take the late shift at Kroger's? You know you can ask me that anytime. I'm glad to help out."

"You wouldn't care to have the kids up here sometimes, then?"

Lusa smiled. "Of course not." It had taken her a year to learn that when mountain people said "I don't care to," they meant the opposite of what she thought. They meant "I wouldn't mind."

Jewel held her eye, shy and bold at the same time. "But they said you're going back to Lexington pretty soon."

"Who did?"

She shrugged. "I can see why you would. I'm just saying I'd miss you."

Lusa took a breath. "Would you get this house and the land then?"

"Oh, no. Mary Edna would, I guess. She's the oldest. I don't even have a man to farm it."

"So Mary Edna wants the place."

"It's yours, honey; you could sell it or whatever you want. Cole didn't have any will, so it goes to you. She said they have that law now, a success statue or something where it used to be the family would get a farm back, but now it goes to the wife."

Lusa felt a rush of adrenaline through her limbs. Only one thing could account for Jewel's acquaintance with "success statues": they were consulting lawyers. "I haven't made up my mind about anything yet," she said. "I haven't been able to think straight since everything happened."

"You seem like you're doing good, honey."

Lusa looked at Jewel, longing to trust, knowing she couldn't. She felt dismayed by the complexities of even the simplest of things, a conversation with a sister—not her own—in a kitchen, also not her own. "Probably you all think I'm not behaving like a decent widow," she said, surprised by the anger in her chest.

Jewel started to protest, but Lusa shook her head. "You see me pushing right along, canning cherries like everything was normal. But when nobody's here, sometimes I have to lie down on the floor and just try to keep breathing. What am I supposed to do, Jewel? I'm twenty-eight. I've never been a widow before. How does a widow act?"

Jewel offered no advice. Lusa took one of the jelly jars in her hand and stared at its ruby redness, that clear, proud color that she knew she loved, theoretically, but that couldn't touch her just now. "I grew up in a family where suffering was quiet," she said. "My father is a man who's lost everything: his family's land, his own father, his faith, and now his wife's companionship. All for unfair reasons. And he's just kept working, all his life. I was always more of a complainer, but I'm learning to be quiet. It seems like the only grown-up way to face this brutal thing that's happened."

Jewel's eyes were so much like Cole's, so earnest and perfectly blue, that Lusa had to look away from her.

"I may look like I'm doing all right, but I don't know if I'm coming or going. Whoever told you my plans knows more than I do."

Jewel put her hand on her mouth—a nervous habit, apparently. "It's none of my business, but there wasn't any life insurance, was there?"

Lusa shook her head. "Cole wasn't planning on dying this year. We'd talked about insurance, but with everything so tight, it just seemed like one extra payment we didn't need. We thought maybe we'd do it after we had kids or something."

"I'll tell you something. Mary Edna and Herb could help with the burial. I would if I could, but they *can*. Herb and his brother are doing good with their dairy over on Six. That's Herb's family's land, paid off. So they're set up pretty good right now."

"I can cover the burial, it's done. That was our savings. Mary Edna didn't offer, and I sure wasn't going to ask."

"Mary Edna's bark's a whole lot worse than her bite."

"It's not that. You know why. I'm not stupid, Jewel, I know what everybody's saying: here I am living in this house you all grew up in, on your family's land. The so-called Widener place, and there's no longer any Widener on the premises. Do you think I'd feel comfortable asking your family for *anything?*"

Jewel gave her an odd look. "Is that true? Lois told me that— that you were going to take your maiden name back now."

"What? No, I never did . . ." Lusa wondered how far the mis-understandings went, and whether any of it would be possible to untangle, after a point.

"Well, anyway," Jewel said, "having a house and a farm's not the same as having money."

"*Tell* me. When I hear people hinting I'm a gold digger, I feel like publishing my damn debts in the newspaper. I've got a barn to reroof before winter, and this house, too, probably in the next year or two. And something's wrong with the spring box; I'm just wait-ing for the day I wake up and have no water. What else? Oh yes, Cole's brand-new Kubota, twenty-two thousand dollars, which won't be paid off for another four years."

"I didn't know he'd financed the tractor."

Was Jewel spying? What difference would it make if they knew she was destitute? None, Lusa decided. "He didn't want to. But we had to have a tractor, and he deserved new. That John Deere of your daddy's was older than Cole, I think. He'd been fighting with it his whole life, holding it together with baling twine and fence wire."

"That tractor *was* older than Cole. Come to think of it."

"And now I'll have to pay somebody to mow hay and put it in the barn, and fix the fences and round up the cows when they get over on the neighbors', and mess with the baler, which breaks down every single time you use it. And run and repair the bush hog and the side-arm mower—or am I supposed to learn to do all that myself? I'm sure there are other costs, too; I just don't know enough to see them coming."

"Lord, Lord," Jewel said softly. Her face was the saddest thing Lusa had seen in a stretch of many sad days. Her forehead was deeply creased, and her eyes looked like an old woman's. At close range she looked much older than Lusa had thought she was.

"No man to farm it," Lusa summarized. "As you put it."

"Herb and Big Rickie will help you out."

"Oh, they've been up here. I guess they're in charge now. Cole's grave isn't yet healed over, and already I'm nobody."

"What do you mean?"

"Well, I need help, sure. But *help.* It would be nice to be asked, instead of bossed around like a child. Do they do that to you?"

"They don't have any business with me. I don't even plant a garden anymore. I praise the Lord for my job at Kroger's and beg Him to strike Shel dead if that check should fail to keep coming for the kids."

"What about Emaline and Frank?"

"Emaline and Frank are officially out of farming for good, they say, and I think they're just as happy about it, to both have factory jobs instead of farming."

"But I heard Frank complaining at the funeral about losing his tobacco lease. And he complains about commuting to Leesport."

"Frank would complain about the moon if it looked at him wrong. He makes good money at Toyota, and he likes everybody to know it."

"So who's still farming, just Lois and Big Rickie? And Herb?

How can I live smack in the middle of you all and not know what's what?"

"Well, because it's not really settled, that's why. About half the time Hannie-Mavis and Joel lease out their allotment to a big grower over to Roanoke, like Herb does. Then the next year, they won't. But Lois and Big Rickie always do their own tobacco, four acres and some. You might not know it, but he and Joel's got land leased all over the county running beef cattle, too. Big Rickie's got farmer in his blood."

Both women jumped at the sound of a crash and breaking glass from the porch. Lusa started for the door, but Jewel stopped her, holding up a pair of tongs. "You take the jars out of the canner and get the syrup boiling. I'll be back in a jiffy."

Lusa could hear Jewel scolding and both kids crying or whining on the porch. She tiptoed to look out the high window over the sink. "Jewel," she called, "if it's those jars of green beans, it's a good riddance. They've been out there since I moved in."

There was no answer, and from this angle she couldn't see Jewel or the kids but could hear a smack and a wail. "That is no way to treat your little brother," she heard. "You keep this up and you're wearing a dress tomorrow. I mean it."

Lusa frowned and turned to the stove. She measured equal parts sugar and hot water into the pot, hoping three quarts of syrup would be the right amount to cover five quarts of raw-pack cherries. She should put in something acidic to lower the pH, for the canning, but she didn't have any lemon juice. Would vinegar work? She added one tablespoon, a wild guess, then took up the tongs to lift the sterilized jars from the water bath. She lined them up on the counter, a raft of widemouthed birds begging to be fed.

"It *was* the green beans," Jewel sighed, coming inside. "I got all the glass. I told them to clean up the rest and throw it out by the creek, and then go play in the barn or something. I don't care if it's raining; they won't melt."

"That's fine. Truly, I'm glad about the beans. I've been scared to eat them and scared to give them away. My luck, I'd kill somebody of botulism."

Jewel reached under the sink to shake a dustpan of broken glass like wind chimes into the trash. "She's going to be my death, if I don't kill her first. Lowell's a handful, but he's just little. Crystal Gail's something else. It's time for her to be growing out of this *stage,* which she's been going through since the day she was born. What?"

Lusa realized she must look comically confused. "Crystal?"

"Crys. Oh!" Jewel laughed, waved her hand. "You thought she was a boy. You and everybody else. When she started kindergarten, the teacher refused to let her go to the girls' bathroom until I rushed down there with her birth certificate."

"Oh."

Jewel looked earnest. "Don't think it's because of Shel leaving, some child-of-divorce thing. She's *always* been this way."

"I don't think anything about it, Jewel; I just didn't realize."

"You can't imagine. It's been going on since she was a baby. Her first word was *no,* and her second was *dress.* No dress. No dolls, no pretty hair bows. I gave in on that haircut because she was cutting it herself. I was afraid she'd poke her eyes out."

Jewel looked so vulnerable, Lusa could practically see the veins through her skin. She wanted to hug her, to trust her completely. "It doesn't matter," she said. "I'm just glad you told me so I won't keep using the wrong pronoun. I can't believe I've known that child a year and nobody ever set me straight."

"You and Cole only ever had eyes for each other, honey. You hardly came to family things anyway, and if you did, it wasn't to look at my crazy mixed-up daughter."

"Ouch," Lusa said, burning her hand slightly on the rim of a jar.

"She's not crazy, don't do that to yourself. I wouldn't worry about it."

"You would if you were her mother. You'd worry yourself sick.

She's about half the reason why Shel left. He blamed me—oh, Lord, did he blame me. He said I was making her a little homo by letting her wear jeans and cut her hair like that. And maybe he was right. But it wasn't my idea. I'd like to have seen *him* try and get her into a dress. That's what I told him: *You* try putting panty hose on a tomcat!"

Jewel and Lusa looked at each other and laughed.

"And anyway," Jewel asked, a little shyly, "isn't a homo a man?"

"Jewel, she's just a tomboy. I was exactly like that at her age."

"You were? But you're so pretty. And you cook!"

Lusa felt awkwardly flattered, though she was also aware that this wasn't the point. "You should have seen me. I skinned my knees and caught bugs and wanted to be a farmer when I grew up."

"Careful what you wish for."

"The syrup's boiling."

"Do you put a dash of vinegar in it, or not? Oh good, you did, I can smell it. Here, you hold the funnel over the jars and I'll pour—where's your ladle?"

Jewel knew exactly where the ladle was, and everything else in this kitchen. The question was a gift of respect. Lusa retrieved the ladle from its drawer and closed it with her hip, feeling acutely grateful.

"Crystal's pretty. The name, I mean."

Jewel shook her head. "It doesn't look like her. She looks like Beaver Cleaver."

Lusa smiled. *"Meeseh maydel, shayneh dame,"* she said, her grandfather's promise—which had finally come true, for what it was worth.

"What?"

"'Ugly ducklings grow up to be swans.'" Lusa felt frustrated again—this wasn't really her wish, to promise that Crys would grow up straight and feminine, because maybe she wouldn't. Her wish was to tell Jewel that the alternative would be fine, too. But Lusa couldn't imagine having *that* conversation with Jewel. "Maybe it's not really about trying to act like a boy," she hazarded cautiously, "but just her way of trying to be herself."

"Let's don't talk about it. Crys is just Crys. Tell me some gossip. Tell me why you're mad at Big Rickie and Herb."

Lusa poured four cups of cherries into each jar, then held the funnel steady over the mouth as Jewel covered them with boiling syrup. "I'm not mad, I don't guess. I mean I am, but I shouldn't be. I know they meant well."

"Well, but what did they *do?*"

"They came up this morning to *inform* me that they're going to set my tobacco on Saturday."

"And?"

"And, I don't want to grow tobacco."

"You don't? Why not?"

"Oh, I'm being stupid, I guess. Farm economics, what do I know? But half the world's starving, Jewel, we're sitting on some of the richest dirt on this planet, and I'm going to grow *drugs* instead of food? I feel like a hypocrite. I nagged Cole to quit smoking every day of our marriage."

"Well, honey, you didn't ask the whole world to quit smoking. And by the way, they didn't."

"I know. It's the only reliable crop around here you can earn enough from to live off a five-acre bottom, in a county that's ninety-five percent too steep to plow. I *know* why every soul in this end of three states grows tobacco. Knowing full well the bottom's going to drop out any day now."

"They're trapped."

"They're trapped."

Jewel paused between jars and pointed the ladle toward the back window, the one that faced up Bitter Hollow toward the mountain. "You've got timber."

Lusa shook her head. "I couldn't log this hollow."

"Well, but you could. That hollow goes up half a mile or more before you get to National Forest land. We used to think those woods went on forever."

"I will not cut down those trees. I don't care if there's a hundred thousand dollars' worth of lumber on the back of this farm, I'm not selling it. It's what I love best about this place."

"What, the trees?"

"The trees, the moths. The foxes, all the wild things that live up there. It's Cole's childhood up there, too. Along with yours and your sisters'."

"That's so. Cole loved it best of any of us."

"*Cole* did? He always acts like—acted like—the woods and the briar patches of this world were enemy number one."

"Well, farming. You know. You've got to do what it takes."

"Yep. And around here that's tobacco, I guess, if I want to keep this farm. I just wish I could be the one person to think of a door out of that trap."

Jewel smiled. "You and Cole. He used to say that."

"What?"

"That he'd be the first one in this county to make a killing off something besides tobacco."

"When did he say that?"

"Oh, he was sixteen, maybe. Future Farmers of America and high school running-back star, what a combination. *Much* too interested in his good looks to smoke a cigarette, mind you, or grow plain old ordinary tobacco. He was going to set the world on fire. He tried red bell peppers one year and cucumbers the next, potatoes the next."

"No. He never told me that."

"I'm telling you. Right out here in Daddy's bottom field. Every year, whatever it was, it failed, and he had to eat a little more of his pride. He grew up in those three years, from dreamer to farmer. Gave up his pipe dreams and started smoking."

Lusa shook her head. "I can't picture that. I know Cole was energetic, but I can't picture that he was ever so—what? starry-eyed."

She laughed. "Plus, I figured he was born smoking. Like a *fish,* he was hooked."

"No, I remember being shocked to see him smoking with the men at Mommy's wake. So it was right around then, when Mommy died. The very next year, Daddy cleaned out the barn and signed the farm over to Cole, and then he died, too. Seemed like he could trust Cole to be a man finally. He'd be able to handle anything that came along, after the red bell peppers, the cucumbers, and the potatoes."

Anything but a steering column through his rib cage, Lusa thought morbidly, recognizing how self-pity could push its nose into any conversation like a tiresome dog. It took so much energy to keep Cole outside her thoughts for a single minute. And yet people still said, "I didn't want to remind you. . . ."

"What could go wrong with potatoes?" Lusa forced herself to ask. "It seems like such a sure thing. Good yielder, easy to transport, and you could spread out the harvest."

"It was the funniest thing. They said he could make a profit if he could get them down to the potato-chip factory in Knoxville. But then when he did, it didn't work out. They liked the Idaho potatoes better. The ones that grow around here have too much sugar in them. It makes them slice ragged and burn around the edges."

"Too much sugar?"

"That's what they said. This bottomland's too rich. I mean, they're good potatoes, just not good for the market."

"Jewel, my life sounds like a country song: 'My roof's a-caving in, my land's too steep to plow, and my bottom's got too much sugar.'"

"Your bottom!" Jewel startled Lusa by smacking her with a dish towel. "Let's get your bottom to cleaning up this mess. You are not going to starve, Loretta Lynn."

Jewel piled things up to carry to the sink while Lusa plunged her hands into soapy water so hot it prickled her skin. The hurt felt like a punishment that would clean the ache out of her chest. The rain was picking up again, starting to hammer a quiet roar on the tin roof, playing Zayda Landowski's music. Yesterday was the anniversary of her wedding, which nobody had mentioned all day, but Zayda had regaled her all through the rainy night playing klezmer tunes on his clarinet—the Jewish wedding she never had. She and Cole had made a small ceremony of it in the Hunt Morgan garden in Lexington, outdoors, to sidestep the issue of religion. That had been fine with Cole. He wasn't churchy like his sisters.

"Jewel, I want to tell you something. Just let me say this. I loved my husband."

"Well, sure you did."

In her mind's eye Lusa pictured the lower field, back when he'd first set out to make it his own: a moving sea of leaves turning lightly in the breeze, the bobbing red bells of ripening peppers, a young man wading through them the way he would walk into a lake. Cole at nineteen. A man she never met.

"We never got a chance to hit our stride, maybe. You all still think I don't really know who he was, but I did, I do. We talked a lot; he told me things. Just a few days before he died, he told me something amazing."

Jewel looked up. "What? Can I ask?"

Lusa crossed her arms over her stomach, holding her breath, transported by the scent-memory of honeysuckle across a field. *Like a moth, here I am, we're here.* She glanced over at Jewel. "I'm sorry, it won't make any sense to you. It's nothing I can say in words."

"Well," Jewel said, turning away. She was disappointed, Lusa could see. Now she thought Lusa was withholding something important, some piece of her brother that would help bring him back.

"Never mind. I'm sorry, Jewel, but really it's nothing that matters now. Just that we were right for each other, for sure. Just like you and Shel were in the beginning. Even though everybody's poisoned it now by taking a bad end and working backward."

Jewel passed the sponge from one hand to the other while she studied Lusa. "Nobody's saying you didn't love him."

"Nobody *thinks* they're saying that." She could feel Jewel's scrutiny but couldn't look up. She turned back to the sink and leaned in to the sticky preserve pot and scrubbed it hard to keep herself from crying or yelling. Her whole body pumped with the effort.

"My Lord, honey. What's this about?"

"That thing about changing my name back, for instance. My husband's hardly cold in the grave, and already I've run to the courthouse to erase his family name from the deed to your family farm? That's for *shit*. What kind of meanspirited lie is that, and who made it up?"

Jewel hesitated. "Lois saw your signature on something at the funeral home."

Loud Lois, she thought uncharitably, picturing that long face permanently puckered with worry that someone else was getting her share. "I always had the same name, before, during, and after Cole. Lusa Maluf Landowski. My mom's Palestinian and my dad's a Polish Jew, and *never*, before I came here, did I think that was anything to be ashamed of. I've had it since I was born. Not that I've ever heard anybody in your family say it. You talk about making somebody disappear? You think they put the vanishing act on Shel? Try living in a family that won't learn your damn name!"

She and Jewel blinked at each other, shocked equally.

"Nobody meant any harm, honey. It's just normal to take your husband's name around here. We're just regular country people, with country ways."

"It never struck me as a regular thing to do, so we just didn't. God, Jewel, did you all really believe I'd take his name and then throw it *back,* a week after he died? Some carpetbagger, erasing your family name and stealing your homeplace, is that how you see me?"

Jewel had her hand on her mouth, and tears were welling up in her eyes; they were back where they'd started. Lusa had raised her voice at this timid woman who was probably the nearest thing she had to a friend in the family or this county. Jewel shook her head and held out her arms to Lusa, who stepped awkwardly into her hug. Jewel's body felt as bony and light as a bird's underneath her apron, all feathers and heartbeat.

They clung to each other for a minute, rocking back and forth. "Don't pay any attention to me," Lusa said. "I'm losing my mind. There are ghosts here. There's one in this kitchen that stirs up fights."

Over Jewel's shoulder she could look straight down the hall through the wavy antique glass in the front door to the outside, the yard and front pasture. This rain would never end, she thought. She could see the fresh beginnings of yet another storm coming: the leaves of the tulip poplar down by the barn trembling and rotating on a hundred different axes, like a tree full of pinwheels. Beneath it Lowell and Crystal orbited the barnyard in their dark, soaked clothes, laughing and galloping on a pair of invisible horses, traveling in circles through the infinite downpour as if time for them had stopped, or not yet started.

9

Old Chestnuts

arnett stood admiring the side of his barn. Over the course of a century the unpainted chestnut planks had weathered to a rich, mottled gray, interrupted only by the orange and lime-colored streaks of lichen that brightened the wood in long, vertical stripes where moisture drained from the galvanized tin roof.

He was haunted by the ghosts of these old chestnuts, by the great emptiness their extinction had left in the world, and so this was something Garnett did from time to time, like going to the cemetery to be with dead relatives: he admired chestnut wood. He took a moment to honor and praise its color, its grain, and its miraculous capacity to stand up to decades of weather without pressure treatment or insecticides. Why and how, exactly, no one quite knew. There was no other wood to compare with it. A man could only thank the Lord for having graced the earth with the American chestnut, that broad-crowned, majestic source of nuts and shade and durable lumber. Garnett could recall the days when chestnuts had grown so thick on the mountaintops of this county that in spring, when the canopies burst into flower, they appeared as snowcapped peaks. Families had lived through the winter on the gunnysacks of chestnuts stored in their root cellars, and hams from the hogs they'd fattened on chestnuts, and the money they'd earned sending chestnuts by the railroad car to Philadelphia and New York City, where people of other nationalities and religious persuasions roasted them for sale on street corners. He thought of cities as being populated with those sorts of people, the types to hunker over purchased coals, roasting nuts whose origins they could only guess at. Whereas Garnett liked to think of his own forebears as chestnut people. Of chestnut logs the Walkers had built their cabins, until they had sons and a sawmill to rip and plane the trees into board lumber from which they then built their houses and barns and finally an empire. It was lumber sales from Walker's Mill that had purchased the land and earned his grandfather the right to name Zebulon Mountain. Starting with nothing but their wits and strong hands, the Walkers had lived well under the sheltering arms of the American chestnut until the slow devastation began to unfold in 1904, the year that brought down the chestnut blight. The Lord giveth and the Lord taketh away.

That was not Garnett's to question, the fall of his family fortunes. He didn't begrudge the sales of land that by the year 1950, when the last chestnuts were gone, had whittled his grandfather's huge holdings down to a piece of bottomland too small to support anything but a schoolteacher. Garnett hadn't minded being a teacher; Ellen certainly hadn't minded being married to one. He hadn't needed to own an empire and did not resent the necessity of close neighbors (save for one). But neither did he ever doubt that his own dream—to restore the chestnut tree to the American landscape—was also a part of God's plan, which would lend to his family's history a beautiful symmetry. On his retirement from the Zebulon County school system a dozen years ago, Garnett had found himself blessed with these things: a farm with three level fields and no livestock; a good knowledge of plant breeding; a handful of seed sources for American chestnuts; and access to any number of mature Chinese chestnuts that people had planted in their yards in the wake of the blight. They had found the nuts far less satisfactory, and of course the tree itself had none of the American chestnut's graceful stature or its lumber qualities, but the Chinese chestnut had proven entirely resistant to blight. This lesser tree had been spared for a divine purpose, like some of the inferior animals on Noah's ark. Garnett understood that on his slow march toward his heavenly reward, he would spend as many years as possible crossing and backcrossing the American with the Chinese chestnut. He worked like a driven man, haunted by his arboreal ghosts, and had been at it for nearly a decade now. If he lived long enough he would produce a tree with all the genetic properties of the original American chestnut, except one: it would retain from its Chinese parentage the ability to stand tall before the blight. It would be called the Walker American chestnut. He would propagate this seedling and sell it by mail order that it might go forth and multiply in the mountains and forests of Virginia, West Virginia, Kentucky, and all points north to the Adirondacks and west to the Mississippi. The landscape of his father's manhood would be restored.

A loud buzz near his ear made Garnett turn his head and look up too fast, causing him to experience such a bout of dizziness that he nearly had to sit down on the grass. The Japanese beetles were thick as pea soup already, and it was only June. He noticed that his Concord grapevines, which he loved to see climbing lazy and lush up the slatted side of the old grain house with their leaves drooping like ladies' hands, were showing a rusty brown aura. From this distance it looked as if they'd been dusted with brown powder, but he knew it was really the brown skeleton of the leaf showing through. It was something he had pointed out to his vo-ag students time and again, the characteristic sign of Japanese-beetle damage. Something to add to his list for the hardware today: malathion. The Sevin dust wasn't killing them dead enough. Or it was washing off in all this rain.

He glanced over toward Rawley's, whence came the plague. She had started several new brush piles along the line fence just to gall him. She called them "compost" and claimed they heated up on the inside to a temperature that would kill beetle larvae and weed seeds, but he doubted it. Any decent farmer who'd spent his life in Zebulon County learning thrifty and effective farming methods would know to set fire to his orchard trimmings, but *she* was too busy with her bug traps and voodoo to get rid of her tree-trash the normal way. Compost piles. "Laziness lots" would be a better name for them. "Stacks of sloth."

Earlier in the week he had attempted to speak to her over the fence: "The source of Japanese beetles seems to be your brush piles, Miss Rawley."

To which she'd replied, "Mr. Walker, the source of Japanese beetles is Japan."

There was no talking to her. Why even try?

He noted that her pitiful old foreign truck was gone from its usual spot between the lilac hedge and her white clapboard house. He wondered where she might have gone on a Friday morning. *Saturday* mornings she always went out with her produce to the Amish market, and Mondays to Kroger's (the Black Store wasn't adequate to her needs, according to Oda Black, who had spied Nannie in Kroger's purchasing soya sauce), and lately she went out on Tuesday afternoons also, for a purpose he hadn't yet discerned. Sundays she went to the Unitarian place; Garnett was not about to call it a church. That was just her cup of tea, he imagined: a den of coffee-drinking women in slacks making high-toned conversation along godless lines. Evolution, transcendentalism, things of that nature. Thank goodness it was over the county line, at least, in Franklin, where they had the college. They had more of that kind over there, and as Garnett understood it, the debauchery in this state just increased at a steady pace along an eastward line that wound itself up in Washington, D.C. It was Oda Black's opinion that the Unitarian women refused to wear proper foundation garments and dabbled in witchcraft. Oda was quick to point out that *she* was not one to stand in judgment (though she was wide enough to stand anywhere she pleased, and no one would argue, save for the floorboards). She'd heard it from somebody firsthand, and furthermore two girls from the college had once wandered into her store talking right out loud to each other about witchcraft, not caring who heard them, while they reached into the cooler for their sodas. Oda reported that their flesh had jiggled under their T-shirts like jelly turned out of its jar.

That was Franklin County for you. That college was asking for it when they let in women.

Garnett stepped up onto his porch and pulled a folded square of paper from his shirt pocket. He had put a good day's work behind him, five hours already this morning hand-pollinating and bagging chestnut flowers. June was his busiest month, and this morning when the sun finally came out after its long confinement, Garnett had risen early and got out into his hybrid seedling fields to make up for lost time. There was still so much to be done: the grass in his yard was high, and weeds were springing up along the creek bank, but he could postpone the mowing and weed killing until later this afternoon. Now it was past eleven o'clock, and he had earned the pleasure of a trip to town. Not that he had any kind of a joyride planned. It was mostly errands: Black Store, Tick's Garage, and Little Brothers' Hardware. He unfolded the square of paper on which he'd made his list for the hardware:

1. *Hacksaw blade*

(The last time he'd used the saw on a stripped bolt, he'd noted it was dull.)

2. *Black plastic for mulching between the tree rows*
3. *AA flashlight batteries (four)*
4. *3 PVC pipe fittings, L-shape, 1/2 inch (broken irrigation line)*
5. *Paint markers for the hybrid trees*

(He resented this item, since he knew he still had some markers down in the barn, but he'd wasted nearly an hour yesterday looking for them and suspected they'd been taken. Maybe by a neighbor child. Maybe by a groundhog.)

6. *Weed killer, one gallon concentrate!!*

The resentment attached to this final purchase was boundless and only feebly expressed by his underlining and exclamation points. But he couldn't delay it any longer. He had to face Oda Black every time he needed bread, Miracle Whip, and bologna, and he knew how they must be tarring and feathering him down there at the store behind his back. "Here comes the county's worst road frontage," Oda probably cried when his truck pulled up out front, chuckling as she shoved herself up from her armchair by the front window and slid her swollen feet toward the register. "Shhh, everybody! It's Mr. Pokeweed." All right, then, he would spray his front bank himself. Bring that forest of briars crashing down around the ears of the snapping turtles. Garnett still turned red to think about it. At least Oda didn't seem to have heard about the turtle.

He added malathion (for Japanese beetles!!) to his list, refolded the paper, replaced it in his shirt pocket, and went into the house, comforting himself with thoughts of Pinkie's Diner. In the front hallway he paused to sort through a stack of mail he had brought in yesterday but forgotten to look at: advertisement circulars, nonsense, not even a bill. He slid the whole lot into the trash and closed the west-facing window in the kitchen against the heat that would arrive this afternoon in his absence. After his errands he would go to Pinkie's for the fish-dinner special that was offered every Friday afternoon: all the fried catfish you could eat with hush puppies and slaw, $5.99. Garnett suspected that since Pinkie's had it on Fridays, it was probably meant for the Catholics, but the diner was a place of business, after all, not a church. Catholics in Zebulon County were few and far between, and anyhow Pinkie Prater would accept $5.99 from a dog or a horse if it came in, and put it in his cash register with no questions asked. Pinkie's on Fridays was a settled matter in Garnett's mind. In fact, on the rare Friday when he failed to keep his appointment with the fish-dinner special, rumors about Garnett Walker's health circulated so fast that when he turned up next at Black Store or the filling station, people were amazed to see him alive.

No matter. A predictable mare beats a wild hare, his father used to say. Pinkie's was Garnett's only extravagance, and he liked to look forward to it. He did not tend to eat well since his wife had died. It had been enough years now that he had gotten used to cold meat sandwiches for dinner and a single place mat on the table, but he had never learned to cook. Certainly not something like a hush puppy. How would you even begin to make a hush puppy, what in the world was in one? Nothing to do with a puppy, surely. Garnett had long known, though he didn't much like to admit it, that God's world and the better part of daily life were full of mysteries known only to women.

He would have to change his shirt before starting out. He had broken a sweat out there in the field, to say the least. He closed the bathroom door (though he lived alone and never had guests) and took off his shirt without looking in the bathroom mirror. After he had washed himself with a cloth, he went to his bedroom bureau to retrieve his last clean undershirt (tomorrow was laundry day) and to the armoire to take down his town shirt from its hanger. (It smelled slightly of Pinkie's fish-dinner specials; he would remember to wash it tomorrow, even though this would also mean fussing with the iron. He had never learned to make it hiss out steam the way Ellen could.) Only after he had buttoned the collar and tucked in the tails did he allow himself a glance in Ellen's dressing mirror. There was nothing wrong with his bare chest, beyond an old man's slightly sunken ribs and an odd nest of white hair in the middle, but modesty was Garnett's habit. He had been a widower for eight years; he kept company with his God. His body was no longer to be looked upon. If the thought caused him sadness—that he would never again know the comfort of human touch—he sensed it was merely a tributary to the lake of grief through which an old man must swim at the end of his days.

He gathered up his ring of keys, counted the cash in his wallet, and locked the kitchen door on his way out. He stole another glance over toward Nannie's, noticing with surprise a large, roughly cow-shaped patch of darkness on her roof. He walked a bit closer and squinted through the tops of his bifocals. It was a patch of the green shingles missing; they must have blown off in the last storm. What a mess that must be, in all this rain, and what a nuisance to replace. Worse than a nuisance: those old, hand-cut shingles were impossible to find nowadays. She would have to redo the whole roof if she didn't want it to look hodgepodge. He touched the corners of his mouth, trying not to harbor pleasure at a neighbor's misfortune. She did not know that in Garnett's own garage there was a stack of those green shingles, from the original lot that Garnett's father and Old Man Rawley had ordered together and shared. Originally, before Garnett had modernized to asbestos in the 1960s, the two houses had borne the same style of clapboard and the same spade-shaped shingles. Garnett's father had been on good enough terms with Old Man Rawley that he'd sold him the fifty-five acres of orchard land with only the one decent house site, which put the Rawleys near enough by to hit with a rock, as the saying went (though no one had ever felt that particular urge until Garnett and Nannie). The house was modest, neat and small, with its hipped roof and gables facing the road. Old Rawley was a good orchard man who'd planted excellent stock. But anyone could have foreseen that his daughter stood to inherit, since he had no sons. That was trouble that Garnett's father should have smelled: a daughter away at school in the 1950s. Before you could say Jack Robinson she'd be back here parading around in loud clothes, having an illegitimate child with mental deficiencies, and making up her mind to grow apples with no chemicals whatsoever, in flat defiance of the laws of nature. Garnett sighed and forgave his father once again. It was not a premeditated crime, only a failure of foresight.

As successor to a lost fortune, Garnett had spent his life glancing away from visions of how things might have turned out differently. Nannie Rawley was the exception. How could he not dwell on her presence in his life and seek its meaning? Garnett had overlooked her as a child (she was a kid, maybe ten years younger); had hardly known her as a young woman since she was away for so many years; and had mainly ignored her as long as his wife was alive. (Ellen liked to have little chitchats with her, and then disapprove afterward.) But now, during these eight years alone, he'd been forced to bear her as a burgeoning plague on his old age. Why? What made Nannie do the things she did, before God and Man and sometimes on Garnett's property? He suspected a connection between that long-ago birth of a deformed child and her terror of chemicals. The troubles had been evident at birth, the Mongol features and so forth, and Nannie had named it Rachel Carson Rawley, after that lady scientist who cried wolf about DDT. Everything in Nannie's life since seemed to turn on the birth of that child, now that he looked back. The woman had probably been normal once. That child had launched her off the deep end.

Where would she be now, on a Friday? She never went out on Fridays. He ducked behind his rose of Sharon and peered around the back of her house to make sure the truck wasn't parked back there. Sometimes she parked in back if she had something to unload. Last week she had parked inside her barn with a load of apple crates piled high in the truck bed. But today there was no sign of her.

He climbed into his own truck, a 1986 Ford pickup, which

started right up (he had cleaned and gapped the spark plugs last week), and steered carefully out onto number 6, purposefully ignoring his disgraceful frontage. Soon enough, soon enough! He needed more Two-Four-D and Roundup both, for the seedling fields, and had neglected to order them wholesale from the company as he had in previous years. He drove very slowly, taking his time with the curves. Garnett did realize his eyesight wasn't what it could have been; this was not something he refused to admit. But there was very little traffic on 6 anymore since they'd made the interstate down King Valley. Anyone who had any business on this road would recognize Garnett's truck. They'd know to give him a wide berth. It wasn't as if he were *blind,* for heaven's sake. He just had some trouble judging distance. There had been a few mishaps.

He would go to Little Brothers' first, then circle around to the filling station to top off the tank of his truck and use the air hose to clean his air filter, two things he did each and every Friday. Today he would also need to buy five gallons of diesel for his tractor, since he would soon have cultivating to do. After his dinner at Pinkie's he would stop at Black Store on the way home. That was it, Black Store should be the last thing, lest the milk curdle in his truck on this warm day, and the eggs incubate and hatch.

He passed by Black Store just then, at the intersection of 6 and Egg Creek Road, though he didn't see Oda wave at him through the window. Images from Garnett's past always lurked and rose up from the ditches as he drove this road, pictures more real to him than the things in plain view. A wild grapevine that had climbed into his mother's arborvitae, covering its rounded top like a shiny green-leather hunting cap. A sport groundhog, blond as wheat, with a black tail and cap, that lived under their barn for a season. All of the children had seen it before their father did, for what do children have to do in their lives but look for sport groundhogs? Father did not believe in its existence until nearly the end of the summer, when he finally saw it, too. Then it was real. He told neighbors about it then. The children felt proud when he did, as if they, too, had become more real. As Garnett navigated Highway 6 he breathed the air of that other time—a clearer time, it seemed, when colors and sound were more distinct and things tended to remain where they belonged. When the bobwhite quail could be counted on to cry his name pensively from the fields of an afternoon. Whatever happened to the bobwhite? You never heard him anymore. Garnett had read something from the Extension about fescue's being the cause, the ordinary fescue grass people planted for hay. It grew too densely for the bobwhite chicks to find their way through. Garnett could remember when fescue hay was the latest thing and the government was paying farmers to convert their fields from their native grasses to this new kind from Europe or somewhere fancy. (They'd thought kudzu was a great idea back then, too—Lordy!) Now fescue was everywhere, and probably no one but Garnett even remembered the bunchgrasses that used to grow here naturally, the bluestem and such. It must seem strange to the animals to have a new world entire sprouting all around them, replacing what they'd known. What a sadness, the baby quails lost in that jungle with nowhere to go. But you had to have hay.

Now here was Grandy's bait store, not a memory but a fact, with its hand-lettered sign: LIZARDS, 10 FOR A $. It perturbed him slightly that people in Zebulon County could not learn to call a salamander what it was. But it perturbed him more that Nannie Rawley stopped in there at least once a month, bought every "lizard" in the tank, and set them all free behind her orchard, in Egg Creek. Everyone knew she did it. Boys seined them and sold them to Dennis Grandy for a penny apiece, laughing all the way, knowing full well that most would be set free again by Nannie Rawley. Why did everyone suffer her so merrily? She claimed there were ten or fifteen kinds of salamanders in Zebulon that were endangered species, and said she was doing her part to save the environment. Implying what, then—that anyone who went bass fishing with salamanders was an enemy of God's plan?

Garnett would like to tell her a thing or two about God's plan.

That the creatures of this earth came to pass and sometimes passed on. That these matters were not ours to control if we were, as she claimed, merely one more species among our brethren, the animals. And if we were *not* the equal of animals, if we were meant instead to be masters and keepers of Eden, as the Bible said, then "lizards" were put here for a man to go bass fishing with, and that was that. She couldn't have it both ways. It was all quite clear to Garnett. Yet his logic always cowered before her curt and snappy replies. He had actually thought, once or twice, of writing her a letter.

He drove past the Pentecostal church, which had a spindly clump of joe-pye weed sprouting up in its parking lot. Oho! Too busy speaking in tongues and throwing babies to get out and weed their parking lot. Garnett smiled, feeling secure in his understanding of what God's word did and did not mean to suggest. He felt a slight press of guilt, then, as he steered his truck onto Maple. He ought to tell Miss Rawley about those shingles in his garage. If only she were the least bit reasonable.

There was the bank, there was the Esso. He was in town now. There was Les Pratt, who'd taught math at the high school when Garnett taught vocational agriculture. He waved, but Les was on the wrong side of the street. There was Dennis Grandy's wife with all those children, who weren't exactly dirty but never seemed quite clean.

And there was Nannie Rawley! Her truck, anyway. Dear merciful heavens, could he not get away from her for at least one pleasant trip into town? That woman was stubborn as cockleburs and a rash of poison ivy.

He slowed down to get a better look. It *was* her truck, parked in the Baptist church lot, where they let the Amish set up their farmers' market on Saturdays. This was *Friday,* though. Yet it was them, all right, the Amish children in their sober black dresses and trousers, politely selling their produce. He didn't see Nannie. He would maneuver his truck around the block and come back for a second look.

Were there so many Amish now that they had to have markets

on Saturdays *and* Fridays? They were a burgeoning people, that much he knew. They'd taken over a long row of farms on the other side of the river, he'd noticed last year. How were they managing so nicely, when every other farmer in the county was selling off his hayfields for house lots and looking for factory work? Well, the Amish weren't in debt up to their ears on chemicals and equip-ment—which gave them an unfair advantage, Garnett supposed. Oh! He missed a stop sign, then slammed on the brakes a hair too late, but it was all right: the car got around him. For quite a while he'd wondered about those farms along the river, which were un-reachable by car and accessible only by swinging bridges—long, narrow ones made of planks with just cables for handrails. It would take some courage to cross that gorge every day. He'd wondered how on earth a man would get his television or his wife's refrigera-tor over there, or even a tractor, to a farm like that. Then Les Pratt had told him the answer in a single word: Amish.

He rounded the corner and took another look at the Amish market. It was tempting to stop. He used to go nearly every Saturday before Nannie started showing up there with her apples or, in the early season, like now, her apple-blossom honey and basil-dasil and whatnot for sale. Evidently you didn't have to be Amish; they shared the space with Nannie and a handful of other farmers from the upper end of the county. The only rule was that everything had to be organic. The Amish didn't use any poisons, which seemed all right to Garnett if it was a religious matter. But Nannie's presence among them had settled it: he couldn't set foot in the place once she became a part of it, for now it was *Organic,* capital *O,* with its placid, irritating sense of holier-than-thou. So! No more stopping by on Saturday mornings to buy a delicious fresh pie and stand among these innocent youngsters with their neat stacks of vegeta-bles, preserves, and rabbits. He missed them, he realized sadly, rec-ognizing the same small ache that came when he thought of his boy's face in innocent childhood—his own son barefoot with a fish-ing pole, the terrible mistakes all lying ahead of him still. Garnett

missed hearing the Amish children count out his change in an accent that seemed vaguely foreign while he covertly looked at their
feet, which were thickly callused, for they wore no shoes all summer long. He knew the Amish didn't send their children to school,
and technically he disapproved of what they called godly simplicity
(actually simple backwardness). Yet he had a soft spot for those boys
and girls. He wondered why the adults sent the children to town to
do their selling. Were the adults elsewhere in town on other business, making the small, spare purchases they must surely need to
make? (A rake, some kerosene, something like that, he imagined.)
Did they feel the children would make better emissaries for repre-
senting their kind? Was it a play for sympathy? It seemed to run
against their habit of isolation, Garnett thought. Letting these children come into town to watch other families pile out of station
wagons, to see other children play with radios or the electronic
thingamajigs they all carried in their pockets now while their
mothers idly handled the melons—what were those Amish children
learning to want, that they could never have?

Half a block up from the market he slowed and pulled his truck
into a parking spot on the side of the street. He sat for a while,
considering his alternatives. He could go and buy a pie. They had
the most wonderful pies. Apple, cherry, and something they called
shoofly. But where in heaven's name was Nannie Rawley? Her
truck was there, and in front of it was a table with her kinds of
things, the frills she'd gotten into when apples were out of season:
lemon basil, lavender sachets, dried flowers—the sorts of things he
considered so unnecessary that it embarrassed him to look at them.
Where was she?

He would walk down to the end of the block and do his errands
at Little Brothers', he decided. On the walk back, if the coast was
clear, he would buy a pie. He would try to find one particular boy
he remembered, with the stiff Dutch-boy haircut and the rabbits in
a cage. He'd chatted with that young fellow and given him some advice about poultry. Ezra, that boy was. Or Ezekiel?

Garnett mounted the concrete steps to Little Brothers' with a light and steady heart, but things did not go well from that point on. Right on the threshold where Dink Little greeted him by name, he realized he'd forgotten his list. He patted his shirt pocket, ready to whip it out with a flourish in answer to Dink's predictable "What'challneed deday?" Then he patted his other pocket. But he'd changed his shirt, of course.

"I just need to look around a minute, Dink," Garnett replied, feeling sure he could quickly reconstruct his list as soon as he saw one of the items on the shelf. But he saw nothing he needed here. The musty, high-ceilinged store suddenly seemed more like an attic than a place of commerce: tall stacks of galvanized buckets leaned this way and that, mops leaned lazily against shelves full of floor polish. Stacks of green work gloves reached out toward him like a host of dismembered hands. He staggered sideways around a display of lawn mowers on sale and bumped his head on the sign above them that was so large and colorful it gave him a headache even without his reading it (JUNE MOWER SALE 10% OFF ALL BRANDS! TORO! GREEN MACHINE! SNAPPER! JOHN DEERE!). Garnett felt so rattled he could hardly stand up. He set his sights on a wheelbarrow down at the end of an aisle and headed for it just to get himself away from the door and the register, out of sight, where he could think.

If he took his time he would remember. Weed killer, of course! Roundup, one-gallon concentrate. He almost laughed aloud. It was coming back: Roundup, malathion, and paint markers for the trees, which he really shouldn't buy; he had some in the barn.

"Now does it sound like more of a whine, or more of a buzz? Because when the gearing pops out of whack, hit'll do that on you." One of the brothers up at the register was chatting with a customer. That would be Big, or Marshall. Dink always stayed by the door.

"What I'm saying is I didn't even hear it," the customer argued. "I turned my back and it ran off down the hill."

Weed killer and malathion. He spied a bottle of malathion on a shelf midway down the aisle past the galvanized buckets. Even though it was a spray bottle and not the size he needed, he walked over and seized it for courage. He was an old man lost in a hardware store, missing the fine print on all he surveyed; he needed to arm himself. What else had been on that list?

"They don't make them any bigger than that, or any meaner. Just a monster, and you'll have to take my word for it," the customer said.

"Well, Big here's the expert on *big*," said Marshall.

"Now, you boys aren't listening to me," the voice said coyly.

The brothers were laughing to beat the band, but Garnett's heart skipped a beat. He knew that voice. Good Lord in Heaven, was he meant to suffer like Job? It was Nannie Rawley.

Garnett stood next to the wheelbarrow at the end of the aisle, listening. How could she be *here* when she'd been down the street selling froufrou at the Amish market ten minutes ago? Was she one of those Unitarian witches, whizzing around Egg Fork on a broomstick? He leaned forward and peered around a stack of galvanized buckets, looking for an escape path. He could just leave, go home, get his list, and come back in half an hour. There would still be time for fish dinner afterward. Pinkie's stayed open till four.

But there was no way out. The register was near the front door, and that was where she was, holding court, making her ridiculous small talk with Dink, Big, and Marshall. He nearly covered his ears, so unbearable was that voice to him. However entertaining it might be proving at the moment to the indolent Little brothers. They were laughing like a pack of hyenas.

"Not a snapper!" one of them cried.

"Yes, a snapper," she replied, sounding both indignant and amused.

Garnett sat down in the wheelbarrow and held his head in his hands. This was too much to bear. This was beyond even what he expected of Nannie Rawley, whose sole claim on any kind of decency was that she was generally not a rumormonger.

"Law, I think I'da had to seen that to believe it," said Marshall, practically doubled over with amusement.

How could she do this to Garnett, her own good neighbor? How *dared* she ridicule him in public over that business with the snapping turtle? When the whole thing had been her fault!

"It was her fault," he said faintly, much too faintly to be heard, from his undignified post in the wheelbarrow. "Her weeds."

They were still braying like donkeys as they rang up her purchases—did it take all three Littles to ring up a blessed purchase? They were acting like schoolboys, making over her as if she were some beauty queen instead of a backbiting hag in a calico skirt. She had this whole town under her spell. Now she was asking for their advice about roofing compounds! Was there to be no end to this torment? Apparently she meant to stand there flirting all day, until Pinkie's Diner closed and the chickens went home to roost.

Garnett was going to have to march past them. This became clear. Suddenly all he could do was picture himself safely home at his kitchen table reading the farm news in the paper. That was where he wanted to be, more desperately than he desired any love or grace on this earth or beyond it: home. He wouldn't even go to Pinkie's. There was no point now. It was all-you-can-eat, and he'd lost his appetite.

Garnett stood tall and marched toward the door, holding his spray bottle of malathion in front of him to clear the path. They turned to stare as he stalked wordlessly and with great dignity past the counter.

"Why, Mr. Walker!" she cried.

Well howdy-do to you, he thought. There you are, caught in your tracks, you old biddy, you and your gossipmongering friends. Let your sins keep you awake at night. He nearly knocked his head a second time on the June Mower Sale sign but remembered to duck—praise Jesus!—in the nick of time.

He found his truck and was two blocks down the street past the Amish market before his heart stopped pounding in his ears. And he was beyond Black Store, halfway up Route 6 to his house, somewhere in front of Nannie Rawley's farm frontage, when it occurred to him that her lawn mower was a Snapper. Her mower that he knew had been giving her trouble, which she'd purchased at Little Brothers'. A Snapper.

He was parked in his own driveway before he realized he had shoplifted a bottle of malathion.

{10}

Moth Love

Swallows looped and dived inside the barn, swooping from their nests in the rafters overhead toward the doorway and out into the bright-purple evening, where the low sun glinted off their streamlined, back-curved wings. They were like little fighter planes, angry at any intrusion, expressing their ire in motion like bullets. Every evening Lusa came into the barn to milk, and every evening the swallows responded this way. Like some people, she thought: short on sense, long on ambition. Sunset canceled all previous gains, and the world was good for a fresh fight every day.

Her thoughts trailed off into a kind of trance as she milked and watched the barn swallows make their repetitious oval flights out over the flat surface of the pond, which the sunset had laminated with gold leaf. Suddenly she jumped, startling the cow. Little Rickie was standing in the doorway, all six and a half feet of him.

"Hey, Rickie. How's it going?"

He ambled toward the stanchion where she sat on a stool working the udder to its end. Down here in the cellar of the barn where the stalls were, the roof was low. Little Rickie's head nearly touched the rafters.

"Good, I reckon."

"Well, good. How's your family?"

Rickie cleared his throat. "Fine, I guess. Dad sent me up to tell you we won't be setting tobacco on Saturday. Tomorrow, I guess he means."

"No?" She looked up at him. "Why not? The ground is drying out. I walked out there on the tobacco bottom this afternoon, and it's not that bad. In fact I called down there to tell him everything looked good for tomorrow, but nobody was home. I think the rain's really stopped, finally."

Rickie looked as if he'd rather be anywhere in the county, pretty much, than in this barn talking with Lusa. A family trait. "Well, Uncle Herb said he's got real busy with his calves. And Dad said you wasn't all that interested in us setting your tobacco anyways, is what they said."

"Oh, I see. I'm supposed to go down there and apologize for my rash attempt at self-rule and beg them on bended knee to come set my tobacco." She saw she was being punished: the tobacco had been *their* idea, and now they were using it against her. Lusa put her shaking hands on her knees to force some calm onto herself. Her sudden anger had upset the cow enough to stop her milk for the moment. There was nothing doing until she let down again. Cows were a lesson in patience.

Rickie shrugged his shoulders inside his jean jacket, that particular movement owned by teenaged boys trying to fit their adult bodies. She shouldn't speak her mind to this kid, she realized; he must already consider her a hysteric. A *redhead*, Cole used to say. The boy kept a nervous eye on Lusa while he shook a cigarette out of his pack and lit it. As an afterthought he held out the pack to her, but she shook her head.

"No thanks, I don't smoke. Which is a misdemeanor in this county, I gather."

He ran a hand through his thick black hair. "I don't think Dad and them is wanting you to get on your knees and beg them or nothing."

"No," she said. "I'm sorry for snapping. I didn't mean that literally."

"Anyways it wouldn't matter if you did, since Dad didn't get sets from Jackie Doddard. There's prolly none left in the whole county by now, I don't reckon."

"Oh. Well, I guess that settles it. My goose is cooked."

She returned her hands to the cow's udder and manipulated it gently to submission. There was no sound in the barn but the rhythmic ring of the milk stream against the metal bucket and the syncopated, soggy-sounding drips from the waterlogged joists where the roof had leaked. Every drip reminded Lusa of the barn-fixing money she didn't have and now would not earn from tobacco.

"Got some leaks," Rickie said, looking up.

"About three thousand dollars' worth, I'm guessing. Maybe more, once they get into those rotten roof beams."

"Hay's going to spoil."

"Oh, don't worry about that. I probably won't even get any hay mowed or put up in the barn this summer. The baler's broken down, and the tractor's probably going to be repossessed. I was thinking I'd just let the cows eat snow this year."

Little Rickie stared at her. His big body was a cool seventeen, but his face looked younger. What was wrong with her, why was she venting her ironic wrath on this child? He was only the messenger. She was shooting the messenger.

"Hey," he said. "I'm real sorry about, you know. Uncle Cole."

"Thank you. Me, too." She exhaled slowly. "It hasn't even been a month. Twenty-seven days. Seems like twenty-seven years."

He repositioned himself against one of the massive old chestnut posts that held up the upper floor of the barn. Upstairs where they hung the tobacco, the barn was lofty as a cathedral, but down here where the animals stayed it was friendly and close with the sweet, mixed smells of grain, manure, and milk.

"Me and Uncle Cole used to go fishing. He ever tell you about that? We'd skip school together and go trout fishing up on Zeb Mountain. Man, it's pretty up there. They've got trees so big you just about fall over from looking at them."

"You'd skip school together?" Lusa considered this. "When you were in first or second grade, Cole was still in high school. I never even thought about that. He was your pal. Like a big brother."

"Yeah." Rickie looked down, being careful where he put his cigarette ash. "He always told me stuff. How to talk to girls and stuff."

Lusa raised the heel of her hand against one eye and turned away, unprepared to cry in front of Rickie. "Yeah. That was one thing he sure knew how to do."

The cow lowed, a small protest in the dripping silence. Her calf in the neighboring stall immediately began to bawl, as if he'd just woken up to the injustice of milk robbery.

"Milking, huh?" Rickie noted.

"Yep."

"Looks like you're good at it."

"Cole taught me; he said I had a talent. Stupid thing to be good at, right?"

"Not really. Animals, you know. They can tell what's what. You can't fool them like you can people."

The calf next door was still bawling, and she crooned to calm him: "Hush now, your mama will be there in a minute." He quieted, and Lusa returned to the milking. There was comfort in this work. Sometimes she felt flooded with the mental state of her Jersey cow—a humble, unsurprised wonder at the fact of still being here in this barn at the end of each day. Lusa actually enjoyed the company. She'd been tempted to name her, until Cole pointed out that they were going to eat her child.

"Uncle Herb, over at his dairy? Him and the cows is like oil and water, he says. He does all the milking with machines. Hooks up bossy to the tank and sucks her dry."

"Yikes. Poor bossy."

"I don't think they mind it none. They're just cows."

"True."

"How many times a day you milk her, twiced?"

Twiced, they all said. *Oncet, twiced.* She wondered if that was a vestige of Old English hanging on in these isolated mountain towns. "I just milk once a day, believe it or not. Even that's more than I need now. Just before you came in that door, I was making up my mind for this to be my last milking."

"Yeah?"

"Yeah. Tomorrow I'm pasturing this girl out with her calf so all that milk can go to the stomach it was made for. It doesn't do much for mine."

"Don't care for milk, do you?"

"It doesn't care for me. I did this for Cole because he loved fresh cream. I like making yogurt, *laban zabadi*—I'll miss that. But I've frozen enough butter and cheese to last me all winter, and fresh milk I just don't need. Unless your family wants it?"

"Nah, we get a gallon a day from Uncle Herb. We drink it, too. Mostly I do."

"Well, good for you. I wasn't raised on it like you were." Lusa was finished. She opened the stanchion to release the cow's head and carefully backed her out of it. The gentle old Jersey ambled straight to the stall that held her calf, and Lusa let her in, giving her broad flank one good pat for good-bye. She felt ridiculous for the tears in her eyes.

"Yeah, Mom said you were . . . something."

"She thinks I'm something, does she? That's nice." Lusa brushed off her jeans and shook bits of hay out of the tails of her stained white work shirt, which reached to her knees. It was one of

Cole's, pulled on over a rust-colored velvet T-shirt she used to feel pretty in, once.

"No, I mean, some nationality."

"I knew what you meant. Rickie, everybody's some nationality."

"Not me. I'm just American."

"Is that why you've got a Rebel flag on the bumper of your truck? Because the Confederacy tried to bust up the American government, you know."

"A southern American, then. What are you?"

"That's a good question. Polish-Arab-American, I guess."

"Huh. You don't look it."

"No? What do I look like to you?" She stood under the light, holding her arms out straight against the planks of the stanchion. Her hair was curly and wild in this humidity, a strawberry-blond halo around her face in the harsh light. Small white moths batted circles around the lightbulb overhead. Rickie inspected her politely.

"You look like a white person," he said.

"My mom's parents were Palestinian, and my dad's were Jews from Poland. I'm the black sheep of your family, and for all that I still sunburn like nobody's business. Just goes to show you, Rickie, you can't tell a book by its cover."

"I heard Mom and Aunt Mary Edna talking about that, that you were one of those other Christianities."

"I can just imagine that conversation." She picked up the flat-head shovel to clean up the floor of the milking parlor, but Rickie took it out of her hands, excusing himself for bumping her shoulder. She never knew how to take these country kids—rudeness and politeness in an unfathomable mix. He scraped the manure into a small pile and carried it a shovelful at a time to the mound just outside the door.

"It wasn't nothing against you, Aunt Lusa," he said from the darkness, giving her a jolt. It had been so long since she'd heard her name spoken aloud. Twenty-eight days, exactly. Nobody else in the family ever said it. Rickie ducked back into the bright milking parlor. "It was just one time when they were just talking about, what if you and Uncle Cole had kids. This was before . . ."

"He died. When kids were more of an option for us."

"Yeah. I think they just wondered, you know, how the church part would work. That it would be hard on his kids."

She gathered up the bucket and rag she'd used to wash the Jersey's udder, and set the lid onto the stainless steel milking bucket. The rim felt warm.

"It wasn't hard on me, being mix-and-match," she said. "I'll grant you we weren't really devout, either way. My dad hated his father and kind of turned his back on his religion. And I'm not a good Muslim, that's for sure. If I were, you'd see me turning"—she rotated slowly in the barn cellar, finding east—"*that* way and kneeling down to pray five times a day."

"You pray towards the chicken house?"

"Toward Mecca."

"Where's that at, North Carolina?"

She laughed. "Saudi Arabia. It's where the prophet Muhammad was born, so you send your prayers in his direction. And you have to wash your hands first, too."

Now Rickie looked amused. "You *wash your hands* before you pray?"

"Listen, you haven't *seen* religious. You're not supposed to touch alcohol or cigarettes, and women cover themselves up totally, all but their eyes." She held her hands in front of her face, peering through her fingers. "If a man sees a woman's *foot,* even, or her shape, it'll lead him to impure thoughts, see? And it's all her fault."

"Man, that's harsh. I thought Aunt Mary Edna was harsh. You believe in that?"

"Do I look like it? No, my mom never even wore the veil. Her parents were already pretty westernized when they left Gaza. But I have cousins who do."

"Yeah?"

"Yep. The American version is a scarf and a long raincoat. I'd always have to do that whenever we went to the mosque with Mom's relatives in New York."

His eyes widened. "You've been to New York City?"

She wondered what that place was in his mind. As far from the truth as this barn was in the minds of her Bronx cousins. "A hundred times," she said. "My parents both came from there. We always tried to go back for their families' holidays. I think the deal on religion between Mom and Dad was that we'd skip the guilt-and-punishment stuff and celebrate the holidays. Feasts, basically." Lusa smiled, thinking of boy cousins and music and reckless dancing among lawn chairs in a small backyard, festivals of love and fitting in. "I grew up on the best food you can imagine."

"Huh. I thought people that didn't believe in God just mostly worshiped the devil and stuff."

"Whoa, Rickie!" She laughed weakly, sitting back down on her milking stool. "Don't you think there might be a couple of options in between?"

He shrugged, embarrassed. "Maybe."

This was her cue, surely, to shrug this boy off and shoo him home. But then what? Wait for Cole to explain her to this family? Her body ached with the burden of her aloneness. Nobody was going to do this for her. She pressed her folded hands between her knees and looked up at him. "Who are you saying doesn't believe in God? Jews believe in God. Muslims believe in God. To tell the truth, most Jewish people and *all* Muslims I know spend more time thinking about God than you do around here. And definitely less of their church time on gossip."

"But different gods, right? Not the real one, not our'n."

"Yes, your'n. Same exact God. His technical name is Jehovah; all three factions concur on that. There's just some disagreement about which son did or did not inherit the family goods. The same-old, same-old story."

"Huh," he remarked.

"Do you know that most of the people in the world are actually not Christians, Rickie?"

"Is that really true?" He grinned sideways like a schoolboy trapped by a trick question. Then lit another cigarette to recover his dignity, raising his eyebrows in a question to make sure it was OK.

"Sure, go ahead."

"Can you say something in Jewish?"

"Hmm. Maybe you mean Yiddish. Or Polish."

"Yeah. Something in a language."

"Between Yiddish and Polish I'm not good for much. My bubeleh lived with us before she died—my dad's mother—but she was, like, classified. Dad wouldn't let her speak anything but English in our house. Wait, though, let me think." She rehearsed the phrase in her mind, then recited aloud, *"Kannst mir bloozin kalteh millich in toochis."*

"What's that mean?"

"'You can blow cold milk up my ass.'"

He laughed loudly. "Your *mammaw* taught you that?"

"She was a pissed-off old lady. Her husband ran off with a coat-check girl in a nightclub. You should ask me about Arabic, my mom taught me a bunch of things."

"OK, what's one?"

"Ru-uh shum hawa. It means 'Go sniff the wind.' Bug off, in other words."

"Rooh shum hawa," he repeated, with dreadful inflection, but Lusa was touched by his effort. His willingness to stand here and talk with her about foreign things.

"Yeah, roughly," she said. "That's pretty good."

Rickie smirked a little. "So," he said, exhaling smoke, "did you have other Christmases? Where you'd get presents and stuff?"

"Other Christmases, other Easters. Yep. It wasn't so much about presents, but definitely about food. Ramadan, that's a whole month where you don't eat during the daytime, only at night."

"No kidding? You'd go all day?"

"Supposed to. We usually didn't. I'd just skip breakfast and try to be good for a month. But the best part is the end, where you have this giant feast to make up for everything you didn't eat that month."

"Like Thanksgiving?"

"Better than that. It lasts three days. Not even counting the leftovers."

"Man. A pig-out."

"A goat-out, is what it is. My family was nix on pork, on both sides—Jews and Muslims agree on that. But we love goat. People think lamb's the Middle Eastern thing but the real, true tradition is *qouzi mahshi,* milk-fed kid. Mom and I would always go visit the Arab cousins for Id-al-Fitr, at the end of Ramadan, and they'd roast a kid over this giant spit in their backyard. Then there's another feast four months later, Id-al-Adha, which requires an even bigger goat."

"I don't think I'd care for goat."

"No? You ever eaten it?"

"Nuh-uh."

"You don't know what you're missing. *Qouzi mahshi,* yum. It's like a sweet, tender calf, only better."

He looked doubtful.

"Hey, I thought you *raised* goats, Rickie. What are those things with horns I've seen back behind your house?"

"Oh, that was a Four-H project."

"And you didn't eat your project at the end?"

"Nah. They're just there to keep down the weeds, I reckon."

"Are they for milk, theoretically, or for meat?"

"They're supposed to be slaughter goats. The idea was to sell them at the state fair while they were still under forty pounds or something. The judges feel their ribs and hipbones and everything and give you a grade."

"And did your goats make the honor roll?"

"They were pretty good. But you can't sell a goat around here.

Heck, you can't give away a goat around here. I know because I tried."

"But I've seen them all over the place. Here in this county, I mean."

"Well, see, there was this big slaughter-goat craze a while back in Four-H. Mr. Walker got people started on it for some reason, and now half the back fields in the county are full of goats people can't give away."

"Huh," Lusa said. "Who's Mr. Walker?"

"He's uncles or cousins to us someways. By marriage."

"Everybody within sixteen miles of here is uncles or cousins to you someways."

"Yeah, but Mr. Walker, he's the livestock adviser for Four-H. Or used to be, when I was a little kid. He's prolly retired now. He's got that farm over on number Six that's all weedy in front? He grows chestnut trees, I heard."

"Chestnut trees all died fifty years ago, Rickie. The American chestnut went extinct due to a fungal blight."

"I know, but that's what people say he's growing. I don't know. He knows all this stuff about plants. Everybody said he should have been the crop-project adviser, not the livestock adviser. That's why he screwed up all these kids on the goats."

"Huh," Lusa said. "You think he could help me find a cheap goat or two for a feast? What the hell, I'd even invite your mom and aunts up, scandalize the family with *qouzi mahshi* and *imam bayildi*."

"What's that?"

"Food of the gods, Rickie. Roast goat and roast stuffed vegetables. Actually *imam bayildi* means 'The emperor fainted.' Which is what your aunt Mary Edna would do if she saw a goat looking at her from the middle of her mother's walnut dining table."

Rickie laughed. He had a wonderful laugh, wide open, the kind that showed molars. "You don't need Mr. Walker to find you a goat. You could just run you an ad in the paper: 'Wanted, free goats. You deliver.' I swear, Aunt Lusa, you'd look out your window next morning and see a hundred goats out there eating your field."

"You think?"

"I swear."

"Well, they'd keep the thistles and briars from taking over my hayfields. I could get rid of my cows. Then I wouldn't have to learn how to run the bush hog."

"'At's a fact, they would keep your briars eat down. They don't take much hay, either; they can feed theirselves pretty good off the brush, most of the winter."

"Are you serious? My God, then I wouldn't even have to run my baler or put up hay? That's the best idea I've heard all day."

"You need *some* hay," he cautioned. "For when it gets bad. Just not so much." He lit another cigarette from the one that was still burning. She walked over and took the pack from him.

"Can I try this?"

"Go ahead. Gives you cancer."

"I think I heard about that." She gave a small, mirthless laugh, peering into the hole in the pack. "I'll tell you, though, hanging on to extra years in my seventies doesn't seem high on my list right now. Under the circumstances." She extracted one white tube and stared at it. It smelled like Cole. "I can't even get excited about seeing thirty, to tell you the truth."

"That's how kids in high school feel. That's why we all smoke."

"Interesting." She put it in her mouth and leaned toward his lighter, which he pulled away, teasing her.

"This really your first time?"

"Yep. You're corrupting an old lady." She tried to inhale the tip of the flame, but her throat recoiled and she coughed. Rickie laughed. She waved a hand in front of her face. "I'm no good at this, obviously."

"It stinks, it really does. You shouldn't start, Aunt Lusa."

She laughed. "You're sweet, Rickie. Thanks for looking out for me."

He met her gaze for a second. He was a striking young man, a handsome union of his father's dark complexion and the Widener looks. Lusa was seized and simultaneously mortified by thoughts of his bare chest and arms, of putting her head there and being held by him. What was she, losing her mind? Was this celibacy, lunacy, or what? She glanced down at her tennis shoes.

"I really don't want to die," she said, a little shaky. "I don't mean to sound like that. I'm depressed, but I think that's normal for a widow. They say it passes. I was more just thinking that if tobacco's the lifeblood of this county, I should support the project."

"Nah, you don't have to." He dragged and puffed away, making tiny whistling sounds with his cigarette. He looked at her sideways. "Aunt Lusa, I hope you'll take this the right way, but you're no old lady. These guys at school, friends of mine? They seen you at Kroger's and said you were pretty hot."

"Me?" She blushed scarlet.

"No offense," he said.

"None taken. I know, you and Cole used to skip school to-gether and he taught you how to sweet-talk girls. I keep forgetting I'm not your mother."

He grinned and shook his head. "You are not my mother."

"Thank you," Lusa said primly, feeling a little guilty for all the names she'd called Rickie's mother in her mind: long-in-the-tooth, leather-lunged Lois. "I'm sure your mother is a better soul than me."

He snorted. "If that's what you call it. My mother believes in no cussing, a good night's sleep, and everything in the kitchen deco-rated with little ducks."

"And how do you know I don't believe in those things?"

"I seen your kitchen."

"Hey, look, I can do this." She took a tiny gulp of cigarette smoke but mostly vamped with it dangling from her fingertips, draping her arm over the top of her head. "How old is Lois, if you don't think she'd mind my asking?"

"She's, lemme think." He looked at the ceiling. "I think she's, like, around forty-one or -two. Aunt Mary Edna's a whole bunch older than her. She's like fiftysomething."

"That's about what I thought, the Magnificent Eldest. And Emaline is between them."

"Yeah, Aunt Emaline's older than Mom. And Aunt Hannie-Mavis is younger. She's not forty yet. I know because she was lording it over Mom about being forty."

"And Jewel's what, between your mom and Emaline?"

"No, Aunt Jewel's the youngest one. She was right before Cole, just two years apart or something like that."

"Jewel? Are you sure?"

"Yeah. She's not that old. I was just a dumb little kid when she got married—I was the ring burier. I don't even remember it that well, but they have these embarrassing pictures. Luckily nobody gets them out anymore since Uncle Shel run off with that waitress."

"Oh yeah, lucky thing that was."

"Oh man, yuk-yuk-yuk." He smacked his head, causing Lusa to giggle. She felt lightheaded, on a nicotine rush, though it was the conversation, too—the company—making her giddy. The last time she'd talked this long with a seventeen-year-old boy, she'd probably been in the back of a car.

She sobered some, though, to think of Jewel. Not about Shel's running off; about Jewel's being thirty and looking fifty. "I *thought* that was right, that she was younger. But lately I was wondering. She looks older."

"She's the littlest sister, though. My mom and them were always jealous of her growing up, because of Cole. He was everybody's favorite, right? And him and Jewel were, like, unseparatable best friends."

"Oh," Lusa said, taking this in. "And then I came along. So they could all resent me instead."

"They don't, Aunt Lusa."

"But they do. You don't have to pretend."

He looked at her, seeming just in that moment more man than

boy, as if he understood pain. She felt her heart stir again, but it wasn't desire, she realized, just a kind of love for who he might someday become. She could see how he would be with a girlfriend: sweet and in charge. Exactly like Cole at seventeen, probably. She leaned against the barn wall beside him, tilting her head back against the planks, both of them facing out the doorway into the evening. Content for a minute to be just where they were. The surface of the pond was the color of blood oranges.

"So," he said.

"So?"

"So, you run your ad. People start showing up to dump off their goats, starting with me. You can have my two."

"Thank you," she said.

"And then what? What are you going to do with your five hundred goats?"

Lusa closed her eyes, tasting and smelling roast goat. Last time she'd celebrated an Id-al-Fitr was years ago, when her mother was still lively and well, someone Lusa could talk to. Someone to cook with. A late-winter celebration, it had been then. The Muslim calendar crept up eleven days on the Christians every year. By now, Id-al-Fitr would be close to Christmas.

She opened her eyes. "Rickie. Can you get a bunch of goats pregnant all at once?"

He blushed, and she burst out laughing.

"Not *you*," she said, when she could speak again. "I mean if you had a bunch of female goats and a—what do you call him? A billy goat?"

"You call them does and bucks. If they're meat goats."

"Does and bucks, right. So, what happens? Don't blush! Rickie!" She swatted his arm. He was giggling like a child. "I'm being practical. I just had an idea. *Two* huge goat-feast holidays are coming up, together, at the very end of the year. And that means Id-al-Adha will be—February, March—early *April!* The same time as Orthodox Easter and Passover. I can't believe this!" She was talking fast, counting on her fingers and getting herself excited. "I need to look at a calendar to make sure. How long does it take to make a kid?"

"How long are they pregnant, you mean? Five months, a little bit less."

She counted on her fingers. "That's November, that's perfect! A month to fatten them up. Can you get them all to, you know—don't blush!" She smoothed her shirttails, made a sober face, and deepened her voice. "We're farmers, Rickie. Farmer to farmer, I'm asking your advice. Could I get one stud billy to knock up a whole field of babes at the same time?"

"Ppphhhhh!" Rickie exploded, folding up on himself.

"I'm serious!"

He wiped his eyes. "I think so, yeah. You can give them hormones and stuff."

"No, no, no. These are religious-holiday goats. No hormones. Can we do it another way?"

"It's been a long time since I was in Four-H, Aunt Lusa."

"But you know about livestock. How does it work?"

"I *think* how it works is, if you've got does that haven't been around a buck at all, and then you put them all in the field with him, they all come into season together. I'm not positive, but I think that's right. You could call up Mr. Walker and find out."

"Oh, right. I'm going to call up some old dude out of the blue and ask him about goat sex!" She and Rickie collapsed again, starting the cow lowing in the stall behind them. Lusa tried to shush herself and Rickie, but she had to hold on to a post just to keep herself on her feet.

"Here, put this out for me," she said, handing him the stub of her cigarette. "Before I burn down my barn."

He tamped it out on the bottom of his shoe, then ran a hand through his hair and straightened up. She saw his eyes glance twice at the open doorway. It was no longer evening now but night, full dark.

"You need to get home," she said.

"Yeah, I do."

"Tell your dad it's OK about the tobacco. He's right, it really is what I wanted, not to set tobacco this year. Thank him for helping me stick to my principles."

"OK."

"Now *get*." She smacked his thigh with the back of her hand. "Your mother will think I'm holding you hostage."

"She won't, either. They're more shy of you than anything, the whole family."

"I know. I'm an outsider occupying their family home. They want their farm back, and I really don't blame them. Most mornings I get out of bed thinking I should pack my car and drive away without even saying good-bye."

He raised his eyebrows. "That'd hurt some feelings."

"Maybe that'd be my point."

"Even if you left, we couldn't be sure of keeping this place. My folks or Uncle Herb and Aunt Mary Edna, they could lose it next year to the bank."

"That's what I was thinking, too. Families lose their land for a million reasons. My dad's parents had this wonderful farm in Poland, which they lost for being Jewish. And my mother's people got run off their land for *not* being Jewish. Go figure."

"Is that true? What type of farming?"

She glanced up at him, surprised by his interest. "The Malufs had olive groves along the Jordan River, or so I'm told. I don't know the details; it was pretty far back. Mom was born in New York. But my dad was actually born on his folks' farm, in the middle part of Poland, which people say looks like a storybook. I think they grew sugar beets."

"That's something, that you come from farming people." He appraised her as though she'd suddenly grown taller or older. "I never knew that."

She saw now that his interest was not in social history but in crops. She'd begun to comprehend this frank pragmatism and to suspect that if she could acquire it—if she could *want* to—she could belong here. She shrugged. "So what, I come from farming people. Doesn't make any difference."

He continued to look at her. "You talk about leaving, everybody says you're going to, but you stay. There's some reason."

She sighed, crossing her arms across her chest and rubbing her elbows. "If there's any reason or rhyme to what I'm doing, I wish I knew it. I'm like a moth, Rickie, flying in spirals. You see how they do?" She nodded up at the lightbulb, where hordes of small, frantic wings glinted through the arc of brightness in circular paths through the air. They were everywhere once you bothered to notice them: like visible molecules, Lusa thought, entirely filling up space with their looping trajectories. Rickie seemed surprised to realize this, that moths were everywhere. He stared upward with his mouth slightly open.

"A calf will run around that way when it's lost its mama and scared to death," he observed at last.

"They're not lost, though. Moths don't use their eyes the way we do; they use smell. They're tasting the air, taking samples from different places and comparing them, really fast. That's how they navigate. It gets them where they need to be, but it takes them forever to get there."

"'Go sniff the wind.' However you said that."

"*Ru-uh shum hawa*. Exactly. That's me. I can't seem to go in a straight line."

"Who says you have to?"

"I don't know, it's embarrassing. People are watching me. I'm figuring out how to farm by doing all the wrong things. And I'm having this retrospective marriage, starting at the end and moving backward, getting acquainted with Cole through all the different ages he was before I met him."

She doubted Rickie was following this, but he was respectful, at least. They stood together watching the dizzying dance of silver wings through the cool air: tussock moths, tortricids, foresters, each one ignoring the others as it wheeled on its own path, urgent and true.

"Aunt Lusa, you worry too much."

"I'm a widow with a farm drowning in debt, standing in a barn that's about to fall on me. You're right. What, I should *worry?*"

He laughed. "About the family, I meant. They're just jealous that Uncle Cole went so crazy over you. But who wouldn't? You're so pretty and smart and stuff."

She made a face at him, a squashed, sorrowful smile, to keep from crying. "Thank you for saying that."

He shrugged.

"And listen, Rickie, thanks for just . . . I don't know. Making me laugh out loud. You don't know how much I needed that."

"Well, listen. If you need help with this goat thing."

"Oh, I'm just dreaming. It's desperation."

"What were you thinking? Tell me." He was a peer suddenly, earnest and kind. She saw something of the older Cole she'd known—not in Rickie's eyes, which were dark, but in the seriousness of his face.

"Well, what I was thinking was, I know this butcher in New York, Abdel Sahadi, he's my mother's cousin. He probably sells—I don't even know, a thousand goats a year? Maybe more."

Rickie whistled, long and low.

"Yeah," she said, "New York City. It's all people, eating all the time. That's basically what you've got going there. But he sells almost all those goats at holiday times. All at once. So he doesn't want them trickling in all year long. He needs five hundred, all in the right week. If it's winter when you want one, you have to order it way ahead of time, and you pay a fortune for it. You wouldn't believe what people in the city will pay for a milk-fed kid at holiday time. It's like the ordinary rules of what you can afford don't apply at those times."

He was listening to her carefully. It made her listen more carefully to herself.

"Rick. Do you mind if I skip the 'Little Rickie'? You're not so little, you know?"

"Hell, I wish somebody would *bury* the damn 'Little Rickie.'"

"OK, Rick. Tell me this. Is there any possible way I could produce fifty or sixty suckling kids by the end of December? And then maybe twice that many in the spring, four months later?"

He didn't hesitate to take her seriously. "You know about worming, ketosis, birthing, all that, right? It's some work. Did you ever raise livestock before?" She tilted an eyebrow at him, but he was suddenly off on his own calculations. "OK. You'd have to have two seasons. Not the same mothers for both kiddings."

"Right."

"How's your fence? A fence that won't hold water won't hold in a goat."

She laughed. "I think I'm OK. It's electric."

"Really? *Shoot,* that's good. When'd you put that in?"

"I don't even know; years ago. Cole did it. It runs all the way around the main cow pasture up there. He had a bad stretch with some roving cows."

"That's lucky, that you've got that. That costs some money to put in."

"I know, he told me. But he said if his cows had got over in Mary Edna's garden one more time it would've cost him his manhood."

Rickie laughed. "All right, then, lady, I think you're set up. Goats'd do fine out there on your brush; you wouldn't need to grain them or hay them much, maybe just give them some fodder after it snows. But kidding in November, they'd need shelter. If it gets real cold, you'll need to get the mothers in your barn when they're ready to spring. You build them a little kidding pen. Jugs, they're called."

Lusa looked up at the ceiling of the barn cellar, envisioning the space above. The door to the main gallery of the barn opened onto the hillside. She could change the fencing just a little to give access to the big pasture. "If I didn't have it full of tobacco up there, or stacked full of hay, I'd have some room."

"That's going to be your trick," he said. "Getting them to settle down and kid right, after it gets cold. That's not the normal season. I've never seen it done, to tell you the truth."

"Oh. That must be why goat's so expensive in the middle of winter."

"Oh, yeah. They'd be worth gold to somebody that wanted them."

"But do you think I could do it?"

He spoke carefully. "It's possible. I think everybody in the county would think you were crazy for trying it."

"How about if nobody but you and me and that cow in there knew what I was up to? And especially if nobody knew about my cousin Abdel and holiday prices in New York?"

"Oh, well, then they'd just think you'd gone off the deep end with too many pet goats. They'd think you were a city gal with her nose in a book and not one lick of sense in her head."

She grinned at her coconspirator. "Not a problem. That's what they think now."

{II}

Predators

rom inside her dark cocoon Deanna listened to the racket of a man in her cabin: the door flung open, boots stomping twice to shed their mud at the door, then the hollow clatter of kindling dropped on the floor. Next, the creak of the stove's hinge and the crackling complaints of a fire being kindled and gentled to life. Soon it would be warm in here, the chill of this June morning chased outdoors where the sun could address it. She stretched her limbs under the covers, smiling secretly. Getting up to a warm cabin on a cold morning without having to go outside for firewood first, *that* was tolerable.

She felt something sharp against her leg: the plastic edge of one of his strings of condoms at the bottom of the bed, twisting there like a strand of DNA. She'd been astounded when he first produced these packets of cheerful little rubber disks in the primary colors, a whole procession of them strung together as if they'd come off some giant reel of condoms somewhere. "That's my stash," he'd said, utterly nonchalant, pulling them out of his pack like a magician's tied-together scarves from a sleeve. He claimed to have gotten them free at some walk-in clinic that urged them onto its clientele. She disliked thinking of his ambling into such a place for treatment of God-knew-what. Didn't really care for the grim realities of this man at all, the fact that he was a seasonal migrant picking up occasional work, salmon fishing, carving knife handles for cash. A male who shacked up for shelter, she suspected. She'd done her best to run him off, flying into her rage at him up in the chestnut log, yet he persisted in her territory. He'd been out several years from Wyoming—with his hunting rifle, following his passion, which they did not discuss. He talked about everything else instead, and she found herself swallowing his stories like bits of live food brought to a nest: the Northern Lights unfurling like blue-green cigar smoke in the Arctic sky. The paraffin-colored petals of a cactus flower. The Pacific Ocean and tidepools, neither of which she'd seen, except for the artificial versions of the latter in the Chattanooga Aquarium. She thought now of the pink anemones waving in that water. Like herself, when he'd first spied on her with her sensitive, fleshy tentacles of thought waving all around her, until he'd touched and made her draw up quickly into a stony fist. But he knew just how to touch her, speak to her, breathe on her, to draw her out again. Physical pleasure was such a convincing illusion, and sex, the ultimate charade of safety.

The stove's metal door banged shut and she heard the hush of his jeans shed onto the floor. Her body tingled with the anticipation of his return to her bed. She waited, though, and for a minute too long there came no body diving headfirst into her world under the quilts. She poked her head out into the morning and blinked at its brightness. It was late morning already. The sun was a dazzling rectangle at the window, where a naked man danced in silhouette, batting both hands at a frightened moth.

"Hey hey, careful!" she cried, causing him to turn to her. She couldn't see his expression because he was backlit, but already she knew that face, its guilelessness.

"I wasn't going to kill him," he insisted. "I'm just trying to catch him and put him outside. Little bugger snuck in here, he's trying to see you naked."

She sat up and squinted at the desperate wings flailing at the window. "No, now that's a female. She's looking at *you*."

"Hussy," he said, trying to clap the moth between his hands. "Look at her, she's terrified. Never saw such a display of manhood in all her days."

"Don't do it like that." Deanna lifted aside the heavy pile of blankets and put her feet on the cold floor. The wood stove radiated a tangible field of heat that her body passed through as she walked to the window. "Best if you don't touch it. The scales will come off its wings."

"And that would be terrible?"

"To the moth it would. I think it dies or something, without them."

He stepped back, deferring to this dire claim. "Is that a scientific fact?"

She smiled. "My dad told me, so it must be true." She tried with her cupped hands to steer the moth away from the window. "Darn it, little wing, I'd open this window for you, but you've picked the only one that doesn't open."

"Who's your dad, a moth scientist or something?"

"Don't laugh, there are moth scientists. I knew of one, in graduate school." She tried to urge the moth toward the window over the bed, but nothing doing. It continued to throw itself eastward like a supplicant toward Mecca.

"Maybe if we close the curtain she'll go to a different window," he suggested.

"Maybe." Carefully she drew the white cotton curtain between the moth and the glass, but she could see that wasn't going to help much.

"She can still see the light," he said.

He'd believed her when she declared the moth a female.

Deanna was touched. "You know what, I can't really sex a moth at twenty paces, I was bluffing. And no, my dad wasn't a scientist. He could have been. He was a farmer, but he was . . ." The moth settled onto the curtain and sat still. It was an astonishing creature, with black and white wings patterned in geometric shapes, scarlet underwings, and a fat white body with black spots running down it like a snowman's coal buttons. No human eye had looked at this moth before; no one would see its friends. So much detail goes unnoticed in the world.

"I can't really even describe how my dad was," she finished. "If you spent a hundred years in Zebulon County just watching every plant and animal that lived in the woods and the fields, you still wouldn't know as much as he did when he died."

"Your hero. I'm jealous."

"He was. He had theories about everything. He'd say, 'Look at that indigo bunting, he's so blue, looks like he dropped down here from some other world where all the colors are brighter. And look at his wife: she's brown as mud. Why do you reckon that is?' And I'd say something dumb, like, maybe in indigo buntings it's the men instead of the ladies that like to get dressed up. And Dad would say, 'I think it's because she's the one that sits on the eggs, and bright colors would draw attention to the nest.'"

"And what did your mama say about it?"

"Yeek!" Deanna howled, startled by the darting shadow of a mouse that burst from behind the woodpile and ran practically across their bare feet before disappearing into a hole in the corner between the log wall and the floor. "Damn." She laughed. "I hate how they make me squeal like a girl, every time." Eddie Bondo had jumped, too, she'd noticed.

"Your mama said 'Yeek'?"

"My mama said not a whole heck of a lot. On account of she was dead." Deanna narrowed her eyes, studying the hole into which the mouse had disappeared. She'd been stuffing holes with scraps of aluminum foil for two years. But anything with mice was a war you couldn't win, she'd learned that much.

She realized Eddie was looking at her, waiting for the rest of the story. "Oh, it's not a tragedy or anything, about my mother. I mean, to Dad it was, I'm sure, but I don't even remember her, I was that little." Deanna spread her hands, unable really to name the hole this had put in her life. "Nobody ever taught me to be a proper lady, that's the tragedy. Oh, now look, she *is* a she." Deanna pointed to the moth, which was pressing the tip of its abdomen against the fabric of the curtain, apparently attempting to lay eggs.

"My mama died, too, quite a while back," he said, as they watched the moth closely. "Happens, I guess. Daddy remarried after about, oh, fifteen minutes."

Deanna couldn't imagine such family carelessness. "Did you get along with her, at least?"

He laughed oddly. "She could have got along without *me*. She had her own kids, that was some of the trouble, who the ranch would go to. The whole ugly-stepsister story, you know."

Deanna didn't know. "My dad never did remarry."

"No? So it was always just you and him?"

Did she want to tell him this? "Mainly me and him, yeah," she said. "He had a friend, but that was years later. They never moved in together, they both had their farms to run, but she was good to me. She's an amazing lady. I didn't even realize until just lately how she'd been through hell and back with us. My dad was a mess on her hands at the end. And she had a little girl, too, with Down's syndrome and a hole in her heart that couldn't be fixed. My half-sister."

Eddie Bondo put his hands on Deanna's shoulders and kissed her. "This is you, isn't it?"

She ran a hand through his hair, newly shorn to a smoother shape—less crow, more mink. On Tuesday, her day of mortification after assaulting him in the chestnut log, she had let him talk her into many things, including cutting his hair with her little scissors. It was surprisingly thick, like the pelt of some northern animal that needed the insulation. The exquisite tactile pleasure of that slow hour spent out on the porch with her hands on his scalp had created between them a new kind of intimacy. Afterward they'd stood quietly watching a pair of chickadees gather up the fallen hairs for their nest.

"Me, no," she said, unsure what he meant, "my half-sister. Rachel was her name."

"It's who you are, I mean. You're telling me a piece of your life."

She looked at his eyes, watched him glance back and forth between her own two pupils. He was that close.

"Our bed's getting cold," he whispered.

"I don't think that's possible."

The fire cracked loudly then, like a shot, startling them like the mouse had, making them laugh out loud. Eddie Bondo ran for the bed and leapt under the blankets, hooting that the posse had found him out. She tugged at the edge of the bed, fighting him to let her in. "I reported you to the Forest Service," she warned. "Keeping a wildlife manager from her work, which is a hanging crime in these mountains."

"I get my last meal, then." He threw aside the covers to reveal himself, solemn and flat on his back. She pounced and tried to pin him, but he was strong and seemed to know real wrestling moves. In spite of her size and longer limbs, he could have her tidily turned with an elbow pinned behind her back every time. In less than a minute she was helpless, laughing as he straddled her.

"What is that, Bondo? Some kind of sheep-herding maneuver?"

"Exactly." He gathered a thick skein of her hair in one hand. "Next I shear you."

Instead he kissed her forehead and then each one of her ribs before nuzzling his head against her waist. But she tugged him back up to the pillow beside her. She needed to look at him. "OK," she said, "you're saved. I'm giving you a stay of execution."

"Governor. I'm your slave."

She wanted to play, but her mood was wrong for it. Speaking aloud of Nannie and Rachel had brought those two into this cabin. And her father, too—especially him. What would he have made of Eddie Bondo? "I told you something about me," she said. "Now you have to tell me one thing about you."

He looked wary. "I choose which thing? Or you get to ask?"

"I get to ask."

"A serious thing?"

"To me it is."

He rolled onto his back and they both stared up at the ceiling, its crooked log beams riddled with the small tunnels of beetles. Deanna thought about the trees they had been once, a long time ago. Suffering more in life than in death, surely. There was a scratching sound coming from the space above the roof boards.

"What's up there?" he asked.

"On top of those boards, cedar shingles—rotten, probably. See all the nails? Then galvanized tin on top of the whole mess."

"I mean that noise," he persisted.

"Mouse, probably."

"The same one that just made you squeal like a girl?"

She narrowed her eyes. "Different one. One of his innumerable friends and relations."

They both stared for a while at the roof, their eyes following the sound as it moved higher, toward the peak. Deanna decided the motion was too slow for a mouse and considered the other possibilities.

"Who built this cabin?" he asked her.

"Guy named Walker, Garnett something Walker. There was this whole line of them, all with the same name. Kind of like land barons in this area, a hundred years ago."

"And this was the baron's luxurious abode?"

"Oh, not hardly. This was just the headquarters for one of his hundred logging camps. He and his sons logged out all these mountains. This was probably one of his last stands; the cabin is nineteen-thirties or so, I'd guess. Looking at the logs."

"What are they, oak?"

"Chestnut, every one. When people realized the chestnuts were dying out, they had this huge rush to cut down all that were left, even the standing deadwood."

He studied the construction more closely. "That's why the logs are kind of small and twisted?"

"Yeah. Deadwood, or maybe some of the bigger limbs off huge trunks they took for lumber. But Eddie, listen." She turned to look at him. "What I'm saying is, they realized the chestnuts were going extinct. So what did they do? They ran up here and cut down every last one that was left alive."

He thought about it. "They were dying anyway, I guess that's what they figured."

"But not all of them would have died. Some of those last chestnuts were standing because they weren't sick. They might have stood straight on through the blight."

"You think?"

"I'm sure. People study this stuff. Every species has its extremes, little pockets of genetic resistance that give it an edge on survival. Some would have made it."

She watched his eyes track the twisted logs as he pondered what she'd just said. This was the thing that surprised her again and again: Eddie Bondo paid attention. Most men of her acquaintance acted like they already knew everything she did—and they didn't.

"If some of the chestnuts had lived," he asked, "how long would they have stood?"

"A hundred years, maybe? Long enough to spread their seeds. Some of them *did* live; there's maybe five or six per county hidden back in the hollows, but there aren't enough to pollinate one another. If more of them had been spared they could have repopulated these mountains over time, but nobody thought about that. Not one person. They just sawed the last ones down, hell for leather."

He turned his acute gaze on Deanna. "That's why you live up here by yourself, isn't it? You can't stand how people are."

She weighed this, feeling its truth inside herself like damp sand. "I don't *want* to feel that way," she said finally. "There's people I love. But there's so many other kinds of life I love, too. And people act so hateful to every kind but their own."

He didn't reply. Was he taking her judgment personally? She'd been thinking of people who refused to be inconvenienced for the sake of an endangered fish or plant or owl, not of coyote killers per se. She forced her next words, knowing that each one had its own cost. "You said I could ask you a question, and now I'm asking it."

"What?"

"You know."

He blinked but didn't speak. Something in his eyes receded from her.

"What brought you down here to the mountains?"

He looked away. "A Greyhound bus."

"I have to know this. Was it the bounty hunt?"

He didn't answer.

"Just say no if the answer is no. That's all I want."

He still said nothing.

"God." She let out a slow breath. "I'm not surprised. I knew. But I will never, ever understand who you are."

"I never asked you to."

No, he hadn't, and she would refrain from trying if she was capable of it. But here he was, naked beside her with his left hand lying above her heart. How could she not need to know who he was? Were male and female from different worlds, like the indigo bunting and his wife? Was she nothing but mud-colored female on the inside? *She* who'd always been sure she was living her life bright blue?

"Where does it come from?" she asked. "I can't understand that kind of passion to kill a living thing."

"Not just a living thing. An enemy."

"Tell me the truth. How many times have you seen sheep killed by coyotes?"

"Enough."

"A hundred?"

"On my own family's ranch? No. A hundred would wipe a man out, even if it was spread out over four or five years."

"On your own family's ranch, in your lifetime, how many? Fifty? A dozen?"

He was still looking up at the roof beams. "Maybe a dozen," he conceded. "We've got sheepdogs, we've got good fences, but even so. Probably that many. You can't always tell what got them, especially if it was a lamb and whatever got it just hauled it clean away."

"So in one or all of those cases it could have been anything. A neighbor's dog. A barn owl. A damn bald eagle."

Eddie Bondo grimaced, declining to agree or disagree.

"A coyote is just something you can blame. He's nobody's pet; he doesn't belong to anybody but himself. So, great, put a bullet in him."

He turned to look at her full on, propping himself up on an elbow. "What you don't understand is that ranching's not like farming. It's not a vegetarian proposition."

She shook her head but said nothing, beginning to feel herself recede in her own way. What was it about the West, that cowboy story everybody loved to believe in? Like those men had the goods on *tough*. She thought of her soft-spoken father, the grim line of his mouth stretched pale as a knuckle while he worked the docking tool and she held the bawling head end. Working to castrate the bull calves.

The moth on the window grew restless again, fluttering against the sheer curtain and the bright outdoors behind it. He saw her watching it and reached up to tug her hair gently. "Miracle of miracles, I do believe I'm in bed with an animal lover."

She looked at him, surprised. If he only knew she'd been reminiscing about castration. It bothered her a lot, his being so sure he had her number. She opened her mouth, closed it, then opened it again, a little startled at what she chose to say. "I'll tell you something. If a feral cat wandered up here from some farm and started wrecking nests and killing birds and having babies in the woods? I'd trap it and drown it in the creek."

He made a face of exaggerated dismay. "You wouldn't."

"Maybe I would. I'd want to."

"Why?"

"Because cats like that don't belong here. They're fake animals, introduced, like the chestnut blight. And just about that destructive."

"Not a cat person," he decided. Once again, sure he knew.

"I had cats as a kid. But people won't be bothered to fix them, so they breed in the barns and prowl the woods, and they don't have any sense about what things to take. They're not natural predators, except maybe in a barn. In the woods they're like a firebomb. They can wreck a habitat so fast, overrun it in a season, because there's no natural control. If there were still red wolves here, the place could hold its own against a stray cat. But there aren't." Or enough coyotes, she thought.

He studied this new Deanna, potential murderess of tabby cats. She met his gaze for a second, then rolled over and rested on her elbows, twirling the end of her hair into something like a paintbrush and touching its tip to the palm of her other hand.

"I don't love animals as *individuals,* I guess that's the way to put it," she said. "I love them as whole species. I feel like they should have the right to persist in their own ways. If there's a house cat put here by human carelessness, I can remedy that by taking one life, or ignore it and let the mistake go on and on."

"How much damage could a cat really do?"

"You wouldn't believe how much. I could show you a list of species that have been wiped out because of people's laziness about cats. Ground-nesting birds, especially."

"Not the kitty's fault."

"No," she said, amused that her hunter seemed to be pleading the kitty's case. "And it's also not a cat's idea that every life including its own is sacred. That's a human idea, and I can buy it for humans. But it's some kind of weird religion to impose it on other animals that have already got their own rules. Most animals are as racist as Hitler, and a lot of them practice infanticide. Cats do—lions. A lot of primates, too."

"Yeah?"

"Yep. And I support their right to go on murdering their babies in the wild if that's how they do it, unpestered by humans. That's the kind of animal lover I am."

He raised his eyebrows and nodded slowly.

"It's not like you thought, is it?"

"Heck, now I'm thinking maybe you'll go hunting with me."

She rolled onto her back. "Forget it. I'd never kill just for fun. Maybe to eat, if I was hungry, but never a predator."

"So a deer but not a fox? Plant eaters matter less than carnivores?"

She thought about this. "They don't *matter* less. But herbivores tend to have shorter lives, and they reproduce faster; they're just geared toward expendability. They can overpopulate at the drop of a hat if nobody's eating them."

He lay on his back next to her, at ease with this kind of talk. "Like rabbits do, sure. But it's complicated. Up north, the lynx go in these cycles. Every ten years, boom, there're thousands, and then they crash."

"All the more reason to leave them alone," she insisted. "There's something going on there you don't want to mess with. Maybe there'd be some plague let loose on the Arctic." She wondered if he'd seen lynx. She'd probably never see one herself.

"I know what you're saying," he conceded. "It's been messed with already."

"What are they like, lynx?" She tried not to sound like a jealous child.

"Oh, baby, there's a cat you'd love. They're just like you."

"How's that?"

He grinned, thinking about it. "About three parts pissed off to four parts dignified. They're gorgeous. If you find one caught in a trap line and let it go, it won't scramble around and run, nothing like that. It'll just stand there glaring at you for a minute, and then turn around real slow and just *strut* away."

She could picture it. "Don't you get it? To kill a natural predator is a sin."

"You've got your rules, I've got mine."

She sat up to look at him. "Right. But then there's the *world,* which has got these rules nobody can change. That's what's wrong with people: they can't see *that.*"

"And what rule of the world says it's a sin to kill a predator?"

"Simple math, Eddie Bondo, you know this stuff. One mosquito can make a bat happy for, what, fifteen seconds before it starts looking for another one? But one bat might eat two hundred mosquitoes in a night. Figure it out, where's the gold standard here? Who has a bigger influence on other lives?"

"OK already, I get it," he said. "Chill."

"Chill yourself," she said. "I didn't make up the principles of ecology. If you don't like them, go live on some other planet." *Doing my best to run this guy off,* she thought. But she couldn't go on biting her tongue. She needed this conversation.

"Fine," he said. "But if I'm a bug rancher it's my right to shoot the bats off my ranch."

She leaned back against the pillow. "What you're thinking about coyotes doesn't make a lick of sense. They're way more important to their natural prey than they are to livestock. I bet there's not one rancher in the whole American West who's gone under because of coyote predation."

"Maybe not *gone under*," he said.

"It's just fear, looks to me like. A bunch of macho ranchers scared of a shadow."

"You've got no idea how tough ranching is."

"I don't see you ranching sheep, Eddie. I don't think I can give you the high ground here."

"I'll inherit fifteen hundred acres one day," he said, sounding unconvinced, and she wondered what divides of kinship were concealed in that flat statement, what dreads and expectations, what it was costing him to hold his place in his family. As the daughter of a farmer who'd lost his land, she felt only measured sympathy.

"Right," she said. "You'll settle down with the little wife, raise up sheep till you're old, that's the plan? Just this one little thing, you need to run around and shoot every coyote in the world first?"

He shrugged, refusing to absorb her irony. "I've still got some time. I like to get around, see a lot of country."

Shoot every coyote, screw every woman, see the world, she thought: the strategy of prolonged adolescence. But that wasn't fair; he was also kind. He'd worked hard this morning to provision her nest, bringing armloads of firewood like bouquets. She tried to put aside the misery of thinking too much. "Well, you're being true to your school," she said. "Willing to travel great distances to make the world safe for Wyoming sheep."

"You make fun, but you don't know. Sheep ranching needs all the help it can get. You're right on the edge of busted all the time."

"*What* don't I know? You start down that mountainside and you'll come to the edge of a field, OK? From that point on, you can't walk right or left without stepping on some family that's lost its farm to bad luck, bad weather, chestnut blight, change, economics, the antitobacco lobby. You name it, there's some farmer I know who got eaten by it. But they're not bitter. They go to work at Toyota and forget about it."

"They don't forget about it," said Eddie Bondo. "They just don't have an enemy they can look at through a rifle sight."

She looked at him for a long time. Thought of her father, drinking to diffuse his grief in the last year before they sold out. If he'd had something to shoot at, what would he have done?

"I can't say you're right," she said finally. "You don't know that."

"If there's coyotes moving into this country now, they'll get shot at."

"I know that. I think about it all the time."

"So they're here. You know where they are."

She returned his clear-eyed gaze. "Is that why you're hanging around me? You're trying to get information?"

His green eyes went dark, a turmoil under the surface briefly revealed. "If that's what you think, I'll get my boots on and leave right now."

"I don't know if it's what I think. I've never known what to think since the first day you showed up here. But if that's what you're after, you should go."

"If that were what I was after, I'd be a fool. I *know* there's coyotes denned up around here someplace where I can't get a bead on them, and not for love nor money are you going to give me a clue."

"That's the story."

"Deanna, don't you think I know that?"

"If I trusted you I would show you where they are, but I don't. Not in that way, not that kind of trust."

"You already told me that. The first day up there on the mountain when I found you tracking that bobcat. You told me what the deal was. I accepted."

"I did?"

"You did."

"So what are we doing here?"

"Having breakfast in bed," he replied. "Trying to catch a moth without harming one scale on its fuzzy little head."

She examined his beautiful face and the exquisite planes of his body, wishing she could look inside him to see what mixture of love and anger and deception resided there, in what proportions. "How old are you?" she asked him.

He seemed surprised. "Twenty-eight. Why? How old are you?"

She hesitated, surprised at herself. Sat forward and drew the covers close around her. It was the first time in her life she'd felt uneasy owning her age. Nearly twenty years older than this man—it made no sense.

"I don't want to say."

"Damn, girl, get over *that*. Look at you. It takes more than thirty years to tune an engine to run like that."

"Way more than thirty," she said. "More than forty."

"Really?"

"Yeah, really."

She thought she saw a flicker of surprise, but he covered well. "So, you're ninety-seven. You're my grandma. Come here, Granny, I want to rub the rheumatism out of your bones." As he pulled her down close to him the fire cracked again, flaring brilliant orange in the stove's small, round window. She could see the flame reflected in his eyes.

"I want to tell you something," she said, holding his stare. "You're a good tracker, but I'm a better one. If you find any coyote pups around here and kill them, I'll put a bullet in your leg. Accidentally."

"That true?"

She knew it wasn't, but maybe he didn't. "Absolutely. I might even follow you a ways to do it, if I had to. That's the kind of accident I'm talking about."

"A leg. Not between my eyes?"

"No."

He smiled and rolled away from her onto his back, clasping his hands behind his head. "OK, then, I'm fairly warned."

"Fairly warned," she agreed.

She got out of bed, trembling internally from the effort of acting so tough. She slipped her long flannel gown over her head and shook it down over her body like a cocoon. She took a wide-mouthed plastic cup from the kitchen cupboard and an envelope from the stack of papers on her desk. She turned it over: an old letter from Nannie Rawley, the only person who still wrote her here. She went to the window and pulled back the curtain gently, sending the disturbed moth back into its frenetic charge at the glass. On the curtain it had left a double row of tiny eggs, as neat as a double-stitched seam. It made Deanna sad to see such a last, desperate stab at survival. She'd read that some female moths could mate with many different males, save up all their sperm packets, and then, by some incomprehensible mechanism, choose among them after the boys were long gone—actually deciding whose sperm would fertilize the eggs as she laid them. Deanna studied this little moth's earnest work on the curtain. Maybe she'd been holding out for some perfect guy she believed was still out there. Too late now.

"You poor thing," she said quietly, "quit bashing your brains out, you've earned your freedom." Carefully she placed the cup over the moth, then slid the letter between the cup's mouth and the glass. The trapped creature clicked against the hard plastic, but it wasn't human hands, so the scales shouldn't rub off. Deanna stepped barefoot into her unlaced boots and clumped outside, negotiating the door with her elbow, feeling Eddie Bondo's eyes on her as she went. A lynx, was that really how he saw her? She didn't feel that elegant or self-contained. He made her talk too much.

The day was gorgeous. This was summer, surely. These morning chills would soon be gone for good, dissolved into the heat of breeding season. She inhaled: even the air smelled like sexual ecstasy. Mosses and ferns were releasing their spores into the air. Birds were pressing the unfeathered brood patches on their breasts against fertile eggs; coyote pups, wherever on earth they lived, were emerging for their first lessons in life. Deanna stood at the edge of the porch and raised the paper from the lid of the cup, giving the cup a gentle heave to send the moth on its way. It tumbled and struggled in the bright air, then swerved clumsily upward for several seconds, grasping at sudden freedom.

A phoebe darted out from the eaves and snapped the moth out of the air. In a vivid brown dash she was gone again, off to feed her nestlings.

{12}

Old Chestnuts

Dear Miss Rawley,

I have been greatly troubled by a suspicion that occurred to me last Friday, June 8, in the Little Bros. Hardware. I could not help but overhear (though I did not wish to, but the conversation was quite unavoidably audible) your remarks to the Little bros. concerning a "snapper." I was wondering whether this conversation referred to your lawn mower, since I am aware this is a brand of mower commonly used in this region and sold by Little Bros. Or is it possible you were discussing a certain event, previously known only to the two of us, involving a snapping turtle?

I write to ask you this, Miss Rawley, not because it is a matter of any great concern to me, but because in keeping with the Lord's counsel I feel I should advise you it is a sin that does not rest lightly on any soul, to slander the good name of a neighbor who has worked long and hard these

many years to serve with wisdom and dignity his county
(vo-ag teacher for 21 yrs, 4-H adviser more than 10 yrs) and
his Lord.

Sincerely,
Garnett S. Walker III

P.S. On the matter of setting free the "lizards" sold at
Grandy's bait store on the grounds that some of them belong
to species that are vanishing from our region, having given it
some thought, I propose three questions:

1) Are we humans to think of ourselves merely as one
species among many, as you always insist in our discussions of
how a person might live in "harmony" with "nature" while
still managing to keep the Japanese beetles from entirely de-
stroying his trees? Do you believe a human holds no more
special authority in this world than, say, a Japanese beetle or a
salamander? If so, then why is it our duty to set free the salamanders, any more than it is the salamander's place to swim
up to the state prison in Marion and liberate the criminals in-
carcerated there?

2) Or are we to think of ourselves as keepers and
guardians of the earth, as God instructed us to do in Genesis
1:27–30, "So God created man in his *own* image; . . . and
God blessed them and said to them, 'Be fruitful and multiply,
and replenish the earth, and subdue it! . . . Behold, I have
given you every herb bearing seed which is upon the face of
the earth, and every tree in which is the fruit of a tree-
yielding seed; to you it shall be for meat. And to every beast
of the earth, and to every fowl of the air, and to every thing
that creepeth upon the earth'"—such as salamanders, Miss
Rawley—"'wherein there is life, I have given every green
herb for meat'; and it was so." If the Holy Bible is to be believed, we must view God's creatures as gifts to his favored
children and use them for our own purposes, even if this oc-

casionally causes this one or that one to go extinct after a while.

3) If one species or another of those muddly little sala-manders went extinct, who would care anyway?

Just wondering,
GW III

That was it exactly, he thought. That was *telling* her. Garnett licked the envelope and pressed it shut, feeling more pleased with himself than he had in many years. As he walked out his front door and down the drive to his mailbox he whistled "Pretty Saro," casting it up to the mockingbird on the grain shed so he might catch up a few of Garnett's notes and weave them into his merry hymn to the day.

13

Predators

hy would you use the word *windfall* to describe something lucky?" Eddie Bondo asked, revealing a peevish edge to his personality that she'd not yet seen.

It was a fair question. She paused to scratch the back of her neck as they fought their way through the impossible maze of sideways trees: now the mosquitoes were finding them. Deanna had made an unlucky choice in an otherwise perfect morning, and they'd ended up here, climbing tediously through the horizontal labyrinth of an enormous windfall. As nearly as she could figure it out, one huge pine struck by lightning on the hilltop had taken down a whole hillside of its brethren by means of their intertwined limbs. Since she'd chosen the route, she was still trying to pretend this was fun.

"A windfall would be lucky," she ventured, "if you'd been meaning to spend six weeks sawing down all these trees for lumber."

"Well, I wasn't," he stated.

They'd come out this morning in search of molly-moochers, as people here called them. He'd laughed at this funny pair of words (as he laughed at her "oncet" and "twiced" and "I might could") but got interested when she explained what they were. Morels were hardly more than a legend out on the arid pine slopes of the West, but here they were real, and he wanted to taste them. She was happy to take him looking. Officially she wasn't supposed to harvest anything out of these woods, but mushroom populations were in no danger in the National Forest, and now was the wrong time to find them anyhow. Her dad had taught her to hunt them in mid-May when oak leaves were the size of squirrels' ears. Even the ravenous will of Eddie Bondo couldn't make one appear in the third week of June. But they'd come looking because that was how it was with him. Some days he packed up and was gone, temporarily or for good she never quite knew, but when he was here he was *here;* if they began a day by waking up delighted together in her bed, it was going to be a new adventure, another reason to ignore her notebooks and the trails she was supposed to maintain. Most days they neglected the trails altogether to clamber into the mountain's wildest places, straight up or down slopes so steep they had to ascend on all fours and descend on the seats of their jeans, sliding like bobsledders on the slick leaves. They discovered groves and clearings even Deanna hadn't known before, where deer browsed quietly on moss and new leaves.

They were reaching the edge of the tangle. Deanna peered through, swatting a mosquito and rubbing her scratched-up knee. The day was warm, but she regretted her shorts at the moment. She could see now where they were: not very far from the Egg Creek trail. She retied her braid into a double knot to keep it out of the branches and pushed on to the end of this tedious maze.

As they emerged from the pine needles, they startled up a grouse, whose coppery tail flashed as its plump body soared horizontally with a noise like an outboard motor. Deanna stood still with her hand flat on her heart, which raised an equivalent ruckus. Grouse always made such an *explosion.* She wished she could have seen their chickenish cousins the heath hens, who used to strut around in clearings with their feathers standing straight up, inflating the yellow balloons on their necks to make booming sounds you could hear for miles. Not anymore, of course. In the same plaintive tone her single friends in grad school used to complain that all the best men were married, Deanna felt like whining, "All the best animals are extinct."

"Is there a season on those?" Eddie asked, marveling at the grouse, his earlier irritation now gone without a trace. She gave him a look, didn't answer. Grouse were fairly rare here. More often she discovered flocks of hen turkeys gabbling quietly in the woods, battering the undergrowth with their wings as they struggled into low branches. They'd seen some yesterday, in fact. And there was one big old tom they often saw in the early morning strutting alongside the Forest Service road, alone, steering clear of female companionship. She unknotted her braid and let it fall down her back while she considered the best route out of here. Eddie Bondo had begun to whistle.

"Shhh!" she hissed suddenly. Someone or something was there in the pines above them. She waited a second to see if it moved like a deer or a man.

Man.

"Hey, buddy," she called. "How you doing today?"

From the dark-green boughs he came forward: tall and a little potbellied, with gray hair down to his shoulders and a small-bore rifle, dressed out for jungle combat. It always killed her how these guys dressed. Like a deer would be impressed by the uniform.

He was squinting at her. "Deanna Wolfe?"

"Yeah?" She squinted back. She'd be darned if she could name him. She could memorize Latin names and birdcalls, but the guys she'd gone to high school with all kind of blended together.

"Sammy Hill," he offered finally.

"Sammy, *sure*," she said, as if that had been on the tip of her tongue. Sammy Hill, could she possibly forget a name like that?

"Dee-anna *Wolfe*," he repeated, directing his pleasure mainly at her legs. "I heard you's up here. I heard you near 'bout got eat by a bear." He spoke too loudly, maybe nervous, or possibly a little deaf. A lot of guys lost their hearing on tractors and mowing machines.

"Yeah? That story's still going around?"

"That's how Miss Oda Black tells it. But hell, I didn't believe it. Gal like you getting cold all by herself up here on the mountain? Hell, you haven't changed a bit."

All by herself. She glanced to the side, listened behind her. If Eddie Bondo could be relied on for one thing, it was to disappear. Well, fine, he didn't need to be part of this. "Not a *bit*, since high school?" she asked sweetly. "You're saying I still couldn't get a date unless everything else female in the county had rabies?"

"No, now, you've got that wrong. We was all in love with you, Deanna."

"Well, heck, Sammy. How come I didn't notice?"

He laughed. "We's just asceared of you."

"Now, is that why you brought your gun up here today?"

He looked at his rifle, dismayed. "What, this?"

"I hate to tell you, Sammy," she said, sounding convincingly sorrowful, "but deer season's in the fall. And now here it is June."

He looked at her, blinking with the effort of his innocence.

"You know what?" she said. "Down at George Tick's gas station? He's giving out free calendars. You could pick you up one on your way back to town."

Sammy chuckled, shaking his head. "Deanna Wolfe. *You.*" He chuckled some more. "You's just as funny as you ever was."

"You, too, Sammy." She kept up the smile, waiting. She knew this routine. They were almost finished.

He seemed to have a bright idea. "Hell, I wasn't aiming on shooting nothing today, I's just looking for sang," he said. "Got me a alimony payment due."

"Oh, well, then," she said, nodding seriously, "good thing you brought that rifle. Sang plants can get real mean in breeding season."

He chuckled and chuckled, Sammy Hill. Tilted his head back and gave her a little wink, and then in a flash she saw him at age sixteen, in a different body altogether. Lean and confident, the cocked wrist tossing a wad of paper into the trash can—*that* Sammy Hill, the basketball player. He had a stuck-up sister, Regina, whom the boys called Queen of the Hill.

Sammy scratched his cheek with a knuckle, betraying a missing molar in his embarrassed grin. "No, now, I needed this rifle for protection," he said, with make-believe conviction. "Bears and stuff. After I heard what happened to you."

"Well, yeah, I can sure understand that. But now, Sammy, you could take a bear one-handed. Athlete like you. You still sink a jump shot like you used to?"

His face brightened. "Naw," he said, blushing under his stubble.

"Well, now, here's the bad news. There's no sang hunting up here, either, anymore—the governor's trying to let everything on this mountain grow back. I'm sorry, Sammy, but I've got to send you on out of here." She truly felt sorry for this heavyset version of Sammy, so early to ripen and now gone so badly to seed. "Maybe there's some sang up on the back of your dad's farm," she suggested, "up there by the fork."

"You know, I bet there is."

"How is your dad?"

"Dead."

"Oh. Not so good, then."

"Not so ornery, neither."

"Well, OK," Deanna said. "Nice to see you, Sammy. Say hey to Regina for me."

"Well, hell, Regina don't speak to me no more but to nag. Since I busted up her Camaro. I reckon you'll have to tell her hello yourself."

"I'll do that," Deanna said, raising one hand in a coy little wave. Sammy touched the brim of his camouflage cap and headed downhill, slow and awkward with his head craned far forward in the way

of tall men with potbellies and bad backs. He had to watch his footing carefully on the steep slope.

She stood waiting a long time for the molecules of Eddie
Bondo to reassemble out of pine boughs and humid air. He wasn't
behind her now, it turned out, but above her, standing a little to the
rear of where Sammy had been. She spotted his grin first, like the
Cheshire cat's.

"Well *hell*, Deanna," he mocked, and spat.

"Watch it. That's my mother tongue."

"I bet those boys *were* all in love with you."

"Uh-huh. Not so much that it interfered with their general disdain."

He moved down the slope toward her as if he'd been born to
slopes. Short men really had the advantage in the long run, she decided, admiring his grace. Their backs held better. And then there
was the matter of shoulders and narrow hips and that grin—the
matter of Eddie Bondo. She felt a strange little interior pride, that
this beautiful male was her mate, at least for a season.

"What the heck is *sang?*"

"Ginseng." She began picking her way toward the Egg Creek
trail, and he followed.

"That's what I thought," he said.

"You ever seen any?"

"I don't know. What's it look like?"

She thought about it. "A five-fingered leaf, littlish plant, dies
back to the ground in winter. It's particular about where it grows.
Only under sugar maples, on a north slope."

"And it's good for ex-wives?"

She was puzzled. "Oh, right, alimony payments. Good for payments of all kinds. It's hard to find, though. It's been overharvested
for about five generations, I guess."

"Daniel Boone had an ex-wife?"

"No doubt. They could always sell it for good money even back
then, get it packed off to China some way."

They walked quietly for a while. "Sammy Hill wasn't looking for sang," she confided.

"No?"

"Nope. He'd have had a spade and a burlap bag, and he'd be a little higher up than this, and he'd be looking in the fall. Not now."

"You can't find it now?"

"I could. *Sammy* couldn't."

Eddie clucked his tongue at her. "Bragging."

"Well, it's just . . . you know. It's easy to find in the fall, and people do what's easy. Spring and summer, ginseng's a real shy plant, and then in October it goes careless and gets bright-red berries and these yellow leaves like highway construction flags."

She didn't mention that whenever she found it in that condition she plucked off the gaudy leaves and tucked them in her pockets to save it from being discovered by hunters. She scattered the ripe berries under new groves, helping the ginseng roots to keep their secrets. Later on, when she did her weekly washing in a tub of scalding water, she'd roll ginseng leaves out of all her pockets like wads of tissue. Eddie would think she was nuts if she told him that. Hoarding this mountain all to herself, was his general accusation, but that wasn't it. If no person ever saw it again, herself included, that would be fine; she just loved the idea of those little man-shaped roots dancing in their world beneath the soil. She wanted them to persist forever, not for the sake of impotent men in China or anywhere else, just for the sake of ginseng.

Eddie Bondo was curious about the roots. When they sat down in the moss on the bank of Egg Creek to eat their lunch of sardines and crackers, she took a stick to the soft black dirt and tried to draw pictures of the different forms she'd seen: one-legged man, one-armed man; they weren't always perfect. Rarely, in fact.

He wasn't looking at her pictures. He was looking at her. "Those guys don't scare you, do they? You chew them up and spit them out between your teeth, smiling the whole time."

She looked down at her ginseng man. "What, you mean Sammy Hill?"

"And the best part was, he loved it. He'll go down and tell everybody he ran into this long-haired she-wolf with legs like a pinup girl."

She didn't like to think about what he'd tell. "I try not to step too hard on their manhood. You do that, next thing you know they're back up here with three or four of their buddies, which can get ugly. But no, they don't scare me." She shrugged. "They're just people I grew up with."

"I can't picture that," he said. "You with those guys. You driving a car, going shopping. I don't really see you anywhere but in the woods."

"Well. I guess it's been a while."

"Don't you miss it, any of it?"

"If you're speaking of high school and the Sammy Hills of this world, no, I don't."

"I'm not. You know what I mean."

She tried to decide if she knew. "There's some people I'd love to spend the day with, sure. And certain things."

"Like what?"

"I couldn't even say." She thought about it. "Not cars or electric lights, not movies. Books I can get if I ask. But walking around in a library, putting my hands on books I never knew about, *that* I miss. Anything else, I don't know." She pondered some more. "I like the beach. My husband's family had a beach house in North Carolina."

"The beach doesn't count. I mean stuff invented by people."

"Books, then. Poems, scary stories, population genetics. All those pictures Mr. Audubon painted."

"What else?"

"Chocolate? And Nannie's apple cider. And my border collie, if he weren't dead. But he counts, domestic pets are inventions of man." She closed her eyes, fishing for the taste of something lost. "And music, maybe? That's something I used to love."

"Yeah? Did you play any instrument?"

She opened her eyes wide. "No, but I listened a bunch. My dad played in a bluegrass band, Out of the Blue. And when I lived in Knoxville there was this little bar where we'd go, bluegrass and country music. People you've never heard of. These sisters used to play there sometimes—man, they were great. They came up from Texas, I think. The Dixie Chicks."

Eddie Bondo laughed out loud.

"Yeah, funny name."

"Funny *you*. You've been out of circulation awhile. They don't play little joints anymore."

"You've heard of them?"

"Me and everybody with ears."

She shook her head. "Amazing. Nothing stays the same down there."

"Nothing stays the same anywhere."

She looked at him earnestly. "Well, but see, up here it does. I guess there's big successes and failures going on, but they're too slow to notice in a lifetime." She crossed her arms, hugging herself. "I guess that's why I like it. Nature's just safer."

He leaned forward and kissed her. "Tell me some more about ginseng."

She concentrated on her drawing of a perfect two-armed, two-legged cocky little man who had no need to dig up ginseng for virility. He laid her down on the ground on top of her artwork and they stayed there awhile in the shifting leafy sunlight, leaving their own impression of human desire. Soon they were headed back toward the cabin with nothing on their minds but their bodies.

That was when they came upon the coyotes, two females hunting in the open. They were a mile or so from the hollow that fed Bitter Creek, not a place where Deanna would have gone looking for them. It was in a clearing where fallen trees had opened the canopy, letting the sun onto a patch of forest floor that now grew thick with a red carpet of new blackberry leaves. At first she thought they were dogs, they were so big: thick-furred behind the ears like huskies, and much stockier than the scrawny specimen she'd seen in the zoo or any western coyotes she'd seen in photographs. These two appeared golden in the sunlight, arching their backs and hopping through the foot-deep foliage, one and then the other, like a pair of dolphins alternately rolling above the waves. They were on the trail of something small and quick beneath the leaves and grass. Probably a vole or a mouse. They paid no attention to the pair of humans who stood with their boots frozen in the shadows. Focused entirely on their pursuit, their ears twitched forward like mechanical things, tracking imperceptible sounds. Like two parts of a single animal they moved to surround and corner their prey against a limestone bank, tunneling after it with their long noses. Deanna watched, spellbound. She could see how efficiently this pair might work a field edge, pursuing the mice and voles they seemed to prefer. No wonder farmers saw them often and feared for their livestock; if only they knew that they had nothing to lose but their mice. It occurred to her as she watched them that this manner of hunting might actually be helpful to ground-nesting birds like the bobwhite, because of the many passages it would open through the tight clumps of fescue.

Then, without any warning that the chase was near an end, the forward guard pounced and then raised her head with a sideways jerk, snapping the mouse just once in the air like a small, damp dust-rag she meant to shake clean, before disappearing into the woods with her catch still writhing in her jaws. Her sister paused at the edge of the woods and turned back on them with a dark, warning glare.

Deanna didn't speak for the rest of the afternoon. What was there to say, to this man whose thoughts she couldn't stand to know? She wanted him to have seen how they really were in that sunny clearing, how golden and perfectly attuned to their own necessities. But she knew not to ask. The sight of them had caused him to withdraw far inside himself, carefully avoiding any touch or glance at her as they stood watching the animals. Afterward, he hadn't offered a word about what they'd witnessed.

They did not go to bed in the afternoon, as it seemed they'd intended. Her body went cold. She put on a kettle for tea, then boiled some rice and reheated yesterday's black beans. She and Eddie had fallen into the habit of eating their meals on the bed, but on this day she claimed back the single chair and the table, covering it with a pile of books and papers and her neglected field notebook, writing while she ate. Eddie Bondo was restless, pacing out on the porch. The loudest sound on the earth, she thought, is a man with nothing to do. Why was he still here?

For the hundredth time she asked herself what madness of mate choice this was. A female prairie chicken would reliably copulate with the cock who inflated his yellow air sacs and boomed loudest. Bower birds went for the guy with the gaudiest nest. What was it in Eddie Bondo that moved her so powerfully to capitulate—his gait that matched hers, finally a man who could keep up? Or was it his smaller stature, after all those years of professors' bossing her around? But he was plenty cocky, as self-sufficient as any creature she'd met. Her match, she supposed, in that regard. She only wished she felt less like a prairie chicken stalking dazed across the lekking ground toward the grand display.

In the evening, when she couldn't stand any more of his proximity, she invented the necessity of walking down to the hemlock grove with a claw hammer. She would work on the trail bridge over the creek that had collapsed back in February. She still had a few hours of sunlight, as it was close to the summer solstice. (She thought about this: had she missed the solstice, in fact?) She would pull the old bridge apart, count the unsalvageable boards, and put in a requisition for the lumber she'd need to repair it, since the Forest Service jeep would be coming up fairly soon to drop off supplies and collect her new list. She would order no more food than usual, nothing extra. She'd left the cabin without a word, unable to imagine his doing anything but cleaning his gun in her absence.

The hemlock grove was on a tributary that fed Bitter Creek, in a strange, narrow hollow where long updrafts carried sound peculiarly well. Sometimes here she'd heard sounds all the way up from the valley: a dog barking, or even the high, distant whine of trucks on the interstate. That was in winter, though, when the trees were bare. Today, as she worked to pry up boards, she heard mostly the heavy quiet that precedes a summer evening, before the katydids start up, when the forest's sounds are still separated by long silences. A squirrel overhead scolded her halfheartedly, then stopped. A sapsucker worked its way around a pine trunk. Eddie Bondo had spoken of acorn woodpeckers he'd seen in the West, funny creatures that worked together to drill a dead tree full of little holes, cached thousands of acorns in them, and then spent the rest of their days defending their extravagant treasure from marauding neighbors. How pointless life could be, what a foolish business of inventing things to love, just so you could dread losing them. She listened to the sapsucker's methodic rapping, which ceased only when the bird paused to flick off sections of bark that landed on the mossy ground near the creek.

She was tearing the last boards off the log frame of the bridge when she heard something else that caused her to stop her hammer and listen. Voices: men talking, it sounded like. She stood up and listened more carefully. Hunters.

She wiped a strand of hair out of her eyes, feeling put out. This *must* be the longest day of the year, for she'd had quite enough of it. Talking meant there was more than one, and this late in the day they'd be up to something stupid like sleeping in a tree all night so they could poach wild turkeys at first light. She sighed and walked the log back across the creek to where she'd thrown her jacket. She'd have to head down there and summon the energy to call their bluff.

The sounds were very distant, maybe as much as a mile off. But they were certain, and continuous. She listened for another minute to the low, steady murmurs. It wasn't words. Growls, they were. Little conversational growls and higher-pitched barks. It wasn't men talking; this was women, *coyote* women, not howling at the moon but snarling quietly in the language of mothers speaking to children. Those two females this morning had taken a live mouse, she'd noticed. They hadn't eaten it or even killed it, just disabled it. Now Deanna knew why. *Those pups are alive,* she sang to herself in a whisper. Alive in the world with their eyes open, learning to hunt. Learning to speak. Coyote children born empty-headed like human infants, needing to learn every skill they'd need for living. Their protectors hadn't vocalized all spring, but now they would have to; no social creature could grow up mute, it wouldn't survive. The pups must be over six weeks old, nearly ready to hunt on their own. What a sight they must be now. Quickly she stacked the good lumber against a hemlock trunk and set off for home, though "home" didn't offer her much right now: a place where she couldn't breathe a word of what she knew tonight, nor even sleep, until she saw those pups with her own open eyes.

In the early-morning light, moving fast down the Bitter Creek trail, she stopped for a minute to listen. Nothing, only silence. Or rather, every kind of sound except what she was listening for. Plenty of noise rustling up from the dry leaves around her feet—that would be a lizard making itself sound as big as a bear. She walked on, knowing now what to listen for and knowing she would hear it. All spring she'd been waiting while her imagination filled with voices that made the small hairs stand up on the back of her scalp: those classic howls to the moon, the yips and polyphonic cries she'd studied on cassette tapes till she'd worn them to crinkled, transparent cellophane. She was beginning to fear she'd worn out her mind the same way, waiting in these mountains, leaning into the silent nights, eventually deciding that the one sound she longed for was not going to come. Here it wasn't necessary for them to speak. Not like out west, where they would have to call to each other from the tops of desert hills for the joy of their numbers because they were so plentiful. They'd have to remind one another of who they were, how many families, and where they stood. Here there was just one single family, and it knew exactly where it stood. Best to keep quiet.

The hardest work of Deanna's life had been staying away from that den, protecting it with her absence. Sometimes she'd felt sure they were gone, maybe headed south toward the Blue Ridge. She tried to believe that was for the best, but really there would be no safe haven for this family. Wherever these coyotes went, they'd have the hatred of farmers to contend with. Here on this isolated mountain they had the strange combination of one protector and one enemy. She didn't trust her power to bargain for their safety. In the six weeks of her acquaintance with Eddie Bondo, including both his presence and his absences, she'd hedged and evaded. Now he'd seen them, and she'd spent last night curled miserably in her chair near the wood stove, thinking, while he snored. By morning her bones ached and her mind was raw, but she was ready to lay her cards on the table.

"I'm going down the hill this morning, alone," she'd said. "If you follow me, you're off this mountain for the rest of your life or mine. Whichever lasts longer."

Without a word he'd packed some cold biscuits in his pack, hitched it over his shoulder, and hiked out whistling along the Forest Service road, in the opposite direction from Bitter Creek. Deanna stood for several minutes looking at his hat, which he'd left hanging on the peg by the door, and at his gun propped in the corner. Then she dressed and flew down the trail, free at last to go see. Now she could listen and not be afraid of hearing the voices that could give away their presence. For all those weeks she'd been holding her breath, listening and wanting not to hear. How had she let that happen?

She stopped again, this time hearing only the manic laughter of a woodpecker pair having too much fun, moving sideways through the woods, hopping over each other from one tree trunk to the next. For a minute she watched this pileated woodpecker couple playing checkers with themselves. They were huge, as big as flying black cats, and impossible to ignore with their big, haughty voices and upswept red crests. She received a vision of ghosts, imagined for a moment the ivory bills—dead cousins to these pileated woodpeckers—who had been even bigger, with nearly a three-foot wingspan and a cold, white-eyed stare. Lord God birds, people used to call them, for that was what they'd cry when they saw one. Never again.

Now, beneath the laughter of ghosts, she began to hear the intermittent vocalizations of the coyotes. She moved toward the sound, another slow hundred steps down the trail, stopping finally in a place where she could peek through rhododendrons and get a clear view of the den. The place had altered since spring; now the woods were thick with leaves. Air and light moved differently, and the den had changed, too. The bank below the cave was an apron of bare dirt, ridged with so many tiny claw marks it looked like light-brown corduroy. She thought she saw some movement inside the dark grin of the den's mouth, but then nothing, only stillness. She counted her own heartbeats to pass a minute, then more minutes, and convinced herself she'd actually seen no movement. There *had* been pups here, that was sure from all the claw marks on the bank, but it was too late, she began to believe. She'd missed them by one day; they'd grown up and gone.

Then she saw a rustling movement in the huckleberry thicket a little distance from the opening. A long, low whine pulled at her heart, an irresistible appeal. An adult was in that thicket, the mother or one of the beta females calling the children out. Instantly they appeared all together in the opening, a row of bright eyes beneath a forest of tiny, pointed ears. Deanna tried to count, but there were too many, and they moved in a rambunctious swarm of ears and tails: more than six, she decided, and fewer than twenty. They tumbled over one another out the doorway as the female approached with something in her teeth, a dark, small thing she tossed into their midst. A wake of tiny growls and yips erupted, and the little golden furballs hopped like popcorn in a kettle. Puppies, she thought; they were nothing but *puppies.* But kittenlike, too, in the way they were pouncing and playing with the half-living vole that had just been delivered to their schoolyard. Deanna sank down on her knees, into the childhood summers when neighbors had brought litters of pups in boxes and the barn cats had delivered their kittens practically into her hands. Without self-consciousness her body became a child's, her teeth holding her braid in her mouth for silence and her hands on her chest to keep her heart from bursting.

She wished so hard for her father, it felt like a prayer: If I could only show him this, oh, please. Let him look down from Heaven, whatever that means, let him look up through my eyes from the cells of genesis he planted in me, let him see this, because he would understand it perfectly. Love was one thing he always knew when it looked him in the face.

She wondered if there was anyone alive she could tell about these little dogs, this tightly knotted pack of survival and nurture. Not to dissect their history and nature; she had done that already. What she craved to explain was how much they felt like family.

14

Old Chestnuts

arnett turned up the hot water and let it scald the muscles shielding his shoulder blades. What an ache he had back there, as if some schoolyard bully had landed a haymaker squarely on his backbone.

He sighed. This life was getting to be too much for one old man. It wasn't so much the work; he loved messing with his chestnut trees. People presumed it was awfully tedious to bag all the flowers in the spring, do the careful cross-pollinating, collect the seeds, and plant the new seedlings, but every inch of that was exciting to Garnett because any of those seeds might grow up to be his blight-resistant chestnut tree. Every white bag slipped over a branch tip, every shake of pollen, each step carried the hope of something wondrous in the making. A piece of the old, lost world returning, right before his eyes.

No, what got him lately was the running into one problem after another, this farm and all its history dragging him down. The farm was a darn junkyard hiding its menace under a thin skin of grass. Every farm around here was, to tell the truth. He'd seen a young couple with a real estate agent looking over the farmhouse down by Oda Black's, and he'd been tempted to holler at them out the window of his truck, "Come looking for some history, have you? Well, this here's the story of how Old Man Blevins buried himself in debts and broke-down machinery, and it's just waiting to tangle up whoever steps on it next."

Well, of course he hadn't told them anything, and they'd buy. They had that strenuously foolish look of city people; the woman was dressed more like a man than the man. Soon they'd be finding out what Garnett knew by heart: on an old farm, every time you sink a spade to plant a tree, you're going to hit some old piece of a broken dish, a length of leather harness, some rusted metal, maybe even a cannonball! When Garnett was a schoolboy his father used to bring cannonballs home from somewhere and the boys would play with them till they ended up forgotten in the orchard or buried in their mama's flower patch, lying in wait to wreak havoc fifty years later on a tiller, a mower blade, or some other piece of equipment costing a day's work and too much money to repair.

This morning his plan had been modest: to finish clearing out the edge of the back field along the fencerow to make room for a single new row of trees. He thought the worst of it would be clearing the weeds, but no. He'd wrecked his bush hog and then his tiller blade. Half buried in that slim patch of ground he'd found six old fenceposts all wrapped up in barbed wire, evidently just thrown down there after they pulled them out to put in the new fence, back in the forties. Once he'd wrestled all that out, he'd discovered underneath it enough nails and carriage bolts scattered around to fill a bucket three times (and three times had carried it to his trash pile in the garage, now growing monstrous). Then, beneath all that, the entire metal chassis of an old wagon—and the worst was still yet to come! All in a mess at the end of the fencerow he'd uncovered a huge roll of black plastic with something heavy inside, which

Garnett began to fear would turn out to be a body (he'd already found everything else there was today, so why not?). But no, it was clumps of white powder, possibly rock salt, though he wasn't sure. Something his father had meant to throw away when Garnett was still a boy. That was the trouble with their thinking back in those days: "away" simply meant "out of sight somewhere," for someone else to run into further down the road. Garnett was fed up to the teeth with it all, and he still hadn't cleared the ground he'd meant to have laid open by midmorning, and now what? Good grief, that was his telephone ringing.

He turned off the shower and listened. Yes, there it was, the telephone on the little hall table just outside the bathroom door, ringing off the hook.

"Hold your horses!" he cried, not very pleased to have to cut his shower short and scurry around drying his head and wrapping himself in a towel. He stepped gingerly out onto the floorboards in the cool hallway and yanked up the receiver.

"Hello," he said, as pleasantly as he could manage while patting down his wet hair. He didn't feel right to be chatting with anyone, even a wrong number, looking like this.

"Hello, Mr. Walker?"

It was a woman. Not from around here, either; she had a town-ish sound to her, that way they have of hurrying up every single word.

"Speaking," he said.

She seemed uncertain for a moment, and he prayed she'd hang up, but then she launched into it: "I was wondering if I could ask you some questions about goats. I'm interested in getting started on kind of a semi-large-scale meat-goat operation, but I don't really have much capital, and some people directed me to you. They said you were the man to talk to, the regional goat maven, and you might even know how to get me started with some . . . I don't know how to put this." She breathed. "OK, plain talk? I'm wondering if you know anybody who'd give me goats for free. To get me started."

Garnett collected himself: the Regional Goat Maven, caught with a towel around his waist and his hair standing up like a chicken in the rain.

"Goats," he said.

"Yes."

"May I ask where you are located? That would be the first consideration."

"Oh, I'm sorry. I forgot my manners. This is Lusa Landowski, I live on the old Widener place, my husband was Cole Widener."

"Oh, Mrs. Widener. I was awfully sorry to hear about your husband. I would have been at the funeral, but there were . . . there are some considerations between our families. I expect you've heard all about that."

She was silent for a few seconds. "You're related to us somehow, aren't you?"

"By marriage," he said. "Distantly."

"I'm sorry; my nephew mentioned it, but I'd forgotten. That's right, one of my sisters-in-law is a Walker. I *think*." She laughed, sounding rather jolly for a new widow. "I'm still learning what it's like to live among six hundred relatives. I'm new to all this—I'm from Lexington."

"And that would be where you plan on raising the goats?"

"Oh no, *here*. I'm trying to keep this farm solvent, which would be the point of this goat business, if I can do it. I'm not at all sure I can, or whether it's crazy to try."

"Oh? Now, don't you have beef cattle up there on the Widener place?"

She sighed, now sounding not jolly at all. "Cattle just seem to be a losing proposition for me, with all you have to put into them. The Ivermec and everything, and I know I'm also supposed to check the cows to see if they're pregnant, but a cow pelvic examination I know from nothing. I'm scared to get close to them. I'm a small woman, and they're so *huge*." She gave an embarrassed laugh. "I guess I'm not much of a farmer yet. I can't even get my hay baler working. Two of my brothers-in-law have this leased-out cattle empire, so I could sell them my cattle, I'm thinking. Get into a smaller breed." She paused. "I was thinking I could handle goats."

"Well. You seem to have a plan, at least."

"It's a lot to go into; I'm sorry. I didn't mean to get into personal business, but listen, maybe this isn't a good time for you to talk. I'm sorry to be bothering you."

"Oh, it's no bother at all," he said, shifting from one bare foot to the other, feeling a draft, and no wonder: under the skimpy towel he was naked as a jaybird. He thought he heard someone rapping at his front door. Oh, dear, was it a delivery? He wasn't expecting a delivery.

"Oh, well, that's good," she said, laughing a little. "At least you haven't said flat out that I'm crazy—yet. I was hoping to kind of pick your brain. If I could."

"Well, pick away," said Garnett, miserably. He heard the knock again, more insistent.

"First of all, do you think it's realistic for me to try to get free goats? How would I go about that?"

"I'd suggest you run an ad in the newspaper. You're liable to find yourself with more goats than you know what to do with."

"Really? You agree that people are dying to get rid of them, then. Which I guess ought to tell me there's no money in it, if I had any sense."

"I can't really encourage you, Mrs. Widener. There's not a man in this county who's made a dollar off a goat, in my recollection."

"That's what my nephew said. But it seems to me the problem is marketing. Like everything else in farming, so I'm starting to learn. Nobody here knows what to do with a goat, they won't even eat them, and we're oversupplied. My nephew said we'd had kind of a goat plague on Zebulon County a while back. Why is that?"

Garnett closed his eyes. Was all this really happening? Some mysterious intruder was banging down his front door, a strange woman from Lexington was attempting to uncover his most embarrassing secret, his back ached like the dickens, and his bare buttocks were hanging out in the breeze. He did not wish he were dead, exactly, just maybe peacefully asleep in his bed, with all the lights out.

"Mr. Walker? Are you still there?"

"Yes."

"Is this . . . are you just thinking I'm some nut?"

"Oh, no, not at all. Your question about the surplus goats isn't an easy one to answer. Six or seven years ago, they started out as a whole slew of Four-H projects that kind of overgrew themselves. That's the best way I can describe it. A mistake that grew like Topsy. I was supposed to be supervising these young folks and should have steered them into hogs or poultry, but my wife had just died—you can understand, being a widow yourself. And my neighbor has a very hard grudge against goats of any kind, and I had a spell of poor judgment there. That's the only way I can describe it."

"Mr. Walker, you don't have to go into that, I'm not a reporter or anything. I'm not even that nosy compared to most people around here. I'm just looking for some free goats."

"Try an ad in the paper, then, that's what I suggest. But don't give out your address in the paper."

"No?"

"Goodness, no, or people will just dump any kind of animal on you, and you'll be sorry. Do you have a pickup truck, Mrs. Widener?"

"Sure."

"Well, then, list your telephone number in the ad, but don't make any mention of the Widener place. Just a phone, and ask people to call you. If they have what you're looking for, then you go pick up the animals yourself. But first ask them some questions. Do you have a pencil and paper?"

"Just a minute." He heard her clunk down the phone and walk across a floor. He wondered which room she was in. Upstairs, or down? Maybe the kitchen. They'd had the wedding right in the front hallway, with the girl walking slowly down those beautiful steps in her little white shoes and short white bridal dress. She'd looked about thirteen. They'd intended to have it out in the yard, but the weather had turned cold and rainy at the last minute. He remembered all of it. Ellen was sick. He hadn't thought about that for years: she'd had a terrible headache, and they'd had to leave early. It was probably connected with the cancer, they just didn't know it yet.

"OK, I'm back."

"Oh," he said, startled. "What was I saying?"

"When people call, I should ask them about their goats . . . what?"

"Oh, yes. First, you want meat goats, do you? Not for milking?"

"Definitely for meat."

"All right, then, you want to produce slaughter kids."

"I guess that's right. In time to sell by, oh, maybe around the end of the year or something like that, I was kind of thinking."

"Oh. Then you have no time to waste."

"Is it even possible? To get them to breed at this time of year?"

"It's not the right time for them, but there is a way to make it happen. If you can be *sure* they haven't been around a buck for all of last fall and winter, they'll be ready to come into season now. I guarantee it."

"Is that reasonable to expect? That people will have does that haven't been with a buck?"

"There are probably a hundred families in this county keeping a handful of goats in their backyard. And people don't generally like billies that close to the house—they have quite a stout odor. Have you ever smelled a billy goat, Mrs. Widener?"

"Not that I recall," she confessed.

"Well, if you had, you would remember it. It's an odor that appeals to a nanny goat, evidently, but not to human beings. Most people only want to keep the does around."

"All right. Good."

"So what you'll want is does—three- and four-year-olds are the best, nothing a whole lot older. Get as many does as you think you can handle, but watch out for bucks. You'll only want one, with your does. Mrs. Widener, can you tell a buck from a doe?"

She laughed. "Mr. Walker, I'm ignorant, but I'm not stupid."

"Well, of course not. I just meant . . . you *are* from Lexington."

He heard her breathe in sharply as if to speak, but then she paused. "OK, just one buck," she said finally. "Got it."

"Well, but you might as well get a spare or two. Once in a while you'll get a buck that doesn't perform, so you may as well have a few on reserve. You'll have to keep them in a separate pasture, out of sight."

"Gentlemen-in-waiting," she said.

Was that a bawdy joke? He didn't know what was what anymore; kids laughed at you even when you said a simple word like *queer.* But she didn't seem to be laughing. She sounded more earnest than most of the boys he'd had in 4-H.

"Now, if your does really haven't been pastured with a buck since before last fall, they'll come into season right away, just a day or two after you put the buck in the field. Some people think it helps to rub down the buck with a rag and then walk around waving it in the she-goats' noses. But I never thought that was really necessary."

"So that's the first thing I'll ask people when they call: 'Have you got does? And are they now or have they ever been pastured with a buck?' Right?"

"That's right," he said.

"If they are, I should just pass?"

"That's up to you. If you want kids by the end of the year, you should."

There was a pause. She seemed to be writing something down. "OK. And the next question?"

"What kind of goats are they? You'll want Spanish, or Spanish crossed with what they call brush goats, which is what most people have around here. Meat goats, just ask if they're meat goats. Your Saanens, your Swiss dairy goats, anything somebody's milking, that's probably an animal you don't want."

"OK. What else, you said the age was important?"

"Nothing over five years, nor less than one hundred pounds."

Again, she was taking notes. "What else?"

"Well, of course, you want them healthy. You don't want parasites. Look them over when you go to pick them up. If you're not one hundred percent satisfied with the looks of them, don't take them."

"That's going to be hard," she said. "To turn up my nose at somebody's offer of free animals? Beggars can't be choosers."

"That's why you have your truck. *You* go to *them*. They're the beggars, they're hoping you'll take the useless beasts off their hands. You'll decide."

"Oh, you're right. That's a very good way to look at it. Thank you, Mr. Walker, you've been extremely helpful. Do you mind if I call you back if I have more questions? I'm kind of learning as I go here."

"Not at all, Mrs. Widener. Good luck to you, now."

"Thanks."

"Bye-bye."

He hung up the phone and cocked an ear toward the front hallway downstairs. Still clutching the towel around his waist with one hand, he tiptoed over to the window and peered out, though he didn't expect to see anything new in back of the house. Who could have been at his door? He dressed very quickly in the doorway to the landing, a place in his house where he seldom tarried, and it gave him pause when he glanced up and caught his reflection inside the chestnut frame of the antique mirror that hung there. He felt he had seen a ghost, but not of himself: it was the mirror frame that provoked him, his surviving face circumscribed by the remains of that extinct tree.

He padded down the stairs in his leather slippers, since he'd left his muddy boots outside the door to clean later, feeling too tired and fed up to do it when he came in from the field. His trousers, covered with green cockleburs, he'd folded over a kitchen chair, dreading the chore of picking them. The sharp burrs would prick his fingertips and leave them with a dull, poisoned ache. Garnett believed that if the Almighty Father had made one mistake in Creation, it was to give us too darn many cockleburs.

At the front door he opened the screen and poked out his head, then looked to the left and the right. Nobody. There were his boots side by side, still waiting muddily by the door. No car in the driveway, no delivery truck or any sign that one had been here. Usually the big UPS truck backed up on the grass and left an awful, curved scar of mud there. That boy they'd hired to drive it had more earring holes than brains in his head.

Garnett stepped out on the porch and squinted through his cloudy corneas at the heavy afternoon air, as if he might be able to decipher traces left in it. He didn't get unexpected visitors very often. Never, in fact—nor unexpected phone calls, for that matter, but mercy, when it rained it poured. Someone had been here, and he'd missed him. It wasn't an easy thing for him to let go of.

Then he saw the pie on his porch swing. A berry pie, just sitting there, taking in the day. It had the pretty little slits in the top from which a berry pie bleeds its purple fluids—oh, what heavenly mysteries were created by female hands. Blackberry pie was his favorite. Ellen had always made one with the first fruits harvested from the fencerows, after ceremoniously sending him out with a pail on the third Saturday of June. Garnett glanced at the sky briefly, asking God what kind of a trick this was.

He went over to take a closer look. It was a pie, all right—fresh. Even if his eyes could trick him, his nose never did. Stuck underneath it, wafting a little in the breeze, was a small collection of papers. He slipped the thin squares of paper out from under the pie, along with a sealed envelope, and scowled at the whole mess. The squares of paper were receipts. Good grief, was someone charging him for this pie? No, they were *his* receipts, one from Little Brothers' and one from Southern States, probably taken out of the small metal box just inside the front door where he always emptied his pockets and tended to let his receipts pile up until tax time. But there were words on the back of these, written in an extremely small, tidy hand. A note, attached to a letter in a sealed envelope.

He looked around the empty porch. Someone had brought him this pie, stood there banging on his door for fifteen minutes while that Widener woman rattled on endlessly about goats, and then finally given up and written him a note and left the pie. Who would do such a thing? As if he didn't know. With a sinking feeling he carried the note inside, pie and all, catching the door with his elbow. He set the pie inside a cupboard where he wouldn't be looking at it while he read the note, and then he fetched his reading glasses and sat down at his kitchen table to read. First, the note on the scraps of receipt:

Mr. Walker,

Well, you needn't to waste a stamp and two hours of Poke Sanford's time—think of that poor fellow having to carry a letter from your box down to the P.O. and back out the same road again to mine! I'm right next door. You could knock. That's what I meant to do today. I had a letter written up to give you in case I couldn't think of everything [. . . and here the note continued onto the second receipt] or if you weren't in the mood to chat, but really I hoped to say most of this in person. But now you aren't home. Oh, fiddle. Your truck is here. Where are you? I'll just leave you the pie and the letter. Cheer up, Mr. Walker. I hope you enjoy them both.

Your neighbor, Nannie Rawley

Next Garnett tore open the long white envelope and slid out the handwritten letter folded inside. He noticed that his hands were shaking when he did it. Cheer up indeed.

Dear Mr. Walker,

    Since you asked, yes, I do believe humankind holds a special place in the world. It's the same place held by a mockingbird, in his opinion, and a salamander in whatever he has that resembles a mind of his own. Every creature alive believes this: The center of everything is *me*. Every life has its own kind of worship, I think, but do you think a salamander is worshiping some God that looks like a big two-legged man? Go on! To him, a man's a shadowy nuisance (if anything) compared to the sacred business of finding food and a mate and making progeny to rule the mud for all times. To themselves and one another, those muddly little salamander lives mean everything.

    Of all things, I'd never expect *you*, Garnett Walker III, to ask, "Who cares if one species is lost?" The extinction of one kind of tree wreaked pure havoc on the folks all through these mountains—your own family more than any other. Suppose some city Yank said to you, "Well, sir, the American chestnut was just *one* tree—why, the woods are full of trees!" You'd get so mad you'd spit. It would take you a day and a night to try and explain why the chestnut was a tree unlike any other, that held a purpose in our world that nothing else can replace. Well sir, the loss of one kind of salamander would be a tragedy on the same order to some other creature that was depending on it. It wouldn't be *you* this time, but I assume you care about all tragedies, not just the ones that affect the Walker fortunes. Do you recall how they mentioned in the paper last year about all the mussel shells in our river going extinct? Well, Mr. Walker, now the mailman tells me he saw on a nature show that every kind of mussel has to live part of its little life as a parasite on the gills of a different kind of minnow. If the right minnow isn't there at the right time, well, sir, that's the end of the story! Everything alive is connected to every other by fine, invisible threads. Things you don't see can help you plenty, and things you try to control will often rear back and bite you, and that's the moral of the story. There's even a thing called the Volterra principle that I read about in my orcharding journal, which is all about how insecticide spraying actually drives up the numbers of the bugs you're trying to kill. Oh, it's an aggravation and a marvel. The world is a grand sight more complicated than we like to let on.

Just think: if someone had shown you a little old seedling tree potted in a handful of dirt coming in on a ship from Asia all those years ago, asked you to peek into it, and remarked, "These piddly little strands of fungus will knock down a million majestic chestnut trees, starve out thousands of righteous mountain folk, and leave Garnett Walker a bitter old man," would you have laughed?

If God gave Man all the creatures of this earth to use for his own ends, he also counseled that gluttony is a sin—and he did say, flat out, "Thou shalt not kill." He didn't tell us to go ahead and murder every beetle or caterpillar that wants to eat what we eat (and, by the way, other insects that *pollinate* what we eat). He did not mean for us to satisfy our every whim for any food, in every season, by tearing down forest to make way for field, ripping up field to make way for beast, and transporting everything we can think of to places it doesn't belong. To our dominion over the earth, Mr. Walker, we owe our thanks for the chestnut blight. Our thanks for kudzu, honeysuckle, and the Japanese beetle also. I think that's all God's little joke on us for getting too big for our britches. We love to declare that God made us in his image, but even so, he's three billion years old and we're just babies. I know your opinion of teenagers, Mr. Walker; just bear in mind that to God, you and I are much younger, even, than that. We're that foolish, to think we know how to rule the world.

I'm partial to the passage from Genesis you quoted, but I wonder if you really understand it. God gave us every herb-bearing seed, it says, and every tree in which is the fruit of a tree-yielding seed. He gave us the mystery of a world that can re-create itself again and again. To *you* the fruit shall be food, he's saying, but just remember, to the tree it's a child. "And to every beast of the earth, and to every fowl of the air, and to every thing that creepeth upon the earth wherein there is life, I have given every green herb for meat." He's looking out for the salamanders there, you see? Reminding us that there's life in them, too, and that even weeds and pond algae are sacred because they're salamander food. You're a religious man, Mr. Walker. Seems to me you'd think twice about spraying Roundup all over God's hard work.

Never mind. We all have our peeves. Myself, I hate goats (as you well know), and I sorely despise snapping turtles. I'm sure God loves them as much as he loves you or me, but I've got new baby ducklings on my pond, and an evil old turtle in there is gobbling them down like the troll under the bridge. I can't stand it. There was one duckling I loved best, white with a brown wing (I named him Saddle Shoe), and yesterday while I stood and watched, that turtle came up right underneath and yanked down poor Shoe as he flapped and wailed for Mama. I bawled like a baby. I'd shoot that old S-O-B in the head if I had a gun and the heart to use it, so help me! But I have neither, and God knows that is surely for the best.

Yours very sincerely,
Nannie Land Rawley

P.S. I had to rack my brain, but yes, I recall my conversation in the hardware. I was telling a tale on myself: I'm not used to the get-up-and-go hydrostat transmission they put in the new Snappers, compared to the old geared ones. Marshall claims he sold me a small, polite little mower, but I say it's a monster with a death wish. I left it running in the front yard one day while I went in to get a drink of water, and when I came back it was gone! I called Timmy Boyer to report it stolen! The poor man had to walk up to my porch with hat in hand and explain to me as how he'd found my mower in a compromising position a hundred yards downhill from where I left it. Evidently while I was inside, my Snapper took a wild hair and decided to fling itself headfirst into Egg Creek.

Mr. Walker, I've always found people love you best if you can laugh at your own foolish misfortunes and keep mum about everyone else's.

Well, thought Garnett. For goodness' sakes. It was a lot to take in at once. He felt a moment's relief about the whole snapper incident and an iota of sympathy for the woman's poor ducklings (oh, Saddle Shoe!), but only an iota, before his blood pressure started to rise. The longer he stared at the letter, flipping backward through its several pages, the more its true meaning began to reveal itself to him among the flimflam phrases of her mock friendliness. Bitter old man indeed!

He forgot the pie completely—would not remember it, in fact, until a day and a half later (at which time he would sample it tentatively and find it still edible). That pie was the furthest thing from his mind as he stomped to his desk and tore a blank sheet from one of his chestnut notebooks. Without a second thought to appearances, for this was no time to stand on ceremony, he plucked a black ballpoint pen out of his pen-and-pencil cup and applied it so hard to the page that its line wavered and skipped like a terrified heart. "Dear Miss Rawley," he scrawled,

I am weary of your grabbing every opportunity as a pulpit for your absurd views on modern agriculture!! If you can prove to me your so-called Voltaire principal, i.e. spraying pesticide is good for the health of insects, then by all means I will drink a quart of malathion, pronto!!

Furthermore, what is this business about God being three billion years old? God is ageless; the earth and its inhabitants were created in 4300 B.C., as can be proved by extrapolating backward from present population to the time of the first two people, Adam and Eve. You were unaware of this scientific formulation, probably, or were perhaps making a veiled reference to Evolutionary Theory. Because if the latter, your words fall on ears too wise for that old scam. I am a scholar of Creation Science, and suggest you think about a thing or two, i.e. who but an Intelligent, Beautiful Creator could have created a world filled with beauty and intelligence? How could Random Chance (i.e. "evolution") have created lifeforms so vastly complex as those that fill our world? I realize you're no scientist, Miss Rawley, but I could explain to you the Second Law of Thermodynamics, which states that all natural things move from order to chaos, quite the opposite of what the evolutionists claim. I could go much further than this, though I am fighting the inclination to wash my hands of you altogether and let you cast your own soul on the brimstone as you seem determined to do, and let you face in the jaws of Satan the same fate suffered by your precious duckling.

Hah! thought Garnett, rather proud of his dramatic twist of the knife and thinking he ought to end right there.

"But no," he wrote, unable to stop himself,

I shall be a good neighbor and send you these thoughts which should be enough for you and your bra-burning

Unitarian friends to ponder, I dare say, for many days to come.

Truly, Garnett S. Walker III

P.S. I am not a bitter old man.

Garnett carefully affixed not one but *two* stamps to the envelope to prove his point (he wasn't sure exactly what point, but he trusted his instincts) and licked its seal shut before he could give himself a chance at failed nerve or courage. Politeness be hanged. This was no longer simply a matter of pride. Garnett Walker was now a Soldier of God on the way to his mailbox, marching as to war.

15

Moth Love

rom where Lusa stood at her upstairs window, the front lawn looked like a bolt of deep-green velvet with just a few moth-eaten patches where the reddish ground showed through. Jewel and Emaline were setting up the lawn chairs while Emaline's husband, Frank, and Mary Edna's Herb carried the big walnut dining table outside. Lusa had invited the whole family for the Fourth of July, claiming she needed to make ice cream out of a month's worth of leftover cream sitting in her icebox. Maybe it was just pity, but they'd all agreed to come— even Mary Edna's son and his wife from Leesport, whom she'd met only at the funeral.

Mary Edna had arrived an hour early with a plate of deviled eggs in each hand (Salmonella waiting to happen, Lusa thought but did not say). Seeing the front hallway suddenly occupied by the Menacing Eldest in a burnt-orange pantsuit and sensible shoes had sent Lusa into a panic; she'd called out some instructions and flown upstairs on the pretense of finding a tablecloth. But of course Mary Edna would know that the tablecloths were in the cherry armoire in the parlor. Right now, in fact, she was outside sailing one of her mother's linens over the table while the men hunkered down near the chicken house with their backs to her, stabbing beers into a tub of ice and opening up long-necked bottles of something home-made. Hannie-Mavis was trying to organize the kids into a labor pool for cranking the ice cream, but at the moment they were circling her like a swarm of bees threatening their queen with mutiny. Lusa stood with one hand on the back of the green brocade chair and looked down on all her in-laws from above, pondering their resemblance to the clucking, parti-colored flock of chickens that was usually scattered out over her yard. The hens had scrammed early to their roosts to avoid this onslaught of relatives. Lusa smiled a small, sad smile, wishing she could watch the whole evening from this window. Finally they were all here, conceding to be her guests. And she didn't have the nerve to go downstairs.

She sighed and shut the window. It had rained earlier. The air had the fetid smell of mushrooms releasing their spores into the damp air. It was evening, though, so the men would be shooting off their fireworks soon, tinting the air blue with that acrid smoke. Having a program would help the evening go by. She glanced in the dresser mirror and ran a hand through her strawberry mane, feeling miserable. Her jeans fit too well, the black knit shirt was too low-cut, her hair was too red—the widow Jezebel. She'd chosen the black top for a drab effect, but it was no small task to look dowdy next to Mary Edna in her waistless polyester pantsuit, or Hannie-Mavis in a red striped top, star-spangled shorts, gold mules, and blue eyeliner. Lusa pointed her feet toward the stairs and made them go. *It time, it's time, too late to change now. A year too late.*

She was right about the fireworks; there was already a movement afoot to begin. Hannie-Mavis's Joel and Big Rickie were peering into a series of brown paper bags they'd set out in a row, arguing about some aspect of the scheme. Lusa was grateful for the rain—she'd been genuinely afraid they'd burn down her barn, and not brave enough to declare a ban on the fireworks (they were a tradition). But May and June had dumped such rain on Zebulon County that the air itself could smother a flame. Bullfrogs had wandered up out of the duck pond and carelessly laid their jellied masses of eggs in the grass, apparently confident that their tadpoles would be able to swim through the lawn like little sperms. Fierce snapping turtles no longer confined themselves to the ponds but wandered the lanes like highwaymen. In all her life Lusa had never seen such an oversexed, muggy summer. Just breathing was a torrid proposition.

"Hey, guys," she called to Joel and Big Rickie, who nodded at her, smiling broadly like schoolboys. They were thrilled about this picnic. Lois the Loud, meanwhile, sat in a folding chair near the food table, chain-smoking and posting a stream of complaints about how much they'd spent on the fireworks.

"One hundred and eighty-one dollars," she boomed in a voice deepened by decades of cigarettes. Mary Edna stood three feet away, ignoring her and scowling at the food table. When Lois spied Lusa coming out of the house, she perked up at the potential of a new audience. "A hundred and eighty-one dollars!" she called out to Lusa. "That's what these little boys spent on their little show for tonight, did you ever hear the like?"

Lusa had already heard it all from upstairs, but she pretended to be dismayed. "Good grief. Did they drive all the way to China, or what?" she said, walking over toward Lois. She was relieved to see that Lois was in the Jezebel camp, too, dressed in jeans and a western-style shirt unsnapped a tad too far.

"Naw," Lois said, "they went over to Crazy Harry's down there off the interstate."

As far as Lusa could tell, the entire border of the state of Tennessee was ringed with shacks advertising cheap fireworks. It had to do with their being legal on one side of the line and not the other, but she wasn't sure which was which.

"I should have gone with them," Lois droned on in her deep, cracked voice. "Or sent Little Rickie and the girls along to keep an eye on them. I didn't think two grown men would act like kids in a candy store." She examined the ends of her hair, which she wore long and dyed coal black—not flatteringly, in Lusa's opinion, since Lois was fair and blue-eyed like Cole, and a little long in the tooth for the straight, dyed look. But maybe having Indian-black hair like her husband and children made her feel like she belonged to them. Who knew?

Mary Edna was fussing tediously with a piece of aluminum foil over a sheet cake. She was a vision in her orange polyester, which seemed itself a heat source in this muggy night; the outfit gave Lusa an odd, uncomfortable sensation that Mary Edna's physical presence would spoil the food.

Mary Edna turned around suddenly, as if reading Lusa's thoughts, but it was Lois she snapped at: "Oh, hush your bellyaching, Lois, they do it ever year. If you're not used to it by now, you never will be."

Lusa winced, but Lois was utterly unfazed. She craned her head sideways toward Mary Edna, flicking ash in the grass. "Why sure, go ahead and talk. Your husband wouldn't go spend a week's grocery money on cherry bombs and Martian Candles and stuff."

"I'd ruther him do that than what he's up to right now, down there poking his nose in the bottles. What kind of hooch have they got down there?"

"Lord, honey, Frank's done made that elderberry wine. You'd think he'd get over that little chemistry project, or Emaline would dump it down the drain, one."

"Oh, it's that business."

"He claims it's a pure wonderful product and maybe he'll sell it one of these days." Lois rolled her eyes.

Mary Edna touched her bluish, tightly coiffed hair and stared at the men with narrow eyes. "I wouldn't know. You ask me, I'd have to agree with the good Lord. All of it bites as the serpent."

Lois snorted, breathing smoke out her nose like a dragon. "After the second bottle of that stuff, turpentine'd taste pure wonderful, I expect."

Lusa watched the sisters volley, surprised that they could be as mean about their own husbands and each other's as they'd ever been toward her. Cole had always insisted that she took his family too personally. She'd never had brothers or sisters of her own, only parents who said "please" and "thank you" to each other and to the child they'd produced late in life and never quite known how to handle. Maybe Cole had been right. She'd never experienced rough-and-tumble, the sharper edges of family love.

She walked down toward the chicken house, deciding to investigate whatever it was that was biting these men as the serpent. They were engaged in the kind of cheerful, energetic argument that tends to happen when all present are agreed and the enemy is absent. Farm policy and government stupidity, most likely. But maybe not. "Blevins would lie, though," Herb was saying. "He'd lie quicker than a dog can lick a plate."

"Howdy, gentlemen," she called from a decent distance as she approached, just in case they were about to say something they wouldn't want her to hear. It embarrassed them to death if they let slip even so much as a "hell" or "damn" in her presence.

"Hey there, Miz Widener," Big Rickie called to her. "I have a crow to pick with you!"

His friendliness caught her off guard. This crow didn't seem very threatening. "What is it now, those cows I sold you and Joel? Did they all run off already? I warned you they were fence jumpers."

"No ma'am, them cattle are behaving just fine, thank you. But now we *leased* them cattle, a percentage on the calves, let's don't forget. We don't owe you unless they all get busy and get theirselves in the family way this winter."

"I recall the terms, and I gave those girls their instructions." Lusa smiled. Rickie and Joel had made her a good deal, and she knew it.

"No, now, our contention is with your antitobacco policy."

"My what? Oh, I see. You've got me chalked up as the enemy of the small farmer."

Rickie hid his cigarette quickly behind his back. Herb, Joel, Frank, and Herb's son all followed suit. "No ma'am," Big Rickie said. "We've got you chalked up with Miss Butcher, our tenth-grade shop teacher. She used to throw screwdrivers at us when she caught us smoking."

"A *woman*, you had for a shop teacher? A *Miss Butcher*? I can't believe that."

"God's honest truth," Frank said. "I had her, Rickie and Joel had her, and Herb's boy here did, too. By the time she retired she was somewheres around a hundred years old, and missing three fingers."

"She should live to a hundred and twenty," Lusa said. "Look at you. Despite her years of trial, you're all still smoking like chimneys. Where's my screwdriver?"

They ducked their heads like little boys. Lusa felt amazed to be the center of their attention. These men had never fully let her in on a conversation before. Possibly it was the elderberry wine, which Frank was now urging her to sample. He'd put it up in beer bottles, so it was hard to tell who was drinking what.

"Wow," she said, after a taste. It was dry and strong, almost like brandy. "Good," she added, nodding, since they seemed very interested in her opinion. "Although I hear it bites as the serpent."

They exploded at that, all of them, even Herb. Lusa flushed a little, pleased to have earned this amity but also surprised to find herself allying with these men against their women. Or maybe it was just Mary Edna. There seemed to be resentment throughout the ranks on the Mary Edna score.

"So, Mr. Big Rickie. What's this crow you have to pick with me, really?"

"Them goats up 'air in your back pasture. Now I see why you

had Joel and me clear out all your cattle: to make way for the goats. I know what you got 'em for, too."

"You do?" She felt a slight panic, for no reason. Had Little Rickie shared her plan? Would it really matter if he had?

"Yep." Big Rickie had a twinkle in his eye.

"OK, why did I get those goats?"

"To make me look bad. They'll eat down all the thistles and rose briars out of your hayfield neat as pickle. And see, now, a man drives by, he'll look on the other side of the fence and say, 'Well, sir, that old Big Rickie Bowling, his hay's nothing but a mess of briars. I wouldn't buy that hay for two cents.'"

"That's *exactly* why I got goats, to wreck your hay trade. I couldn't stand to sit here and watch you get rich selling hay."

"Lord, Rickie," Joel said, "woman's going to ruin you. You'd just as well get out of farming altogether, with her running the competition."

Were they making fun of her now? But this was how they spoke to each other, too—in a complicated mix of rue, ridicule, and respect that she was just beginning to grasp. They were also appreciating her figure rather frankly, especially Big Rickie and Herb's son from Leesport, whatever his name was. Lusa pulled at her shirt, wondering if her nipples showed through somehow. She racked her brain for the son's name, which she couldn't have guessed if her life depended on it. She kept hoping he would reintroduce himself, but instead he handed her a second bottle of Serpent, as they were now calling their drink. Had she downed the first one so fast? And why did Rickie keep smiling at her? He was a handful—she'd never imagined this side of him. She could see why Lois would want to keep her hair young and her eye peeled.

"Is 'at there barn made of chestnut?" Herb's nameless boy was asking her now.

"You're asking *me?*"

"Your barn, ain't it?"

She was startled by this turn in the conversation that had now, suddenly, given her authority over her barn. Their wives wouldn't even acknowledge Lusa's ownership of her kitchen. But of course, these men were in-laws, too; they hadn't grown up in these buildings any more than Lusa had. She'd never really thought of this—they weren't Wideners, either.

"Yeah, I think it is chestnut," she said. She pointed at the joinery under the peak of the gable end. "You see how the roof got raised up at some point? That was more recent, and I think they used oak. It's not weathering as well. All the rafters need to be replaced."

Herb whistled. "That's going to cost you."

"*Tell* me," she said. "If you hear of anybody who likes to replace barn roofs, tell him you know a lady who's looking to make him rich."

"You ought to have him build you a gabazo up there on your hill, while he's at it," said Frank. "So you could set up there in it and watch your goats."

"I know a man that had two gabazos," Rickie said. "But they died."

"Rickie Bowling, you're a damn fool."

They all stood silent for a moment in the early-evening light, studying the barn with its many seams of age and repair. From the depths of the chicken house behind them came the low, world-weary moan of a hen slowly accomplishing an egg. In the ambient air the choir of summer insects was tuning up its infinite clicks and trills. By nightfall they'd be deafening, loud enough to drown out the fireworks. But for now Lusa and the men could still hear the constant voice of Lois, who had flagged down Hannie-Mavis and was now bending *her* ear about the price of gunpowder.

"I'm a damn fool," Rickie said solemnly, "what spent a hundred dollars on fireworks, and won't hear the end of it till Christmas."

"I heard it was a hundred and eighty-one dollars and twelve cents," Lusa said. "Approximately."

"No, now, the eighty-one dollars and twelve cents, that was Joel."

"Come on," Joel said, suddenly excited. "Let's go shoot."

"Hold your horses, Mr. Sexton. We can't start till it gets good and dark." But Joel was already walking back uphill. They all watched him go, observing as his path intersected with that of the starred-and-striped Hannie-Mavis, who had broken free of Lois and was headed in her husband's direction carrying a hot dog on a bun. Lusa started to make a remark about her outfit also looking better in the dark, but she thought better of it as Hannie-Mavis stood on tiptoe in her little gold shoes, letting Joel give her a kiss before he took the hot dog from her. There was such a wealth of simple fondness in his hand as it touched her back, in her stretched calves and her head turned to receive his kiss. A vast loneliness crept over Lusa. She needed Cole to negotiate this family. With him it had made sense. Or could have, maybe, eventually.

Joel began poking into the paper bags, holding the hot dog high in his other hand as he bent over. Rickie seemed nervous about letting him do it alone. "I hate to leave such pleasant company," he said, making a courtly bow and giving Lusa a look in the eye that shocked her with suggestion. "But I have to go keep an eye on my brother-in-law. He is not to be trusted."

"I don't think you are, either," she said.

He winked. "I believe you may be right."

Lusa turned her face away to hide a blush, pretending to look uphill toward the food table. She felt incensed—here she was not six weeks a widow, and her brother-in-law was flirting. Although he may have just been trying to cheer her, and the alcohol muddled everything, of course. Just for a minute, she herself had forgotten to be sad. She felt guilty and hopeful both, realizing that beyond these numb days lay an opposite shore where physical pleasure might someday surprise her with its sharp touch. Where she would see colors again.

"Gentlemen. I'd better go act like a decent hostess and see if we're going to have any ice cream," she said. Frank reached out to snag the empty bottle out of her left hand and press a full one into it.

"We are sinking deep in sin," she sang quietly as she walked past Mary Edna with a Serpent in each hand, heading down toward the barn to check on the progress of the ice cream crankers. She felt a tightness in her lower abdomen, not from the elderberry wine but from something else, a body sensation she recognized but couldn't place. She'd been feeling it all day—a fullness, not really unpleasant but distracting, and a constant small twinge on the left side of her belly. And then it came to her, just as she spied the bald pate of an enormous whole moon rising above the roof of the barn. Of course. What she felt was her cycle coming back. She'd been on the pill for years, since college, but she'd tossed out the pink dial-pack several weeks ago when she finally made herself clear Cole's tooth-brush and shaving things out of the bathroom. Now, after years spent suppressed in hibernation, her ovaries were waking up and kicking in. No wonder the men were fluttering around her like moths: she was fertile. Lusa let out a rueful laugh at life's ridiculous persistence. She must be trailing pheromones.

Halfway down the hill, Jewel's five-year-old flew into her legs, causing her to spill wine on herself and nearly lose her footing.

"Good grief, Lowell, what is it?"

"Crys made me cut my leg!" he wailed, pointing frantically. "It's bleeding! I need a Band-Aid."

"Let me see." She sat down on the ground, set both her bottles firmly into the grass, rolled up Lowell's pants leg, and scrutinized the unbroken skin for damage. "I don't see anything."

"It's the other leg," came a weary voice through the darkness. It was Crys, trudging up the hill after her brother. "He scratched it on a nail in the barn cellar."

Lusa was flustered by the child's hysteria. To calm both him and herself she held him in her lap while she examined his other leg.

She found a scratch on the ankle, but it hadn't even broken through the second layer of epidermis. Definitely no blood. "You're OK," she said, hugging him tightly. She picked up his leg and kissed it. "This will heal before your wedding."

Crys flopped onto the ground beside Lusa. "Did he say it was all my fault?"

"No, he did not."

"Well, he will. That's what he'll tell Mama. But I didn't ask him to climb under the barn with me. I told him not to. I *told* him he's a tattletale sissy and he always gets hurt and cries."

"I am not a tattletale sissy!" wailed Lowell.

"Shhh," Lusa said, putting an arm around Crys's shoulders while Lowell quieted to an occasional racking sob in her lap. He clung to Lusa endearingly, clutching her around the waist with his small hands. "Nothing's anybody's fault," she said. "It's hard to have a big sister who can do everything in the world. Lowell just wants to try to keep up with you, honey."

Crys shrugged off Lusa's arm without a word.

"Lordy, is that my Lowell hollering?" It was Jewel calling out from behind them, sounding worried.

"We're OK," Lusa called back. "Down here by the barn. Wounded in action but headed for recovery, I think."

Jewel appeared and sat down heavily on the grass, reaching out to stroke Lowell's forehead. He practically leapt from Lusa's lap into his mother's embrace. Crys stood up and disappeared.

"He just got a little scratch," Lusa reported. "He was trying to climb around in the barn with his sister. No B-L-O-O-D, but I've got Band-Aids in the bathroom upstairs if you think that would help the patient's morale."

"Who wants ice cream?" a female voice beckoned through the darkness—one of Lois and Rickie's teenaged daughters, Lusa guessed. The two of them had taken over supervising the kids after Hannie-Mavis washed her hands of it.

Lowell took a deep breath, heaved himself up, and struck out with a loping limp in the direction of the ice cream. Jewel leaned against Lusa's shoulder for just a second. "Thanks, hon."

"I didn't do anything."

"You didn't smack them, that's something."

"God, Jewel, don't say that. I like your kids. They're something else, both of them."

"Something else, all right." Jewel tilted her head and chanted, "The boy's a girl, and the girl's a boy."

"Maybe that's what I like about them."

"They've had it tough. Poor kids. I wish I could have done better for them."

"Every kid has it tough," Lusa said. "Being a little person in a big world with nobody taking you very seriously is tough. I can relate."

Jewel shook her head, giving Lusa to know there was a much larger sadness here that she should not try to explain away. Lusa went silent. She'd borne enough of people's do-goodnik consolations lately that she knew when to stop. For a minute they sat staring at the moon, which was now an astonishing bronze disk hanging above the barn. No words seemed pure enough to touch it. Out of the blue darkness, from the depths of her memory, she heard Zayda Landowski's voice say, *"Shayne vee dee levooneh."* A song, or maybe just a compliment to a beloved child: "Beautiful like the moon."

"Jewel, I want to ask you a weird question. This house where you all grew up. Has anybody ever seen ghosts in it?"

"Stop that! You told me that time that Mommy was hainting the kitchen, and it gave me the all-overs."

"This is different. I'm talking about happy ghosts."

Jewel waved her hand, as if to chase away gnats.

But Lusa persisted: "When it rains, I hear children running on the stairs."

"That'd be the roof, I expect. That old house is noisy as the dickens in the rain."

"I know what you're talking about. I hear music and words sometimes when it's raining; that's the tin-roof noise. I've been having whole conversations with my grandfather, who used to play the clarinet. But this is different. Sometimes even when it's not raining, I hear children climbing the stairs, really fast, in a kind of a tumble, the way several kids would come up the stairs all at once. I've heard it a bunch of times."

Jewel just looked at her.

"You think I'm nuts, don't you?"

"No-oh."

"You do, too. Too much time alone, a widow losing her marbles. Which is true, I am. But if you heard what I'm talking about you'd be amazed. It's so real. Every time I hear it, I swear I have to stop my work and go to the steps, and I absolutely expect to see real children coming up. I'm not saying it's 'kind of like the sound of footsteps.' It *is* the sound of feet on the steps."

"Well, who is it, then?"

Lusa looked at Jewel, really examined her. Even in the dark she could see steep lines carved into her face that hadn't been there a month ago. It was as if some wires had got crossed, and all the grief Lusa felt inside were showing on Jewel's exterior. "Are you all right?" she asked.

Jewel gave her a guarded look. "What do you mean?"

"I mean you don't look so hot. Too tired, or something."

Jewel adjusted the flowered scarf tied over her hair, a sort of babushka that didn't help any. "I *am* tired. Sick and tired." She sighed.

"What of?"

"Oh, honey. It's all right. I'm managing. Don't ask, because I don't want to talk about it tonight. I just want to come up here and eat ice cream with you all and watch the fireworks and have fun, for once." She sighed deeply. "Ask me tomorrow, OK?"

"OK, I guess. But you've got me worried."

"I better go see if Lowell's going to need hospitalized. He's probably forgotten about it, but if I don't put a Band-Aid on it now he'll wake up at three in the morning thinking he's going to die." She tried, slowly, to push herself to her feet. Lusa jumped up and helped her, then scooped up her two bottles off the grass. One was still full.

"Did you see me parading around here with a bottle of booze in each hand? I expect Mary Edna's praying for my eternal soul."

"Mary Edna's praying for her *husband's* eternal soul, because those jeans fit you like the bark on a tree, and Herb Goins hasn't taken his eyes off your bottom all night."

"Jewel! *Herb?* I thought Herb was a gelding."

"You'd be surprised. He's not the only one, either."

Lusa grimaced. "Get out of here, you're embarrassing me. Go check and make sure there're enough plates and stuff for the ice cream, would you? And make sure they put the peaches and black-berries in it, there're fresh peaches in that cooler already cut up. You put the fruit in last thing."

"We'll figure it out."

"OK. I'll be up in a minute. I just want to walk down to the pond for a second and look at this moon."

The grass laid a cool dampness between the soles of her feet and her rubber thongs. She moved herself along the bank until the moon's reflection hung dead center in the pond, a white, trembling promise as old as night. She felt the enormous sadness inside her waking up. Sometimes it slept, and then she could pretend at life, but then it would rise and crowd out anything else she might try to be, hounding her with the hundred simple ways she could have saved him. He'd had a cold that day. He could have laid off, declined to take that trip over the mountain. If she'd been a better wife she would have kept him home.

"Cole," she said out loud, just to put the round word in her mouth, but then she regretted it because it summoned his presence so fully that her heart began bleeding out wishes: *I wish you were here tonight. I wish I could have back every minute we wasted being mad at each other. I wish we'd had time to make a baby together. I wish.*

"Ssssst."

She turned her head. The wall of the barn that faced the moon was whitewashed in light, but she couldn't see anything else. She smelled smoke, though. Then saw the red bouncing ball of a cigarette's lit tip.

She wiped her eyes quickly, though it was quite dark. "Who is that?"

"Me," came a whisper. "Rickie."

"Little Rickie?" Her coconspirator. She walked toward him, navigating carefully around the marshy spots at the edge of the pond. "Did you see what I got?" she asked him, trying to be glad about this distraction from her self-pity. "Did you check out my field up above the tobacco bottom when you drove in?"

"Shhh!" His hand closed around her wrist in the darkness and he pulled her around the corner of the barn, into deep moon shadow.

"What are you doing, being a bad boy, smoking behind the barn? Here, look how bad *I'm* being." She held out the bottles, which he refused to sample.

"Pew, that hooch of Uncle Frank's is nasty."

"You think? I was just about to decide I liked it."

"That means you're skunked."

"Possibly. Who on earth are you hiding from?"

"Mom."

Lusa laughed a little. There was no end to family charades. "Your mom, the Queen of Camels—from *her* you're concealing your evil habit?"

"Not mine, yours," he said, lighting a cigarette and putting it in her hand. Lusa frowned at it for a few seconds, then put it to her lips and inhaled. After a few seconds she felt a pleasant, tingling rush running through her arms and under her tongue.

"Uh-oh," she said. "I'm liking this. You are a very bad influence. Did you see my goats?"

"Yep. Looked like about forty or fifty up 'air."

"Fifty-eight, I'd like you to know, and not one of them previously pastured with a buck. They've got one now, though, you better believe. If he gets busy and does his job I'll have fifty suckling kids in time for Id-al-Fitr, and my new barn roof paid for."

"Dang, that's something. All from just that one ad in the paper?"

"My telephone ringer *broke,* Rickie. I swear I'm not kidding, that's how much it rang. Have you ever heard of a telephone wearing out? I was in the pickup pretty much dawn to dusk all last week."

"Yeah, Aunt Mary Edna said she seen you coming in and out. She prolly knows how many trips. How much you have to pay out, total?"

"A dollar sixty-five for the ad is my total investment so far. Goose-egg for the goats. You wouldn't believe how thrilled people were to give me these animals. You'd think I was hauling toxic waste off their land."

"You can thank Mr. Walker for that. He's like the granddaddy of all the goats in this county."

"I do thank him—I *did.* I called him up on the phone. He was very nice."

"Nice, huh? That's not what they used to call it up at school."

"Well, I think he's a swell old guy. Totally helpful. You know what he told me? Sometimes you have to rub the buck with a rag and then dance around waving it in the girls' noses, to turn them on."

"O-oh . . . yeah," Rickie said, nodding slowly. "I believe I heard about that down to Oda Black's. Somebody said they seen you up here doing naughty things with goats."

Lusa got elderberry hooch in her nose when she laughed. "They did not."

"Oh, OK. My mistake." He smoked and gazed out at the field. The grass looked white in the moonlight, as if touched with hoarfrost. "Would that really *help*, you think? I mean, why would it?"

"Pheromones," she said.

"What's that?"

"Smells. A whole world of love we don't discuss."

"Huh," he said. "So. Fifty-eight does. Think you'll get fifty kids out of 'em?"

"You bet. And you know what else? You won't believe what else."

"What?"

"Over in the little pasture where I used to keep the calf? Three bucks—my backup men. *And* in the old pasture, the one behind the orchard that's gotten way overgrown with briars? Guess."

"What, more goats?"

"Seventy-one does."

"Shit, girl! You're in business."

"Looks like it. Those are all does that have been pastured with a buck at some point recently, or that people couldn't be sure of. Mr. Walker said not to take them since I couldn't make them come into season right away. But I thought, why not just take them and keep them over there? In October I'll turn my boys loose on them, and then I'll have my second batch of kids born and fattened up in time for Greek Easter and Id-al-Adha."

Rick whistled. "You've done your math."

"A regular goat-breeding genius." She tapped her head. "You're not supposed to count your chickens before they hatch, but I talked to my cousin already, the butcher. He's so excited you wouldn't believe it. He's going to start taking orders in September. He thinks we can make a killing."

"Yeah? How much?"

"Well, not a killing. Enough. Enough to cover the big stuff— the barn repairs I need to get done right now, for instance."

"Per pound, what are we talking about?"

"A dollar sixty, maybe a dollar seventy-five?"

She had no real frame of reference for this price, but Rickie evidently did because he whistled approvingly. "Man. That's *good*." He grinned at her. Her eyes were fully adjusted to the darkness, and she could see him clearly: not exactly a carbon copy of his father, but with exactly the same gleam in his eye. She turned up her bottle and let the tail end of the Serpent bite her tongue.

"Look," he said, pointing up toward the moonlit hillside. She could see the pale, hump-backed shapes of her goats spread evenly over the pasture, the way a child would put them in a drawing. Eventually her eyes made out something else: the movement of the dark billy. He was working his herd, methodically mounting one doe after another. Lusa watched in awe.

"You go, boy," she cheered solemnly. "Make me a new barn roof."

Rick laughed at that.

She looked up at him. "Have you ever noticed what goats do in the rain?"

"Yeah. They get all hunkered up into a horseshoe shape."

"It's the funniest thing. I never knew that before. Yesterday morning when it was pouring rain, I looked out my window and thought, *This* I need, all my goats have come down with polio or something. But then as soon as the rain stopped, they all straightened out again."

"Just goes to show you. You never pay much attention to a goat till he's fixing your barn roof for you."

"How right you are, my friend."

The moon was high now, and smaller, and she felt her grief shrinking with it. Or not shrinking, never really changing, but ceding some of its dominance over the landscape, exactly like the moon. She wondered why that was, what trick of physics made the moon appear huge when it first came up but then return to normal size after it disentangled itself from the tree branches. In its clear light she watched her goats hard at work increasing themselves. She felt that Cole would approve of her ingenuity. But for the first time in all her plotting she also now felt a twinge of sadness for these mothers and for their babies who would all come to naught, at least from a maternal point of view. Yes, it was food, and people needed food and their merry feasts, but from this end it seemed like so much effort and loss just to repair a barn and pay off some debts on an old, sad farm. For the hundredth time Lusa tried and failed to imagine how she was going to stay here, or why. When she tried to describe her life in words, there was nothing at all to hold her in this place. And words were all she could offer over the phone to her father, to Arlie and her other friends, to her former boss: "Less than a year," she was starting to say, "I'll be out of here."

But there were so many other things besides words. There were the odors of honeysuckle and freshly turned earth, and ancient songs played out on the roof by the rain. Moths tracing spirals in the moonlight. Ghosts.

"Rick," she said, "do you ever see ghosts?"

"You mean real ones?"

"As opposed to imaginary ones?" She laughed. "I guess that means no. Sorry I asked."

"Why? You been seeing ghosts?"

"They're in my house. It's full of them. Some are mine, people from my own family—my dead grandfather, specifically. And some are your family. Some I can't identify."

"Scary."

"No, that's the funny thing, is they're not. They're all really happy. They're good company, to tell you the truth. They make it seem less lonely in the house."

"I don't know, Lusa. Sounds a little bit cuckoo."

"I know it does." He'd used her name—no one else in the family did, ever—and he had not called her *Aunt* Lusa. Whatever this meant, it stopped the conversation for a minute.

"Well," she said finally. "I just wanted to tell somebody. Sorry."

"No, it's OK. It's kind of interesting. I never seen any ghosts, but I never seen Alaska, either, and it's probably up there."

"That's a sensible philosophy."

"What do they look like?"

She glanced at him. "Are you really interested?"

He shrugged. "Yeah."

"They're not like in the movies. They're like actual people, in my house. Kids, to be exact. Mostly they play on the steps. This morning I heard them whispering. I got up and looked down over the banister and they were sitting there on the second step from the bottom, with their backs to me."

"Who was?" Now he was interested.

"Promise you won't tell anybody this."

"Cross my heart."

"Cole and Jewel. A boy and a girl, and that's who they were. About four and seven years old, maybe."

"Nuh-uh. You sure?"

"Yes."

"You never knew Cole when he was little, though," he pointed out.

She gave him a look. "You're questioning my scientific accuracy? They were *ghosts!* I don't know how I knew it was him, I just did. I've seen pictures, and you know, or maybe you don't, but when you've been that close to somebody you can learn to know their whole life. It was him, OK? And your aunt Jewel, brother and sister. She had her arm around his shoulders like she meant to protect her kid brother from the whole big world. Like she knew she'd lose him someday. All of the sudden I understood this whole new thing about both of them, how close they'd been. And I felt really sad for Jewel."

"Everybody feels sad for Aunt Jewel. Talk about getting the short end of the stick."

"What, because her husband left her?"

"Yeah, Uncle Shel hitting the road, and then Cole dying, and her kids' being messed up, and now getting sick."

"What sick, *how* sick?"

"I don't even know. Honest to God, they don't tell me anything. They act like I'm a little kid. But I have eyes, I can see her hair's falling out."

"Oh no," Lusa whispered, looking down. "God. Is it cancer?"

"I think so. Of the . . ." He touched his chest. "She had that operation last year, on both sides, but it's still got all through her."

"Last *year*? After I moved here, or before?"

"I'm not really sure. It was all hush-hush, even in the family. Nobody knows down at church. Not even her boss at Kroger's. He'd prolly fire her."

Lusa found no words; she could only shake her head from side to side.

"Aunt Hannie-Mavis's been taking her to Roanoke for these treatments. I only know that because she brings both their kids over for Mom and my sisters to baby-set when they go. They never told me anything, really, I just put two and two together."

"They haven't told me, either," Lusa said. "I knew something serious was wrong. Damn it, I *knew* that, and they won't even let me help." Her voice cracked. She felt flushed and weak-kneed from this awful news and feared that if she started to cry she might not stop. He put his arm around her. Just from the simple comfort of that gesture, tears flooded her eyes.

"They don't want to put more worries on you," he said. "You've already been through the worst there is."

"Not the worst. I'm still alive."

"I think it'd be worse losing the person you love than dying yourself."

To her embarrassment, this made her cry helplessly. He was so young, how could he know that? She pressed her face against the cotton of his white T-shirt and the warmth of his chest and let herself stay there, sobbing, wishing she could fly away from here. In her mind she could easily picture it: throwing things in a suitcase, books and clothes, practically nothing—she'd leave behind all the heavy family furniture. Just run down the steps and away. But those two children were on the landing with their backs to her, impossible to get around. They stopped her.

Rick had been standing silent for a long while, she realized, holding her patiently, stroking her hair with his other hand. She took a breath.

"I'm sorry," she said, pulling her face away and avoiding his eyes.

"Don't be. It got my arm around you for a minute. I'd like to do more than that: I'd like to fix your whole barn roof." He put his finger under her chin and to Lusa's utter shock leaned down and kissed her very quickly on the lips.

"Rick," she said, feeling some form of hysteria rise through her body, "*Little Rickie.* I'm your *aunt.* For God's sakes." This was like a movie, she thought. The woman with no desire left in her, pursued for an evening by every man.

"I'm sorry," he said, really meaning it. He actually took a step back from her. "Oh, Lord, that was dumb. Don't be mad. I don't know what I was thinking, OK?"

She laughed. "I'm not mad. And I'm not laughing at you, I'm laughing at me. You're a very handsome man. Your girlfriend is very lucky to have you."

He didn't comment on that. He was looking at her, trying to guess what damage he'd done. "You won't, like, tell anybody, will you?"

"No, of course not. Who would I tell?" She smiled, shaking her head and wiping her eyes with her palm. "Here's the really funny thing: your dad was considering making the same pass half an hour ago."

"My *dad?* Him and *you?*"

"Don't act so shocked. Is that any worse than *you* and me?"

But now he was angry. "God*damn*, my dad! He didn't get any-where, did he? I mean, what did he try?"

She regretted her indiscretion; she'd forgotten somehow that this was a child and his father. Lusa had no instincts for such things—she wasn't a mother. "He didn't really try anything," she amended calmly. "He didn't get past the planning stages."

"Man! That old lech," he said, shaking his head sadly. "And now look at him. He's up there jacking off in front of everybody with bottle rockets instead."

"You're very bad."

"I am."

"But you're right. I guess I'd better go supervise the show. So I can write up a good report for the insurance after they burn the place down."

He touched her shoulder, stopping her. "Just don't be mad, OK. I like us being friends, Aunt Lusa. I'm sorry I messed up."

"Rick, I'm not mad." She looked at her hands and clinked her bottles together, hesitating. She still felt startled by the taste of his mouth, the smoke and human pungency that had struck through her numbness into some living place at her core. "You know some-thing? I'm lonely, I'm losing my mind, and it felt so good to have your arms around me, I can't even think about it. I should be thank-ing you. That's it, end of subject." She gave him a quick hug and left him there in his cloud of smoke.

She mounted the hill slowly, amazed by the vision of lights opening out ahead of her. Hundreds of luminous fireflies were ris-ing out of the grass while red and blue sparks rained down from the sky. All her sisters-in-law were busy feeding children or cleaning up, but the men were glued to their lawn chairs, hooting as the bombs went off. One after another the missiles rocketed crazily out over the pond or into the catalpa tree, setting dozens of small, hissing fires among the leaves.

"Aaaw," the male voices cried in unison when one misfired

sideways into the grass. Then came a solid, beery cheer when the next one shot straight up with a loud hiss, popping open above their heads, flinging its sparkling seeds to the wind.

Lusa bit her lip against the strange ache in her belly. This night was out of control completely, she thought, but what could you do? We're only what we are: a woman cycling with the moon, and a tribe of men trying to have sex with the sky.

{16}

Predators

oof!" she cried aloud, jerking backward as if she'd touched electricity. That right there was a copperhead. Slowly she pulled her weed hook back from the briars she'd been clearing away from the edge of the trail. In one slow, steady motion she brought the tool's handle up to rest on her shoulder while the rest of her body held perfectly still, catching up with its lost breath. Not all snakes did that to her anymore. She'd seen enough of them now to conquer the instinctive recoil; normally, when a slender-headed snake raced underfoot, a dark nose tapering to body in a streamlined profile, her mind instantly recognized a friend. But a triangular head made her go cold. Like a yield sign, she'd thought once before, only here in the woods it means *stop*. Here every bird and mammal knew that shape advertised a venomous status—the profile common to pit vipers in general and copperheads in particular. This one sunning itself at the trail's edge was especially fat-bodied, marked in a diamond pattern like a long argyle sock in coppery hues of brownish pink and deep rose. They were beautiful colors, but they did not add up to an appealing creature.

Easy, stand your ground, her dad would sing in a low monotone. The first copperhead of her life they'd found in the barn, coiled under a hay bale they were fixing to carry outside for the cattle. She'd yelped and darted for the loft door that once, but never again. *You can't run away till you know where "away" is. You could be headed straight for his maw.* Now she kept her boots planted as she watched this fellow coil lazily over himself, headed in several directions at once, in no hurry to choose a course. She breathed deeply and tried not to hate this snake. Doing his job, was all. Living out his life like the thousand other copperheads on this mountain that would never be seen by human eyes; they wanted only their one or two rodents a month, the living wage, a contribution to balance. Not one of them wanted to be stepped on or, heaven forbid, to have to sink its fangs into a monstrous, inedible mammal a hundred times its size—a waste of expensive toxin at best. She knew all this. You can stare at a thing and know that you personally have no place in its heart whatsoever, but keeping it out of *yours* is another matter.

Finally the wide-jawed head nudged out of the sunlight into the tall grass. The body elongated and followed in a sinuous line, flowing downhill. Shortly the head reappeared, tongue flickering, ten feet away, in another patch of sunlight. The fixed line of its mouth ran back from the blunt nose in a little upcurve, like an ironic smile. It was just an illusion created by the deep jowls with the fangs tucked inside, she knew, but it filled her with sudden emotion. The fear and anger and queasiness in her stomach made her feel weak, but there it was. She hated the thing for its smile.

"You stay there," she said to its unblinking stare. "Wipe that grin off your face." She turned and headed uphill toward the cabin with the stout scythe balanced over her shoulder. Her legs felt as heavy as water. There was no reason to feel this tired, except maybe the aftermath of an adrenaline rush, but she was ready to quit for the day. Eat a late lunch, curl up with a book. Rain was coming. She'd heard unexpectedly loud thunder several times already this morning (each boom had made her jump, as the snake had): a storm rolling in from Kentucky. She took a shortcut back to the jeep road through a ten-year-old clear cut that was overgrown now but still sunny, and full of cockleburs. She tried to avoid this route in summer so she wouldn't have to spend an hour afterward picking the burrs off her jeans. But she didn't want to get caught in the storm. She swiped her weed cutter at the dense stands of bristly seedpods, taking her own perverse satisfaction in their presence, here and everywhere. Parakeets' revenge, was how she liked to think of them. They'd coevolved with an expert seed eater, the Carolina parakeet, which had gone extinct so soon after Europeans settled that little was known about it but this one thing, its favorite food. John James Audubon painted the birds' portrait with their mouths full, feasting among cockleburs, and he wrote of how the bright flocks would travel up and down the river valleys searching the burrs out, descending noisily wherever they found the bristly stands and devouring them until hardly any were left. That was hard to imagine, a scarcity of cockleburs. Now they went uneaten and would continue so for the rest of time. Now they grabbed the ankles of travelers and spread into fields and farms, roadside ditches, even woodland clearings, trying to teach a lesson that people had forgotten how to know.

She picked up her step when the first fat raindrops began to spatter through the leaves. An hour ago she'd been sweating, but as the storm moved in she felt the air temperature plummet as if she were swimming deep into a lake. She stopped to untie her windbreaker from around her waist and put it on, pulling the hood forward to her eyebrows before taking off again at a trot. By the time the trail met the Forest Service road that ran up from the valley, she'd picked up her pace to a dead run.

She slowed down on the road because its ruts could turn an ankle, and because the mountain was steep; she needed to catch her wind. Why did people always run in the rain? She still had half a mile to go, so she'd be soaked when she got home, regardless. She smirked at herself, then stopped to listen.

It was a vehicle. She stood waiting for it to round the corner so she could see what manner of human intrusion this was to be. Sad to say, she assumed people meant trouble. She knew the Forest Service wouldn't approve of her inhospitable outlook, but this mountain would be a superior place if people stayed off it altogether. She waited, feeling her shoulders tense up, and was surprised when the flat green flank of the Forest Service jeep appeared through the damp tree trunks. *Today?* What was it, July already?

She thought about this. Yes, well into the first week of July. Darn it, they'd sent up her supplies, and she'd missed what's-his-name again. Jerry Lind was his name, the guy who usually drove up with her mail and groceries. She needed to give him her requisition. Her heart was pounding, and not just from running uphill. Eddie Bondo was up there. This morning she'd left him sitting on the porch in his bare feet reading her *Field Guide to the Eastern Birds*. Oh, hell.

"Hey, Deanna! You look like the Grim Reaper." Jerry was driving with his head stuck out the open window.

"Hey, Jerry. You look like Smokey the Bear."

He touched his hat brim. "Keeps the rain off." He cut the engine, slowing to a roll next to Deanna and then pulling the brake on hard, causing the whole vehicle to jerk. The road here was deeply cut with ruts that were starting to run like small chocolate rivers. She cocked her left foot up against the jeep to tie her soggy bootlaces.

"What'd you do with my stuff, just plunk it down on the porch stoop?"

"Nah, I put it inside. With rain coming. Your mail's on the table with the food boxes. I put your bottled gas for your stove on the porch."

She studied him for some sign of what he'd discovered at the cabin. "You run into any trouble?" she asked cautiously.

"What, you mean that door? I'd say so—those hinges are ninety percent rust. You got any WD-40, or should I bring you up some next month?"

That was all he'd run into? Trouble getting the door open? She watched his face. "I got oil," she said slowly. "I do have a list for you, though, for next month. I need some lumber to patch up a bridge, and I've got a list of books I need."

Jerry shifted his hat and scratched his forehead. "Man alive, more *books*. Don't you ever want, like, a TV?"

"A TV that runs on batteries? Don't tell me they make such a thing. I don't even turn on the radio I've got."

"You don't listen to the *radio?* Man. The President could get shot or something and you wouldn't know it for a month."

She dropped her left foot and hiked up her right to retie her other bootlace. "Tell me something, Jerry. If the President got shot this afternoon, what would you do tomorrow that'd be any different from what you'd do if he hadn't?"

Jerry considered the question. "Nothing whatsoever, except probably watch a bunch of TV. On CNN, see, they'd tell you every fifteen minutes that he was still dead."

"Why I like my life, Jerry. I watch birds. They do something *different* every fifteen minutes."

"Get in," he said. "I'll drive up and get your req list. I promise I won't tell you any news from the world."

"All right." She walked around behind the boxy metal truck to climb in on the passenger's side, tossing her weed hook onto the floor behind the seats with a loud clang. "What were you going to do if you didn't run into me, just repeat last month's requisition?"

"Wouldn't be the first time." The jeep lurched forward in pulses as Jerry lifted his foot off the brake. The road was extremely steep.

"That's true, it wouldn't," she agreed. "I'm still eating the rice you doubled up on me in November." What had he seen in the cabin? She felt embarrassed and raw, as if Jerry had seen her naked. She studied him for signs of his thoughts while receiving whiplash in small doses as the jeep pitched downhill. Jerry seemed like his usual self—a kid, in other words. She resisted telling him to gear down and use the transmission instead of the brake. Who was she to backseat-drive? She hadn't driven a car in two years.

He squinted at the single-lane track. The shoulder dropped off steeply to the left, while the mountain rose straight up to the right. "I never had to backtrack on this road before. Is there someplace wide enough to turn around?"

"Not for about a mile and a half. Down at that farm's the first place it widens out." She shifted in her seat. "Who owns that place at the bottom of the hollow? I guess you wouldn't know."

"I do, though; it's the Widener place. Cole Widener. Forest Service had to get a right-of-way through him when we rehabbed this cabin. Before you came."

She looked off to the side, thinking about it. "Wideners," she said, nodding slowly. "They've got some kind of timber, let me tell you. There's some virgin stuff in there, I swear, right back up against our border. Every year I'm scared to death they'll discover what they've got and log it. It'd cut the heart out of some wonderful habitat, all the way up this side of the mountain."

"Hey, he died, I heard. Truck blew two tires on the same side at once and he hit a bridge piling or something. On Seventy-seven, going over the mountain."

"Jerry, no news. You promised."

"Oh. Sorry."

"That's sad, though. I wonder who that farm will go to now. They'll log it, I bet anything."

"That I can't tell you."

"Widener. What was his first name? You said it a minute ago."

"Cole, like Old King Cole. Except I heard he was pretty young."

"Cole. I'm trying to think if I knew him. I went to school with Wideners, but they were girls." Not a very friendly bunch, either, as she recalled. They came to school in handmade dresses and kept to their own company like a club.

"Don't ask me," Jerry said cheerfully.

"I know. You're from Roanoke, and you're twelve."

"Yes ma'am, that's almost right. Twenty-four, actually. So," he said, still rolling very slowly downhill. "A turnaround?"

"Oh, sorry. There's really no place reasonable—your best bet here's to just put it in reverse and back uphill real slow."

Jerry followed her advice, though it was a tricky business to negotiate the road uphill and backward. "Dang," he said repeatedly, driving with his body half turned around, frequently turning the wheels the wrong way. "This is like writing your name in a mirror."

"You know what, Jerry? You could just park. I'll walk up and get my list."

"That's OK, sit tight, I'll drive you."

Deanna felt uneasy approaching the cabin. He'd missed running into Eddie his first time up, apparently, but good luck didn't strike twice. "No, really," she said, "I don't care to walk it. Stop here, it'll just take me ten minutes."

"You don't *care to?* Or you wouldn't *mind?*"

She looked at him, exasperated. "Would you please just let me out?"

He continued his slow backward progress, letting one tire run off the road for a second. "It'd take you an hour, and it's raining cats and dogs. What's wrong with you, you got the all-overs?"

"Whatch'all doin', Jurry, takin' a college course somewheres in hillbilly English?"

"My mammaw says that, 'You've got the all-overs.' She's from Grundy."

"Fine. I've got the all-overs from sitting here waiting for you to rear-end a tree or plow over the cliff. Will you just let me walk?"

"No."

She gave up. Fighting with Jerry to be allowed walk in the rain seemed ridiculous. She faced forward and watched the road wind out in front of them like a film running backward in slow motion. Could he really be that blind? Even if Eddie Bondo hadn't been there, the cabin was full of him. His coffeepot on the stove, his pack under the bed. Come to think of it, there were very few signs. There was next to nothing. She relaxed.

"Hey, I met your boyfriend."

"*What!*"

"He's pretty cool. I never met anybody from Wyoming before."

"What'd you do, interview him? He's not my boyfriend, Jerry. He's just a friend who hiked up to see me for a couple days. He's packing out tomorrow."

"Yeah, right."

"What?" she asked.

"Nothing. He's packing out tomorrow."

Well, Deanna thought, he might be, for all she knew. She shifted her legs; this jeep wasn't built for tall people. Soldiers must have been short in World War II. "Why does everybody assume *boyfriend* when a girl and a guy are friends?"

Jerry touched his fist to his mouth and cleared his throat. "Maybe because of the twenty-five-pack of rubbers laying on the floor by the bed?"

She turned to face him, openmouthed. "*Lying* on the floor. Jesus, Jerry, that's none of your business. He's just a friend, OK? People see a single woman and think she's got to have a man hidden somewhere."

Damn him, she thought, why couldn't he have been gone? Last month when Jerry brought the mail he was gone, *usually* he was gone, last week he'd stormed out and stayed away for four days, in the rain, just because she'd looked at him wrong. Of all the days for Eddie Disappearing Act Bondo to get domestic.

"OK," Jerry said. "Whatever you say."

Deanna stared ahead. "He probably thought *you* were my boyfriend."

Jerry blushed.

"Scary thought, huh, Jur? Gives you the all-overs, don't it?"

"I didn't say that."

"OK, just pull in here by the cabin. I'll run in and get my req list. And don't you be telling the boss I've requisitioned extra food for a visitor, OK? Because I haven't."

"I'm not going to tell on you, Deanna. Government employees are allowed to have a life. At the office I think they'd all be *glad* if you were shacking up with some guy up here. They worry about you."

"Oh, do they?"

"They think you should come down on furlough more often. You've got about a hundred vacation days saved up that you've never used."

"How do you know I've never used them? Maybe I'm on vacation right now."

"You *live* here," he said firmly. "You *work* here. You take a vacation in *civilization*. TV, electricity, city streets, cars, honk honk. Remember?"

"Not my idea of civilized, pal." She slammed the jeep door and headed her long-legged stride toward the cabin. She flung open the door with no heed for its rusty hinges and stood for a second inside the doorway, glowering at Eddie Bondo in his blue corduroy shirt, unbuttoned. He was reading, leaning so far back in the chair that it was balanced on its two hind legs like a dancing dog. She pointed a finger at him.

"As soon as he's out of here, I've got a crow to pick with you."

Eddie raised his eyebrows.

She snatched the requisition list off the desk and was out the door again. Through the kitchen window he could see her out there standing in the rain, talking a mile a minute to the kid in the hat. She could picture how she looked to him; her hood had slid off the back of her head, her hands flew as she spoke, and her braid hung out the bottom of her jacket, lashing at the backs of her knees like the tail of an animal setting off at a gallop. When she bent over to pull her long-handled scythe from behind the seat, the kid cowered as if he thought she might take his head off. Eddie Bondo would be smiling.

She hung up her tools on the outside of the cabin with a hard thump while the jeep turned out and puttered down the hill.

"What are you grinning at?" she demanded when she came back in. "I saw a copperhead a while ago, making a face just like that."

"I'm grinning at you, girl. Just like that snake was."

"Should I chop you into pieces like I did him?"

"Don't lie, tough girl. You didn't hurt a hair on his little copper head."

She looked at him. "*What,* then?"

"Nothing. You're just beautiful, that's all. You look like some kind of a goddess when you're mad."

What did he think she was, some high school girl he could sweet-talk? Tight-lipped, she began to shove pots and pans around, putting away cans from the wooden crates Jerry had left on the table. She lugged the huge, mouseproof canisters out from under the pantry shelves and heaved in the sacks of beans and corn flour. Eddie Bondo couldn't stop grinning.

"I'm not kidding," she warned him. "I'm just about mad enough to throw you out, rain or no rain."

He looked amused by this toothless threat. "What did I do now?"

She turned around to face him. "You couldn't have gone out? You couldn't just step into the outhouse or something for ten minutes when you heard the jeep?" She stood with her hands on her hips, amazed, as if confronted with a fabulously unruly child. "For once it didn't occur to you to disappear?"

"No, it didn't. May I ask why I'm supposed to hide?"

She went back to slamming cupboards. "Because you don't exist, that's why."

"Interesting," he said, looking at the backs of his hands.

"I mean here you don't. You're not a part of my life." She unzipped her parka and came out of it like a snake shedding its skin, shaking out the full length of her miraculous hair. She hung the windbreaker on a peg, wrung out the end of her braid, sat down on the bed with a put-out sigh, and began unlacing her soaked boots. With one damp, wool-stockinged foot she kicked the long string of condoms back into the darkness under the bed. "Jerry was impressed with your supply of prophylactics," she said.

"Oh, I see. I blew your cover. Deanna the Virgin She-wolf has her reputation to think about."

She glared at him. "Would you put all four legs of that chair on the floor, please? I've only just got the one. I'd thank you for not breaking it."

He obliged, with a thump. Closed his book, looked at her, waited.

"Rainy day got you down?" he asked finally. "PMS? What?"

The PMS joke made her wrathful. She had a mind to tell him the truth, that she was apparently menopausal. July's early full moon had snuck past her with no ovulation, and she couldn't even recall when she'd menstruated last. Her body was going cold on her. She tossed her boots at the door and stood up to pull off her soaked jeans. She didn't care if he watched or not, she didn't even feel like being modest. She was no virgin she-wolf, just an old woman with no more patience for keeping a boy around.

"What reputation?" she said, hanging her wet clothes on a peg near the stove and getting a clean towel out of the cabinet. "Other than Jerry and the guy who cuts my paycheck, there's hardly anybody who remembers I'm up here. I'm that far gone."

As she toweled her hair, she bent over toward the wood stove. Her chilled-to-the-bone body was treating it as a source of warmth, she realized, even though there was no fire there. She also noticed he was watching every move of her naked limbs, taking in the long muscles of her thighs.

"If you don't care what people think," he said, "then what's the problem? Why was I supposed to hide from young Smokey?"

"He's not that much younger than you are. You're both just a couple of kids. Button your shirt, my God, it's freezing in here."

"Yes, Mother." He made no move to button his shirt.

She stood up, hugging the towel to her chest. "Why are we playing house here, you and me? Do you know I'm forty-seven years old? The year you were learning to walk, I had my first affair with a married man. Does that not freak you out?"

He shook his head. "Not really."

"Does me. All of it does. That I spent six years researching an animal you'd like to see purged from the planet. That I'm half a foot taller than you. Nineteen years older. If we walked down the street together in Knoxville, people would gawk."

"As far as I know, walking down the street together in Knoxville is not in the plans."

She sat on the bed in her underwear, shivering, feeling suddenly too exhausted even to sit up. She got under the blankets and pulled them up to her chin. She tried that out, looking at him sideways from the pillow. "As far as I know, there *are* no plans."

"Is that a problem?"

"No," she said, miserably.

He put his bare feet flat on the floor and leaned forward with his elbows on his knees. When he spoke again he used a new version of his voice, quieter and kinder. "I guess we might seem like a weird pair to anybody who was looking. But if nobody's looking, there's no weirdness. I thought it was pretty simple."

"If pride falls in the forest and nobody hears it, did it really fall?"

He blinked. "What?"

"You're ashamed of me," she said. "*I'm* ashamed of me, of us. Otherwise we'd be able to walk down the street anywhere."

He studied her face, seeming momentarily older—as if he could will himself into moments of maturity, she thought, but normally just didn't bother. He was twenty-eight, a juvenile male. Like a yearling red-tailed hawk with his dark adult feathers just starting to show through. On the matter of mate choice, she was apparently addled.

"Where I come from, people keep their treasure under the mattress," he offered finally. "They don't have to advertise it all over creation."

"But if they keep it hidden they never get to use it."

"What is there to *use* about you and me? Where are we supposed to be spending ourselves besides here?"

"Nowhere. I don't know what I'm saying. Forget it."

He sat up against the straight chair back and crossed his arms over his chest. "I know what you're saying. I'm really not all that stupid. My immaturity notwithstanding."

She lay still for a long time, looking at him from her prone position. His blue-green eyes, the exposed skin of his chest, the white bone buttons on his corduroy shirt—all of his planes and angles held a clear light whose beauty cut her like a knife.

"Eddie. It's not like I want to get married and live happily ever after."

He winced a little, she thought, at the blunt mention of that possibility, even in the negative. "If you did," he said slowly, "I'd be in Alberta about now."

"Alberta, Canada?" she asked. "Or Alberta, Kentucky? Just how repellent are we talking about here?"

He stared at her, offering no answer.

She shook her head. "You're not big enough to break my heart. I'm not some schoolgirl, give me a little credit. But I'm not sure I can be like you, either."

"What does that mean, 'like me'?"

"Living with no plans at all. I keep bumping into walls." She rolled onto her back, unable to look at him anymore. "When I moved up here I thought I'd be just like the phoebes and wood thrushes. Concentrate on every day as it came, get through winter, rejoice in summer. Eat, sleep, sing hallelujah."

"Eat, sleep, screw your heart out, sing hallelujah."

"Well, yeah." She covered her face with both hands and rubbed her eyes. "The birds were getting a lot more action than me. But you know what? Turns out they *do* have a plan. I'm an outsider, I'm just watching. They're all doing their own little piece of this big, rowdy *thing*. Their plan is the persistence of life on earth, and they are working on it, let me tell you."

"You're persisting."

"In a real limited way. When I'm dead, what have I made that stays here? A master's thesis in the U.T. library, which eleven people on the face of the earth have read or ever will."

"I would read it," he said. "So, twelve people."

"You don't want to." She gave a short, unenthusiastic laugh. "It's the last thing you'd ever want to read. It's about coyotes."

"What about them?"

She turned her head to look at him. "Everything about them. Their populations, how they've grown and changed over time. One of the things it shows is how people's hunting them actually increases their numbers."

"That can't be."

"You wouldn't think so. But it's true. I've got a hundred pages of proof."

"I think I ought to read that."

"If you want to. It'd be a nice gesture." A gift before parting, she thought. She turned back to the ceiling and closed her eyes, feeling the distant pressure of a headache coming on. His reading it, or not, wouldn't buy her a place in the scheme of the planet. She pressed her fingertips to her eyelids. "Maybe it's my age, Eddie. You've got more time to pretend your life is endless. Before you face up to the bigger picture."

He didn't ask her about the bigger picture. And he didn't get up and walk out the door. He asked if she would like him to make a fire, and she said she would. Her body was shivering visibly. She pulled the blankets over her head, leaving a small window through which she could watch his careful, steady hands place kindling inside the stove. She thought about the things people did with their highly praised hands: made fires that burned out; sawed down trees to build houses that would rot and fall down in time. How could those things compare with the grace of a moth on a leaf, laying perfect rows of tiny, glassy eggs? Or a phoebe weaving a nest of moss in which to hatch her brood? Still, as she watched him light a match and bring warmth into the cabin while the rain pounded down overhead, she let herself feel thankful for those hands, at least for right now. When he climbed into bed beside her, they held her until she fell asleep.

"You're getting sick," he told her when she opened her eyes again.

She sat up, groggy and unsure of the time of day. He was up and dressed, shirt buttoned, even, working at the stove. He'd hooked up the new bottle of propane—a regular handyman. "What time is it?" she asked. "What do you mean I'm getting sick?"

"You sneezed in your sleep. Four times. I never heard anybody do that before."

She stretched her limbs, feeling very tired and a little achy from the weed cutting, but nothing else. No headache; that threat had passed. "I think I'm OK." She inhaled the rich, convivial scent of onions frying in oil, something wonderful. Occasionally it took all her wits to resist loving this man. She thought of coyotes; that helped. Something big enough to break her heart.

"You sneezed in your sleep," he insisted. "I'm going out to get some more firewood." He dumped two handfuls of chopped vegetables into the pot, poured in water from the kettle, and settled the iron lid on it with a happy little ring.

"Is it dark? Wait! What time is it?" She scratched her scalp and squinted at the window.

"Dusk. Why?"

"Be careful about the phoebe nest on the porch. Don't scare her off the nest. If she goes off it this late she might stay off all night, and the kids will freeze."

"It's not that cold out. It's July."

"For a featherless little quarter ounce of bird it's cold out. They'll die overnight if she's not on them."

Eddie seemed to have trouble believing in the summertime cold up here, what people called blackberry winter. But he knew the truth of her warning, that a bird chased off its nest at dusk wouldn't come back. She might sit fifty feet away from it, crying out to her babies all night, stranded. Deanna had never known exactly why, but Eddie had told her what a hunter knows about animal perceptions: most birds can't see in the dark. From one minute to the next, at dusk, they go blind and can't see at all.

He smiled at her from the doorway. "I don't need four dead babies on my conscience, on top of all my other sins."

"It's important," she persisted.

"I know it is."

"It *is*. She's already lost one brood, thanks to us tromping around out there."

"I'll be careful," he said. "I'll tiptoe."

He did, apparently. She didn't hear another sound until he came back in and stoked up the fire. She felt the mattress shift when he sat down on it, heard the hiss of the match, and smelled its sulfur when he leaned over to light the kerosene lamp on the table beside the bed. "Roll over, I'll rub your back where it hurts."

"What'd you do, eat some Mr. Nice Guy mushrooms?" She opened her eyes. "How do you know my back hurts?"

"I'm always a nice guy, you just fail to see through my irritating demeanor." He kissed her forehead. "You're coming down with something. The flu or something. You felt hot as a furnace a while ago. Roll over."

"The epizooty," she said. "Nannie used to say that. It's a catchall disease category." She rolled over and lay with her face buried in the pillow, smiling, suffocating with comfort as he massaged her shoulders. "Nannie was my dad's girlfriend," she said into the pillow, which muffled her words completely.

"What?"

She turned over onto her back. "Nannie was my dad's girlfriend."

"Oh. I thought you said, 'Eddie is a mad birdbrain.'"

"Well, yeah. That, too."

"The apple-orchard lady, I know. You got free apples, and old Dad got lucky." His hands moved expertly down her sides, working gently from rib to rib but pausing just under her breasts and finally resting there, distracting her senseless. When she could no longer stand the suspense, he unzipped his jeans and got under the quilts. For a long time he stroked her without speaking.

"So," she said. "You remember this junk I tell you about my life?"

"She had a baby with a hole in her heart. But she wouldn't marry your dad."

"You do remember. I'm never sure if you're listening."

"No future doesn't mean I'm not here *now*."

She wanted to believe it but couldn't, quite. "I don't know why you'd invest the effort," she said. "If you're just going to have to forget it all later."

"You think I'm going to forget you when we're finished here?"

"Yes."

"No." He kissed her for a long time. She kept her eyes open, watching. Kissing her with his eyes closed, he looked so vulnerable and yielding that it was nearly painful to see it.

"I'll forget you," she lied softly into his mouth. "The minute you're gone."

He pulled away from her a little, looking at her eyes to see what she meant. She couldn't focus as close as he could. That was age, again.

"I'll make sure you don't," he promised, and she shivered, feeling the prescience of some deep change or damage. He would make sure. The coyotes came unbidden to her mind: children in the woods, huddled in their den away from the storm.

But Eddie Bondo's mind seemed to be here, focused on her, making amends for whatever hurt he felt he'd delivered earlier—the Alberta crack, she supposed. This was their strange dance. More than once now she'd flown into a rage at him and then spent days afterward offering food, cutting his hair, washing his socks, her unguents of apology. It made her think of the bobtail cat she'd had in childhood that would sometimes get mean when they played and scratch her, drawing blood; afterward he would always hunt down a mouse and bring her its liver.

Eddie had rolled on his side and propped himself up on one elbow, the better to uncover her body and look at it. It had taken some getting used to, this. She fought the persistent urge to cover herself with the sheet.

"How come they never got hitched up?" he asked, tracing her aureoles with his index finger. "Your dad and his lady friend."

"Nannie never did want to. I'm not sure why. I guess I admired her for it, though, for knowing her mind and wanting to be on her own. The county gossip was always that *Dad* wouldn't marry *her*."

"You girls always get the losing end of gossip."

"Oh, you noticed. Yeah. And Nannie was kind of an odd bird. She still is. But he would have married her in a second. He was like that, just a plain honorable guy."

"Unlike me."

"Very. I think it turned him sad in the long run, that she wouldn't marry him. Especially after Rachel turned out so sickly.

When she died, it tore everybody up. Dad was losing our farm at the time, and he just fell to pieces drinking. I'm sure it broke Nannie's heart, too, but she wore it better."

"And what about you? She was your sister. Half-sister."

"Yeah, she was. I can't explain it, but I always knew she was going back to Heaven. She'd just come to be my little sister for a while. Rachel was this angel. We'd play pirate ship and I'd be the captain and she'd be the angel. She was happy all the time. She had this kind of creamy skin you could almost see through. It was a local tragedy when she died."

Deanna closed her eyes, feeling weirdly hollow inside from this talk. It might be a fever, making her so loose and dreamy. "Nannie's tough, though; she's carried on all these years. She lives her life how she wants to, no matter what people say."

"So that's where you learned it from."

Deanna laughed. "Oh, boy. You should see what a mess I made out of life. I went to college and proceeded to go to bed with my professors left and right."

He moved his body against hers, all of it, hard and warm and impossible to ignore. "You were pursuing higher learning."

"Low learning. I don't know what I was doing. I think I had this daddy complex. I listened to my instructors. I married one of my instructors. He thought I was brilliant, so I married him. He said I talked like a hillbilly, so I stopped saying 'Hit's purty' and 'Oncet in a while.' He said I should be a teacher, so I got certified and taught school in Knoxville and spent my twenties and half my thirties going out of my gourd."

"What did you teach?"

"Science and math and Please Shut Up, to seventh graders."

While they'd been speaking he had moved on top of her, supporting his weight on his elbows, and gently slid inside her without changing the tone of his voice or the conversation. She inhaled sharply, but he touched a finger to her lips and kept talking. "No, I can't see you with an apple on your desk. I see you throwing chalk."

She lay perfectly still, catching her breath. As if she'd seen a snake.

"Maybe I threw some chalk, I don't remember. I liked the kids sometimes, but mostly I felt like I was under siege." She spoke slowly and calmly, and it all seemed very secret, as if their bodies were hiding from their minds. "I'm an introvert," she continued carefully. "I like being alone. I like being outside in the woods. And there I was. Living in a little brick house in a big-city suburb, spending my days with hundreds of small, unbelievably loud human beings."

He had begun to move inside her, unhurriedly. It took some concentration to keep her voice steady. She felt the corners of her mouth drawing back involuntarily, like the copperhead's smile. "You'd think I could have figured it out, but I was restless for ten years before it dawned on me that I needed to go to graduate school and study wildlife biology and get myself out of there."

"And here you are." He held her eyes, smiling, while he slowly, slowly moved his hips. Her pelvis tilted, reaching for him.

"And here I am."

"And you and the professor never had kids?"

"Oh, that was out of the question. He'd been married before. He had two teenagers already when I met him. The way he did the math, he and his ex-wife had replaced themselves. There was no more room on the earth for him to put another kid."

"Wow. That's some pretty strict math."

"He was like that. German."

"But you hadn't replaced *yourself.*"

"I guess that wasn't his problem. He had a vasectomy."

"And that was that. No regrets?"

"I'm not all that maternal."

He slipped a hand under the small of her back and pushed himself up very far inside her until she began to lose her train of thought. He had a way of reaching against her pelvic bone, creating a kind of pressure in a place no man had found before. Intercourse with Eddie Bondo was a miracle of nature. He held her there, with her back arched, and chuckled softly against her cheek.

"*You.* You spend more time making sure you don't hurt a spider or a baby bird than most people do taking care of their kids. You're maternal."

He was still listening to her. She couldn't even remember what she'd said.

"Shhh," he said suddenly, tightening his grip on her and going perfectly still. "What *is* that?"

They listened to the soft sliding noise overhead in the roof boards. It was a dry, rough, papery scrape, almost like sandpaper moving through slow circles over a rough board. The sound had become nearly constant these days, in the evenings, when the rain wasn't drowning it out.

"It's not a mouse," Deanna conceded finally.

"I know it's not a mouse. You always say it's a mouse, but it's not. It's something long and slidey."

"'Slidey'?" she asked. "And *you* make fun of the way *I* talk?"

"Long and scaly, then."

"Yeah," she said. "It's a snake. Probably a big old blacksnake that came in out of the rain one day, hit the mouse jackpot, and decided to stay."

Eddie Bondo shivered. She felt him going soft inside her, and she laughed. "Don't tell me you're scared of snakes? You are!"

He rolled off of her, throwing an arm over his face.

"Why, my lands, Eddie *Bon*do. A brave guy like you."

"I'm not scared of them. I just don't like the idea of one crawling around above me while I sleep."

"Oh, well, don't sleep, then. Just lie here listening for it. Tell me if he's headed down here for the bed. Good night!" She leaned over, feigning to blow out the lamp.

"Don't do that!" He struck a tone of true panic at the combination of snake and darkness. But then he grabbed her pillow and whacked her with it, to cover his embarrassment. She let the lamp burn and fell back on the bed, delighted with herself.

"Lady," he said, "you are one mean son of a gun."

She took the pillow from him and settled it back under her head, relishing the upper hand. All her life in Zebulon County she'd known big, husky men who worked dispassionately with fierce machinery and steers big enough to kill them, but who freely admitted to a terror of snakes of any kind. At nine years of age Deanna Wolfe had made a legend of herself by bringing an eight-foot blacksnake to school.

"It just does not make any sense to despise that snake up there," she told Eddie. "He's on our side. I hate mice, is what I hate—getting into my food. Making their nest in the drawer so my socks stink like mouse pee. Running over my feet in the morning and making me throw my coffee against the wall. If you took all the snakes out of this world, people would be screaming bloody murder at the rodent plague. Not just here. In cities, too."

"Thank you, Miss Science Teacher. Too bad we're not all as logical as you are. You know what?" He rolled over and whispered in her ear, "You're scared of thunder."

"I'm not, either."

"You are. I've seen you jump."

"That's a startle response, not fear. Thunder is nothing but two walls of split-apart air coming back together, which could not hurt a fly."

He lay back against the pillow beside her, grinning fiercely. "Which causes you to jump out of your skin."

"Mice make me jump, too, but that's not fear, that's disgust."

"OK, then. Snakes aren't scary, they're just disgusting."

"Foolish choices, Eddie. People make them every day, but hating predators on principle is like hating the roof over your head on principle. Me, I'll take one snake over fifty mice in my house any day. A snake in every roof."

He shuddered.

"Snakes have manners, at least—they stay out of your way."

"Stay out of my way," Eddie Bondo said to the roof.

"Don't worry." She pulled the covers up and put her head on his shoulder. It was true that she had her own irrational fears. She spoke quietly, stroking the hard, indented midline of his chest and thinking of the cartilage that sheltered his heart. "It's a single-minded predator, and its prey is not us. From a snake's point of view, we don't even exist. We're nothing to him. We're safe."

They lay still for a minute, listening to the cricket music of a midsummer night. From somewhere nearby she heard the quiet little chirping call of a screech owl. It was not the breathy hoot of the great owls but a more private sound, a high-pitched descending chuckle. She listened for the answer and immediately it came, a series of soft, quick barks the little owls use at close range in breeding season. They were finding each other out there in the darkness, making their love right under the window. Deanna grazed the length of Eddie Bondo's collarbone with her lower lip. "So," she said, "could we go back to our previous conversation?"

"I'm not sure." He lifted the blankets and looked. "Yes."

She rolled away from his arms just long enough to blow out the lamp. In a habit carried over from childhood, her mind whispered a prayer of thanks, as small and quick as the extinction of lamplight into darkness: *Thanks for this day, for all birds safe in their nests, for whatever this is, for life.*

{17}

Old Chestnuts

he bank of Egg Creek was soaked like a sponge with rain. Garnett could only look the hillside up and down and shake his head. The ground had gotten so soft that a fifty-year-old oak growing out of it had leaned over, pulled its roots out of the mud like loose teeth, and fallen over before its time. What a mess. Somebody would have to be called, some young man with a chain saw who could tame this tangle of trunk and branches into a cord of firewood. Oda Black's son, now there was a polite boy who could do it in one morning and not charge a fortune.

The cost wasn't the problem, though. Finding a man to do it wasn't even the problem. This section of Egg Creek stood as the property line dividing Garnett's land from Nannie Rawley's, *that* was the problem. It was only fair that she pay for half the cleanup— or more, really, since it was *her* tree that had fallen on *him*. But they would have to come to some agreement, and for the likes of *that* no precedent existed in the history of Garnett and Nannie.

He stared at the mess and sighed. If only she would come up here and notice it so he wouldn't have to be the one to take the first step. If Garnett brought it up, she would act like he was asking for a favor. Which of course, he was not. He was calling attention to her negligence, was all. Any farmer worth his salt walked his property lines after every storm to look for damage like this. But then there was Nannie Rawley.

"Oh, me," he declared aloud to the birds, some of whom were merrily singing from the branches of the fallen oak without a care over their world's sudden shift from vertical to horizontal. For that matter, the fallen tree still burgeoned with glossy oak leaves—probably still trying to scatter its pollen to the wind and set acorns as if its roots were not straggling in the breeze and its bulk doomed to firewood.

Birds and oak trees have minds like hers, he thought, surveying this profoundly deluded little world with an odd satisfaction.

He noted that more than half a dozen trees along this bank were leaning precariously downhill from her side toward his. The next storm would likely bring down more. One old cherry seemed particularly threatening, with nearly a forty-five-degree lean to it, right out over the path he used to get up here. He made a mental note to walk fast and not tarry anytime he had to pass under it. "Oh, me," he said again, as he turned back down the path toward his house and whatever he had to do next.

It would have to be face-to-face. Not over the telephone. She was never in her house, and she had one of those confounded machines that beeped at you and expected you to speak your whole mind on the spot without even warming up to the subject. His heart couldn't take those things; whenever one surprised him these days he'd have to go lie down afterward. No, he would walk over there today and get Nannie Rawley over with, like a dose of castor oil. Garnett felt a flutter of anger against his fate. Anytime he thought he'd washed his hands of the woman, she'd turn up again somewhere else nearby. She was worse than mildew. Why did God insist on running this woman smack up against him, time and again? He knew the answer, of course: Nannie Rawley was a test of his faith, his cross to bear. But when would enough be enough?

"Haven't I done what I could?" he asked as he walked, raising the palms of his hands and mouthing the words without sound. "I've written letters. I've explained the facts. I've given her scientific advice, and I have given her the Holy Word. Good God, have I not done enough on behalf of that woman's mortal soul?"

One of the leaning trees in the bank shifted hard, with a groan and a crack, causing the old man's heart to leap in his chest like a crazed heifer trapped in the loading chute. He stopped dead on the trail, laying a hand on his chest to calm that poor doomed beast.

"All right," Garnett Walker said to his God. "All *right!*"

Garnett did admire a well-set orchard, he'd give her that much. He liked the cool, shaded ground spread under the trees like a broad picnic blanket, and he liked how the trunks lined up for your eye as you walked through: first in straight rows and then in diagonals, depending on how you looked. A forest that obeyed the laws of man and geometry, that was the satisfaction. Of course, these trees had been planted by old Mr. Rawley back in 'fifty-one or so, while she was off at her college. If *she'd* done the planting, why, they'd surely be all higgledy-piggledy like trees in a woodland glade. She'd have some theory about that being better for the apples.

He knew for a fact she was putting in a new section of trees in the field on the other side of her house, though he hadn't been over there, so he couldn't say if they were straight or not. She'd mentioned that they were scions cloned off one of the wildings that had sprung up in the fallow pasture on the hill behind her orchard. That field looked awful, the way she was letting it grow up, but she claimed it was her and the birds' big experiment and that she'd discovered a particularly good accidental cross up there, which she'd patented under the name "Rachel Carson." What did she think she was doing, patenting a breed and grafting out a whole new orchard? Those trees wouldn't start to bear apples for another ten years. Who did she think would be around to pick them?

Garnett's plan today had been to go right up and rap on her screen door, but on his way up the drive he'd spied her ladders and picking paraphernalia scattered around out here in the orchard on the west side. He crossed over just below her big vegetable garden, which looked well tended, he had to admit. By some witchcraft she was getting broccoli and eggplant without spraying. Garnett didn't even plant broccoli anymore—it was just fodder for the looper worms—and his eggplants got so full of flea beetles they looked like they'd taken a round of buckshot. He inspected her corn, which was tasseling nicely, two weeks ahead of his. Did she have corn earworms, at least? He tried not to hope so. He'd gone almost as far as the line fence that separated their fields when he heard her humming up in the foliage and saw her legs on the ladder, sticking out below the ceiling of green leaves overhead. *This is how a duck must look to a turtle underwater,* he thought wickedly. Then he took a deep breath. He wasn't going to dally around here.

"Hello! I have some news," he called. "One of your trees came down on me."

Her dirty white tennis shoes descended two rungs on the ladder, and her face peered down at him through the branches. "Well, you don't look that much the worse for it, Mr. Walker."

He shook his head. "There's no need to behave like a child."

"It wouldn't hurt you, though," she said. "Now and then." She climbed back up into the boughs of her apple, a June Transparent— he could tell from the yellow fruits lying on the ground. She was picking June apples in the middle of July. It figured.

"I have a piece of business to discuss with you," he said sternly. "I would appreciate talking with you down here on solid ground."

She climbed down her ladder with a full apple basket over her arm, muttering about having to work for a living instead of collecting a retirement pension. She set her basket on the ground and put her hands on her hips. "All right. If you're going to be sanctimonious about it, *I* have a piece of business to discuss with *you!*"

He felt his heart stutter a little. It aggravated him no end that she could scare him this way. He stood still, breathed slowly, and told himself that what he beheld was nothing to be afraid of. This was no more daunting than a piece of ground that needed plowing—a small, female terrain. "What is it, then?"

"That god-awful Sevin you've been spraying on your trees every blooming day of the week! You think you've got troubles, a *tree* came over on you? Well your poison has been coming down on me, and I don't just mean my property, my apples, I mean *me*. I have to breathe it. If I get lung cancer, it will be on your conscience."

Her hail of words stopped; their gazes briefly met and then fell to the grass around each other's feet. Ellen had died of lung cancer, metastasized to the brain. People always remarked on the fact that she never had smoked.

"I'm sorry, you're thinking about Ellen," Nannie said. "I'm not saying your poisons caused her to get sick."

She had thought it, though, Garnett realized with a shock. Thought it and put it about so other people were thinking it, too. It dawned on him with a deeper dread that it might possibly be true. He'd never read the fine print on the Sevin dust package, but he knew it got into your lungs like something evil. Oh, Ellen. He raised his eyes to the sky and suddenly felt so dizzy he was afraid he might have to sit down on the grass. He put a hand to his temple and with the other reached for the trunk of a June Transparent.

"This isn't going well," Nannie observed. "I didn't mean to start off hateful, right off the bat. I thought I'd give us some room to work up to it." She hesitated. "Could you maybe use a glass of water?"

"I'm fine," he said, recovering his balance. She turned over a pair of bushel baskets and motioned for him to sit.

"I've just been festering about it too long," she said. "Just now I was up there stewing over a whole slew of things at once: your poison, the bills I need to pay, the shingles off my roof I can't replace. Dink Little claims they don't make that kind anymore, can you imagine? It's just been one darn thing after another this week, and when you came hollering at me all of a sudden, I let the dam burst." She reached between her knees and scooted her bushel forward so they faced each other directly, within spitting distance. "What we need is to have a good, levelheaded talk about this pesticide business, farmer to farmer."

Garnett felt a pang of guilt about the shingles but let it pass. "It's the middle of July," he said. "The caterpillars are on my seedlings like the plague. If I didn't spray I'd lose all this year's new crosses."

"See, but you're killing all my beneficials. You're killing my pollinators. You're killing the songbirds that eat the bugs. You're just a regular death angel, Mr. Walker."

"I have to take care of my chestnuts," he replied firmly.

She gave him a hard look. "Mr. Walker, is it my imagination, or do you really think your chestnuts are more important than my apples? Just because you're a man and I'm a woman? You seem to forget, my apple crop is my living. Your trees are a *hobby*."

Now, that was low. Garnett should have called on the phone. Talking to a brainless machine would beat this. "I never said a thing about your apples. I'm helping you out by spraying. The caterpillars would be over here next."

"They *are* over here. I can keep them under control my own way, normally. But your spraying always causes a caterpillar boom."

He shook his head. "How many times do I have to listen to that nonsense?"

She leaned forward, her eyes growing wide. "Until you've *heard* it!"

"I've heard it. Too many times."

"No, now, I haven't explained it to you right. I always had a hunch, but I couldn't put it in words. And, see, last month they had a piece on it in the *Orchardman's Journal*. It's a whole scientific thing, a principle. Do you want me to get you the magazine, or just explain it in my own words?"

"I don't think I have any choice," he said. "I'll listen for the flaw in your reasoning. Then you'll have to hush up about this for good."

"Good," she said, shifting her bottom on the basket. "All right, now. Goodness, I feel a little bit nervous. Like I'm back in college, taking an exam." The anxious way she looked up at him reminded Garnett of all the years of boys who'd feared him in his vo-ag classes. He wasn't a mean teacher; he'd just insisted that they get things *right*. Yet they'd dreaded him for it. They were never his chums, as they were with Con Ricketts in shop, for instance. It made for a long, lonely life, this business of getting things right.

"OK, here we go," she said finally, clasping her hands together. "There are two main kinds of bugs, your plant eaters and your bug eaters."

"That's right," he said patiently. "Aphids, Japanese beetles, and caterpillars all eat plants. To name just a few. Ladybugs eat other small bugs."

"Ladybugs do," she agreed. "Also spiders, hornets, cicada killers, and a bunch of other wasps, plus your sawflies and parasitic hymenoptera, and lots more. So out in your field you have predators and herbivores. You with me so far?"

He waved a hand in the air. "I taught vocational agriculture for half as long as you've been alive. You have to get up early in the morning to surprise an old man like me." Although, truth to tell, Garnett had never heard of parasitic hymenoptera.

"Well, all right. Your herbivores have certain characteristics."

"They eat plants."

"Yes. You'd call them pests. And they reproduce fast."

"Don't I know it!" Garnett declared.

"Predator bugs don't reproduce so fast, as a rule. But see, that works out right in nature because one predator eats a world of pest bugs in its life. The plant eaters have to go faster just to hold their ground. They're in balance with each other. So far, so good?"

Garnett nodded. He found himself listening more carefully than he'd expected.

"All right. When you spray a field with a broad-spectrum insecticide like Sevin, you kill the pest bugs *and* the predator bugs, bang. If the predators and prey are balanced out to start with, and they both get knocked back the same amount, then the pests that survive will *increase* after the spraying, fast, because most of their enemies have just disappeared. And the predators will *decrease* because they've lost most of their food supply. So in the lag between sprayings, you end up boosting the numbers of the bugs you don't want and wiping out the ones you need. And every time you spray, it gets worse."

"And then?" Garnett asked, concentrating on this.

She looked at him. "And that's it, I'm done. The Volterra principle."

Garnett felt hoodwinked. How could she do this every time? In another day and age they'd have burned her for a witch. "I didn't find the fault in your thinking," he admitted.

"Because it's not there!" she cried. "Because I'm right!" The little woman was practically crowing.

"The agricultural chemical industry would be surprised to hear your theory."

"Oh, fiddle, they know all about it. They just hope *you* don't. The more money you spend on that stuff, the more you need. It's like getting hooked on hooch."

"Pssht," he scolded. "Let's don't get carried away."

She leaned forward, elbows on her knees, and looked at him very earnestly with eyes that had the color and deep shine of a polished chestnut. He'd never noticed her eyes before.

"If you don't believe those fellows are bad eggs, then you're a dupe, Mr. Walker. Have you been getting those fliers from the Extension? Now all the companies are pushing that grain with its genes turned out of whack, and fools are growing it!"

"Modern farmers try new things," he said. "Even in Zebulon County."

"Half the world won't eat that grain; there's a boycott on it. Any farmer that plants it will go bankrupt in a year or two. *That's* modern farming for you."

"That's taking a dim view."

She slapped her hands on her knees. "Look around you, old man! In your father's day all the farmers around here were doing fine. Now they have to work night shifts at the Kmart to keep up their mortgages. Why is that? They work just as hard as their parents did, and they're on the same land, so what's wrong?"

Garnett could feel the sun's insistent heat on the back of his neck. Nannie, facing him, was forced to squint. They'd started this conversation in the shade, but now the sun had moved out from behind a tree—that was how long they'd been sitting here on bushel baskets speaking of nonsense. "Times change," Garnett said. "That's all."

"*Time* doesn't change; *ideas* change. Prices and markets and laws. Chemical companies change, and turn your head along with them, looks like. If that's what you mean by 'time,' then yes, sir, we have lived to see things get worse."

Garnett laughed, thinking for some reason of the boy who drove the UPS truck. "I won't argue with that," he said.

She shaded her eyes and looked right straight at him. "Then why do you make fun of my way of farming for being old-fashioned, right to my face?"

Garnett stood up, brushing invisible dirt off the knees of his trousers. There was a high, steady buzz that he'd thought was his hearing aid, but now he decided it was coming from the trees and the air itself. It made him feel jumpy. This whole place was giving him the all-overs.

She stayed seated but followed him around the glade with her eyes, waiting for an answer he couldn't assemble. Why did Nannie Rawley bother him so? Dear Lord, if he had world enough and time, he still couldn't answer. He stopped pacing and looked down at her sitting there wide-eyed, waiting for judgment. She didn't look old-fashioned, exactly, but like a visitor to this day from an earlier time—like a girl, with her wide, dark eyes and her crown of braided hair. Even the way she was dressed, in denim dungarees and a sleeveless white shirt, gave her the carefree air of a child out of school for summer, Garnett thought. Just a girl. And he felt tongue-tied and humiliated, like a boy.

"Why does everything make you so mad?" she asked finally. "I only wish you could see the beauty in it."

"In what?" he asked. A cloud passed briefly over the sun, causing everything to seem to shift a little.

"Everything." She flung out an arm. "This world! A field of plants and bugs working out a balance in their own way."

"That's a happy view of it. They're killing each other, is what they're doing."

"Yes, sir, eating others and reproducing their own, that's true. Eating and reproducing, that's the most of what God's creation is all about."

"I'm going to have to take exception to that."

"Oh? Are you thinking you got here some way different than the rest of us?"

"No," he said irritably. "I just don't choose to wallow in it."

"It's not *mud*, Mr. Walker. It's glory, to be part of a bigger something. The glory of an evolving world."

"Oh, now," he cried. "Don't even get started on your evolution. I already put you straight on that." He paced in a circle like a dog preparing to lie down, and then stopped. "Didn't you get my letter?"

"Your thank-you note for the blackberry pie I baked you? No, I don't believe I got any such a thing. I got some evil words about bra-burning Unitarian women and casting my soul to the jaws of Satan like the snapper that ate my duckling. I think some crazy man must have addressed that letter to me by mistake. I threw it in the trash."

He had never seen her get quite this agitated before. Garnett said nothing. She got up and picked up an apple from the grass, then tossed it from hand to hand. "That was mean, about my duckling," she added. "And the Unitarian position on underwear is none of your business, if there even *was* one, which there isn't. Nobody's seen *my* underwear since Ray Dean Wolfe died, so you can keep your thoughts about my body to yourself."

"Your body!" he said, mortified. "That letter was not how you're telling it. It was about your mistaken belief in a flawed theory of the earth's creation, answered clear and plain beyond a shadow of a doubt."

"You live your whole darn life beyond a shadow of a doubt, don't you?"

"I have convictions," he said.

She tilted her head, looking up at him. He could never tell if she was coy or just a little hard of hearing. "You want to make everything so simple," she said. "You say only an intelligent, beautiful creator could create beauty and intelligence? I'll tell you what. See that basket of June Transparents there? You know what I put on my trees to make those delicious apples? Poop, mister. Horse poop and cow poop."

"Are you likening the Creator to manure?"

"I'm saying your logic is weak."

"I'm a man of science."

"Well, then, you're a poor one! Don't tell me I can't understand the laws of thermodynamics. I went to college once upon a time, and it was *after* they discovered the world was round. I'm not scared of big words."

"I didn't say you were."

"You did, too! 'I realize you're no scientist, Miss Rawley,'" she mocked, in an unnecessarily prissy version of his voice.

"No, now, I just meant to set you straight on a few points."

"You self-righteous old man. Do you ever wonder why you don't have a friend in the world since Ellen died?"

He blinked. He may have even allowed his jaw to go a little slack.

"Well, I'm sorry to be the one to break it to you. But just listen to yourself talk!" she cried. "'How could random chance—i.e. evolution—create complex life-forms?' How can you be so self-satisfied and so ignorant at the same time?"

"Goodness. Did you *memorize* my letter before you threw it in the trash?"

"Oh, phooey, I didn't have to, I've heard it all before. You get your arguments straight out of those dumb little pamphlets. Whoever writes those things should get some new material."

"Well, then," he said, crossing his arms, "how *does* random chance create complex life-forms?"

"This just seems ridiculous, a man who does what you do claiming not to believe in the very thing he's doing."

"What I do has nothing to do with apes' turning helter-skelter into thinking men."

"Evolution isn't helter-skelter! It's a business of choosing things out, just like how you do with your chestnuts." She nodded toward his seedling field and then frowned, looking at it more thoughtfully. "In every generation, all the trees are a little different, right? And which ones do you choose to save out for crossing?"

"The ones that survive the blight best, obviously. I inoculate the trees with blight fungus and then measure the size of the chancres. Some of them hardly get sick at all."

"All right. So you pick out the best survivors, you cross their flowers with one another and plant their seeds, and then you do it all over again with the next generation. Over time you're, what, making a whole new kind of chestnut plant?"

"That's right. One that can resist the blight."

"A whole new species, really."

"No, now, only God can do that. I can't make a chestnut into an oak."

"You could if you had as much time as God does."

Oh, if only I did, Garnett thought with the deep despair of a man running out of time. Just enough years to make a good chestnut, that was all he wanted, but in his heart he knew he couldn't expect them. He had thought sometimes of praying for this but trembled to think what God would make of his request. Ellen had not been granted time enough even to make peace with her own son.

But he was drifting. "I don't know what you're talking about," he said irritably.

"What you're doing is artificial selection," she replied calmly. "Nature does the same thing, just slower. This 'evolution' business is just a name scientists put on the most obvious truth in the world, that every kind of living thing adjusts to changes in the place where it lives. Not during its own life, but you know, down through the generations. Whether you believe in it or not, it's going on right under your nose over there in your chestnuts."

"You're saying that what I do with chestnut trees, God does with the world."

"It's a way to look at it. Except you have a goal, you know what you want. In nature it's predators, I guess, a bad snap of weather, things like that, that cull out the weaker genes and leave the strong ones to pass on. It's not so organized as you are, but it's just as dependable. It's just the thing that always happens."

"I'm sorry, but I can't liken God's will to a thing that just *happens*."

"All right, then, don't. I don't care." She sounded upset. She sat back down on her bushel, tossed the apple away, and put her face in her hands.

"Well, I *can't*." He tried to hold still instead of pacing around, but his knees hurt. "That's just a godless darkness, to think there's no divine goal. Mankind can't be expected to function in a world like that. The Lord God is good and just."

When she looked up at him, there were tears in her eyes. "Mankind functions with whatever it has to. When you've had a child born with her chromosomes mixed up and spent fifteen years watching her die, you come back and tell me what's good and just."

"Oh, goodness," Garnett said nervously. The sight of a woman's tears in broad daylight should be against the law.

She fished in her pocket for a handkerchief and blew her nose loudly. "I'm all right," she said after a minute. "I didn't say what I meant to, there." She blew her nose again, like nobody's business. It was a little shocking. She rubbed her eyes and stuffed the red bandanna back in her pocket. "I'm not a godless woman," she said. "I see things my own way, and most of it makes me want to get up in the morning and praise glory. I don't see you doing that, Mr. Walker. So I don't appreciate your getting all high and mighty about the darkness in my soul."

He turned his back on her and looked out over his own land. The narrow, bronze-tipped leaves of the young chestnuts waved like so many flags, each tree its own small nation of genetic promise. He said, "You called me a bitter old man. That wasn't nice."

"Any man who'd cut off his own son like a limb off a tree is bitter. That's the word for it."

"That's none of your business."

"He needs help."

"That's not your business, either."

"Maybe not. But put yourself in my shoes. I'd give up the rest of my life in one second if it could help Rachel, and I've lost that chance. If I could have gotten the doctors to cut out my heart and put it into her, I would have. So how do you think it feels to watch other people throw away their living children?"

"I have no children."

"You did have one for twenty years. And he's still alive, last I heard."

Garnett could feel her eyes on the back of his shirt like the noonday sun, but he couldn't turn around. He just let her go on hitting him with her words, blunt as rocks. "He's walking around somewhere carrying your genes and Ellen's." She paused, but he still didn't turn around. "Even your same *name,* for heaven's sakes. And you won't help him, or claim him? Looks to me like you've given up on the world and everything in it, including yourself."

Garnett wanted nothing but to walk away from there. But he couldn't let her be right about this, too. He turned to face his neighbor. "I can't help that boy. He has to help himself. There comes a time."

"You think he's still a boy? He must be in his thirties by now."

"And still a boy. He'll be a man when he decides to act like one. It's not just me that thinks that. Ellen went to those meetings for years, and that's what they told her. With the drinking and all that, they have to decide for themselves to get better. They have to *want* to."

"I understand," she said, crossing her arms and looking down at all the bruised apples strewn through the grass. She kicked at one with the rubber toe of her small white canvas shoe. "I just hate to see you forget about him."

Forget? Garnett felt a sting of salt in his eye and turned his head away, looking for something to look at. What a useless, pathetic business, the human tear duct! His cloudy vision settled on a square white wooden box at the edge of her garden. He puzzled over it for a minute and then remembered that Nannie kept beehives. She was in thrall of bees, as of so many other things. It was true what she'd said: she was a surprisingly happy woman most of the time. And he was often quite glum.

"We had that boy too late in life," he confessed, keeping his back to her. "We were like Abraham and Sarah. At first we couldn't believe our luck, but a baby worried us to death, and a teenager plain bewildered us. Sometimes I wonder what Abraham and Sarah would have done if they'd had their son in the day of hot rods and beer."

He was startled by her hand, laid gently on his upper arm for just a few seconds. She had surprised him by coming up on him that way, from behind. After she took her hand away he could still feel its pressure there, as if his skin were somehow changed underneath the cloth of his shirt.

"There's always more to a story than a body can see from the fence line," she said. "I'm sorry."

They stood side by side with their arms crossed, looking over toward her blossoming garden and his field of young chestnuts behind it. At such close range, standing quiet this way, Nannie lacked her usual force. She just seemed small—the crown of her head barely came up to his shoulder. *Goodness, we are just a pair of old folks,* he thought. *Two old folks with our arms folded over our shirtfronts and our sorry eyes looking for heaven.*

"We've both had our griefs to bear, Miss Rawley. You and I."

"We have. What worse grief can there be than to be old without young ones to treasure, coming up after you?"

He cast an eye out over his field of robust young chestnuts yearning for their future. But the pain was so great, he could not look that way for long.

An indigo bunting let out a loud, cheerful song from the fencepost, and the strange buzzing sound also rose in the clear air. Why, that was her bees, Garnett realized. A world of busy bees doing their work in field and orchard. Not his hearing aid.

When he felt sure most of the emotions had safely passed over, Garnett cleared his throat. "The reason I came down here, like I said, is because one of your trees has come down on my property. Up in the back." He nodded toward the rise of the mountain.

"Oh, up there across the creek?"

"Yes."

"I'm not surprised. There's trees galore up there threatening to come down. I won't miss it much. What kind was it?"

"An oak."

"Well, that's sad. One less oak in the world."

"It's still in the world," he pointed out. "On my property."

"Give it a year," she said. "The carpenter ants and bark beetles will take it on back to good dirt."

"I was thinking of something more expeditious," he said. "Such as Oda Black's boy and a chain saw."

She looked at him. "Why on earth? What harm is that tree doing you up there in the woods? For heaven's sakes. The raccoons can use it for a bridge. The salamanders will adore living under it while it rots. The woodpeckers will have a heyday."

"It looks unsightly."

She sighed, overdramatically in Garnett's opinion. "All right," she said, "call Oda's boy if you want. I expect you'll want me to pay half."

"Half would be fair."

"The firewood's mine, though," she said. "All."

"It's on my land. It's my firewood."

"My oak!"

"Well, now. A minute ago you wanted it to rot into topsoil. Now you want the firewood. You don't seem to know what you want."

She let out a little explosion of air through her nose. "You are a sanctimonious old fart," she announced, before stooping to pick up her basket of June Transparents and tromping off toward her barn. Garnett watched her go. He stood there for quite a while, in fact, letting his shoes inhabit Nannie's green, manure-drunk orchard grass while he pondered the risky terrain of a woman's mind.

He really had intended to thank her for the pie.

{18}

Moth Love

In the summer after her husband's death Lusa discovered lawn-mower therapy. The engine's vibrations roaring through her body and its thunderous noise in her ears seemed to bully all human language from her head, chasing away the complexities of regret and recrimination. It was a blessing to ride over the grass for an hour or two as a speechless thing, floating through a universe of vibratory sensation. By accident, she had found her way to the mind-set of an insect.

Like so many tasks that had always been Cole's, the mowing was something she'd initially dreaded taking on. For the first weeks postfuneral, Little and Big Rickie did it alternately without a word. But then the day came when she noticed that the yard was calf-deep in grass and dandelions. The world grows quickly impatient with grief, she observed, and that world seemed to think her chores were her own now. Lusa would have to put on her sunglasses and boots and go see if she could get the mower started.

At first she'd been dismayed by the steepness of the slopes and by how perilously the riding mower tilted toward creeks and ditches, but she'd concentrated on finding the Zen of a straight, even roadside or a spiral of tightening concentric circles in a yard. After her first few hours she realized she had stopped thinking altogether. She was just a body vibrating like one of Heaven's harp strings in the sharp, green-scented air. The farmhouse was surrounded by acres of yard, side yard, and barnyard, not to mention a mile of shoulder on both sides of her road that she had to keep clear. In a summer as rainy as this one she could hardly afford to pass a dry day without spending some part of it on the mower.

So that was where she was on the morning Hannie-Mavis and Jewel drove up to drop off Crys before heading to Roanoke for another chemo. Not both Jewel's kids, only Crystal. The plan was for Lois to pick up Lowell from T-ball and keep him overnight while his sister stayed here. Evidently Crys had used up all her other aunts: her last time at Lois and Rickie's she'd had a fit, broken a porcelain praying-hands statue on purpose, and hidden out overnight in the barn. This was reported to Lusa along with the claim that Emaline's new work schedule made her too tired to take the kids, and Mary Edna wouldn't have the child in her house, period, until she quote-unquote straightened up and flew right. Lusa understood that they must be desperate to ask for her help; she didn't know the first thing about taking care of a child like Crys. But at least she didn't enforce a dress code.

She killed the mower engine as they pulled up, but the two women waved frantically and called out that they were running late for Jewel's appointment. Crys got out of the back of the sedan, Hannie-Mavis reminded her to get her overnight bag, and Jewel yelled at her to be good, all in the same instant, and then they were off, sending gravel flying. Crys stared at Lusa with her eyes narrowed and her chin tucked down, like a guard dog on the brink of its decision. Lusa could only stare back at this sullen, long-legged urchin in her Oliver Twist haircut and high-water jeans. In her hand she clutched a small, white, squarish overnight case from another era—probably something her mother or aunts had used in their teens for happier sleepovers than this one. Here we are, Lusa thought, widow and orphan, at the mercy of a family that takes no prisoners.

"Hi," Lusa said, trying not to sound too much like she was from Lexington. She would never get the long, flat *i*, though, not the way they said it around here.

"Hi-y," the child mimicked, sure enough, eyeing Lusa with disdain.

Lusa licked her lips and thumped the steering wheel a couple of times with her thumbs. "You want me to show you your room? So you can unpack your bag?"

"'S got nothing in it. I just brung it so Aunt Hannie-Mavis would think I had clean underpants and stuff."

"Oh," Lusa said. "Then I guess you don't need to unpack. Just pitch it up there on the porch, then, and come help me finish the mowing."

Crys tossed the hard little cube toward the porch, underhand, like a softball pitch. It hit the step and flew open, letting fly a square of mirror that broke to pieces on the stone steps. A banty hen scratching in the flower bed next to the porch let out a squawk and scrambled for safety. Lusa felt shaken by this child's untempered hostility, but she knew enough not to show it. "Oh, well," she said carelessly. "There's seven years of bad luck."

"I already done had ten years of it," said Crys.

"No way. How old are you?"

"Ten."

Lord help me get through the next thirty hours, Lusa pleaded to any God who would listen.

"You know what, Crys? I've just got a few minutes left to go on this yard. You want to sit here on the seat with me and help me mow? Then we'll be done with this chore and we can find something more fun to do."

"Like what?"

She racked her brain wildly; suggest the wrong thing here and she might lose an eye. "Hunt bugs, maybe? I love bugs, they're my favorite thing—did you know I'm actually a bugologist?"

The child crossed her arms and looked elsewhere, waiting for Lusa to say something interesting for a change.

"Oh," Lusa said, "but I guess you hate bugs. All the other women in this family fear and despise bugs. I'm sorry, I forgot."

Crys shrugged. "I ain't asceared of bugs."

"No? Good, that makes two of us, then. Thank God I've finally got somebody to go bug hunting with." She pressed the clutch, turned the key, and started the engine roaring again, then sat and waited. After a second of hesitation Crys crossed the yard and climbed onto the seat of the mower in front of Lusa.

"Uncle Rickie says you can't do this 'cause hit's dangerous," she declared loudly as they backed up a little and headed into a circular path around the lower yard.

"Yeah, it's probably dangerous for little kids," Lusa yelled over the engine noise. "But holy smokes, you're *ten,* you're not going to fall off and get run over or anything. Here, put your hands on the steering wheel, like this." They bounced down a small embankment. "OK, you're driving now. Don't run over the chickens, or we'll have chicken salad. And watch out for the rocks. Go around, OK?"

She helped Crystal steer around a limestone outcrop on the bank between the barn and the henhouse. Lusa had learned to give it a wide margin, to spare the mower blade and also because she loved the flowering weeds that had sprung up in this little island.

"What's them orange flowers?" Crystal asked loudly. She seemed unperturbed to be having a conversation at this decibel level.

"Butterfly weed." Lusa tried not to be shocked by her grammar, which was noticeably worse even than that of the other kids in the family. She wondered if everyone had given up on Crystal, and if so, how long ago.

"What's butterflies do, smoke it?"

Lusa ignored this. "They drink nectar out of the flowers. And there's one kind, the monarch, that lays its eggs on the leaves so the caterpillars can eat butterfly weed when they hatch out. And you know what? The leaves make them poisonous! The whole plant's full of poison."

"Like 'at stuff the doctor's putting in Mama," Crystal said.

It was unnerving to have this sad, bony little body so close to her on the seat; it was all Lusa could do to keep from wrapping her arms around it. "Yeah," she said. "Kind of like that."

"It makes Mama poison. Whenever she comes home from Roanoke we can't go in her room or touch nothing in the bathroom after she goes pee. Or we'd die."

"I don't think you'd die. You'd get sick and throw up, maybe." Lusa allowed her chin to brush against the crown of the blond, cropped head that bobbed just in front of her chin. It was brief, a gesture that could pass for an accident. They stopped talking for a minute while Lusa helped steer the mower around the shrinking swath of remaining grass. "You know what?" Lusa said, "That's exactly what happens to the monarch butterflies."

"What does?"

"The caterpillars eat the poisonous leaves, and their bodies turn toxic. So if a bird eats them, it vomits! It's kind of a trick the butterfly plays on the birds to keep her caterpillars from getting eaten."

Crystal seemed unimpressed. "But if a bird eats it and vomits, the caterpillar's already done keelt."

It took a second for Lusa to interpret this. "It's already been killed? Well, yeah, *that* one has. But the birds learn their lesson, so most of them don't get eaten. It's a scientific fact. Birds avoid eating the caterpillars of monarch butterflies."

"So what," Crystal said after a minute.

"So that's one weird way that mothers can take care of their children," Lusa said. "Making them eat poison."

"Yeah, but so what for the one that's dead."

"Good point," Lusa said. "So what for him." She would not go into the current theories on kin selection. She reached under the seat and pulled the lever that lifted the blade. "Let's head into the barn. We've done enough mowing for today; let's go hunt bugs." She helped guide the mower in through the door of the barn cellar and parked it inside.

When she cut the engine, her ears were left singing the high, ringing complaint of assaulted eardrums. She and Crys climbed off the machine and stood dazed for a minute while their eyes and ears adjusted to the dim, dusty silence. Crys was peering up at the steps that rose to a trapdoor in the floor of the barn above them. It was more of a permanent stepladder than a staircase, and so twisted by a hundred years of this structure's settling that none of its angles squared with gravity anymore. It always made Lusa think of an Escher drawing of a spiral staircase whose every flight seemed to define "up" in a different direction. This thing looked so crazily hazardous that she had never used it, even though it was a long walk around to the ground-level entrance on the hillside.

"Can we go up there?"

"Sure." Lusa swallowed a taste of panic. "Good idea. We need to go up to the storage room anyway, to get nets and collecting jars."

The girl grasped the rickety, splintered wood and started to climb in the many different directions this staircase called "up." On a wing and a prayer, Lusa followed. The trapdoor gave easily when they shoved it. They stuck out their elbows like chickens spreading their wings in the dust, pulled their bodies up through the hole, and emerged into the main room of the barn. Lusa inhaled its perfume, a faint petroleum pungency but mostly the mellow sweetness of old tobacco. A fine brown dust of crumbled leaves inhabited every crevice of this place where Wideners had stripped, hung, and baled tobacco for over a hundred years.

The storeroom was a former corncrib, framed out in a corner of the barn and carefully rodent-proofed by means of wire mesh nailed over every square inch of its floor, walls, and ceiling. Lusa unlatched the door and felt depressed by the sight of this dusty, quiet room full of equipment. Everything here had been touched by Cole's hands at one time or another. He'd moved it, stored it, kept it in repair. A lot of it she didn't even know how to use: sprayer arms and tractor attachments, a long row of chemicals stored on the shelf. Vehicle parts. Stranger things, too: an antediluvian oil furnace and an assortment of horse and mule tack left from the days before tractors. An empty piano, just the wooden case, with nothing inside. Lusa stored her own things in this room but had never really looked around at everything else. Before this moment, it had never all belonged to her. She pinched her nose against a sneeze that was bringing tears to her eyes and tried to stave off whatever sadness was coming on; this child would brook no self-pity. And given the set of woes *she'd* been handed at ten years of age, why should she? Lusa wedged herself through an aisle between the piano case and some large bundles of baling twine and stooped to blow some dust off the huge iron hulk of an ancient machine.

"Holy cow. Look at this, Crys."

"What is it?"

"A grain mill. An old-fashioned one—look, it has all these cloth belts and things." She studied the way it was put together. "I guess they hooked it up to some kind of a turning axle to power it. Maybe a mule in a yoke, walking in a circle."

"What for?"

"No electricity. This thing's a hundred years old. It was your great-great-grandfather's, probably."

Crys sounded scornful, as if Lusa were very slow to keep up: "I mean, what'd they use it for?"

"It's a mill. They used it to grind their flour."

Crys squatted underneath the machine and looked up inside of it. "To grind up flowers?"

She pronounced it "flars," puzzling Lusa for a second.

"Oh, no, *flour*. You know. To make bread. Everybody around here used to grow their own wheat and corn for bread, plus what they needed for their animals. Now they buy feed at Southern States and go to Kroger's for a loaf of god-awful bread that was baked in another state."

"Why?"

"Because they can't afford to grow grain anymore. It's cheaper to buy bad stuff from a big farm than to grow good stuff on a little farm."

"Why?"

Lusa leaned against a fifty-five-gallon drum that had solidified creosote in the bottom. "Boy, that's hard to answer. Because people want too much stuff, I guess, and won't pay for quality. And also, farmers have to follow rules that automatically favor whoever already has the most. You know how when you play marbles, as soon as somebody starts getting most of the marbles then they're going to win everything?"

"No."

"No?"

"I don't play with marbles."

"What do you play with?"

"Game Boy." Crys had drifted away and was putting her hands on things, drawing circles in the dust, looking under tables. "What's'is?"

"A bee smoker."

The child laughed. "For smoking bees? Do you get high off 'em?"

Lusa wondered what this child knew about getting high but decided again not to react. "No. Smoke comes out of there, and it drugs the bees, as a matter of fact. It makes them dopey and lazy so they won't sting you when you take the top off their hive and steal their honey."

"Oh." Crys leaned back and bounced herself against a bed-spring that was standing on its end, propped against the wall. "That's where honey comes from? People steal it?"

Lusa was surprised at the extent of the girl's ignorance—her generation's ignorance, probably. "People raise bees, for honey. Everybody around here used to, I'm sure. You see old broken-down bee boxes everywhere."

"Now it just comes in a jar."

"Yep," Lusa agreed. "From Argentina or someplace. That's what I mean about big farms far away taking the place of little farms right here. It's sad. It's not fair, and it stinks." She sat down on a side-arm of the ancient grain mill, which startled her by giving way an inch or two before it held. "Nobody cares, though. I used to live in a city, and I'll tell you, city people do not think this is their problem. They think food comes from the supermarket, period, and always will."

Crys continued to bounce herself sideways against the bed-spring. "My mama works at Kroger's. She hates it."

"I know." Lusa looked around at the dim boneyard of obsolete equipment and felt despair, not only—or not *specifically*—for the loss of her husband, but for all the things people used to grow and make for themselves before they were widowed from their own food chain.

"She hates it because it makes her tired. They won't give her no days off."

"I know. Not enough, anyway."

"Mama's sick."

"I know."

"I can't stay at Aunt Lois's no more. Lowell can, but I can't. You know why?"

"Why?"

Crys stopped throwing herself against the bedspring. She stepped carefully into a broken baling box and out the other side.

"Why, Crys?" Lusa repeated.

"She made me try on stupid dresses. Hand-me-downs from Jennifer and Louise."

"Yeah? I never heard that part of the story."

"She said I had to wear them. They's ugly."

"Probably out of style, too. Jennifer and Louise are a lot older than you."

Crys shrugged her shoulders, a quick, unhappy jerk. She sat down on a tractor tire and put her feet into the center of it, with her back to Lusa. "They were stupid."

"Who was?"

"The dresses."

"Still. Breaking Aunt Lois's knickknacks on purpose, that might not have been the best way to handle it."

"She made me go in the bathroom and give her out my clothes, while I was supposed to be trying the dresses on. And you know what she done? Cut up my corduroys and plaid shirt with scissors so I couldn't put 'em back on."

Lusa was appalled. She stared at the back of the child's head, feeling her sore heart open up to this dejected little creature whose straw-colored hair stood up at the crown of her head like a porcupine's quills. "I think that's awful," Lusa said finally. "Nobody told me that part. Those were your favorite clothes, your old faithfuls, right? I don't think I ever saw you in anything but those corduroys and that shirt on the weekends."

Crys shrugged again, offering no reply.

"So then what? I guess you had to put on one of the dresses."

She shook her head. "I run out of the house neckid. Just underpants. I went and hid in the barn."

"What about the praying-hands statue? How did that get broken?"

"I don't know."

"Just kind of happened, on your way out?"

The porcupine head nodded.

"I'd say that was a fair trade. Her treasure for yours."

Lusa saw the hair on the back of the girl's head shift subtly, from a change in the musculature under her scalp. Smiling, was a good guess.

"I'm not saying it was *helpful*," Lusa amended. "It's made things kind of tense between you and your aunt, which doesn't make life any easier on your mother. She's the one you probably need to be thinking about right now. I'm just saying I understand."

"I told Jesus if I wore them clothes every day he'd make Mama get better. Now they're cut up in Aunt Lois's ragbag, and Mama's going to die."

"Just thinking something like that doesn't make it happen."

Crystal turned around and looked at Lusa through a diagonal shaft of light that fell from a hole in the roof to the floor between them. Dust motes danced up and down in the light, inhabiting their own carefree universe.

"How are things with Lowell?" Lusa asked gently. "He must be pretty scared about your mom's being sick."

Crys picked at a ribbon of loose rubber where the sole of her tennis shoe was coming apart. "He don't like it over there, either. He's asceared of Aunt Lois. She's mean."

"*How* mean? Does she hit him or anything?"

"Nuh-uh, they don't usually paddle us. She just won't be nice to him like Mama is. She won't put his clothes on the chair the right way and make him what food he likes and stuff. Her and Jennifer and them just all holler that he's a big old baby."

Lusa's hand went to her mouth, but she kept her voice nonchalant. "Next time why don't you both come over here? Would that be OK, if I asked your mom to let you do that?"

Crys shrugged, continuing to pick her shoe apart. "I guess."

"OK. But today, since it's just the two of us, we can do whatever we want. I'd like to catch some bugs, if it's OK by you." Lusa pulled two short-handled collecting nets out of her box. "Here's yours. Let's go, the day's wasting out there."

Crys took the net and followed Lusa out of the barn. They began by skirting the edge of the goat pasture. Lusa led, running as fast as she could uphill, sweeping her net through the tall grass along the fence. They were both breathing hard when they reached the hilltop. Lusa flung herself on the ground, panting, and Crys sat down cross-legged.

"Careful," Lusa said, sitting up and reaching for the other net. "Here, fold the net over the frame like this so they won't get out. Now, let's see what you've got." She carefully let a few bugs crawl out onto the outside of the mesh. "These are grasshoppers, and this is a buffalo leafhopper. Big difference, see?" She held out a bright-green grasshopper with its legs writhing in the air. To her surprise, Crys took it and held it up a few inches from her face.

"Hey," she said. "It's got wings."

"Yeah. Most insects have wings—even ants, in one stage of their life. Grasshoppers definitely. This guy can fly if he wants to. Look." She lifted the green wing case with her fingernail, extending the brilliant red cellophane fan of wing underneath.

"Whoa," said Crys. "Are they always that color?"

"Nope. There're twenty thousand kinds of grasshoppers, crickets, and katydids in the world, and no two kinds are alike."

"Whoa!"

"My sentiments exactly. Here, look at this one." She reached into the net and extracted a flat, cross-eyed creature that looked like a leaf with legs. "That's a katydid."

Crys took it, looking it in the eye. She glanced up at Lusa. "They make all 'at racket at night? *Keety-did! Keety-didn't!*"

Lusa was impressed with the imitation. "That's right. You never saw a katydid before?"

She shook her head rapidly. "I thought katydids was some'n *big*. A big old whopper bird or some'n."

"A *bird?*" Lusa was truly shocked. How could rural kids grow up so ignorant of their world? Their parents gave them Game Boys and TVs that spewed out cityscapes of cops and pretty lawyers, but they couldn't show them a katydid. It wasn't neglect, Lusa knew. It was some sad mix of shame and modern intentions, like her own father's ban on Yiddish. She watched Crys study this creature's every infinitesimal feature, handling it with utmost care, eating it with her eyes. Like a good taxonomist.

"How's it holler so loud with that little mouth?" she asked finally.

"Not with its mouth. Look, see this? Wings again." She extended them carefully. "There's a scraper on one and a little ridged thing like a file on the underside of the other. He rubs them together. That's how he sings."

Crys practically put her nose against the thing. "Where at?"

"Those parts are hard to see. Really teeny."

Crys looked skeptical. "Then how's it so *loud?*"

"Did you ever hear a little teeny piece of chalk screech on a blackboard?"

She raised her eyebrows and nodded.

"That's how. A rough thing pushed against a hard thing. Big isn't everything. I should know: I'm only five foot one."

"Is that little?"

"Yeah. For grown-ups, that's little."

"How big's Aunt Lois?" *Ain't* Lois, she always said, as if to negate the woman. Lusa could appreciate the sentiment.

"I don't know; big. For a woman. Five foot ten, maybe. Why?"

Crys looked warily down the hill. "She said you was pushing everybody too far."

Lusa lay back on the grass, crossed her arms behind her head, and watched a cloud loll in the sky. She wondered whom Crys wished to hurt with this betrayal. "Some of your aunts think I shouldn't have this farm. That's what that's all about."

Crys lay down, too, with the top of her head a few inches from Lusa's. "How come?"

"Because I'm different from them. Because I wasn't born here. Because I like bugs. You name it. Because your uncle Cole died and I'm still here, and they're mad because life's not fair. I don't know exactly why; I'm just guessing. People don't always have good reasons for feeling how they do."

"Is my mama going to die?"

"Wow. Where did that come from?"

"Is she?"

"I don't know the answer to that. That's the truth, I swear. Nobody knows. I do know she's doing everything she can to get better, for you and Lowell. Even going up to Roanoke and taking poison once a week. So she must love you pretty much, huh?"

No answer came.

"Another thing," Lusa said. "I know for a fact that Jesus will not hurt your mother just because Aunt Lois chopped up your clothes. If he was in a position to punish somebody, which is debatable, I think it'd be Aunt Lois, don't you?"

"So will he kill Aunt Lois instead of Mama?"

"No, he won't, that one I *can* answer. Life is definitely not like that. God doesn't go around calling fouls like a referee, or else we'd have a different world by now. Ice cream three times a day and no spankings and no stinky dresses if you didn't want them."

Crys chuckled. For the first time since she'd planted herself fiercely on Lusa's driveway that morning, she sounded clear and transparent, like a child. Like the crystal she was. Lusa couldn't see her face, but she could feel her body next to hers in the grass and hear her relaxed breathing.

"Hey. Did anybody ever tell you what a crystal is?"

"A stupid thing. Jewry."

Lusa was startled for an instant. *Jewelry,* she must mean. "Nope. It's a kind of rock. Hard, sharp, and shiny. There are a lot of different kinds, actually. Salt is a crystal, even." She sat up. "Hey! Our bugs got away."

Crystal sat up, too, looking desperately disappointed.

"It's OK," Lusa said, laughing. "We were going to let 'em go anyway. We can catch more." She waved at the pasture. "All the bugs you'll ever need, right there. Can you believe people spray insecticide all over their fields?" She shook the last stragglers out of the two nets. "Look at all the beautiful creatures that die. It's like dropping a bomb on a city just to get rid of a couple of bad guys. See, that's what's so great about my goats—I don't have to use any chemicals to grow them. I only have to kill fifty animals, not fifty thousand."

Crys frowned through the fence at Lusa's goats. That field was shaping up, Lusa noticed. All the gangly thistles left standing by the cows were getting mowed down evenly, pretty as a Lexington lawn.

"For real, how come you got all them goats?"

"Well, it's true what I said, I hate pesticides, and I have to raise something here to make some money. Plus, I said some bad words about tobacco, so that's out. And I don't like sticking my hand up a cow's butt."

The child's mouth flew open and she laughed a beautiful laugh.

"Well, you asked. That's one thing you have to do if you want to raise cows."

"*Yuck!*"

"I'm not kidding. You have to make a fist and stick it way up in there and feel if they're pregnant. And that's not even the worst of it. Cows are big and stupid and dangerous and nothing but trouble, in my opinion." She laughed at the face Crys was making. "Why? You been hearing your uncles talk about me and my goats?"

The child nodded, looking slightly guilty. "They said you was a dope."

Lusa leaned over toward Crys, grinning. "Your uncles took over my *cows*. So who's the dope?"

~

Sometime near midnight, Lusa was surprised to hear a car in the drive. She'd fallen asleep on the parlor couch reading a W. D.

Hamilton article on monarch mimicry and kin selection. The knack for sleep must be returning to her—she hadn't conked out on the couch since before Cole died. She had to sit up and think for a minute to get her bearings. It was Tuesday night. Crys was settled on the daybed upstairs. Jewel was supposed to call tomorrow, as soon as she felt up to having the kids back. Lusa smoothed her shirt-tail and went to the window. It was Hannie-Mavis's car. She hurried to the front door and flipped on the porch light. "Hannie-Mavis? Is it you?"

It was. The engine stopped and her small figure got out. "I just come up to see if y'all was all right. I figured if all the lights was out, fine, then, I'd go on home."

"You haven't been home yet? Goodness." Lusa looked at her wrist, but she wasn't wearing her watch. "What time is it?"

"I don't even know, honey. Late. I've been down there with Jewel, she's bad this time. I couldn't leave her till she was good and settled. But she's asleep now. If you're all right with the young'un, I'll go on home. I just thought I better check."

"Oh, we're fine. She's asleep. I was just reading on the couch." Lusa hesitated, worried by the strain in her sister-in-law's voice. "What is it? What are you saying, then—that Jewel's been sick all afternoon and evening? Ever since you got back from Roanoke?"

Lusa heard a long, strange exhalation in the darkness. "We couldn't even get in the car to come back for three and a half hours. Even then we had to make a stop ever ten miles for her to up-chuck."

Lusa shivered in the chill air. Tiny moths whirled around her head. "My God, you've been to hell and back. Come in for a minute. Let me make you a cup of tea."

Hannie-Mavis hesitated on the walkway. "Oh, it's late. I hate to pester you."

"It's no trouble." Lusa came down the steps to meet her sister-in-law and was surprised when the small woman nearly tumbled into her arms. Lusa held her for a minute, there on the steps under the porch light. "She's really bad, isn't she?"

She was shocked to see, at closer range, that Hannie-Mavis was weeping. "They said it's no good, the chemo's not helping her. Everything she's went through, vomiting and losing her hair, for nothing. She's *worse*."

"How can that be?" Lusa asked numbly.

"It's all over her, honey. Her lungs and her spine. The doctor told me today."

"God," Lusa whispered. "Does she know yet?"

Hannie-Mavis shook her head. "I didn't tell her. How could I? I started telling her the doc said no more chemo, and she thought that was *good* news. 'Oh, Han,' she says, 'wait'll I tell the kids. Let's go get us a ice cream to celebrate!' Mind you, this was between throwing up and throwing up, when she said that." Hannie-Mavis took a deep, racked breath, then let out a long wail. Lusa just held on, feeling awkward, not yet sensing in her body the full weight of this new grief.

"How will she leave her babies!" Hannie-Mavis cried.

"Shhh, one of them's asleep upstairs." Lusa took her by the shoulders and steered her up the last step, across the porch, and in through the front door. In the bright hallway Hannie-Mavis seemed to pull into herself, appearing suddenly more contained and absurdly cheerful in her red-and-white-striped dress made of some silky material. She even had on snappy red high heels, Lusa noticed. The image of her two sisters-in-law dressing up this morning to go to the city, for this awful trip, was devastating. She watched Hannie-Mavis dab at her ruined eye makeup with a ball of tissue that appeared to have been in her hand for much too long.

"Come on. Come in the kitchen and sit down."

Hannie-Mavis hesitated again but then moved slowly toward the kitchen door under her own power while Lusa ran upstairs for a box of tissues. When she came back down to the kitchen and put on the kettle, her sister-in-law had vanished. Lusa heard intermittent nose-blowing from the bathroom. By the time Hannie-Mavis emerged, hairdo and makeup fully repaired, the kettle had already boiled and Lusa was steeping the tea. Seeing her standing in the doorway brought Lusa a sudden, harsh memory of the funeral, of looking at all that blue mascara and saying something cold. She wished she could take it back, whatever it had been. She felt penitent for all the times she'd nearly called her Handy Makeup out loud. You had to be so careful with large families. Who knew how things would turn around, whom you'd need in the end, and what could cause you to see even eye shadow in a different light? At this moment Lusa had to admire the woman's art and energy in the face of heartache. After Cole died, it'd probably been three weeks before she herself had even managed to put a comb to her hair.

Hannie-Mavis sighed as she put her palms flat on the table and eased herself down like an old woman. "Well. How'd *your* day go?"

"Fine."

She looked at Lusa. "What do you mean, 'fine'?"

Lusa shrugged. "I mean it went fine. We had fun."

"You don't have to tell me a tall tale, honey. That child's stinking as a polecat. I'd never say this to Jewel, but I took over driving her to the doctor's mainly so I wouldn't have to keep her kids."

Lusa got spoons, sugar, and teacups—just everyday mugs, not her china cups with moths painted on their rims—and opened her mouth to begin at the beginning, with the broken mirror on the front steps. But a sudden loyalty caught hold of her, imposing its own decision: they could keep some secrets, she and Crys. She sat down without speaking and poured out the tea. "She's a tough nut to crack, yeah," she said at last. "But I kind of like her. I was exactly that same kind of kid. Strong-willed."

"OK, then, honey. You get the Purple Heart." Hannie-Mavis unsnapped her purse and rummaged inside. "Is it all right if I smoke in here?"

Lusa jumped up and got an ashtray from the small drawer by the sink. Put there last by Cole, she realized, feeling a small, electric sting at the thought of his hands on this object. Each little stab like this seemed to move the larger pain further away from her center. She was beginning to understand how her marriage would some-day be fully apparent to her memory's eye and yet untouchable. Like a butterfly under glass.

"What'd y'all do?" Hannie-Mavis asked, clicking her lighter.

"Well, first we mowed. Then we looked at old junk in the storeroom, and then we caught bugs for a couple of hours. I taught her how to identify insects, if you can believe it. Does she make good grades in school? She's very sharp."

"She makes grades when she feels like it. Which is not very often."

"I'll bet. So then we made a bonfire and weeded the garden in the dark, which was actually fun, and then we came in and ate *eggah bi sabaneh* at ten o'clock."

"Well, mercy. That sounds fancy."

"Not really. Just greens and hard-boiled eggs."

"You got that child to eat *greens?* Good God in Heaven."

"It was the purslane and pigweeds we pulled out of the bean patch. Weeds for dinner, she thought that was just dandy. She said, and I quote, 'This here'd make Aint Lois shit her britches.'"

Hannie-Mavis clucked her tongue. "Oh, boy. No love lost be-tween those two."

"Listen, do you know what Lois did to make her so mad?"

"Made her try on a dress, is what I heard."

Lusa rested her elbows on the table. "Yes, and while she was at it she took Crys's favorite corduroys away from her and cut them up for rags."

"Oh, now, that's bad."

"Crys had made some deal with Jesus about wearing those clothes till her mother got better. Poor kid."

"Oh, no. That is bad. Lois should not have done that."

"No, she shouldn't. That kid needs all the love she can get right now, and that's just hateful."

Hannie-Mavis smoked in silence for a minute. "It is. But it's Lois all over for you. Lois is just mad at the world, and she takes it out on anybody."

"Why? She's got a good husband, nice kids. Ten million knick-knacks. What's her complaint?"

"Law, honey, I don't know. She was always that way. Mad she wasn't born prettier, I guess. Mad because she's big-boned."

"But Mary Edna's big-boned, too—even more so."

"Yes, but see, Mary Edna don't know it. And Lord help the poor soul that ever tells her so."

Lusa hazarded a weak laugh, rubbing her eyes. She suddenly felt exhausted. These were serious revelations, though. Even without having known their parents, she could see the two different bloodlines: Hannie-Mavis, Jewel, and Emaline were sensitive and fine-featured; Mary Edna and Lois were confident, big-handed, long-jawed, hefty. Cole was all these genes come together perfectly at last, the family's final measure. Cole Widener, adored by all, won by Lusa, stolen by death. No wonder this family was still quaking in the aftermath. It was a Greek tragedy.

The two women sat looking at each other across the table, then dropped their eyes and sipped their tea. "I'm fine to keep Crys till tomorrow or the next day, even," Lusa said. "Truly, it's fine with me, if Jewel needs the rest. Tell Lois she can send Lowell up here, too. I think they'd be better off together."

"Those poor children," Hannie-Mavis said.

"They'll be all right. Whatever happens, they'll be OK. Big families are a blessing, I can see that."

Hannie-Mavis looked at her, surprised. "You think we're all right?"

"Who, your family? I think you're a hard club to join, is all."

She laughed a little. "That's what Joel said for years after we got married: 'Going to a Widener get-together is like a gol-dang trip to China.' Why is that? We don't seem like anything special to me."

"Every family's its own trip to China, I guess. For me it's been extra hard because of everything. I know it must have been a shock when he took up with me so fast."

"Now, that's so. He was hightailing it up to Lexington ever chance he got, and for a while there we didn't even know why. Mary Edna was worried he was going to the racetracks. We all just about dropped our drawers when he sets right there in that chair one Sunday supper, I think Jewel and me were cooking for everybody, and he says, 'Next Sunday you get to meet the smartest, prettiest woman ever to walk on top of this world, and for some reason she's agreed to be my wife.'"

"It was kind of a shock to me, too," Lusa said quietly, willing her thoughts to go blank. "And then, now, this." She glanced up at Hannie-Mavis. "Me inheriting the place. I do understand why the family resents me."

Hannie-Mavis looked at her with a gaze Lusa recognized—that same lost, helpless, blue-lashed stare from the funeral. She'd said, *I don't know what we'll do without him. We're all just as lost as you are.*

"We don't resent you," she said.

Lusa shook her head. "You resent that I inherited the farm. I know that. I know you even talked to a lawyer about it."

Hannie-Mavis gave her a worried glance.

"Or somebody did," Lusa dodged. "I don't know who."

Hannie-Mavis smoked her cigarette and poked at the edges of her polished nails, which were as shiny and red as her shoes. "It was Mary Edna," she replied finally. "I don't think she meant you any harm. We just wanted to know what would happen, you know, *after*. Since he didn't have any will."

"Look, I don't blame you. I live every day in this beautiful old house you all grew up in, on the best of your family's land, feeling like I stole it from you. But there are problems, too. This farm has debts. I sure didn't plan on having my life turn out this way."

"Nobody planned what happened to Cole." She smoked

awhile, letting that sentence hang alone in the stratified blue haze above their heads. Then she asked suddenly, "You want to know what I really think?"

"What?" Lusa said, a bit startled.

"Daddy knew what he was doing. He did us girls all a favor by giving us pieces too little to live off of."

"How can you say that?"

"It's true! We're better off. Think about it. Which one of us would rather be up here trying to keep body and soul together with this farm? We don't want it, me and Joel—Lord, he's just cars, cars, cars. That's the only work that makes him happy. I'd hate us to be tied down to this place. And not Jewel, even if she was still married and not sick. She loves the house better than any of us, but Sheldon was no farmer, honey. And Mary Edna and Herb, see, they have his family's dairy—they're set up just fine, they couldn't handle another farm. Emaline and Frank, I think they're just as happy both working jobs instead of farming. I *know* they are."

"What about Lois and Big Rickie? They're still farming."

"Big Rickie loves to farm, that's true. But he's got no more call to own this place than you do. He's married in, just the same as you."

"Well, but Lois. They could be up here."

Hannie-Mavis blew air through her lips like a horse. "First of all, Lois couldn't grow a tomato to save her life, nor do the canning, either. She hates to get dirty. I don't think Lois gives a hoot about this place, really and truly. She might act like it. But if it was hers, I tell you what, she'd tear this house down and build her something brick with plastic ducks in the yard and a three-car garage."

Lusa could see that whole picture in a flash.

"They don't any of them want it, really," Hannie-Mavis said earnestly. "Here's what it is: They just don't want anybody else to have it."

"Me, you mean."

"No, I don't mean *you*, honey. But see, we all know what's going to happen. First we thought you'd leave and the farm would come back to us. Now it looks like you're staying. Well, that's good. That's fine, that you're here. But see . . ."

Hannie-Mavis reached for the box of tissue, dabbed the corners of her eyes carefully, and added another small white wad to the population that was growing on the table. Lusa could see that whatever she meant to say next was very difficult.

"What?" she asked gently. She felt frightened.

"Well, a few years down the line you'll marry somebody around here. Then this farm will be *his*."

Lusa let air burst through her teeth. "That's ridiculous."

"No, it is not. Nobody says you shouldn't get married again. You will, and that's fine. But see, it'll pass on to his children. It won't be our homeplace anymore. It won't be the *Widener* place."

Lusa was stunned. She'd never dreamed this was the problem. "How can you think that?"

"Think what?"

"I don't know, all of it. Who around here am I going to marry?"

"Honey, honey, you're not even thirty yet. We all loved Cole, but nobody thinks you're going to carry a torch for him the rest of your life."

Lusa looked down into the bottom of her empty teacup, which was blank. No leaves, no future to read. "I have to think about this in the light of day," she said. "I have no idea what to say. I just had no idea."

Hannie-Mavis tilted her head. "I didn't aim to hurt your feelings."

"No, you didn't. I thought the problem was *me*. I didn't realize the problem was—what would you call it? Progeny. The family line."

"Well," she said, slapping her hands flat on the table. "I'm going to call it a night. This day's done me enough damage already."

"I think it's tomorrow already."

"Law, so much the worse. I've got to get home and feed the cats, 'cause I'm sure Joel forgot, and then get back over to Jewel's." She gathered up her balls of Kleenex and stuffed them in her purse. Lusa wondered if this was a country custom, to take your own secretions with you when you left. They stood facing each other for a second but held back from a hug.

"Please tell Jewel I'd be happy to keep both kids for another day. And if she needs *anything*—I mean it. You can't do all the nursing by yourself. You get some rest."

"I will, honey. And I'll tell Lois to bring up Lowell, if he wants to come. Thank you, honey."

"*Lusa,*" Lusa said. "I'm your sister now, you're stuck with me, so you could all start using my name."

Hannie-Mavis stopped and turned back in the hallway, touching the sleeve of her dress. She seemed hesitant to speak. "We're scared of getting it wrong, is why we don't say it. Is that a Lexington name?"

Lusa laughed. "Polish. It's short for Elizabeth."

"Oh, well, I thought so. That it was foreign."

"But it's not hard to say," Lusa insisted. "What kind of name is Hannie-Mavis?"

Hannie-Mavis smiled and shook her head. "Just strange, honey. Just awful, awful strange. Daddy was original, and Mommy couldn't spell. You get what you get."

In the morning Lusa was startled awake, once again, by the sound of car tires on the gravel drive. She sat up in bed, looked at the light in the window, and checked the clock. She'd slept late. Whoever it was out there was going to catch her in her nightgown at ten o'clock, a mortal sin in farm country.

But she heard the car door slam and the tires slowly roll away down the hill again. She heard footsteps come toward the house at a clip, and footsteps in the next room as well, bare feet muffled by the hall rug and then slapping quickly down the steps. Lusa got up and walked quietly out into the hall but heard nothing more. Then voices, whispering. She looked down over the banister and her face went hot, then cold. There they were again, side by side, sitting very close together on the second step from the bottom. A small boy and a bigger girl with her arm around his shoulders to protect him from the world. He was not the little boy she'd believed she would know anywhere, at any age, and the older one was not his sister Jewel.

Not Jewel and Cole. Crys and Lowell.

Predators

he sound of a shot startled Deanna awake. She froze, listening to the after-ring of that sound through the hollow and the forced, universal silence that spread out behind it. There was no mistaking it for anything but a gunshot. She sat forward and looked around groggily, trying to shake the wool out of her head. This was the third or fourth occasion she'd fallen asleep smack in the middle of the day, this time in the old overstuffed brocade chair on the porch, where she'd sat down to rest just for a minute.

She rubbed absently at the viny pattern of the nubbly green upholstery, tracing with her fingers the long brown stain that ran across one of the arms onto the seat—she sometimes wondered how this chair had plunged from an elegant former life in someone's parlor to humble service on this porch. And how had *she* gotten here today, catnapping in this chair? Deanna tried to reconstruct her afternoon. She remembered only plopping down in the chair and pulling the knots out of her bootlaces to appease her aching feet; that was the last thing. Before that, a morning-long battle with exhaustion. It had felt like walking through neck-deep pond water just to drag herself up here from the hemlock bridge where she and Eddie had been working earlier. Two big trees had fallen across the trail and had to be cleared. Eddie happily took up the ax and set to limbing and chopping while she wielded the chain saw, and yes, she'd been glad for the help. But she hated the way he showed her up, stripping off his shirt so the sweat ran down the planes of his neck and working cheerfully all morning without a break. She didn't like being skunked. She hated feeling older than him and like a weakling, a girl. An old lady, if the truth be told. After the first hour her arms had ached and her knees had been set to buckle and the roar of the chain saw had drowned out her grumbling at the sweat and sawdust in the collar of her T-shirt. By noon her one and only wish was to go flop down in the middle of the cold creek branch, clothes and all. When the chain saw ran out of gas, she was deeply grateful.

Her plan had been to sit down here on the porch for a minute before hurrying to refill their water jug and the gas can and get straight back down there. Right. She shaded her eyes and frowned at the sun, which was touching the crowns of the poplars. She'd slept for hours. Then she noticed the ax lying at the end of the porch. She studied it, puzzled. He must have come back up here looking for her when she didn't return. Saw her asleep, left again, and now was—where? Panic rose into her throat. The gunfire, that would have been *him*. Eddie Bondo had shot something while she slept.

She jumped up and paced the porch, gripped with the surreal possibility that her obsessive dread had come true. But there had been only the one shot; he couldn't have killed much with just one shot, since they weren't all together anymore. They were leaving the den to hunt now, all of them. She'd seen one or two young at a time running with an adult, as high up as the hemlock grove and all the way down to the boundary line. Most nights now she heard their yips and tremulous, rising howls. They were all over this mountain. She couldn't keep them safe anymore. Dragging her untied boot-laces, she went quickly inside the cabin and checked the corner where his rifle had stood for most of two months. No surprise: it was gone. *Bastard*.

She went to her desk and yanked open the drawer where she kept her pistol, but then she just stared at it. What did she think she was going to do? She slowly closed the drawer and stood with her head back and her eyes closed, stood that way for a long time while tears crept onto her temples. No more shots rang out. Only the one.

She was still not ready to face him—maybe would never be—when she heard him whistling at a distance, coming up the Forest Service road. She glanced out the window, went to the door and bolted it, sat back down on the bed, put her boots back on, stared some more at the book she'd been staring at, then went to the window again. Here he came, grinning like a polecat, resting his gun on one shoul-der and in his other hand toting some object that resembled a dark jacket. She squinted. Something black. Something feathered, with wings, bouncing along limply in his hand as he carried it by its feet. A *turkey*. She ran outside, banging her forehead hard against the door in her haste to get through it, having completely forgotten she'd bolted it shut a minute before. She watched him from the porch, holding her head. The pain burned tears into her eyes, but relief made her laugh like a child.

When he saw her there he hitched a small, extra step into his gait and held up his trophy. "Happy Thanksgiving!"

"Happy Easter's more like it. Turkey season was done with in April." She touched her fingers to her forehead and looked at them, but she wasn't bleeding. She felt delirious, unable to stop laughing. He halted ten feet away and appraised her.

"Well, hell. You're going to let me live. I thought you'd skin me for this."

"I'm mad as hell," she declared, trying to sound like it. "It's high summer. That turkey could be brooding a whole clutch of young. If that's so, you've killed a family."

"Nope. This was Daddy."

"It's a tom? Did you know that *before* you shot it?"

He gave her a wounded look.

"Well, I'm sorry. You've got a good eye, and you know better than to shoot a hen turkey in July. But still, look at you, poaching. Smack under the nose of a game warden."

He walked straight toward her, turkey and all, and kissed her mouth with such enthusiasm that she had to take several steps backward. "This is the warden's dinner," he said.

"You don't need to be shooting me any dinner. And it's too late for dinner anyway, it's suppertime."

"It's your *supper*, then"—he kissed her again—"and I did need to do it. I've been bumming off you all summer. You don't even know what a good provider I am. I considered bringing you a deer."

She laughed. "Oh, boy. That'd be hard to hide if one of my colleagues happened to show up."

He handed her the bird and checked the chamber of his rifle before he set it carefully against the wall. "You need protein," he said. "You've been living too long on bird food, and you're peaked. You're walking around here with iron-poor tired blood."

She laughed. "You're too young to even know what that means. *Now* what are you doing?" He'd picked up the shovel and was over at the edge of the clearing by the boulder, eyeing the ground around it. "You thinking to give it a Christian burial?"

"We need a fire pit. I've been hankering to do this all summer."

She smiled at his *hankering*. "Where'd you learn to talk like 'at, young fella?"

"Some beautiful long-haired hillbilly girl."

He poked the point of the shovel into the soft dirt. Deanna studied the bird in her hand, holding it out at arm's length. It weighed more than a gallon jug of water—ten or twelve pounds, maybe. "So what are your exact plans for tom here?"

"Pluck him."

"Right. But you have to scald him in hot water first to get the feathers loose, and I don't think I have any pot big enough to dunk this old boy in."

"Yes, you do—one of those big metal cans you keep the beans and rice in," he said without looking up. He was excavating a good-sized pit. "We'll boil the water to scald it in there first, and then we can empty it out and cook the bird inside there, with the coals piled all around it."

She looked at Eddie, surprised. "You *have* been thinking about this all summer."

"Yep."

"Carnivorous fantasies," she said.

"Yep."

She went inside, smiling in spite of herself as she checked the bottoms of the storage canisters and emptied out the one that looked more watertight. She felt excited. She'd passed so many days now on forest time, timeless time, noting the changes in leaf and song and weather but imposing no human agenda. Even her own birthday she'd let pass without mentioning it to Eddie. But something in her body had been longing for a celebration, or so it seemed right now. He'd guessed right. She *wanted* this feast. An extravagant event to mark this extravagant summer.

When she carried the empty canister outside, Eddie had already lined the pit with rocks and was starting the fire. While he built up kindling and the rising flame licked around the tall metal can, she carried water one kettleful at a time from the pump spigot inside the cabin. The cold water hissed and sheared into columns of steam as she poured it down the inside of the hot cylinder. On her trips back and forth she paused just once to examine the turkey. She let herself touch the bumpy red skin on his head and wattles and his translucent eyelids, then stroked the iridescent sheen on his dark feathers. Not a human's idea of beauty, maybe, but she felt something for all the days he'd passed in the filtered sunlight of this forest, meditating on fat berries and the far-off sound of a mate. Eddie was right, they'd done no damage to anyone's childhood here—turkey paternity was the hit-and-run kind. But she wondered what mark this grand male had left on his mountain. She hoped the last of his genes were warm in a nest being brooded somewhere.

It was going on dusk by the time the water finally boiled. They argued about whether it was really necessary to scald the bird before plucking, and Deanna went ahead and pulled the long, stiff wing and tail feathers; she couldn't remove the softer breast feathers without tearing the flesh, since the bird was already cold. Eddie deferred to her expertise. She was surprised her hands still knew the motions of plucking and squeezing out pinfeathers after so many years of grocery-store birds or none at all. In recent years she'd hardly eaten meat. But nearly every weekend of her childhood she'd helped butcher a chicken or two. This carcass was impressively large by comparison, even after she'd stripped it naked. Eddie helped her to lift it by the feet and dunk it into the boiling pot for a full minute, and later, to hold it over the flame to singe off the down feathers, and he steadied the bird while she used the ax to chop off its head and feet. He also managed to drag the heavy pot to the edge of the fire pit and continued to build up the coals while she settled down on the flat boulder to eviscerate their prey.

"Leaving the dirty work to the womenfolk," she muttered, not really minding the task but still faintly put out with Eddie for being so cheerful this morning while she was dying on her feet. She put both hands deep inside the bird and gently loosened the membrane that attached the intestines and lungs to the body wall. He watched, impressed, as she pulled the entire mass out in a single glistening package and used her knife to cut carefully around the excretory vent, freeing the mess of viscera, which she set on the boulder beside the carcass. She poked through it, extracted the heart, and looked at it closely, then pitched it to Eddie, causing him to yelp. She laughed. "Anything you're willing to eat, you ought to be willing to look under its hood first. That's what Dad used to tell me."

"I'm not squeamish; I just never cared for bird guts. I'll gut a deer over a turkey any day."

"Why's that?"

"I don't know—personal preference. It's not so delicate. You don't have all those crops and craws and things to deal with."

"Oh, I see. This is a more skilled surgery than you're qualified to handle." She cut the skin all the way down the length of the tom's long neck after carefully examining the wounds that had killed it. It was a good, clean head-and-neck shot: Eddie had done well. The carcass wouldn't be riddled with the hazard of tooth-cracking bird shot, as had so often been the case with the squirrels and turkeys that neighbors gave to her dad. She reached in with two fingers to pull out the damaged esophagus and windpipe. "Boy, he had a voice, this guy. Look at that."

"He has gobbled his last."

"He has," she agreed.

"I can't believe you," he said. "The happy carnivore."

She looked up. "What? Humans are omnivores. We've got meat teeth and fiber teeth and a gut that's fond of both. I know a little bit too much about animals to try to deny what I am."

"But I shot a bird off your precious mountain. I thought for sure you'd grab the gun and shoot *me*."

"Then why'd you do it?"

He flashed his one-sided grin. "You know me. I like a challenge."

She rinsed her hands in a bowl of water, then set to the task of washing every inch of the carcass, looking it over for the last pinfeathers. After it was clean and dry she would rub its skin with salt and a little oil. "It's just a turkey," she said after a minute.

"What do you mean, 'just a turkey'? You won't even let me squash a spider in the outhouse with my shoe."

"A spider's a predator. You kill that gal and we'll have a hundred flies in there, which is not my idea of a good time."

"Oh, right, predators matter more." He went to the firewood pile for another armload of kindling.

She shrugged. "I won't say this guy didn't matter. Everybody in Zeb County can't be up here shooting turkeys, or they'd all be gone by full dark. But something would have gotten him sooner or later. An owl, maybe, if he stuck his neck out after dark. Or a bobcat."

Eddie was picking through the pile, pulling out medium-sized hickory logs, but he stopped to stare at her with raised eyebrows.

"What?" she asked. "It's a prey species. It has fallen prey to us. I can deal with that. Predation's a sacrament, Eddie; it culls out the sick and the old, keeps populations from going through their own roofs. Predation is *honorable*."

"That's not how Little Red Riding Hood tells it," he said.

"Oh, man, don't get me started on the subject of childhood brainwash. I *hate* that. Every fairy story, every Disney movie, every plot with animals in it, the bad guy is always the top carnivore. Wolf, grizzly, anaconda, *Tyrannosaurus rex*."

"Don't forget Jaws," he said.

"Oh, yeah: shark." She watched him return to the fire with his carefully stacked armload of wood. He squatted and began feeding the flames again with such tender care, examining each stick on both sides before extending it toward the tongues of the fire, that he might have been feeding a cranky toddler. "I will never understand it," she said. "We're the top of *our* food chain, so you'd think we'd relate to those guys the *best*. Seems like we'd be trying to talk them into trade agreements."

Eddie laughed at that. "So you're telling me that as a kid, you were rooting for the wolf to eat the Riding Hood babe?"

"My last name was Wolfe. I took it all kind of personally." She finished drying the carcass inside and out with a rag and inspected the cavity. "I sure as heck wanted Wile E. Coyote to get that stupid roadrunner."

"But then the show would be over," he protested.

"Amen to that." She stood up and dried her hands on her jeans. "I'm going to get some salt."

Inside the cabin she poured some olive oil from the square metal container into a jar and dug out her moisture-proof can of salt. She peered into the vegetable bin: plenty of onions, and some potatoes left, too, burgeoning with pink sprouts. Four carrots. She would throw all these into the pot with the turkey once it was halfway cooked. And then drop in a few smoldering hickory twigs and put the lid on to give it a nice smoky flavor. She glanced at the clock on the bookshelf and tried to guess how long this would all take. Hours, of course. And she was ravenous. They would get to smell the heavenly, mounting fragrance and anticipate their feast for hours. Nothing was more wonderful than waiting for a happiness you could be sure of. The pleasure of food was something she'd nearly forgotten. Her sympathy for Jaws and *T. rex* notwithstanding, Deanna was a little surprised at herself—to be engaged in this act of carnivory and just thrilled about it.

When she came outside she saw that Eddie had managed to dump the hot water out of the pot without dousing the fire, which was now roaring. He was piling on logs the size of arms and legs. Luckily her woodpile was in no danger of depletion: there were oak and hickory and poplar logs neatly split and stacked head-high against the cabin's west wall, in spite of its being only July. Splitting firewood seemed to be Eddie's favorite exertion—or second-favorite, anyway. She paused to admire his body as he stood back from the heat and brushed bark off his hands. It was so easy to let go of their animosity in these moments of animal grace. She felt moved by what he'd done for her, his act of provision.

He turned and caught her watching. "What are you thinking about?" he asked.

"Hankerings," she said. "Eating that bird. You may be right about me, I may be a little anemic. Why, what are you thinking about?"

"The gospel according to Deanna. It's a sin to kill a spider but not a turkey."

She walked over to the boulder and settled down beside her next meal. "Oh, *sin*, who knows what that is? Something invented by mothers, I guess. And me never having one." She glanced up. "What?"

He shook his head. "Just you. I was trying to be serious. For once."

"What, about spiders and turkeys? You know about that as well as I do, it's not complicated. Removing a predator has bigger consequences for a system."

"Than taking out one of its prey. I know. Numbers."

"Simple math, Eddie Bondo."

He seemed thoughtful, squatting by the fire with his hands between his knees. "How many big carnivores on this mountain, you think?"

"What does 'big' mean? Mammals, birds?" She looked down the narrow cleft of the hollow, where lightning bugs were beginning to rise in irregular yellow streaks. "Maybe one bobcat per five hundred acres. One mountain lion per mountain, period. Big birds of prey, like great horned owls, one pair needs maybe"—she thought about this—"two hundred acres, I'd guess, to feed itself and raise two or three young in a year."

"And how many turkeys?"

"Oh, gosh, there's gaggles of them walking around this hollow. A turkey lays fourteen eggs without half thinking about it. If something gets one of her babies she might not quite notice. If a fox gets the whole nest, she'll go bat her eyes at tom here and plunk out fourteen more eggs." She pondered the equation for a minute as she worked. "But still, turkeys are scarce compared to their prey. Grubs and things, there's *millions* of them. It's like a pyramid scheme."

Eddie was silent, poking at the fire but still listening. He seemed to understand that this was not a casual conversation to her. She shook a handful of salt out of the can into her palm and rubbed the bird's stippled skin, first with the gritty salt and then with the smooth, cool oil. When she spoke again, she took care to keep the emotion out of her voice.

"The life of a top carnivore is the most expensive item in the pyramid, that's the thing. In the case of a coyote, or a big cat, the mother spends a whole year raising her young. Not just a few weeks. She has to teach them to stalk and hunt and everything there is to doing that job. She's lucky if even one of her kids makes it through. If something gets him, there goes that mama's whole year of work down the drain."

She looked up, catching his eye directly. "If you shoot him, Eddie, that's what you've taken down. A big chunk of his mother's whole life chance at replacing herself. And you've let loose an extra thousand rodents on the world that he would have eaten. It's not just one life."

He was looking away. She waited until she had his eye again. "When you get a coyote in your rifle sight and you're fixing to pull the trigger, what happens? Do you forget about everything else in the world until there's just you and your enemy?"

He thought about it. "Something like that. Hunting's like that. You focus."

"'Focus,'" she said. "That's what you call it? The idea that there's just the two of you left, alone in the world?"

"I guess." He shrugged.

"But that's wrong. There's no such thing as *alone*. That animal was going to do something important in its time—eat a lot of things, or be eaten. There's all these connected things you're about to blow a hole in. They can't *all* be your enemy, because one of those connected things is you."

He reached into the fire pit with a stout, forked limb, carefully rearranging the burning logs into a square with a space in the center where the pot would go. "I would never shoot a bobcat," he said without looking at her.

"No? Well, good. You're not as stupid as some predator hunters, then. Let's give you a medal."

He glanced up sharply. "Who stepped on *your* tail?"

"I know about this stuff, Eddie." She wiped her hands with the rag and listened to her heart beating in her ears. Two months she'd known this man, and for two months she'd been nursing an outrage without giving it a voice. She spoke quietly now, as her father used to when he was angry. "They have those hunts all over. It's no secret; they advertise in gun magazines. There's one going on right now in Arizona, the Predator Hunt Extreme, with a ten-thousand-dollar prize for whoever shoots the most."

"The most what?"

"It's a predator kill, period. Just pile up the bodies. Bobcats, coyotes, mountain lions, foxes—that's their definition of a predator."

"Not foxes."

"*Yes* foxes. Some of your colleagues are even terrified of a little gray fox. An animal that lives on mice and grasshoppers."

"It's not about fear," he said.

"Can you feature the damage those men will do to the state of Arizona in just one weekend, the plague of mice and grasshoppers they'll cause? If you can't feel bad for a hundred mother-years left to rot in a pile, think of the damn *rats*."

He didn't respond. She lifted the bird with care, cradled it against her forearms, and carried it over to the empty canister, which seemed large enough but not quite the right shape. She stood looking down into it for a minute and decided to stand the bird more or less on its head—or rather, the region of its former head. She shifted the carcass around until its drumsticks stuck up satisfactorily, but the joy of this celebration had ebbed. "Here," she said, "help me get this on the fire."

Between them they lifted the heavy pot and lowered it down

into the center of the fire. She poured in a little water from the kettle and settled the lid onto the pot, then washed her hands with the rest of the water. There was a faint chill in the evening air, enough that the cold water stung her hands. But then her hands and feet were always cold, lately. She held her palms up to the fire's warmth. Almost immediately the pot began to hiss with satisfactory little crackles, the age-old conversation of steam and fat. Deanna sat down on the ground on the opposite side of the fire pit from Eddie, facing him through the flames. He poked at the fire a little more, seeming restless. He was squatting on his heels, not sitting.

"It's *not*," he finally said.

"What's not what?"

"Hunting predators. It's not about fear."

She pulled her knees up to her chest and put her arms around them, holding her elbows in her palms. "Then what's it about? Do tell. I'm ready to be enlightened."

He shook his head, got up to collect two more logs from the woodpile, then shook his head again. "You can't be crying over every single brown-eyed life in the world."

"I already told you, that's not my religion. I grew up on a farm. I've helped gut about any animal you can name, and I've watched enough harvests to know that cutting a wheat field amounts to more decapitated bunnies under the combine than you'd believe."

She stopped speaking when her memory lodged on an old vision from childhood: a raccoon she found just after the hay mower ran it over. She could still see the matted gray fur, the gleaming jawbone and shock of scattered teeth so much like her own, the dark blood soaking into the ground all on one side, like a shadow of this creature's final, frightened posture. She could never explain to Eddie how it was, the undercurrent of tragedy that went with farming. And the hallelujahs of it, too: the straight, abundant rows, the corn tassels raised up like children who all knew the answer. The calves born slick and clean into their leggy black-and-white perfection. Life and death always right there in your line of sight.

Most people lived so far from it, they thought you could just choose, carnivore or vegetarian, without knowing that the chemicals on grain and cotton killed far more butterflies and bees and bluebirds and whippoorwills than the mortal cost of a steak or a leather jacket. Just clearing the land to grow soybeans and corn had killed about everything on half the world. Every cup of coffee equaled one dead songbird in the jungle somewhere, she'd read.

He was watching her, waiting for whatever was inside to come out, and she did the best she could. "Even if you never touch meat, you're costing something its blood," she said. "Don't patronize me. I know that. Living takes life."

A fierce hiss came from inside the pot, inspiring her to listen for a minute to this turkey's last lament.

"Good, we agree on that," he said. "Living takes life."

"But it can be thoughtful. A little bit humble about the necessity, maybe. You can consider the costs of your various choices. Or you can blow big holes in the world for no better reason than simple fear."

He held her eye. "I'm not *afraid* of a coyote."

"Then *leave* it . . . the *hell* . . . *alone.*"

They glared at each other through the trembling haze of heat above the fire.

"Why does it come down to this?" he asked.

"Because I'm going to change your mind or die trying."

"Die trying, then. Because you can't and you won't change my mind. I'm a ranching boy from the West, and hating coyotes is my religion. Blood of the lamb, so to speak. Don't try to convert me, and I won't try to convert you."

"I won't go shoot your lambs in the head, either."

"You are, though," he said. "In a way you are. If you're trying to save those bastards, you're slaughtering lambs."

She uncrossed her arms and threw a handful of dry grass into the fire, watching each strand light up and glow like the filament of a lightbulb. "If you only knew."

"Knew what?"

"You said you'd read my thesis. You promised me you would, one time."

He shook his head, grinning. "You never give up."

"You *did*. You gave me your word."

"I must have been trying to get you into bed."

"I think we were already there."

He leaned sideways, looking at her around the edge of the flames. "Likely."

"So?"

"So? Tell me why I should read it." Still on his heels, he made his way around the fire pit like some bent-kneed insect and stopped a few feet away from her. "What will I learn about coyotes that I don't already know in my mean little fearful heart?"

"That they have one of the most complex vocal systems of any land mammal. That they live on rodents and fruits and seeds and a hundred other things besides lambs."

"Lambs are on the list, though."

"Lambs are on the list."

"I already knew that."

She tossed another handful of grass into the fire. "OK. And they have elaborate courting rituals that involve a lot of talking and licking, and they bring each other presents of food. Meat, especially."

He looked at the pot on the fire, and then at Deanna.

"And once they form a pair bond," she said, "it's usually for life."

"And I'm supposed to admire that?"

"You're not supposed to feel any way about it. It's just information."

He nodded. "OK, what else?"

"They're the most despised species in America. Even the U.S. Government is in the business of killing them, to the tune of maybe a hundred thousand animals a year, using mainly cyanide traps and gunning from helicopters. Not to mention the good work done by your pals at the predator-hunt extravaganzas."

"Yep. Go on."

"And after a hundred years of systematic killing, there are more coyotes now than there have ever been, in more places than they ever lived before."

"There. Stop right there. Why is that?"

"It's a mystery, isn't it? We kill grizzlies, wolves, blue whales, and those guys slump off toward extinction as fast as they can. Darn coyotes, though, they're more trouble. I think the Indians are right: they're downright tricky."

"And?"

"And the more we attack them, the more of them there are. I can't tell you exactly why, but I have a lot of ideas."

"Give me one good guess."

"OK. Coyotes aren't just predators, they're also a prey species. Unlike the blue whale or the grizzly, they're real used to being hunted. Their main predator before we came along was wolves. Which we erased from the map of America as fast as we could."

"Oh."

"Yeah, *oh* is right. Wolves. There's no such thing as killing one thing, that's what I'm trying to tell you. Every dead animal was somebody's lunch or somebody's population control."

He took up a longer stick and jabbed at the framework of burning logs surrounding the pot, sending an impressive display of sparks swirling high into the air.

"Will you quit that?" she said, laying a hand on his arm. "You're going to burn down the woods. Just leave it alone."

"I'm trying to get the coals to settle."

"Gravity does that." *This fire can burn itself,* she wanted to tell him, *without a man in charge of it.* "My dad used to say if you play in the fire, you'll pee in the bed."

"Worth it," Eddie said firmly, jabbing and sending up more sparks.

"Quit it," she said, taking away his stick. "Here, *sit*, you're making me nervous."

He sat with his shoulder against hers. They listened to the elaborate sounds of the fire and the cooking bird. There was even a high, musical whistle—steam escaping from somewhere. Deanna's hunger had grown to a sweet, gnawing ache in her belly.

"So we helped them out by killing the wolves," he said, unexpectedly. "And what's your next good guess?"

"It's not a guess, it's a fact. Coyotes breed faster when they're being hunted."

He stared straight ahead, into the fire. "How?"

"They have bigger litters. Sometimes they'll even share a den, so where you'd normally see just the alpha female breeding, now one of her sisters breeds, too. They work in family groups, with most of the adults helping to raise one female's young. It might be that when some adults are killed out of a group, there's more food for the young. Or maybe there's a shift in the reproductive effort. *Something* happens. What we know for sure is, killing adults increases the chances of survival for the young."

"Wow."

She turned toward him. "Hey, Eddie Bondo."

He turned to face her. "What?"

"Boo. Life's not simple."

"So I'm told."

"Hey. Read the book. It'll keep you on the edge of your seat. My major professor claimed he remained conscious through the whole two hundred pages."

Eddie looked back at the fire. "I don't think I'm going to care for the ending."

⌒

The moon was up somewhere, and big, just a little past full. It hadn't yet climbed above the mountains that shadowed this hollow, but the sky was collecting a brightness Deanna could sense through her closed eyelids. She willed her body to find a flat plane of repose instead of turning and turning like a rolling pin on a piecrust. On these sleepless nights she got the blanket in a tangle that left Eddie exposed to the elements.

They'd dragged the mattress outside before collapsing on it in a turkey-stuffed delirium. But she'd always slept outside in summer, whenever the nights were warm enough; moonlight didn't usually disturb her sleep. *Nothing* usually disturbed her sleep. She'd never known insomnia before these last few weeks. She'd never known falling asleep in the daytime, either. Something had gotten her out of whack. Deanna wasn't sure whether these worries roaming her brain were keeping her awake nights or whether they had just moved into the vacant apartment of an insomniac head.

The urge to roll over consumed her like pain, she couldn't resist it any longer, so she moved cautiously from her side to her back. Immediately that felt uncomfortable, too. She tried to forget her body, her immensely full stomach, and Eddie beside her—all these troublesome symptoms of being human. She tried, slowly, to inhale and absorb this night instead. It was an extraordinary time to be awake, if you gave in to it: these hours of settled darkness when the insects quieted and the air cooled and scents rose delicately out of the ground. She could smell leaf mold, mushrooms, and the faint trace of a skunk that must have come poking around the turkey bones in the woods right after she and Eddie fell into bed and she fell asleep, hard, briefly, before popping indelibly awake again.

Now her brain settled on phoebe worries: they might have scared the mother off her nest before dark, or a baby might have fallen out, something that had already happened twice. The fledglings were nearly old enough to fly and slightly bigger even than adults now because of their fluffy juvenile feathers—big enough to make it way too crowded in there. Two days in a row, Deanna had picked up a fallen nestling off the ground and tucked it back in on top of its siblings. Eddie claimed a bird wouldn't return to a nest once a human had touched it; Deanna knew better from experience, but she let the mother bird answer. She swooped back onto her nest just seconds after Deanna stepped away from it.

Please gather your feathered courage and fledge soon, she beseeched these babies, for they were getting to be a handful. She'd been tiptoeing around underneath the phoebe nursery for weeks and forcing Eddie to do the same. This mother had already lost her first brood to their carelessness, and it was too late in the season for her to start again if this one failed. In a few more days, maybe tomorrow, their worries would be over. These children would stretch their wings and leave home for good.

She flexed her left foot against a cramp and fought the urge to roll over onto her stomach. Impossible to keep still in this mess of blankets. The only thing to do with such a restlessness was get up and keep it company. She would walk in the woods. There would be enough light with this moon, once it had crested the mountaintop. But first she would check on the phoebes. Taking great care not to disturb Eddie, she got up quietly, found her boots next to the mattress, pulled on her jeans and buttoned them under her nightshirt, then went into the cabin to fetch the flashlight. She moved very quietly around to the porch to take a peek. The flashlight wouldn't disturb the mother if she was on the nest; this late at night it wouldn't make her fly. Deanna searched the eave for the neat, round mound of woven grass. As she'd dreaded, the mother's brown-feathered head and little pointed beak weren't there where they ought to have been. Quickly she checked the porch floor for fallen angels, but none were there. She went inside and brought out the ladderback chair, then climbed up carefully, steadying herself with one hand on the roof joist. Nothing! The inside of the nest was a tidy pocket, perfectly empty. How could that be? Deanna had watched the mother catch bugs all afternoon, a slave to those four huge appetites. They wouldn't fledge at night. So where were they? She shone the beam on the floor again, searching all around the legs of the chair and farther away, in case they'd traveled as far as the edge of the porch in a feathery little panic. Nothing.

She clicked off the flashlight and thought a minute. Clicked it back on again. With the focused halo of light she scanned every inch of the top of the joist all the way out to the end of the eave, then searched along the other rafters. She passed over and then came back to what looked like a pile of black tubing. Studied it. Found the small, round, wide-set eyes shining back at her, perched smugly on top of the partially coiled body. She swept the light very slowly down the dark body until she found them: four discernible lumps.

She breathed hard against the urge to scream at this monster or tear it down from the rafters and smash its head. Breathed three more times, blowing out hard through her lips each time, feeling a faint coil of nausea inside her anger. This was her familiar, the same blacksnake that had lived in the roof all summer, the snake she had defended as a predator doing its job. Living takes life. *But not the babies,* she cried in her mind. *Not these; they were mine. At the end of the summer the babies are all there will be.*

She climbed down from the chair, clicked off the flashlight, and headed out into the woods, tense with fury and sadness. She didn't understand how far her emotions were running away with her until she felt the coolness of tears running down her face. She wiped them with the heel of her hand and kept walking, fast, away from the cabin and the scent of fire and flesh, up into the dark woods. What was this uncontrollable sorrow that kept surging through her body like hot water? In the last few days she had cried over everything: phoebes, tiredness, the sound of a gunshot, the absence of sleep. Idiotic, sentimental tears, female tears—what *was* this? Was this what they meant by hot flashes? But they didn't feel hot. Her body felt full and heavy and slow and human and *absent,* somehow, just a weight to be carried forward without its enthusiastic cycles of fertility and rest, the crests and valleys she had never realized she counted on so much. Deadweight, was that what she was now? An obsolete female biding its time until death?

Why did she feel so miserable about this? She'd never entirely approved of human beings and all their mess to begin with. Why would she have wanted to make more of them?

Halfway up the hillside she stopped to wipe her eyes and nose on the hem of her nightshirt. When she turned back toward the cabin she understood that the moon must have risen behind her. The trees on the opposite side of the hollow were washed in brilliant white light. They glowed like a fairy forest or a hillside of white birches far from home. She breathed in slowly. This was what she had. The beauty of this awful night. She listened for small yips in the distance, something to put in her heart beside the lost phoebes and the dread of another full moon rising with no more small celebrations from her body, ever again. She kept herself still and tried to think of coyote children emerging from the forest's womb with their eyes wide open, while the finite possibilities of her own children closed their eyes, finally, on this world.

{20}

Old Chestnuts

arnett paused halfway up the hill to take a rest. His heart was beating harder than seemed entirely necessary. He could hear the grumble and whine of the boy's chain saw already at work up there. She would be there, too, by now. They'd agreed to meet at noon to work out dividing the firewood and so on, and it was fourteen after, if his watch could be trusted. Well, she could wait. He was her elder; she could have a little respect. He sat down on a log next to the creek, just for a minute.

A damselfly lit on the tip of a horsetail reed very close to his head, near enough for him to see it well. He couldn't remember looking at one of these since he was a boy—they'd called them snake doctors—and yet, after all those years, here one was. Probably they'd been flittering around this creek all along, whether he paid them any notice or not. He leaned closer to inspect it: it was just about like a dragonfly, except that its wings folded back when it sat still instead of sticking out to the sides. This one's wings were black, not quite opaque but sheer like lace, with a pearly white dot at each wingtip. It reminded Garnett somehow of the underthings of women he'd known long ago, back when women wore garter belts and other contrivances that took some time and trouble to remove. Maybe women still did wear such things. How would he know? Ellen had been dead eight years, and for decades before that he certainly had had no occasion to learn about women's undergarments. He was a faithful man, a good Christian, and Ellen had been, too. She'd believed in the kind of sturdy cotton you could hang on the line without shame.

Now, why on earth was he sitting here in the woods thinking about women's underthings? He felt deeply embarrassed and prayed hastily to the Lord to forgive the unpredictable frailties of an old man's mind. He found his feet and headed on up the hill.

She was there, all right, having some kind of jolly conversation with the boy, who had put down the chain saw and fallen into her thrall as people always did. Like lambs to the slaughter, Garnett thought, but he found himself unexpectedly amused by the sight of this immense young hoodlum nodding courteously to the tiniest gray-haired woman ever to stalk the woods in a long skirt and hiking boots. They both turned to greet him.

"Mr. Walker! Now, you remember Oda's son Jarondell, don't you?"

"Of course. My regards to your mother." Remember *Jarondell*, he thought. That was a name for you. He was more likely to remember the expiration date on his can of Sevin dust.

"We were discussing maybe taking down a few more of these leaners," she told Garnett. "As long as we've got Jarondell up here. That cherry down the path, for one. It's over so far, I'd be surprised if it made it to the end of summer."

Oh, dear Lord, that cherry! Garnett had forgotten all about it, had sat right under it five minutes ago when he paused to rest by the creek. He'd forgotten to worry about the tree falling on him! The thought set him nearly into a panic, so that he was much too aware of the beating of his heart. He laid a hand on his chest.

"What's wrong? Are you attached to that cherry?" She watched him with a worried look, causing him a strong and unwelcome recollection of the day she'd bent over him in the grass and declared that he hadn't had a stroke, he had a turtle.

"Goodness, no," he said huffily. "That's fine, you might as well take that tree down. It's a danger and a nuisance."

She looked relieved. "Oh, I wouldn't go that far. It's just a tree." Her eyes twinkled. "Now of course you'll agree that if Jarondell gets it to fall on my side of the creek, the firewood is all mine."

How that woman loved to aggravate him! She was like a little banty hen just spoiling for a fight. Garnett forced a smile, or the nearest thing to it. "That sounds fair."

She gave him a second look before turning back to Oda's boy (already he'd forgotten the name). The boy stood with his muscular arms crossed and his shaved head gleaming like that Mr. Clean-Up man on Ellen's ammonia bottles, so tall and strapping that Nannie had to shade her eyes from the sun when she looked up at him, though of course that didn't slow her down any. She talked nonstop, pointing this way and that and up into the trees as they chatted (did she not realize they were paying this boy by the hour?). She seemed very interested in the process of felling trees. But of course, that was Nannie Rawley. She was interested in what your dog ate for dinner. Garnett shook his head dramatically—for no audience, it turned out, since she and the boy had already forgotten he was there. He might as well be a tree himself. When the chain saw roared up again, he had to raise his voice considerably to get her attention. "If you get the cherry," he called, "then this one is going to be mine, I gather."

She held her hands over her ears and motioned that they should go down the path. He followed her around a bend where the roar receded to a whine, but she kept walking, all the way down to the log where he had rested earlier. The damselflies were still hovering, a great many of them now, collecting as if for a social event.

"Not here," he said with alarm, pointing up. "We really mustn't tarry here."

"Good *night*," she cried. "Don't tell me you think that cherry's going to fall on you! You think you're that special?" She sat down on the log beside the creek, fluffing her yellow print skirt modestly down over her calves. She looked up at him expectantly. "Well, come on, take a load off."

He hesitated.

"It would sure make the paper, wouldn't it? 'Two Old Fogies Felled by a Single Tree.'"

"All *right*," Garnett said, sitting down grumpily a yard away from her on the log. The woman could make you feel a fool just for minding your own business.

"Don't mind me," she said. "I'm in a tizzy today."

Today, he thought. "Over what, now?" He tried to sound like a father indulging a child, but the effect was lost on her. She launched eagerly onto her soapbox, leaning forward and clasping her hands on her knees and looking him straight in the face.

"It's *bees*," she said. "Down at the Full Gospel church they've got themselves in a pickle from killing their bees. *Killing* them— they fumigated! Why didn't they call me *first*? I'd have smoked them and got the queen out so they'd all come out of the walls in time. I could use another hive on my place. Goodness me, I could use twenty more hives—the way people are using insecticide around here, I can use every bee I can get to pollinate my apples. But no, *now* they call me. After they've got a mess on their hands that any child could have predicted."

Garnett worried over her phrasing. What mess was caused by killing bees that any child could predict? He was evasive. "Well. That must be a bother for them at the worship services." He cast a nervous eye up toward the leaning tree.

But Nannie was heedless of their peril. "Honey two inches deep on the floor of the whole church, oozing out of the walls, and they're blaming the poor dead bees."

Oh, goodness, what a picture. Garnett could just see the women in their church shoes. "Well," he contended, "it *was* the bees that made the honey in the wall."

"And it's the bees that need to vibrate their wings over it night and day to keep it cool in July. Without workers in there to cool the hive, that comb's going to melt, and all the honey will come pouring out." She shook her head sadly. "Don't people *know* these things? Are we old folks the only ones left that think twice about the future?"

He felt a small thrill to be included in her compliment. But he studied her face and couldn't quite work out whether she meant him in particular or old people in general. And now she was headed off on her own tangent.

"You'd think young people would be more careful. They're the ones that are going to be around in fifty years. Not *us*."

"No, not us," Garnett agreed mournfully. He tried not to think of his chestnut fields overgrown with weeds, waving their untended, carefully crossbred leaves like flags of surrender in a world that did not even remember what was at stake. Who would care about his project when he was gone? Nobody. That was the answer: not one living soul. He had kept this truth at a distance for so long, it nearly made him weep with relief to embrace the simple, honest grief of it. He rested his hands on his knees, breathed in and out. Let the cherry tree fall on him now, get it over. What did it matter?

They sat silent for a while, listening to the wood thrushes. Nannie pulled a handful of cockleburs from her skirt and then, without really appearing to give it much thought, reached over and plucked half a dozen from the knees of Garnett's khaki trousers. He felt strangely moved by this fussy little bit of female care. He realized vaguely that as a mortal man, he was starved. He cleared his throat. "Did it ever cross your mind that God—or whatever you want to call him, with your balance of nature and so forth—that he got carried away with the cockleburs?"

"There's too many of them. I'll have to agree with you on that."

Garnett felt faintly cheered: she agreed. "You can't blame me for that one, now, can you? People's spraying or meddling. For the cocklebur problem."

"Oh, I probably could if I tried. But it's a nice day, so I won't."

They sat awhile longer in silence. "Why did they call *you?*" he asked finally, thinking of the woman who had been phoning him up lately for livestock advice. A *goat maven,* she had called him. He glanced over at Nannie, but she seemed lost in her own thoughts. "The church ladies, with their bee problem?"

"Oh, why me and not somebody else? I guess I'm the only one around here that keeps them anymore. Isn't that sad, that nobody in this county under the age of seventy knows how to work bees? Everybody used to. Now they've all let their hives go."

Garnett did think this was sad. As a child he had enjoyed putting on the bee bonnet and helping his father with the honey chores, spring and fall. He honestly couldn't say why he had let that go. "What did you tell them? About the honey on the floor?"

She grinned and looked at him sideways. "I'm afraid I wasn't very nice. I told them that the Lord moves in mysterious ways, and that among all his creatures he loves honeybees just about the best. I told them it was in the Scripture. I expect they're all leafing through their Bibles right now to see what it says about God's sending down a plague on the killers of bees."

"What does it say?"

"Oh, nothing. I just made that up."

"Oh," Garnett said, suppressing a smile in spite of himself. "Then they probably just called all the ladies to come down with mop buckets."

Nannie Rawley snorted. "What a lot of sweetness wasted on a bunch of sourpusses."

Garnett declined to comment.

"It was that Mary Edna Goins that called me. Mad as hops, like the whole idea of a honeybee was my fault." She glanced over at him, then looked away. "Mr. Walker, I don't like to say an unkind word about my fellow man, and I hope you won't think I'm a gossip. But that woman has about the worst case of herself I've ever seen."

Garnett laughed. He had known Mary Edna Goins since before she was a Goins. Once she had called up to tell him that having goat projects in 4-H was giving young people an undue opportunity to think about Satan.

He carefully kept an eye on the cherry tree. "We were going to discuss firewood," he said. "You can have this one."

"Thank you, it's mine already," she said primly. "Are you going to give me my house and land, too?"

"All right, no need to get huffy," he said.

"I agree. I don't need that much firewood anyway. I'll take the wood from this one, you take the oak, and we'll split whatever Jarondell charges us to cut up both."

He knew better than to accept her offer without thinking it over first. He gazed up into the dimness of her woods and was surprised to notice a sapling waggling its leaves in the breeze, uphill from the creek. "Why, look, that's a chestnut, isn't it?" He pointed.

"It is. A young one," she said.

"My eyes aren't good, but I can spy a chestnut from a hundred paces."

"That one's come up from an old stump where a big one was cut down years ago," she said. "I've noticed they always do that. As long as the roots keep living, the sprouts will keep coming out around the stump. But before they get big enough to flower, they always die. Why is that?"

"The blight chancre has to get up a head of steam before it sets off other little chancres and kills the tree. It takes eight or nine years out in the open, or longer in the woods, where a tree grows slower. The fungus inside there is more or less proportional to the size of the trunk. But you're right, they're just about sure to die before they get up enough size to set any seeds. So biologically speaking, the species is dead."

"Biologically dead. Like us," she said with no particular emotion.

"That's right," he said uncomfortably. "If we consider ourselves as having no offspring."

"And unlikely to produce any more at this point." She let out an odd little laugh.

He didn't need to comment on that.

"Now, tell me something," she said. "I've always wondered this. Your hybrids are American chestnut stock crossed with Chinese chestnut, right?"

"That's right. And backcrossed with American again. If I can keep at it long enough I'll get a cross that has all the genes of an American chestnut except for the one that makes it susceptible to blight."

"And the gene for the resistance comes from the Chinese side?"

"That's right."

"But where did you get the American chestnut seed stock to begin with?"

"That's a good question. I had to look high and low," Garnett said, pleased as punch. No one had asked him a question about his project in many a year. Once Ellen had talked her niece into bringing her third-grade class out to see it, but those children had acted like it was a sporting event.

"Well, such as where?" she asked, truly interested.

"I wrote letters and made calls to Forest Service men and what all. Finally I located two standing American chestnuts that were still flowering, about as sick and old as a tree can get but not dead yet. I paid a boy to climb up and cut me down some flowers, and I put them in a bag and brought them back here and pollinated a Chinese tree I had in my yard, and from the nuts I grew out my first field of seedlings. That gave me my first generation, the half-Americans."

"Where were the old trees? I'm just curious."

"One was in Hardcastle County, and one was over in West Virginia. Lonely old things, flowering but not setting any seeds because they had no neighbors to cross with. There are still a few around. Not many, but a few."

"Oh, I know it."

"There were probably plenty, back in the forties," Garnett went on. "Do you remember when the CCC was telling us to cut every last one down? We thought they were all going anyway. But now, if you think about it, that wasn't so good. Some of them could have made it through. Enough to make a comeback."

"Oh, they would have," she agreed. "Daddy was adamant about that. Those two up here in our woodlot, he was determined not to let anybody get. One night he stopped a man that was up here aiming to cut them down and haul them off with a mule before the sun came up!"

"You had chestnut trees in your woodlot?" Garnett asked.

She cocked her head. "Don't you know the ones I mean? There's the one about a quarter mile up this hill, just awful-looking because of all the dead limbs it's dropped. But it still sets a few seeds every year, which the squirrels eat up. And the other one is way on top of the ridge, in about the same shape."

"You have two reproductive American chestnuts in your wood-lot?"

"Are you fooling with me? You didn't know?"

"How would I have known that?"

She started to speak, then paused, touched her lip, then spoke. "I never really think of the woods as *belonging* to us, exactly. I walk all over your hills when I feel like it. I just assumed you did the same with mine."

"I haven't trespassed on your land since the day your father bought it from mine."

"Well," she said cheerfully. "You should have."

He wondered if this was really possible, what she was telling him. Certainly she knew apples, but did she honestly know a chestnut from a cherry? He glanced up at the offending cherry tree again and became convinced it was leaning farther than it had been this morning. A squirrel bounded carelessly up its trunk, which was just too much for Garnett. The sound of a loud crack overhead caused him to look straight up, even though he knew better and had long been in the habit of avoiding that movement. Oh, oh, oh! The curse of his dizziness came crashing down. He held his head and moaned aloud as the woods spun around him crazily. He leaned over and put his head between his knees, knowing it would do no good for him to close his eyes—that would only make him want to throw up.

"Mr. Walker?" She leaned down and looked into his terror-stricken face.

"Nothing. It will pass. A few minutes. Don't mind me. Nothing you can help."

But she was still peering into his face. "Nystagmus," she pronounced.

"What?" He felt annoyed and foolish and weak and fiercely wished she would go away. But she kept looking right at his eyes.

"Your eyes are jerking to the left, over and over—it's called nystagmus. You must be having a doozy of a dizzy spell."

He didn't answer. The spinning tree trunks were slowing up now, like a merry-go-round winding down. It would pass in a few more minutes.

"Do you get it in bed, too, lying on your back?"

He nodded. "That's the darnedest. It wakes me up if I roll over in my sleep."

"You poor thing. That's a misery. You know how to fix it, don't you?"

He moved his head very carefully to face her. "There's a cure?"

"How long have you had this?"

He didn't like to say. Forever. "Twenty years, maybe."

"You never saw a doctor for it?" she asked.

"At first I thought it must be something awful gone wrong inside my head," he confessed. "I didn't want to know. Then the years went by, and it didn't kill me."

"It won't; it's just a nuisance. BPV is what they call it. 'Benign positional vertigo,' or something close to that. I can't remember. Rachel had it bad. Usually old people get it, but you know, everything on Rachel that could fall apart, did. Look here, here's what you do. It's simple. Lie down here on this log."

He protested, but she already had him by the shoulders and was guiding him down onto his back. "Turn your head to the side, as far as it will go. Let it drop backward a little, down off to the side. That's right." He gasped and clutched at her hands like a baby when the dizziness descended again, worse than ever. No matter how he braced for it, that feeling of careening through space never failed to terrify him.

"It's OK, that's good," she crooned, holding on to his hand with one of hers while she cupped her other palm behind his head, steadying him. "Stay there if you can stand it, just hold right still till it stops." He did as he was told. It was a minute, maybe two, before the world slowed and arrested its dance.

"Now," she said, "roll your head straight back till it starts up again. Don't be scared. Go slow, and freeze when it hits you."

He became so terribly aware of her hands. She was holding his head in her competent, tender grip like a mother, pressing his face against her skirt. It was all he could think about as he passed through one more bout of dizziness, then turned his head and endured another. He wondered if he would ever be able to look Nannie Rawley in the eye after this.

"You're almost done," she said. "Now. Listen. I'm going to help you. Sit straight up and tilt forward like this." She put her chin on her chest to demonstrate. "Ready?"

She helped lift him back to a sitting position and guided his head forward. He waited, feeling a strange sensation of reassembly in his head. When it passed he relaxed his shoulders, raised his head, and looked around at a world that seemed to have been made new. She watched him intently. "OK," she said. "You're done."

"Done with what?"

"You're fixed. Try looking up."

He was skeptical, but he did it, cautiously. He felt a feint of movement, but it was small. Compared with the usual, it was hardly anything. No real dizziness. He looked at her, astonished. "Are you a witch? What did you just do to me?"

"It's the Something maneuver—Epley, maybe?" She smiled. "Rachel and I discovered it by accident. I used to roll her around and tickle her to distract her from her dizzy spells. Then a long time later Dr. Gibben told me there was an easier way to do it, and a name for it. You'll have to do it again, every so often. Maybe every day at first."

"What did you fix?"

"It's caused by these little tiny crystals—"

"Ohhh! Don't even tell me. If it's your hocus-pocus theory of everything."

"No, now, listen. It's little hard crystals like rocks that form in the balance-what'sit thingamabob inside your ear. That's a scientific fact."

"Well, how did they get there?"

"Some people just get them, that's all I can tell you. What do you want me to say, that they're caused by orneriness? Listen here, old man, did I fix you up, or not?"

Garnett felt chastened. "Did."

"All right, then, listen to me for a change. You've got you some little rocks in there that float around and make trouble if you tilt your head the wrong way. The trick is to roll them up into a dead-end corner where they can't get out and bother you."

"Are you sure? Is this real, what you're telling me?"

"Real as rain, Mr. Walker."

"All these years?"

"All these years, that's been your trouble. You've had rocks in your head."

They sat without speaking for a long while, listening to the gasoline-powered sounds of an oak turning into a cord of wood. At length she asked, "Would you like to walk up on the hill with me and see those two chestnuts? Would it do you any good to have two more seed sources for your breeding program?"

"Do you have any idea?" he asked, amazed and excited once again. He'd momentarily forgotten the chestnuts. "It would double the amount of genetic variation I have now. I would have a faster, healthier project by a mile, Miss Rawley. If I had flowers from those two trees."

"Consider them yours, Mr. Walker. Anytime."

"Thank you," he said. "That's very kind of you."

"Not at all." She folded her hands on her lap.

Garnett could picture the two old chestnuts up there, anomalous survivors of their century, gnarled with age and disease but still standing, solitary and persistent for all these years. Just a stone's throw from his property. It was almost too much to believe. He dared to hope they still had a few flowers clinging on, this late in the summer. What that infusion of fresh genetic material would do for his program! It was a miracle. In fact, now that he thought about it, if those trees had been shedding pollen all along they might already have helped him out, infusing his fields with a little bit of extra diversity. He thought he'd been working alone. You just never knew.

He turned his head to the side and received an unbidden picture of the rocks in his head, stashed out of harm's way for the moment but poised, surely, to roll back out and make trouble. Without meaning to, he also remembered the stack of green shingles in his garage, hiding there, burning a hole in his conscience like a cigarette dropped on a couch.

21

Moth Love

ne of the skills of grief that Lusa had learned was to hold on tight to the last moments between sleep and waking. Sometimes, then, in the early morning, taking care not to open her eyes or rouse her mind through its warm drowse to the surface where pain broke clear and cold, she found she could choose her dreams. She could call a memory and patiently follow it backward into flesh, sound, and sense. It would become her life once again, and she was held and safe, everything undecided, everything still new. His arms were real, carrying her over the threshold as he joked that she weighed more than one bag of groceries but less than two. Cicadas buzzed and the air was hot and sticky—June, just after the wedding. She still had on her blue rayon skirt but had taken off her stockings and shoes in the car on the drive down from Lexington. The light-blue skirt flowed like cool water over her thighs and his forearms as he carried her up the stairs. He stopped on the landing, kissed her there, and slid his hands under her so her whole weight was nothing held in his hands. She was weightless, floating in air with her back to the window and his strong arms beneath her thighs. The air around his head seemed to shiver with the combined molecules of their separate selves as he entered her and she gave in to the delirium of flight, this perfect love made on the wing.

Sometimes the dream changed itself then, and his comforting presence had the silky, pale-green wings of the stranger who had first come to her after the funeral, on the night Jewel gave her the sleeping pill. He always said the same thing to her: "I know you." He opened his wings and the coremata rose from his abdomen, fragrant and intricately branched like honeysuckle boughs, and once again she felt the acute pleasure of being chosen.

"You knew me well enough to find me here," she said.

And his scent burst onto her brain like a rain of lights, and his voice reached across the distance without words: "I've always known you that well."

He wrapped her in his softness, touched her face with the movement of trees and the odor of wild water over stones, dissolving her need in the confidence of his embrace.

~

"Aunt Mary Edna says they're praying when they do that," Crys reported doubtfully.

"I guess you could say that. Butterfly church."

Lusa and Crys had stopped in the dirt road to admire another dense crowd of swallowtail butterflies congregated on the ground surrounding a muddy spot. Every fifty feet or so they came upon another of these quivering pools of black and yellow wings that rose and scattered as they approached, then settled again on the same spot after they'd passed by. It had rained again yesterday, so there was no shortage of puddles.

"I'll tell you something, though," Lusa said. "It's a no-girls-allowed church. All those butterflies you see there are probably boys."

"Why?"

"What *why?* Because they have little peckers!"

Crys yelped out her sharp bark of a laugh. Lusa lived for this, to crack her up. It had become her pet secret challenge, to try for these moments when you could see all the lights come on, ever so briefly, in this child's dark house.

"I know what you meant," Lusa said. "Why do just the males do that. It's called puddling, believe it or not. That's what real-live bug scientists call it."

"Yeah? Why do just the boy ones do it?"

"They're sucking up a certain mineral or protein from the mud, some special thing butterflies need to be healthy. And then they actually give it to the girl butterflies, like a valentine."

"How do they give it to them?"

Lusa paused, then asked, "Do you know how babies get made?"

Crys rolled her eyes. "He sticks his pecker in her pee hole and squirts in stuff and the baby grows in there."

"*O-kay,* you know the story, all right. So that's how he gives her the minerals. When he gives her the baby-making stuff, he actually puts it together with this whole package of other goodies she likes. It's called the spermatophore."

"Boy. That's weird."

"Isn't it? You know what? Nobody else in Zebulon County knows that, except you and me. Even your teachers don't."

She glanced up. "Really?"

"Really. If you want to know about bugs, I can tell you things you will not believe."

"Are you mad at me for saying 'pecker' and 'shit' and stuff?"

"Nah, not at all. *Hell,* no," she swore, to make Crys laugh. "As long as you know where *not* to say those words. Like in church, or at school, or within one and a half miles of Aunt Mary Edna. But here, who cares? It won't hurt my ears."

"Well, hot damn," the child declared. "Shit fire."

"Hey. Don't use them all up in your first five minutes."

Crys picked up a small stone and tossed it toward the crowd of butterflies, just to see them rise.

"Come on," Lusa said, "let's hunt moths. Today I'm going to find you a luna moth or bust." They walked slowly toward the puddle, passing straight through the cloud of quivering butterflies the way Lusa remembered Superman walking between the molecules of a wall in the cartoons. She and Crys were hiking up the old cemetery road into the woods behind the garage, for no reason in particular, just out for a little adventure while Lowell napped on the parlor couch. Jewel was having a very bad day and had asked Lusa to watch them for the third time in two weeks. Lusa was happy to oblige, though she wondered what kind of a parental substitute she was— encouraging Crys to swear like a tinker, for instance. She didn't know the first thing about kids. But no one else in the family could get a word out of Crys at all. You get what you get in this world, as Hannie-Mavis had once told her. Lusa and Crys had gotten bad luck and the judgment of the righteous. And apparently, each other.

"What's that?"

Lusa looked into the woods where Crys pointed. Birdsong rang like bells in the rainwashed air, but Lusa couldn't see anything in particular. "What, that plant?"

"Yeah, 'at booger one climbing up the trees."

"'*Booger* one'?"

Crys shrugged. "Uncle Rickie says 'em's boogers. Them vines that gets all over everwhere. He hates 'em."

"This one's nice, though; it's *supposed* to grow here. It gets covered with white flowers at the end of summer, and then it makes millions of seedpods that look like little silver starbursts. It's called virgin's bower."

"Virgin's like Jesus's mama, right?"

"Right. Or any girl or woman who's never gotten the pecker business we were talking about."

"Oh. Virgin's power?"

"No, virgin's *bower*. It means her bed." Lusa smiled. "Same thing in this case, actually."

Crys leapt ahead of Lusa with a dozen or so strange, stiff giant steps. She seemed to like trying out different ways of walking, which Lusa just watched, bemused. She was wearing the same outgrown pair of jeans she always wore now, and also, today, a strange, ragged creation over her T-shirt. It looked like a man's denim work shirt with its tail and sleeves cut to ribbons with a pair of scissors.

"I like bugs better than flowers," Crys said decisively, after a while.

"Good, then you're in luck, because I know a million times more about bugs than I do about flowers. And we're looking for a luna moth, remember? Look on the trunks of the trees, on the side that's in shade. Do you know what a hickory tree looks like? With the really shaggy bark?"

Crys shrugged.

"Luna moths especially like hickories. Those and walnuts. They lay their eggs on the leaves because that's what their caterpillars eat."

"How come?"

"That's just how their stomachs are made. They specialize. You can eat the seeds of wheat, for instance, but not the grass part."

"I can eat all kinds of stuff."

"Other animals should be so lucky. Most of them have pretty specialized diets. Meaning they can eat only one exact kind of thing."

"Well, that's dumb."

"It's not dumb or smart, it's just how they're built, like you have two legs and walk on your feet. A dog probably thinks *that's* dumb."

Crys didn't comment.

"But yeah, specialization makes life more risky. If their food dies, they die. They can't just say, 'Oh, never mind, my tree went extinct, so now I'll just order a pizza.'"

"Lowell has that."

"Has what?"

"The special-food problem."

"Yeah?" Lusa was amused by this analysis of her brother. "What does he eat?"

"Just macaroni and cheese. *And* chocolate malted-milk balls."

"Well. That is a specialized diet. No wonder he didn't eat my lentil soup the other night. I should have put malted-milk balls in it."

Crys let out a tiny laugh, just air escaping between her teeth.

"Look here, on the mossy side of this tree. See these little white moths?" They both bent close as Lusa prodded gently at a translucent wing. The moth roused and crawled a few inches up the rough bark. Crys was backlit by the sun, so Lusa could see the pale down on her curved cheek, like the fuzz on a peach. There was a softness to her features in these moments of concentration that made Lusa wonder how so many adults—herself included—could ever take this child for a boy.

She looked up. "What are they?"

"These are called cankerworms. The worm stage got noticed first with these guys, so mama moth is stuck with not such a nice name. She's kind of pretty, though, isn't she?" Lusa let it crawl onto her finger, then held it up and blew on it lightly, sending it fluttering in a crooked arc toward another tree. Crys stood for a minute longer watching its sleepy colleagues on the tree before she was willing to move on. "How come you know so much about bugs?" she asked.

"Before I married your uncle Cole and moved here, I used to be a bug scientist. In Lexington. I did experiments and learned stuff about them that nobody knew before."

"They got a lot of bugs in Lexington?"

Lusa laughed. "As many as anywhere, I guess."

"Huh. Aunt Lois said you's a miner."

"A miner?"

"Gold miner."

Lusa puzzled over this. "Oh. A gold digger." She sighed. This time she was sure Crys hadn't meant to hurt her.

"Is it true?" Crys asked.

"Nope. No gold mines for me, past or future. Aunt Lois has got her head up her butt on that particular subject."

Crys closed her mouth in a tight, conspiratorial grin and rolled her eyes at Lusa. They were finding their ways of living with the judgment of the righteous.

"This is a good spot, let's look up here," Lusa said, pointing up a steep embankment to a grassy clearing above the road, bathed in dappled light. They'd come as far up this road as she wanted to go. They shouldn't stray too far from the house since Lowell was napping alone. Also, Lusa really didn't want to face the family cemetery that waited around the next bend. Cole wasn't in it, but too many other Wideners were.

Crys was already scrambling ahead of her through the plumes of the daylilies that had escaped from someone's garden long ago and were now as common as weeds. They were pretty, though. Their straplike leaves spilled like waterfalls over the banks, crowned with circles of bright orange-eyed flowers and long, graceful buds. They grew in bobbing rows along nearly every unmowed roadside in the county, punctuated with the intermittent purple-pink of sweet peas. Before they started to bloom a few weeks ago, Lusa had never noticed either one of these plants. The whole county was one big escaped flower garden.

Crys yanked the head off one of the lilies as she mounted the bank. "Watch this." She rubbed its center against her chin before tossing the bedraggled flower on the ground.

"Very nice. Now you've got an orange beard," Lusa observed.

Crys attempted an evil grin, touchingly childish. "Like the devil."

"You know what that is, that orange stuff? Pollen. You know what pollen is?"

She shook her head.

"*Spe-erm.*" Lusa exaggerated the word thrillingly.

"Eew, yuck." She wiped her chin fiercely.

"Don't worry. It won't make you get pregnant and have flowers." She walked past her to the edge of the clearing where a stand of hickories had caught her eye. She began to search the trees' north sides systematically, moving deeper into the woods.

Crys trailed along behind her at a little distance. "D'you think it's, like, going to hail?" she seemed to be asking.

Lusa glanced up at the bits of sky she could see between trees. "No way. There aren't any rain clouds in the sky."

"I'm talking about *hail*," the child insisted.

Lusa moved deeper into the woods, scanning limbs and the undersides of leaves with a practiced eye. "It takes a big storm to bring hail. Why do you care, anyway? You don't have a crop in the ground."

"*Hail,* I said!"

There was enough frustration in her voice to bring Lusa out of her own thoughts and make her turn around. Crys had her feet planted and was glaring at her, aggravated.

"What about hail?"

"*Hail!*" the child said, frankly annoyed. "Where the *devil's* at."

Lusa slowly turned over this mystery. "Are you asking me about *hell?*"

The child shrugged. "Just for*git* it."

"Well, I'm sorry. I guess we kind of missed our moment there to talk about the afterlife." Crys had tromped ahead, yanking sassafras leaves off the bushes as she passed.

"I'm just curious," Lusa said, catching up to her. "How do you tell the difference between 'hail' that falls from the sky and 'hail' where the devil is?"

Crys stopped and looked up at her, stupefied. "Duh! They're *spailed* different!"

351

"Oh," Lusa said. "Duh."

Crys studied her for a moment. "Aunt Lusa, did you know you talk really funny?"

"Yeah. It's starting to sink in."

Lusa cajoled Crys into sparing the sassafras bushes and helping her look for a luna instead. "It will be the biggest green moth you can imagine. They're amazing." Crys seemed unwilling to believe in the possibility of finding magic, here or anywhere, but she did come running when Lusa finally let out a yelp and cried, "Oh, look, look, *look!*"

"Where?"

"Way up there—it's too high for us to get. Do you see it, though? Right in the crotch of that branch sticking out."

Crys squinted, seeming less than impressed. "We could poke it with a stick."

"You don't want to hurt it," Lusa argued, but she'd already had the same thought and was twisting a long, skinny limb off an oak sapling. She reached as high as she could, jumping a little, waving the switch like a broom to brush against the hickory trunk just below where the luna rested with its wings serenely folded. It twitched a little and took flight. They watched it dip and climb, dip and climb, high into the branches until it was gone.

Lusa turned to Crys, her eyes shining. "*That* was a luna."

Crys shrugged. "So?"

"So? So *what?* You want it should sing, too?" Crys laughed, and Lusa felt a little startled. They took her by surprise, these moments when her zayda slipped right past her father's guard into her own tongue. "Come on, let's go look in the grass for things we can get our hands on." She led the way back to the grassy clearing on the bank above the road and flopped down in the center of it. She was content for a minute just to lean back on her elbows and look at the toes of her sneakers and past them, down through the enticing woods. She'd been cooped up in the house or weeding or mowing or checking the health of her goats for too many days. She ought to get herself into the woods more often. The grass in this clearing was a little damp—she could feel it soaking her shorts—but the sun felt so good. She closed her eyes and tilted her face toward the sky.

"What's this one?"

Lusa leaned over and looked closely at the shield-shaped green bug that Crys had coaxed onto her wrist. "Southern green stinkbug," Lusa pronounced.

Crys studied it closely. "Does it stink?"

"That's a matter of opinion."

"Is it kin to that red and black one we found on the peach tree?"

"The harlequin bug? Yes, it is, as a matter of fact. Same family, Pentatomidae." She looked at Crys, surprised. "That's very good. You have a really good eye for this, did you know that? You're a good observer, and you remember things well."

Crys flicked the bug off her wrist and rolled over onto her stomach, looking away from Lusa. She parted the grass carefully with her hands, here and there, like an animal grooming its kin. Lusa left her alone, rolling over to study her own patch of grass. Crys eventually gave up the chase and lay on her back, staring into the treetops. After a while she declared, "You could cut down all these trees and make a pile of money."

"I could," Lusa said. "Then I'd have a pile of money and no trees."

"So? Who needs trees?"

"About nineteen million bugs, for starters. They live in the leaves, under the bark, everywhere. Just close your eyes and point, and you're pointing at a bug."

"So? Who needs nineteen million bugs?"

"Nineteen thousand birds that eat them."

"So? Who needs birds?"

"I do. You do." She so often wondered whether Crys was really heartless or only trying to be. "Not to mention, the rain would run straight down the mountain and take all the topsoil off my fields. The creek would be pure mud. This place would be a dead place."

Crys shrugged. "Trees grow back."

"That's what you think. This forest took hundreds of years to get like this."

"Like what?"

"Just how it is, a whole complicated thing with parts that all need each other, like a living body. It's not just trees; it's different *kinds* of trees, all different sizes, in the right proportions. Every animal needs its own special plant to live on. And certain plants will only grow next to certain other kinds, did you know that?"

"Sang only grows under a sugar maple tree."

"What does? Ginseng? Where'd you learn that?"

She shrugged again. "Uncle Joel."

"So he's a sang digger, is he?"

She nodded. "Him and his friends like to go up 'air on the mountain and dig it up. There's a lady up 'air hollers at 'em for it, too. You're not supposed to dig it up. He says she's prolly fixing to shoot his hide if she catches him one more time."

Lusa looked up the mountain. "Some lady *lives* up there? Are you sure? That's just supposed to be Forest Service land, above this farm."

"Ask Uncle Joel. He'll tell you. He says she's a gol-dang wild woman."

"I'll bet. I think I'd like to meet her." Lusa poked an inchworm out of the grass and let it make its way up her finger. "What does Uncle Joel say about me? Is he the one who thinks I should cut down my trees?" She felt only slightly guilty about exploiting this new source of inside information.

"No. He's the one says you've gone plumb goat-crazy."

"Him and everybody else. They're all just dying to know why, aren't they?"

Crys shrugged and looked over at Lusa, a little guarded. But she nodded. "I guess you wouldn't tell, though."

"I'd tell *you*," Lusa said quietly. She would love to give this child a gift that mattered. Her confidence, that would be something.

Her face lit up. "You would?"

"Only if it was just you, not Uncle Joel or anybody else. You couldn't tell them no matter what. Can you keep a secret, cross your heart?"

With earnest solemnity, Crys drew a cross on her chest.

"OK, here it is. I've got this cousin in New York City, he's a butcher, and we've made a deal. If I can get all those goats up there on the hill to have babies a month before New Year's, he'll pay me so much money for them your uncle Joel will keel over."

The child's eyes grew wide. "You'll be *rich?*"

Lusa grinned and hung her head. "No, not really. *But* I'll be able to pay the guy who's redoing all the plumbing in the house, and that friend of your uncle Rickie's who's fixing the barn right now."

"Clivus Morton?" Crys made an awful face. "He's got B.O."

Lusa tried not to laugh. "Well, that's no reason not to pay him, is it? If so, I just wasted nine hundred dollars, because I wrote him a check this morning."

Crys seemed astonished by this figure. "Shit fire. I guess now *he's* rich."

"It takes a bunch of money to keep a farm in one piece. Sometimes you don't make as much in a year as you have to pay out. That's why people moan and groan about farming. Just in case you were wondering."

"What if your goats don't do that—have their babies?"

"I'll still have to pay Clivus Morton a whole bunch more money when he's finished. Whether or not he takes a bath." Lusa lay down on her back in the damp grass, crossed her arms behind her head, and sighed. "It's risky. But the goats are the only way I could think of this year to make some money off a little patch of briar scrub and keep the farm in one piece." She glanced at Crys, who didn't seem to be listening, though it was hard to tell. "So that's what I'm doing with the goats. Just trying to keep my little piece of heaven from going to *hail*."

"Uncle Joel said you was throwing the place away."

"He's welcome to make a suggestion if he has a better idea—he and my vegetarian friends Hal and Arlie in Lexington, who've informed me I'm a sellout. There's not one crop I can put in the ground here that'll earn as much as it costs to grow. Other than tobacco."

Crys looked at her. "Are you that?"

"Am I what?"

"Veg-arian."

"No, I'm one of the other Christianities. As your cousin Rickie put it."

Crys had taken up a stalk of long grass and was very lightly touching Lusa's skin in the spot where her T-shirt rode up and exposed her belly. It was the closest thing to intimacy she'd ever seen this child share with anyone. Lusa held her breath and lay very still, stunned by luck, as if a butterfly had lit on her shoulder. Finally she breathed out, feeling a little dizzy from watching the high, thin clouds race across the blue gap in the trees overhead. "Listen to me moan and groan. I guess I must be a real farmer now, huh?"

Crys shrugged. "I guess."

"If my goats don't work out, I'm what you call screwed. I hate to think about it. I'd feel like a murderer logging this hill, but I'm not sure how else I can keep this farm."

Crys turned suddenly from Lusa and tossed the grass stem away. "Why do you have to keep it?"

"That's a good question. I'm asking myself that question. You know what I come up with?"

"What?"

"Ghosts."

Crys leaned over and peered down into Lusa's face. She looked puzzled, briefly, before her expression went neutral. "That's stupid."

"Not really. You'd be surprised."

Crys pulled a handful of grass out of the ground. "Ghosts of who?"

"People who have lost things, I think. Some are your family, and some are from mine."

"Real people? *Dead* people?"

"Yes."

"Like who?"

"My zayda, my grandpa on my dad's side. Once upon a time he had this beautiful, beautiful farm, right? And people took it away from him. It was a long time ago, before I was born. My mother's grandparents had a farm, too, in a whole different country, and the same thing happened: gone. Now they've all wound up here."

"Are you scared of them?" Crys asked quietly.

"Not at all."

"Do you really believe in ghosts?"

Lusa wondered why on earth she was talking about this with a child. But she needed to speak of it, as badly as Crys needed to curse. They both had their reasons. She sat up and looked at her until at last she caught her eye. "I'm not scaring you, am I?"

The girl shook her head rapidly.

"Maybe I shouldn't even call them ghosts. It's just stuff you can't see. *That* I believe in, probably more than most people. Certain kinds of love you can't see. That's what I'm calling ghosts."

Crys wrinkled her nose. "What do you do, then, *smell* 'em?"

"I do. And hear them. I hear my grandfather playing music when it rains. That's how I know he's here. And your uncle Cole's here, too. I smell him all the time. I'm not kidding: three or four times a week. I'll open a drawer or walk into the corncrib in the grain house, and there he is."

Crys looked truly unhappy. "He's not there for real, though. If you can't see him, he's not."

Lusa reached out and rubbed her shoulder, a hard little point of bone beneath a tense little blanket of muscle. "I know, it's hard to think about," she said. "Humans are a very visual species."

"What's *that* mean?"

A monarch butterfly drifted into the shaft of light in front of them and batted lazily into the cleared path through the trees toward the fields below. Lusa said, "What that means is, we mainly love things with our eyes."

"You mean like Rickie does with those girl magazines under his bed?"

Lusa laughed hard. "That is exactly what I mean."

They both watched the monarch, a bouncing orange dot receding downhill until it was nothing, just a bright spot melting into the light of day.

"A lot of animals trust their other senses more than we do. Moths use smell, for instance. They don't have to see their husbands or wives at all to know they're there."

"So? You're not a moth."

"So. I guess you're right. Pretty stupid, huh?"

Crys shrugged her shoulders. "When you die will you be a ghost hanging around here, too?"

"Oh, yeah. A good one."

"And who'll be here then, after you?"

"That's the sixty-four-dollar question. The ghosts of my family and yours are having a big disagreement over that one. Mine say stay, yours say go, on account of who comes after me. I have no idea how to make everybody happy."

Crys studied her. "Which side you figure to pick?"

Lusa stared and shrugged back at her, the same quick, introverted jerk of the shoulders that Crys kept ready at hand to answer all questions. A stolen gesture.

"Come on," she said then, jumping up and pulling Crys up by the hand. "We'd better go see if Lowell's awake."

"He'll still be asleep. He'd sleep forever if you let him."

"Maybe he's just a little sad about your mom. Sometimes people need to sleep more when they're sad." She reached over to give Crys a hand down the bank into the road cut, but the girl took the plunge by herself in one huge leap.

"Not me," she said, landing on her feet.

"No? What do you do?" Lusa climbed more slowly through the daylilies down onto the road, feeling like the turtle trailing the hare.

"Nothing. I don't think about it."

"Really. Not ever?"

Crys shrugged, then caught herself at it. They didn't speak for several minutes as they walked side by side downhill, through puddles of light in the road spilled by gaps in the forest canopy. Every fifty feet or so they scattered up another cloud of swallowtails—the choirboys turned out of church. Lusa liked the idea of butterfly church. Frankly, it was no more far-fetched than the notion of a communal sucking-up of sodium for sperm valentines. She wondered what would happen if she submitted a paper to *Behavioral Ecology* on the spiritual effects of swallowtail puddling. Lusa was still amusing herself with the idea when they rounded the corner above the house and she was stopped dead in her tracks.

"Oh, no, *look*," she cried.

"Shit, Aunt Lusa. The damn booger honeysuckles et your garage."

Lusa could not think of a better way to put it. The mound of dark-green leaves was so rounded and immense, there was hardly any sign that a building lay underneath. An ancient burial mound, Lusa might have guessed. A Mayan temple crumbled to ruin. Could this really have happened in just one wildly rainy, out-of-control summer? She hadn't been up the cemetery road for as long as she could remember, and certainly hadn't looked at the garage from the back side since before Cole's death. Now she could only stare, recalling the exact content of their argument about honeysuckle before he was killed: the absurd newspaper column about spraying it with Roundup; her ire on the plant's behalf. How could she have gotten so sanctimonious about honeysuckle? It wasn't even native here, it occurred to Lusa now. It was an escapee from people's gardens, like the daylilies—like most weedy things that overgrew, in fact. No local insects could eat it because it was an introduction from someplace else—Japan, probably. *Lonicera japonica,* that would be right, like Japanese beetles and chestnut blight and the horribly invasive Japanese knotweed and the dreaded kudzu. One more artifact of the human covenant that threatened to strangle out the natives.

You have to persuade it two steps back every day, he'd said, *or it will move in and take you over.* His instincts about this plant had been right; his eye had known things he'd never been trained to speak of. And yet she'd replied carelessly, *Take over what? The world will not end if you let the honeysuckle have the side of your barn.* She crossed her arms against a shiver of anguish and asked him now to forgive a city person's audacity.

Her head filled with the scent of a thousand translucent white flowers that had yellowed and fallen from this mountain of vine many months before. Maybe years before.

Crys was looking up at her so anxiously that Lusa touched her own face to make sure it was still intact.

"Don't worry, it's nothing," she said. "I saw a ghost."

22

Predators

og days. Deanna sat on her freshly completed bridge in the hemlock grove, nervously picking off splinters from the end of a pine plank and tossing them into the water, listening to the clan of red-tails screaming at one another up in the sky. Sometimes the birds dipped into the trees overhead, and their reflections glanced briefly across the surface of the water below her feet. She pulled her bandanna out of her back pocket and wiped sweat out of her eyes, leaving a trail of grime and sawdust across her forehead. A hawk goes blind in the dog days, people used to say. And her dad said different: *Nothing about a hot summer day could make a bird lose its sight. They're pushing their young out of the nest in August, is all. The parents fly around crazy, diving into the treetops to try to get away from their full-grown young following them around screeching to be fed, unwilling to hunt on their own.* Her dad didn't know the word *fledge,* but he knew what it meant. *Look close,*

he always used to tell her. *If it doesn't sound true, it isn't. There's always a reason for what people say, but usually it's not the reason they think.*

Deanna was at a loss to invent any more work for herself today. Nothing she'd be able to keep her mind on, anyway. She'd finished this bridge. She'd also collected four wheelbarrow-loads of firewood from the pile here, where they'd cut up the trees, and pushed them all the way up to the cabin. She'd cleared weeds and re-trenched the steepest part of the upper mountain trail. She had run into a pair of hikers up there on the ridge, a young, very dirty couple who seemed delighted with the world and each other. They'd wandered over here as a side trip from the Appalachian Trail. Hiking the whole A.T. this summer from Maine to Georgia was their plan, as they'd eagerly relayed it to her. They had gotten this far, worn out a pair of boots each, and were looking forward to picking up a care package from one of their mothers, including new boots, down where the trail came out in Damascus, before continuing on south. They thanked Deanna, impressed with the upkeep of the trails here in the Zebulon Forest—as if she'd done all the work just for them. Which answered *one* of the two questions she'd been asking herself all summer, anyway. As she watched the pair hike away in their baggy, colorful shorts, she wondered how that would feel, to have a mother leaving you care packages when you ran out of boot leather. Or to hike hundreds of miles beside another person, always knowing which way the trail ahead of you ran, and exactly how far.

He was sitting up there right now in the green porch chair, reading her thesis. She had not felt this nervous since the day of her final oral defense, when her committee made her go out in the hall-way while it deliberated her case.

This humidity had to break. There was a storm in the air, which was probably making the hawks act up even more. She didn't want to be down here when it hit. In her tenure on this mountain she'd been caught outside in a lightning storm exactly twice: once she'd made it into the shelter of the big chestnut log (back when it was still her own), and the other time she'd had to cower against the trunk of a hemlock in the lowest spot she could get to. Both times had been more awful than she liked to admit. He was right about her and thunder. She wasn't afraid of snakes, but thunder paralyzed her. There wasn't any reason, it just was. Even as a girl she'd dreaded loud noises, could not fire a gun without breaking a cold sweat, even just for target practice at a can on a fencepost. Her dad used to sit with her through storms. Eddie had done that, too, and almost the same way, though she didn't tell him so: rubbing her back as she lay with the pillow pulled over her head, counting out loud with her the distance between flash and boom. One fifth of a mile per second.

If not for that, she thought, this would be easy. If not for those nights and early mornings and half minutes when he was suddenly kinder and truer than seemed possible, given everything. Given what he couldn't understand. What did she really think he would do now, when he finished reading the book of her knowledge and beliefs? *Change*? No. Tear his hair for guilt? No. Stay, or walk out the door? Which did she want him to do?

That was the question. When a body wanted one thing wholly and a mind wanted the opposite, which of the two was *she*, Deanna?

She leaned far forward from the bridge so she could see her face in the water. Her braid swung over her shoulder and hung down, nearly touching the water, swaying like a bell rope. *Pull me in,* she said silently to the girl in the water. *Make up my mind for me. Take from me this agitation, the likes of which I have never known in all my life.*

This morning she had wept for no reason she could possibly name. The forest hadn't seemed large enough for her grief. She'd startled up a white-spotted, flag-tailed fawn and sent it crashing downmountain from the bed of leaves where its mother had carefully hidden it. Deanna curled herself into the spot it'd fled, and sensed the small body's warmth still there in the brown leaves. There was no loss here, she told herself; the fawn would bleat for its mother and be found. But she'd suddenly felt so despairing and tired, such an utterly lost cause, that she'd lain on the ground and put leaves in her mouth.

Bang! A thunder boom hit now like a hammer on the back of her spine, jerking her up onto her feet on the raw wooden planks of the bridge. She was grateful for that, at least—one decision made for her. By the time the second boom hit, rolling up the hollow like a wave and crashing over her head, her feet were already headed up the mountain. They would get her to the cabin before the lightning arrived. *What do I want, what do I want?* her feet on the trail demanded, the rhythm of her breathing demanded. If she couldn't say what she wanted, she could say nothing—wouldn't look at him, would have to go on feeling trapped with him in that place, like predator and prey closed tight in a box, waiting for word on which was to be which.

She was breathing hard by the time the cabin came into sight. Why had she been getting out of breath at the drop of a hat lately, was that age, too? Was she running faster than she used to? Through the trees she could just see the south face of her house, where the logs had been completely overgrown this summer by a single Virginia creeper vine. She'd pondered whether to rip the hairy little tendrils off the logs or just leave them there to protect the old wood from wind and rain, like a lively green skin.

She angled up the hill, coming up on the cabin from the back. Her mind was running ahead of her and off to the side, but it snapped back when she saw something odd at the place where the roof gable butted against the uppermost log in the cabin's wall. The small hole there she'd noticed before, but now something was moving out of it, a dark loop. She approached slowly, catching her breath and keeping her eyes on the spot.

She could see now exactly what it was: the cabin's summerlong resident guardian angel who kept down the mice, the devil who took the phoebes, the author of that slow sandpaper sound in the roof—her blacksnake. He was leaving. Deanna planted her feet and watched the entire, unbelievable length of him pour out the small hole in the side of the roof gable. He oozed down the log wall in an undulating, liquid flow like a line of molasses spilling over the edge of a pitcher. When most of his length had emerged, he suddenly dropped into the tall grass, which trembled and then went still. Then he was gone, for good. Just like that, today of all days, for reasons she would never be able to know. Whether she had loved or hated this snake was of absolutely no consequence to his departure. She considered this fact as she watched him go, and she felt something shift inside her body—relief, it felt like, enormous and settled, like a pile of stones on a steep slope suddenly shifting and tumbling slightly into the angle of repose.

The pounding of *What do I want* went still in her breast. It didn't matter what she chose. The world was what it was, a place with its own rules of hunger and satisfaction. Creatures lived and mated and died, they came and went, as surely as summer did. They would go their own ways, of their own accord.

{23}

Old Chestnuts

arnett had made up his mind. He was going to tell her about the shingles. *Today,* he would tell her. Nothing was going to get him off the track this time: she could go ahead and be rude, shocking, or blasphemous, it wouldn't matter, he was still going to give her those shingles. He was a Christian man hovering near eighty, and there was no telling when a fellow his age might just keel over. It had happened to younger men, Lord knew. It was not going to happen to Garnett Walker with those shingles moldering in his garage and the sin of spite staining his soul like an inkblot.

Maybe, while he was at it, he would remember to thank her for the pie.

As he walked across his yard toward the gate, he paused to take stock of a pokeberry weed that had shot up in the ditch beside his driveway, out of reach of the mower. He'd been meaning to get down here with the Weedwhacker, but somehow this poke plant had slipped past his good intentions and grown into a monster. It was a *tree,* practically, ten feet tall, dangling its big, slick leaves and bunches of green berries—all that growth accomplished in just four months, from the ground up, since poke was killed to the ground by frost. He stood with his hands on his hips, scrutinizing its purple trunk. He hated a weed on principle but could not help admiring this thing for its energy. His eye wandered up toward the row of trees that towered along the fencerow, giant leafy masses like tall green storm clouds, and he felt unexpectedly awestruck. A man could live under these things every day and forget to notice their magnitude. Garnett had gradually lost the ability to see individual leaves, but he could still recognize any one of these by its shape: the billowy columns of tulip poplars; the lateral spread of an oak; the stately, upright posture of a walnut; the translucent, effeminate tremble of a wild cherry. The small, lacy locusts were faintly brown this late in summer, and the catalpa at the corner post wore a pale-green color you could pick out on a hillside a mile away, or even farther when it was dangling all over with the long pods that made people call it a bean tree. The sourwood had its white flowers reaching out like skeleton hands in the spring. Trees. Every kind assumed a different slickness in the rain, its particular color in the fall, its own aspect—something you couldn't describe in words but learned by heart when you lived in their midst. Garnett had a strange, sad thought about his own special way of seeing trees inside his mind, and how it would go dark, like a television set going off, at the moment of his death.

What in heaven's name was he doing out here in his driveway looking at trees and thinking about death? He started to turn back toward his house, but from the corner of his sight he registered the rounded shapes of the regularly spaced apples beyond the fencerow and knew, of course, that was it. His mission was Nannie Rawley and the shingles. He thought of going to the garage to check on them first, just to make sure they were in a condition to be offered. But he suspected he might merely be postponing the inevitable. *Just pull up your knickers and go, young man,* he scolded himself, and obeyed.

He found her in back of the house, where he knew she would be. He'd been keeping an eye out this morning and had seen her carrying an old locust fence rail back there. He'd actually grown a little curious about what she was up to, though he knew curiosity had killed the cat, and that was probably even without the assistance of Nannie Rawley.

She waved merrily when she saw him coming. "Mr. Walker! How's your BPV?"

His what? Was she asking him about underwear? "Fine," he said, with reserved commitment.

"No more dizzy spells? That's wonderful. I'm happy to hear it."

"Oh, *that,*" he said, and the memory of her firm, tender hands cradling his head sent a shock of adrenaline through his old body. He'd had a dream about her, so real to him that he'd awakened plagued with the condition he hadn't known for years. He blushed now to recall the whole business again. He nearly turned tail and ran.

"Are you all right?"

"Much better, yes," he replied, getting his bearings. "I'm not used to it yet. I was so used to getting dizzy, it's taking me a while to get used to *not* being dizzy."

"That's old age for you, isn't it?" she asked. "If I got out of bed one morning and my knees didn't hurt, I'm not sure how I'd know to walk."

He stared at her, distracted. She wasn't wearing much. He'd noticed that earlier, when he saw her dragging the locust rail up from the ditch. Just a little yellow sleeveless-blouse sort of thing, and short pants. *Short pants,* on a woman of her age. It was hot, but not so hot as to drive a person to indecent exposure.

"I prayed about that dizziness," he confessed to her. "For several years, I did."

"God moves in mysterious ways," she replied breezily, probably without meaning it in the least. Next she'd be suggesting *she* was the answer to Garnett's prayers.

"Personally, I've found that my prayers seldom go unanswered," he said, a little more haughtily than he'd meant. "Last August, when it was so dry and so many people were about to lose their tobacco, I got down on my knees and prayed for rain, Miss Rawley. And I want you to know, the very next evening it rained."

She looked at him strangely. "Right before you came over here I had a sneezing fit. I guess my sneezing caused you to come."

"That's a very peculiar thing to say, Miss Rawley."

"Isn't it, though," she replied, turning around and taking up her hammer again.

"I take it you don't put much stock in miracles."

"I'm not in a position to believe in miracles," she said without turning around. She sounded a little angry, or perhaps just a little sad. She was building something, all right, working on that locust rail he'd seen her dragging about. Now she had it propped up onto a sawhorse here in the doorway of her garage and was nailing a crossbar to it. Goodness, it looked like the cross the Romans used for crucifying Jesus Christ. He wasn't going to ask—he made his mind up on that. His second vow of the day; he'd better get to the first.

He cleared his throat and then said, for no good reason, "Did you know there's a pokeberry bush by my driveway that must be eleven feet tall? I've never seen the like."

She paused her hammer and turned back around, eyeing him carefully. "Is that what you came over here to tell me?"

He thought about it. "No. It's just an incidental piece of information."

"Oh. Well, that's something, an eleven-foot pokeberry. If they gave out an award for weeds at the county fair you'd have a contender there. Wouldn't they all be surprised: Garnett Sheldon

Walker the Third, first place in the weedy annual category." The usual good cheer had returned to her voice, and he couldn't keep from smiling a little himself. Poke was a half-hardy perennial, not an annual, he was pretty sure, but he refrained from correcting her.

"If I'd thought about it," he said with mock seriousness, "I'd have given it a little ammonium nitrate. I think I could have gotten it up to fourteen feet."

She put down her hammer and seemed to relax. Her trousers, he could plainly see, were a pair of old work pants cut off with scissors. What a thing to do. "You know what I really admire, this time of year?" she asked him.

"I wouldn't dare to guess, Miss Rawley."

"Blackberry canes," she said. "Now you go ahead and laugh at me, because everybody else does; I know they're an awful nuisance. But they're amazing, too."

"I expect they're the fastest-growing plant this side of China," he said.

"*Yes,* sir! They shoot up out of the ground and by mid-June they're eight feet tall. Then the top starts to bend back down to the ground, and by August they've made an arch of a size to walk under, if you wanted to. Did you ever notice how they do that?"

"I've noticed, and noticed," he said. "I've gone through about eight bush hogs in my lifetime, noticing how blackberries grow."

"I know. I'm not *defending* them. They'd eat up my whole orchard if I didn't keep them cut back to the fence. But sometimes in winter I just have to stand back and stare at those arches going down the road, up and down, like a giant quilter's needle sewing its way across Zebulon County, one big arched loop per year. You can love them or hate them, either one, but there's no stopping them." She looked at him sideways, like a mother scolding. "And you have to admit, the berries make the best pie there is."

He flushed. "Oh, I've been meaning for the longest time to mention that pie. I thank you for that pie." *Short pants,* on a woman of her age. From what he could see, she had the legs of a much younger woman. Certainly not what he would have expected in the way of *Unitarian* legs.

"You're welcome," she said. "Better late than never. If recent trends continue, maybe I'll bake you another one next year."

He looked at her long and hard, wondering frankly if they would both be here next summer. After a certain point, you had to think that way. "Miss Rawley," he declared, "I can't say as I've ever seen short pants on a woman your age."

She looked down at her knees—which were maybe a little pale and knobby, on second thought. If one were to pay attention. She looked back up at him with a girlish grin. "I got hot, Mr. Walker. I got inspired by the UPS boy. He drives that truck in nothing but his swimming suit. I figured if that's legal, then surely an old lady can take a pair of scissors to her old khakis once in a while."

Garnett shook his head. "Dignity is the last responsibility of the aged, Miss Rawley."

"Fiddlesticks. *Death* is the last responsibility of the aged."

"Don't get fresh with me," he warned. "And don't expect to see me running around in short pants, either."

"I'd sooner expect to see a pig fly, Mr. Walker."

"Well, good, then," he said. But then asked, "Are you saying I'm a pig?"

She crossed her arms. "Are you saying I'm immodest?"

"If the shoe fits," he replied curtly.

"Self-righteous, tedious," she said. "There's a couple of shoes *you* can try on."

That was it, then. They had stooped to name-calling, like a pair of grammar school children. He took a deep breath. "I think I'm finished here."

"No, you're not," she said firmly, looking at him with a menacing eye. "Tell me what's wrong with me. Let's just get it out. All these years you've been picking at me like a scab. What have you really got against me?"

She stood there fearless, daring him to tell the truth, exciting him toward actually doing it. Garnett turned the thought over in his mind and sighed. With profound sadness, he understood that he could never tell her the answer because he didn't know it himself.

He said, feebly, "You don't act normal for your age."

She stood with her mouth a little open, as if there were words stuck halfway between her mind and the world around. At last they came out: "There isn't any *normal* way to act seventy-five years old. Do you know why?"

He didn't dare answer. Was she really seventy-five, exactly?

"I'll *tell* you why," she said. "Considering everything—the whole history of things—people are supposed to be dead and buried at our age. *That's* normal. Up till just lately, the Civil War or something, they didn't even know about germs. If you got sick, they slapped leeches on you and measured you for a coffin. I wouldn't doubt but hardly anybody even made it to fifty. Isn't that so?"

"I suppose it is."

"It *is*. Our mammaw and pappaw got to keep their dignity, just working right up to the end and then dying of a bad cold one day, with most their parts still working. But then along comes somebody inventing six thousand ways to cure everything, and here we are, *old,* wondering what to do with ourselves. A human just wasn't de- signed for old age. That's my theory."

He hardly knew what to say. "That's *one* of your theories."

"Well, think about it. Women's baby-business all dries up, men lose their hair—we're just a useless drain on our kind. Speaking strictly from a biological point of view. Would you keep a chestnut in your program if it wasn't setting seeds anymore?"

He frowned. "I don't think of myself as obsolete."

"Of course not, you're a man! Men walk around with their bald heads bare to the world and their pony put out to pasture, but they refuse to admit they're dead wood. So why should I? What law says I have to cover myself up for shame of having a body this old? It's a dirty trick of modern times, but here we are. Me with my cranky knees and my old shriveled ninnies, and you with whatever you've got under there, if it hasn't dropped off yet—we're still *human*. Why not just give in and live till you die?"

Garnett was so hot under the collar he could scarcely breathe. He had never sworn in front of a woman in his life, not since grammar school, anyway, but this was a near occasion. She was asking for it. Nannie Rawley needed a willow switch, was what she needed. If they'd both been sixty-five years younger, he'd have turned her over his knee. Garnett swore a silent oath, turned on his heel, and walked away without so much as a word. For an occasion like this, there just weren't any words that would do.

An hour and ten minutes later, Garnett returned to Nannie's backyard with one asphalt shingle in his hand. She was carrying a bushel of Gravensteins to her pickup truck, starting to load up for the Amish market tomorrow, and was so startled to see Garnett Walker that she stumbled and almost dropped her basket.

He held up the shingle, showing her the peculiar heart-shaped profile that matched the ones on her roof, and then he threw it at her feet. It lay there in the grass next to a puddle, this thing she needed, like a valentine. A bright crowd of butterflies rose from the puddle in trembling applause.

"There are two hundred of those in my garage. You can have them all."

She looked from the shingle to Garnett Walker and back to the shingle. "Lord have mercy," she said quietly. "A miracle."

Moth Love

It was nearly noon on a Sunday when Jewel came up to collect the children. Lusa was in the garden picking green beans when she saw her coming up across the yard, moving slowly. "Honey, it's the Lord's day of rest," Jewel called out when she reached the gate. "You shouldn't be working this hard."

"What was God thinking, then, when he made green beans and August?" Lusa replied, trusting that her sister-in-law wasn't really scolding her for sacrilege. Jewel looked pale but jaunty in a little blue cloche someone had crocheted for her. She hadn't ever bothered with a wig but just wore scarves and hats. "Come on through the rabbit fence," Lusa called to her. "The gate just has a wire around the top."

Jewel fiddled with the chicken wire and found her way in. "Lord, this is pretty," she remarked. Lusa sat back on her heels, feeling proud. Red and yellow peppers glowed like ornaments on their dark bushes, and the glossy purple eggplants had the stately look of expensive gifts. Even the onions were putting up pink globes of flower. During all the years of childhood she'd spent sprouting seeds in pots on a patio, she'd been dreaming of this.

"You must be a slave to this garden," Jewel said.

"Just about. Look at this." She gestured at the long row of unpicked beans. "I've done forty quarts of beans already, and I've still got two more rows to go."

"You'll be glad, though. Come next February."

"That's the truth. Between this and my chickens, I may not have to go to Kroger's again till next summer. I've got tomatoes put up, spaghetti sauce—maybe twenty quarts—and I'm freezing broccoli, cauliflower, you name it. *Tons* of corn. Your kids ate their own weight each in corn last night, by the way."

Jewel smiled. "They would. Lowell will even eat roasting ears, and he is Mister Picky. They didn't put much dent in your broccoli, though, did they?"

"No."

"You could quit on the green beans right now," Jewel said. "If you've got forty quarts, you could just stop picking and say, 'Well, sir, I'm done.' It's not against the law."

"I could," Lusa said. "But Cole planted these beans. He put in most of this. Remember how it got warm early, in May? I feel like as long as I'm up here picking stuff, he's still giving me presents. I hate to think of the fall, when I'll have to turn it under."

Jewel shook her head. "It's your work, too, though. I swear, this is *pretty*. It looks like a woman's garden, some way. It doesn't look like other people's gardens."

Lusa thought, but did not say, that this was because she was an outsider. She planted different things: five-color Swiss chard instead of collard greens, and several rows of fava beans to dry for falafel meal. She'd grown four different kinds of eggplants from seed, including the pink-and-white-streaked "Rosa Bianca" for her beloved *imam bayildi* and *baba ganouj*.

Jewel was examining the tomato plants, rubbing their healthy leaves between her fingers. "What do you kill the hornworms with, Sevin dust?"

"No, not that. It kills too many of my friends."

Jewel looked over at her with a horrified face, and Lusa laughed. "Bugs, I mean. I know you all laugh at me, but I'm so fond of bugs, I can't stand to use a general pesticide like Sevin. I use different things. I use Bt on the tomatoes."

"B-T?"

"It's a germ, *Bacillus thuringiensis*. A bacterium that gives hornworms indigestion when they eat my tomatoes but doesn't hurt bees or ladybugs."

"Are you pulling my leg?"

"Nope. Well, *bad* indigestion—the hornworms die. It works on cabbage loopers, too. Here, there's a peck basket by the fence there, why don't you pick some tomatoes for you and the kids to take home?"

"I won't eat them; my stomach's shot for anything acid, I guess from the chemo. I still can't even drink orange juice. But I'll pick you the ripe ones, instead of just standing here useless. Something else for you to put up."

"I *have* quit on canning tomatoes. Now I just slice them up with basil and olive oil and eat them for breakfast."

"Oh, shoot, I stepped right on your marigolds."

"That's okay, I don't care what they look like. I just put them in to keep nematodes away from the roots of the tomato plants."

"Now, that is something. That is really something. Cole was starting to get real interested in all that the last couple years. How to poison things without using poison. He went up to U.K. to take a class on that."

"That's how we met," Lusa said, looking down. "I was his teacher."

"Oh!" cried Jewel, as if she'd been stung by a bee. Was she jealous? Lusa wondered. She didn't usually seem to be, not so much as the other sisters, even though she and Cole had been so close. Jewel alone had always seemed willing to share him. Lusa bent close to her beans to keep the sun out of her eyes as she neared the end of her row. She moved along on her knees, dragging a nearly full paper grocery bag along beside her.

"Believe it or not," she said to Jewel, "I had both your kids up here for half the morning handpicking the bean beetles and squashing them. I told them I'd pay them a penny apiece if they kept track, and would you believe, they did a body count. They're going to go home rich today. You got any overdue bills you need paid, talk to Crys and Lowell." She glanced up. "Jewel? *Jewel?*"

Lusa scanned above the whole row of tall tomato plants for Jewel's head, but it wasn't there. She stood up and walked along the end in a panic, looking down between the rows. There Jewel was on the ground, gripping her knees and rocking with her face tight with pain and a basket of tomatoes spilled out on the ground beside her. Lusa flew to her side and put both arms around her to steady her.

"Oh, God," Lusa said, several times. "What should I do? I'm sorry, I'm not one of those people who're good in emergencies."

Jewel opened her eyes. "It's no emergency. I just need to get to the house. I guess I overdid it. I've got pain pills in my purse."

Leaving beans and tomatoes strewed on the ground and the rabbit fence wide open, the two small women struggled down the slope and across the yard to the house. Lusa practically carried Jewel up the steps. Upper-body strength had come to her unbidden in the last months: nearly every day she did something she used to have to ask Cole to do, and it startled her, always, to glance at her body in the mirror and see planes where soft curves used to be. Carrying a relative up the porch stairs, though, was a first.

They paused in the front hallway, hearing the children's voices. Lowell and Crys were in the parlor with a stack of ancient board games Lusa had pulled out of a closet. Their favorites were Monopoly and the Ouija board, which they pronounced "Ow-jay."

"Where are your pills?" Lusa asked.

"Oh, shoot, my purse is in the car."

"Let's get you onto the parlor couch, then. I'll run and get it."

Jewel gave Lusa a pleading look. "Could we go upstairs? I hate for the kids to see me like this."

"Of course." Lusa felt stupid for not thinking of that. Jewel gripped the banister with a tight, white hand, and Lusa carried most of her weight up these stairs, too. She guided Jewel into the bedroom, deciding not to care that the bed wasn't made and clothes were on the floor. "Here, you sit and I'll be right back."

She flew down to the car and back, breathless, just taking a quick glance at the kids to see that they were occupied. They were arguing over Monopoly money, so they hadn't noticed anything. Keeping her voice as calm as she could, she asked them to go out and close the rabbit fence around the garden and then gather the eggs, which she knew Lowell loved to do, so long as his sister protected him from the rooster. Then she ran back upstairs, pausing in the upstairs bathroom to draw a glass of water from the tap. When she returned to the bedroom she found Jewel settled into the green brocade chair by the window, Lusa's reading chair. She was running her fingers over the vine pattern on the nubbly green fabric, as if reading something written there in Braille. Lusa handed her the glass of water and sat on the floor at her feet to work on the child-proof cap.

When she got it open at last, Jewel swallowed the pills and drank the whole glass of water, obediently, like a child. She set down the glass and went on rubbing the arms of the chair, thoughtfully. "We used to have two of these," she said. "A pair. Mommy's good parlor chairs, till they got old. Lois finally spilled something on one of them. Or, no, she cut her leg open with a pocketknife and got a big streak of blood from here to there. Lordy, she was in trouble."

"For cutting her leg?"

"Well, no, see, for doing it in that chair. She was trying to make a soap carving of Marilyn Monroe! We weren't supposed to be in the parlor at all; it was just for company. That was a whole mess of trouble. Mommy about had a fit. She couldn't clean it for anything. She had to throw that chair out! Lord, I wonder where it ever ended up."

"Probably in the barn, along with everything else in the free world. Do you know there's part of a piano in there?"

"No," Jewel said quietly, her eyes fixed on the wallpaper over the bed. "She put it down by the road. That's the way you did back then, when we were kids. Somebody would always come along that was worse off than you and didn't mind putting a sheet over a stained chair, and they'd take it. It's somewhere now. Somebody's using it someplace." Her eyes focused and came down like a pair of blue butterflies to light on Lusa's face. "Isn't it funny how you never know how things are going to wind up? I get so mad, thinking about not having a chance to get old. Darn it. I want to see what Lois looks like with white hair."

"I don't think any of us will live to see *that*. As long as Lady Clairol's still in business."

Jewel let out a weak laugh, but Lusa felt bad for trying to cover this awful, important moment with a joke. She had suffered so much herself from people's platitudes and evasions of death, yet here with Jewel she had no idea what else to say. "You never know, Jewel, you still might outlive us all," was what came out.

Jewel shook her head, keeping her eyes steady on Lusa. "I'm not going to see another summer. I'll be gone before you're done eating the canned goods in your pantry."

"I'm sorry," Lusa whispered. She reached up to take both of Jewel's hands in hers and held on to them without speaking for several minutes. An occasional syllable of the children's shouts drifted in through the open window. The position eventually became awkward for Lusa and she had to let go, stroking her sister-in-law's fingers gently as she did. She looked back up at Jewel's face, which seemed empty now. The hat looked sad and undignified indoors, seeming to mock her seriousness, but Jewel had been adamant about not spending money on a wig. Lusa had wondered whether it signified optimism that her hair would grow back or realism, an acknowledgment that there wouldn't be much time. Now she knew.

"Jewel, I want to ask you a question. Something I've been thinking about. You don't have to answer today; you can think it over as long as you need to. Or maybe you'll just say no, and that's fine, too. But I want to ask."

"Ask me, then."

Lusa's heart pounded. She had imagined asking this in a more casual setting, maybe while she and Jewel did something together in the kitchen. She hadn't realized before today that it was too late for casual. And this was not a casual thing.

"What is it, then?" Jewel seemed troubled now by the pause.

"I wondered if, when the time came, *if* the time came . . ." Lusa felt her face grow hot. "Forgive me if this is inappropriate to ask, but I wondered what you'd think about the idea of my adopting Crys and Lowell."

"Taking care of them or adopting them?"

"Adopting them."

Jewel studied Lusa's face, surprisingly unshaken. She didn't seem angry, anyway, as Lusa had feared she might be.

"We don't have to talk about this if you don't want to," Lusa said. "I can't imagine anything harder to think about."

"Don't you think I think about it every minute of the day?" Jewel said in a flat voice that frightened Lusa.

"I guess you do. *I* would. That's why I brought it up."

"Well, it's not something you ought to feel obligated about," she answered finally. "I've got four sisters."

Lusa looked at the floor, at her callused knees and dirt-streaked thighs beneath the hem of her shorts, and then she took Jewel's hand back in hers without looking up. "You've got *five* sisters. I'm the only one without children." She glanced up then at Jewel, who was listening. "But that's not the reason. That wouldn't be a good reason. I love your kids, that's the reason. I love Crys and I love Lowell. I'm not sure I'd be the greatest mother, but I think I could learn on those two. Lowell's easy, he's a heart stealer, and Crys . . . Crys and I are two peas in a pod."

"You'd have plenty of help, right down the hill," Jewel said equivocally.

"*Plenty* of help," Lusa agreed, encouraged by Jewel's use of the conditional. She hadn't said no. "More help than you can shake a stick at. Although to be honest I don't think Lois and a stick should be allowed near those kids. At least till they're older."

"Not till they're older," Jewel echoed, closing her eyes and leaning her head back against the big green chair. "Can you picture Crys at the senior cotillion?"

"Believe it or not, I can," Lusa said gently. "But she might be wearing a tux. She's got the world by the tail; she just needs help figuring out what to do with it. It's going to take an open mind. When I look around this family, the best candidate I come up with is me."

Jewel opened her eyes and looked down at Lusa with a new expression. "There's some papers I have to get their father to sign before I can really decide the next step. I've been thinking about all this since I first got sick. I had the papers drawn up already at the lawyer's."

"For what, releasing them for adoption?"

"Well, just releasing them to me. He doesn't even know I'm sick. There's no telling what he'd do. I don't think he'd really come scoop them up, but you never know with him. With Shel, that's the one thing you can count on, is that you never can tell. He might think he wanted them, for a week or two, and then he'd dump them out like kitties by the side of the road when he figured out a kid has to eat and shit."

She closed her eyes again and winced. Lusa stroked the backs of her hands until whatever it was passed over. She wondered what this invisible beast was doing to Jewel on the inside, what parts of her it already owned. She thought of an old tale her zayda used to tell about the beast that ate the moon every month and then slowly spat it back out. A happier ending than this. She could feel the heat and ire of Jewel's monster right through her thin skin.

"So I'll get those sent off to Shel," Jewel said after a minute. "Just to get that part squared away. I'll do that today. I've been putting it off."

"Nobody could blame you," Lusa said, and then they sat still again while the clock out in the hallway chimed half past the hour. Lusa collected several questions in the silence, but she waited until Jewel opened her eyes again before asking them. It was impossible to be too eager about any of this. She tried to talk slowly.

"Do you even know where Shel is? And will he sign the papers?"

"Oh, yeah, I know where he's at. He moves around a lot, but the state's got a garnishee on his wages. See, I had to go to court for that, after he took off. Any employer that writes him a paycheck has to take out three hundred dollars a month and send it to me. That's how I keep track of him."

"Gosh," Lusa said. She had never remotely pictured Jewel in court, standing up to her abandonment. She could imagine the gossip that must have generated. And there were people in this county who would shun Jewel to the end of her life on account of it.

"That's exactly why he'd sign off his claim to the kids," Jewel said. "So he could quit paying. I think he'll sign in a heartbeat. But would you want him to?"

Lusa studied Jewel's furrowed brow, trying to follow the quick turns this conversation had made. "Would I take the kids without the money, you mean?" She thought about it for less than ten seconds. "It's the safest thing. Legally, I think it would be best. Because I'd like to be able to put their names on the deed to this farm. So it would go to them, you know, after me." She felt a strange movement in the air as she said this, a lightness that grew around her. When she gathered the will to look up at Jewel again, she was surprised to see her sister-in-law's face shining with tears.

"It just seems right to do that," Lusa explained, feeling self-conscious. "I'm thinking I'd add 'Widener' to their names, if that's all right with you. I'm taking it, too."

"You don't have to. We all got over that." Jewel wiped her face with her hands. She was smiling.

"No, I want to. I decided a while ago. As long as I live on this place, I'm going to be Miz Widener, so why fight it?" Lusa smiled, too. "I'm married to a piece of land named Widener."

She got up and sat on the arm of the green chair so she could put her arm gently across Jewel's shoulders. They both sat looking out the window at the yard and the hayfield behind it, across which Lusa had received her husband's last will and testament. Today her eyes were drawn to the mulberry tree at the edge of the yard, loaded with the ripe purple fruits that Lowell had christened "long cherries" when he discovered and gorged himself on them, staining his teeth blue. At this moment in the summer the mulberry had become the yard's big attraction for every living thing for miles around, it seemed. It dawned on Lusa that this was the Tree of Life her ancestors had woven into their rugs and tapestries, persistently, through all their woes and losses: a bird tree. You might lose a particular tree you owned or loved, but the birds would always keep coming. She could spot their color on every branch: robins, towhees, cardinals, orchard orioles, even sunny little goldfinches. These last Lusa thought were seed eaters, so she didn't know quite what they were doing in there; enjoying the company, maybe, the same way people will go to a busy city park just to feel a part of something joyful and lively.

"I'm going to have to talk to my sisters about it," Jewel said suddenly. "The other sisters," she amended.

"Oh, sure. I know. Please don't feel any hurry or pressure or anything. God knows I don't want to hurt anybody's feelings. If they don't think I'm in a position."

"You're in a position."

"Well, I don't know. I've never had any idea how I fit into this family picture."

"You have an idea, honey. More than you think." Jewel pressed her lips together in thought, then spoke again. "They'll act hurt for a minute, because they have to. But as soon as we leave and close the door behind us, they will praise the Lord. We will all praise the Lord."

{25}

Predators

or the rest of her own life and maybe the next one after, Deanna would remember this day. A cool snap had put a sudden premonition of fall into the air, a crisp quality she could feel with her skin and all the rest of her newly heightened senses: she could smell and taste the change, even hear it. The birds had gone quiet, their noisy summer celebration hushed all at once by the power of a cold front and the urge rising up in their breasts to be still, gather in, wait for the time soon to come when they would turn in the darkness on a map made of stars and join the vast assembly of migration. Deanna clung to her perch on the rock, feeling the same stirring in her breast, a sense of finished business and a longing to fly. She had climbed up onto a lichen-crusted boulder fifty feet above the spot where the trail ended at the overlook. From here she could look down on everything, the valley of her childhood and the mountains beyond it. If she stood and spread her arms, it seemed possible she would sail out beyond everything she'd yet known, into new territory.

From the branches behind her she heard a sociable gathering of friends hailing each other with their winter call: chicka *dee-dee-dee!* The chickadees, her familiar anchors. Deanna would not fly away today; this thrill was only something left over from childhood, when a crisp turn in the weather meant apple time, time to hunt for paw-paws in Nannie's woodlot. At some point between yesterday and today the air had gone from soggy to brittle. The Virginia creeper on the cabin had begun to turn overnight; this morning she'd noticed a few bright-red leaves, just enough to make her pause and take note of history. This was the day, would always be the day, when she first knew. She would step somehow from the realm of ghosts that she'd inhabited all her life to commit herself irrevocably to the living. On the trail up to this overlook today she had paid little mind to the sadness of lost things moving through the leaves at the edges of her vision, the shadowy little wolves and the bright-winged parakeets hopping wistfully through untouched cockleburs. These dispossessed creatures were beside her and always would be, but just for today she noticed instead a single bright-red berry among all the clusters of green ones covering the spicebushes. This sign seemed meaningful and wondrous, standing as a divide between one epoch of her life and the next. If the summer had to end somewhere, why couldn't it be in that one red spicebush berry beside the path?

She slipped the small, borrowed mirror—his shaving mirror—from her back pocket and looked closely at her face. With the fingertips of her left hand she touched the slightly mottled, darker skin beneath her eyes. It was like a raccoon's mask, but subtler, spreading from the bridge of her nose out to her cheekbones. The rest of her face was the same as she remembered it, unmoved if not untouched. Her breasts were heavier; she could feel that change internally. She turned her face to the sun and slowly unbuttoned her shirt, placing his hands like ghost fingers where hers were now. His touch on her skin would be a mantle she could shed and put on again through the power of memory. Here on this rock in the sun she let him enter her like water: the memory of this morning, his eyes in hers, his movement like a tide pushing the sea against the sand of its only shore. Her body's joy was colored darker now from knowing that each conversation, every kiss, every comforting adventure of skin on skin might be the last one. Each image stood still beside its own shadow. Even the warmth of his body sleeping next to her afterward was a dark-brown heat she stroked with her fingers, memorizing it against the days when that space would be cold.

Fifty feet below her was the overlook where she'd nearly ended her life in a fall two years ago, and then, in May, where she'd fallen again. *Sweet,* he'd said. *Did you ever see a prettier sight than that right there?* And she'd replied, Never. She was looking at mountains and valleys, all keeping their animal secrets. He was looking at sheep farms.

She touched her breast and took up the mirror again to look closely at the deep auburn color of her aureole. It seemed like a miracle that skin could change like this in color and texture in such a short time, like caterpillar skin taking on the color and texture of moth. Briefly, as if testing the temperature of water, she touched her abdomen just under her navel, where the top button of her jeans no longer conceded to meet its buttonhole. Deanna wondered briefly just how much of a fool she had been, for how long. Ten weeks at the most, probably less, but *still.* She'd known bodies, her own especially, and she hadn't known this. Was it something a girl learned from a mother, that secret church of female knowledge that had never let her in? All the things she'd heard women say did not seem right. She had not been sick, had not craved to eat anything strange. (Except for a turkey. Was that strange?) She'd only felt like a bomb had exploded in the part of her mind that kept her on an even keel. She'd mistaken that feeling for love or lust or perimenopause or an acute invasion of privacy, and as it turned out it was all of those, and none. The explosion had frightened her for the way it loosened her grip on the person she'd always presumed herself to be. But maybe that was what this was going to be: a long, long process of coming undone from one's self.

Deanna tried to imagine the night of her own conception, something she'd never before had the courage to consider. The rumpled Ray Dean Wolfe making love to the mother she'd never known. That woman had been flesh and blood—a person who'd moved like Deanna, maybe, who'd walked too fast, or dreaded thunder, or bitten the ends of her hair when she was too happy or too sad. A woman who'd gripped life in naked embrace and gone on living past any hope of survival.

Deanna had not been a fool, she decided. She'd just lacked guidance in matters of love. Lacking a mother of her own, she'd missed all the signs.

Nannie had done her best, and that wasn't bad—just a broader education, by far, than most daughters were prepared for. Nannie Rawley, as reliable and generous as her apple trees, standing in her calico skirt in the backyard calling Deanna and Rachel down out of a tree, not for fear of their climbing but because she could occasionally offer them something better, like cider or a pie. Only then. They'd lived in trees, Rachel low to the ground on a branch where Deanna put her for safekeeping while she herself climbed enough for the both of them, mounting the scaffold limbs like the girl on the flying trapeze. If she looked down, there was Rachel, peering up through the leaves with her sweet, sleepy eyes and her lips parted in eternal wonder, permanently in awe of her airborne sister.

"What made Rachel that way?" she'd asked Nannie, only once. The two of them were up on the hill behind the orchard.

Nannie answered, "Her genes. You know about genes."

Deanna was an adolescent girl who loved science and read more books than anyone she knew, so she said yes, she did.

"I know," Nannie said quietly, "you want a better answer than that, and so do I. For a long time I blamed the world. The chemicals and stuff in our food. I was reading about that when I was carrying her, and it scared me to death. But there's other ways of looking at Rachel."

"I love her how she is," Deanna said. "I'm not saying I don't."

"I know. But we all wish she didn't have so many things wrong with her, besides her mind."

Deanna waited until Nannie decided to speak again. They were walking uphill through an old, weedy hayfield. Deanna was taller than Nannie now, had passed her around her twelfth birthday, but by walking ahead of her on this steep hill Nannie had regained the advantage.

"Here's how I think about it," Nannie said. "You know there's two different ways to make life: crossing and cloning. You know about that from grafting trees, right?"

Deanna nodded tentatively. "You can make a cutting of scionwood from a tree you like and grow it out into a new one."

"That's right," Nannie said. "You call that a scion, or a clone. It's just the same as the parent it came from. And the other way is if two animals mate, or if two plants cross their pollen with each other; that's a cross. What comes of that will be different from either one of the parents, and a little different from all the other crosses made by those same parents. It's like rolling two dice together: you can get a lot more numbers than just the six you started with. And that's called sex."

Deanna nodded again, even more tentatively. But she understood. She followed the path through the tall grass that Nannie was tramping down in front of her.

"Sexual reproduction is a little bit riskier. When the genes of one parent combine with the genes of the other, there's more chances for something to go wrong. Sometimes a whole piece can drop out by mistake, or get doubled up. That's what happened with Rachel." Nannie stopped walking and turned around to face Deanna. "But just think what this world would be if we didn't have the crossing type of reproduction."

Deanna found she couldn't picture the difference, and said so.

"Well," Nannie said, pondering this, "probably for just millions of years there were little blobs of things in the sea, all just alike, splitting in two and making more of themselves. Same, same, same. Nothing much cooking. And then, some way, they got to where they'd cross their genes with one another and turn out a little variety, from mutations and such. *Then* starts the hullabaloo."

"Then there'd start to be different kinds of things?" Deanna guessed.

"More and more, that's right. Some of the kids turned out a little nicer than the parents, and some, not so hot. But the better ones could make even a little better. Things could change. They could branch out."

"And that was good, right?"

Nannie put her hands on her knees and looked Deanna earnestly in the eye. "That was the *world,* honey. That's what we live in. That is God Almighty. There's nothing so important as having variety. That's how life can still go on when the world changes. But variety means strong and not so strong, and that's just how it is. You throw the dice. There's Deannas and there's Rachels, that's what comes of sex, that's the miracle of it. It's the greatest invention life ever made."

And that was it, the nearest thing to a birds-and-bees lecture she'd ever gotten from Nannie, the nearest thing to a mother she had. It was a cool fall day—September, probably—and they were making their way through the hillside field that had gone derelict since Nannie took over running the farm. It was full of sapling apple trees sprouted from seeds left here in the droppings of the deer and foxes that stole apples from the orchard down below. Nannie claimed that these wild trees were her legacy. The orchard trees planted by her father were all good strains, true to type, carefully grown out from cuttings so they'd be identical to their parent tree. All the winesaps in the world were just alike. But Nannie's field saplings were outlaws from seeds never meant to be sown, the progeny of different apple varieties cross-pollinated by bees. Up here stood the illegitimate children of a Transparent crossed with a Stayman's winesap, or a Gravenstein crossed with who knew what, a neighbor's wild apple or maybe a pear. Nannie had stopped mowing this field and let these offspring raise up their heads until they were a silent throng. "Like Luther Burbank's laboratory," was how she'd explained it to an adolescent girl who wanted to understand, but Deanna could think of them only as Nannie's children. On many an autumn Saturday, the two of them had beat their way through the grass of this overgrown field from one tree to the next, tasting apples from these wild trees, the renegade products of bee sex and fox thievery. They were looking for something new: Nannie's Finest.

Deanna knew what to do; she had a plan. This was the first week of August, which meant Jerry would be coming up soon with her groceries and mail. She could send a letter back to town with him. Instead of putting on a stamp, which she wasn't even sure she had, she'd draw a map of Egg Fork Creek and Highway 6 on the back of the envelope so Jerry could find the orchard and deliver it straight. Deanna smiled to think of Nannie's opening the envelope with the map on the back. Maybe she would pause first to study that line of blue ink connecting Deanna's cabin to her own orchard, like a maze in a child's puzzle book painstakingly completed. Maybe, just from that, Nannie would be able to guess the contents of the message inside.

Deanna already knew how the letter would begin:

Dear Nannie,
I have some news. I'm coming down from the mountain this fall, in September, I think, when it starts to get cold. It looks like I'll be bringing somebody else with me. I wonder if we could stay with you.

{26}

Old Chestnuts

arnett was on his way home from a trip to town, thinking about the fish at Pinkie's Diner and whether it had been as good as usual, and just arriving at the place where Egg Fork joined up with Black Creek and the road dipped into a little piece of woods, when he was stopped by an animal in the road. There it stood in broad daylight, causing Garnett to brake hard and stop completely. It was a dog, but not a dog. Garnett had never seen the like of it. It was a wild, fawn-colored thing with its golden tail arched high and its hackles standing up and its eyes directly on Garnett. It appeared to be ready to take on a half-ton Ford pickup truck with no fear of the outcome.

"Well, then," Garnett said aloud, quietly. His heart was pumping heartily, not from fear but from astonishment. The creature was looking into his eyes as if it meant to speak.

It turned its head back toward the side of the road it had come from, and out of the weeds crept a second one, walking slowly. Its tail was held lower, but its color and size were about the same. It hesitated out in the open, then picked up its pace and crossed the road quickly at a neat trot. The first one turned into line behind it and followed, and they both disappeared into the chickory at the edge of the road without so much as a glance back at Garnett. The blue-flowered weeds parted and then closed like curtains in a movie house, and Garnett had the strangest feeling that what he'd witnessed was just that kind of magic. This was no pair of stray dogs dumped off bewildered beside the road and now trying to find their way back to the world of men. They were wildness, and this was where they lived.

He sat for a long moment gazing at the ghosts of what he had seen on the empty road ahead of him. Then, because life had to go on and his prostate wasn't what it used to be, he put the truck into gear and pressed on, minding his own business and keeping fairly well to his own side of the road. He had nearly closed in on the safety of his own driveway when a young man flagged him down. Garnett was still thinking about the dogs, so much so that he went right on past the Forest Service jeep and on down the road a piece before it registered that the boy in the jeep had meant for him to stop.

He pulled over slowly until he heard the chickory weeds in the ditch brush the side of his truck, which told him he was well off the road. Then he shut off the ignition and sat peering nervously into the rearview mirror. The Forest Service people weren't the police. They couldn't *make* you stop. This wasn't like Timmy Boyer's pulling a fellow over and giving him a lecture on old age and bad eyesight and threatening to take away his driving license. Goodness, maybe those animals he'd just seen were something the Forest Service had lost and was looking for? But no, of course not, that was a ridiculous idea. This was just a little, green, open-sided army jeep, not a circus train. If anything, this boy had likely been signaling to Garnett to get back over the center line. He'd been so preoccupied with what he'd just seen back at the fork that he wasn't paying a lot of attention to anything else. Garnett knew he strayed; he would admit to that, if asked.

He was still stewing over whether to try to back up and speak to the young man or just go on down the road and forget about it when the fellow hopped out of his jeep and came walking toward him at a brisk pace. He had some kind of a paper in his hand.

"Oh, for pity's sake," Garnett muttered to himself. "Now they're letting children from the Forest Service hand out driving tickets."

But that wasn't it. Goodness, this boy seemed too young to be operating a vehicle, much less claiming any authority whatsoever over other drivers. He stood next to Garnett's open window studying some kind of scribbling on the paper he had there, and then he asked, "Excuse me, sir, would this be Highway Six?"

"It *would* be," Garnett replied, "if the fools that run the nine-one-one emergency-ambulance business hadn't decided to put up a road sign calling it Meadow Brook Lane."

The young man looked at him, a little startled. "Well, that's exactly what the sign back there said. Meadow Brook Lane. But I've got this map here that says I'm supposed to be on Highway Six, and it seems like that's where I'm at."

"Well," said Garnett. "There isn't any *meadow*, and there isn't any *brook*. What we've got here is just a lot of cow pastures and a creek. So most of us go right on ahead and call it number Six, since that's what it's been ever since God was a child, as far as I know. Just showing up here one day and banging up a green metal sign doesn't make a country road through a cow pasture into something it isn't. I've always had the impression the nine-one-one emergency-ambulance people must be from Roanoke."

The young man looked even more surprised. "*I'm* from Roanoke."

"Well, then," Garnett said. "There you have it."

"But," he said, seeming to waver between confusion and irritation, "*is* this Highway Six, then, or *isn't* it?"

"Who wants to know, and who would he be looking for?" Garnett asked.

The fellow flipped over his paper, which looked like an envelope, and read, "Miss Nannie Rawley. Fourteen hundred twelve, Old Highway Six."

Garnett shook his head. "Son, is there some reason why you can't do your business with Miss Rawley through the United States Mail, like everybody else? You've got to go bothering her yourself? Do you have any idea how busy that woman is this time of year, with an orchard to run? Has the Forest Service got such a shortage of forests to service nowadays, that it needs to be getting into the postal-delivery business?"

The young man had his head cocked and his mouth partly open, but he seemed to have run out of questions and answers both. Whatever business he had with Nannie, he wasn't going to speak of it to Garnett.

"All right, go on, then," Garnett finally said. "That's it right up there. That mailbox sticking out of the bank at a funny angle with all the butterfly weeds around it."

"That's Nannie Rawley?" the boy asked, practically jumping out of his skin.

"No," Garnett said patiently, shaking his head as he started up the ignition in his truck. "That's her *mailbox*."

⁓

It was only reasonable to be curious, Garnett told himself, taking his cup and saucer from this morning off the drainboard and putting them away. Strangers didn't come up this way much, and that boy was young. People of that age were liable to do anything— if you read the newspaper at all, you knew they scared elderly ladies just for sport. And she *was* busy. In another month apples would be falling from the sky like hail over there, and she had just such a short while to get them all in. Half her crop she sold to some company in Atlanta Georgia with a silly name, for apple juice without any pesticides in it. She got the price of gold for her apples, he'd give her that much, even if she did let the bugs have free run of her property. But it always worried Garnett when those pickers came in to work for her during the peak harvest. Last year half her pickers had been those young Mexican banditos who came up here for the tobacco cutting and hanging and stayed on until stripping time. Which right there, to begin with, was a sure sign of things gone out of whack: farmers had so little family to count on anymore that they had to turn to a foreign land to get help with their tobacco cutting and stripping. You could hear those boys in town, summer or fall, making themselves right at home and speaking in tongues. Apparently they meant to settle in. The Kroger's in Egg Fork had started selling those flat-looking Mexican pancakes, just to lure them into staying here year-round, it seemed. That was how you really knew what the world had stooped to: foreign food in the Kroger's.

Garnett held aside the curtain in his kitchen window and angled for a better view, though it was fairly hopeless at this distance. Dr. Gibben had been pestering him for years to get the surgery for the cataracts, and up until right about now Garnett hadn't even considered it. His thinking was, the less he could see of this world of woe, the better. But now he realized it might be the gentlemanly thing to do, to let those doctors take a knife to his eyes. For the sake of others. With so many bandits running loose, you never knew when a neighbor might need you to come to her aid.

Well, the boy had left, he'd seen to that. Garnett had stood his ground right here by his kitchen window and watched while that boy gave her the envelope and then high-tailed that little green jeep back to Roanoke, where people had nothing better to do than think up ridiculous new names for old roads.

But Nannie was acting strange. That was what worried Garnett. She was still standing out on the grass in front of her house as if that boy had said something awful enough to glue her to the spot. He'd driven away five minutes ago, and she was still standing there with the letter in her hand, looking up at the mountains. The look of her wasn't right. She seemed to be crying or praying, and neither one of those was a thing you reasonably expected from Nannie Rawley. It weighed on Garnett's mind, wondering what the young man had said or done to upset her this much. Because, really, you never knew who might be next.

When Garnett positively couldn't wait any longer he went to the bathroom, and when he came back to the window she was gone. She must have gone into the house. He tried to putter around his kitchen and get his mind on something else, but there weren't any dishes to wash (he'd just had dinner at Pinkie's). And there was no point even thinking about what to cook for supper (Pinkie's was all-you-can-eat!). And he didn't dare go outside. It wasn't that he meant to spy on Nannie outright. Whatever was going on over there, it really didn't matter to him one way or the other. He had plenty of other things to do, and people who were counting on him to do them. That girl over at the Widener place with her goat troubles, for one. Poor little thing, a Lexington girl! Petunia in the onion patch. He would go upstairs right now and get down his veterinary manual and look up about the vaccine, check whether those goats would need seven-way or eight-way. He hadn't been sure when he told her. They didn't get red-water disease in goats around here, but there might be some other reason to go with the eight-way. Now he couldn't even remember which one he'd told her to use. It had felt so strange going over there to that house again. It had put his head in a peculiar twist, as if Ellen could be alive again, just for the time being.

Her greatest regret was that she'd never gone to see that baby— that was what she told him, last thing, there in the hospital bed. *Greatest* regret, as if there'd been a whole host of others a husband couldn't be told about. And now there were two babies, a boy and a girl, Garnett believed. Ellen never even knew about the second one. Garnett had come so close to asking the Widener girl about them, the other day when he went over there. He'd stood right there on that porch and had it in him to do it, the words in his mouth, but then he'd turned uncertain. Who was this gal with her goats, anyhow? She was nice enough for a city person, surprisingly nice, but how in tarnation had she wound up here in a man's long-tailed shirt in the middle of a field of thistles and nanny goats? Garnett had asked several polite questions but never had been able to work out exactly what business she had running that farm by herself. It was still the old family homeplace, but the people in it seemed to have shifted. Were those two children even still around? What if they and the mother had moved to Knoxville like every-body and his dog seemed to be doing these days? What if Garnett had been sitting twiddling his thumbs and in the meantime lost his chance to find out about those kids? People were just piling up their belongings and racing for Knoxville like it was the California gold rush, since day one after they put in that Toyota plant over there. Pretty soon there'd be no one left in this county but old folks wait-ing to die.

The hall window upstairs gave a good view of the side orchard and Nannie's backyard, and a little later on toward evening he was able to spot her from there, working in her garden. She was picking her tomatoes. She had more tomatoes than you could shake a stick at and sold them for a scandalous price at the Amish market. He squinted through the wavy, ancient glass of this window.

Well. There was somebody out there with her! That blue and white blotch at the edge of her garden was, now that he looked at it, a man in a hat leaning on the fence. It wasn't the Forest Service boy, it was somebody else, a heavier-set kind of fellow that Garnett didn't recognize as a neighbor. Could it be one of the pickers, ar-rived too early? Who else on earth could it be? Clivus Morton had been coming around lately to work on hammering up the new shingles for her, and even Oda Black's boy what's-his-name had come by once to visit her, for reasons unknown to Garnett. So! Was Nannie Rawley suddenly attracting men of all ages, from miles around? A seventy-five-year-old woman puts on a pair of short pants, and the fellows come swarming around her like bees to a flower, was that it? (Although Clivus Morton was no honeybee. Garnett had known honey*dippers* who smelled better, even after they'd pumped out your septic tank.) *Was* this Clivus? He squinted. Darn this window, he swore mildly, it was as hazy as his eyes. Dirty, too. He hadn't cleaned it since—well, he'd never cleaned it, period.

He moved to the other side of the window, but it didn't help much. He could see she was out there filling her bushel basket and evidently talking up a storm because that stranger, whoever he was (and no, it was *not* Clivus), just stood there leaning forward with his elbows on the top rail of her garden fence as if he had nothing in this world to do but stand there leaning on her fence. He didn't seem to have a speck of manners, either. He could have at least offered to carry the bushel basket while she picked. Garnett would have done that much. You didn't have to agree with everything a person said, or approve of the condition of her soul, to show some simple consideration.

Garnett felt his blood pressure going up. It began to agitate him so, he had to step away from the window. For goodness' sakes, whoever that man was out there, he had no business with her. Garnett felt a murky, un-Christian feeling clouding in his heart. He hated that man. He hated his whole bearing, leaning on that fence as if he had nothing better to do with his life than listen all day to Nannie Rawley and look at her picking tomatoes in short pants.

Moth Love

Thursday dawned cool again, and stayed cool all day. Lusa felt energized by the change in weather, which was lucky for her since the work never stopped. If she'd known how much work there would be in August, she would have considered July a vacation. The garden was like a baby bird in reverse, calling to her relentlessly, opening its maw and giving, giving. She spent the whole morning with the canner rumbling on the stove, processing quarts of cling peaches, while she cut up and blanched piles of carrots, peppers, okra, and summer squash for the freezer. She had put up thirty pints of kosher dills and still had so many cucumbers that she was having desperate thoughts. Here was one: She could put them in plastic grocery sacks and drive down the road hanging them on people's mailboxes like they did with the free samples of fabric softener. She tried the idea on Jewel when she came up to bring Lusa her mail.

Jewel asked, "Have you done any pickles yet?"

Lusa leaned forward on her stool until her forehead rested on the cutting board.

"I take it that means yes," Jewel said. "Lord, I can't believe what you've done here." Lusa sat up and caught Jewel's nostalgic admiration. The jars of golden peaches lined up on the counter looked like currency from another time. "Nobody's done this much putting up since Mommy died. You should be real proud of yourself. *And* you should quit. Don't kill yourself. Give it away."

"I *have*." Lusa gestured with her paring knife. "People down the road run the other way when they see me coming. I caught Mary Edna behind her house throwing the squash I'd given her on the compost pile."

"Don't feel bad. Some summers just overdo it like this and there's a little too much of everything. You can let some of it go."

"I can't, though. Look at those peaches, I should throw those away? That would be a sin." Lusa smiled, self-conscious but proud of herself. "The truth is, I like doing it. I won't have to spend money on food this year. And it seems like hard work is the only thing that stops my brain from running in circles."

"Isn't that the truth. I'd be up here helping you if I had the energy."

"I know you would. Remember that day you helped me with the cherries?"

"Lord, Lord." Jewel sat against the table. "A hundred and ten years ago."

"Seems like that to me, too," Lusa said, recalling her ravaged psyche that day when widowhood had still been new and fierce: her helplessness against life, her struggle to trust Jewel. Crys and Lowell had been strangers she was a little afraid of; Crystal, in fact, had been a boy. A hundred and ten years ago. "You can just throw the mail on the table. Looks like junk and bills—all I ever get."

"All anybody ever gets. Who'd think to write a letter anymore?"

Lusa swept her pile of sliced carrots into the colander for

blanching. Thirty seconds of steam did something to their bio-chemistry that colored them as orange as daylilies (so why did the canning book call this step *blanching?*) and kept them perfect in the freezer. "How are you feeling today, Jewel?"

Jewel put a hand against her cheek. "Pretty good, I think. He's letting me take more of the painkillers now. It makes me stupid as a cow, but boy, I feel great." She sounded so sad, Lusa wanted to go sit down next to her and hold her hand.

"Anything I can do for you today? I'm going to bring down your mother's vacuum and do your rugs when I get a chance. That thing works miracles."

"No, honey, don't put yourself out. I need to get back to the house. I left Crys in charge of burning the trash, and you know where that could lead. I really just came up to show you some-thing."

"What?" Lusa wiped her hands on her apron and crossed to the kitchen table, curious to see what Jewel was pulling out of an enve-lope.

"It's the papers from Shel. He signed them. I knew he would, but still, it's a load off my mind. It's good to be done with it. I wisht I'd done it a year ago." Jewel unfolded the sheaf of stiff-looking pa-pers and handed them to Lusa for her inspection. She sat down and looked them over, her eyes skimming through words invented by lawyers that seemed to complicate something so pure and simple. These children belonged to their mother. Soon, probably sooner than anyone was prepared to believe, they would come to live with Lusa.

A signature was scrawled in blue ink at the bottom of two of the pages, in a hand that was masculine but childish, like a fifth-grade boy's, with the name typed underneath. Lusa stared, aston-ished, then read it aloud. "Garnett Sheldon Walker *the Fourth?*"

"I know," Jewel said with a dry little laugh. "It sounds like the name of a king or something, doesn't it? Anyways not a little old rat with a blond mustache."

"No, but . . ." Lusa struggled to put knowledge and words together. "I know that name. I'm friends with his, well, his grandfather, it must be. With that same name. He's this funny old man who lives over on Highway Six." Lusa looked from the signature to Jewel. "He's even been over here, to this house. He helps me with my goat problems."

"Oh, well, see, Mr. Walker, that's Shel's daddy. He was my inlaws, him and his wife, Ellen. He's come up here, when? Lately?"

"Yeah. Not ten days ago. He came up to diagnose my worm problem. He didn't act like he'd ever set foot on this place before. He wouldn't even step through the barn door till I'd invited him in, like it was a living room."

"Well, that's just like him. They were funny people, him and Ellen. Just kindly old-fashioned I guess. And old, period. I think Shel was a change-of-life baby that came after they'd given up, and they never got over the shock."

Lusa realized this was more or less what she'd been to her own parents. They'd never known what to do with her.

"She died of cancer," Jewel added.

"Who did, Mr. Walker's wife? When?"

"Right around when Shel ran off. No, a couple of years before. Lowell wasn't born yet. She never had a thing to do with Crystal, either, but I guess she was already right sick by that time." Jewel sighed, too familiar with the lapses caused by illness.

Lusa was amazed. She'd simply pegged the old man for a lifelong bachelor. "He's your father-in-law. I can't believe it. How come you never told me?"

"Because I had no earthly notion you even knew him, that's why. We haven't any of us spoken to the old man since her funeral, as far as I can think. I've got nothing against him. It's more like he was funny towards us."

"He's funny toward everybody," Lusa said. "That's my impression."

"What it is, I think, is they were embarrassed to death by Shel's drinking. Shel Walker has shortchanged about everybody in this county, one way or another. He used to paint houses and do odd jobs, and after we got married he got to where he'd take their money for a deposit, go drink it up, and then never come back and do the work. I felt like I couldn't hardly show my face in town. His daddy probably feels worse."

"I had no idea," Lusa said.

"Oh, yeah. Shel spent many a year running around wild. And see, I was part of the *wild,* to begin with, in high school. Then after Shel left me and ran off, that was just finally the last straw. I think old Mr. Walker decided to put that whole chapter on the shelf and pretend me and the kids never happened."

"But he's their grandfather, right?"

"That's sad, isn't it? They never really got to have any mammaw or pappaw. Daddy and Mommy died before they got the chance. And if Shel's got no legal tie to them anymore, Mr. Walker's not hardly obligated to start being a pappaw now, is he?"

"Not obligated, no. But would you care if I called him up? Maybe not right now, but sometime. The kids might like to go over there; he's got a beautiful farm, he grows trees. And there's an apple orchard right nearby, I saw. Wouldn't it be fun to take the kids over there to get cider in October?"

Jewel looked pained, and Lusa could have bitten her tongue off for taking a thing like "October" for granted. "You could call today, I don't care," she told Lusa, "but I wouldn't get my hopes up. He's a sour old pickle."

Lusa didn't say anything. She wasn't sure where Jewel's heart lay in all this. Jewel was looking out the window now, miles away. "They came to our wedding," she said. "It was here, in this house. But they left before the reception—that's how they were. They never approved, they said we were too young. We *were* too young. But just think." She looked back at Lusa, intense. "What if I'd been sensible and waited, instead of marrying Shel? There'd be no Crystal and Lowell."

"That's true," Lusa said.

Jewel narrowed her eyes. "Remember that. Don't wait around thinking you've got all the time in the world. Maybe you've just got this one summer. Will you remember that? Will you tell the kids for me?"

"I think so," Lusa said. "Except I'm not sure I understand what you mean."

"Just make sure they know that having them, and being their mother, I would not have traded for anything. Not for a hundred extra years of living."

"I will."

"*Do*," Jewel said urgently, as if she meant to leave the world this very afternoon. "Tell them I just got this one season to be down here on the green grass, and I praise heaven and earth that I did what I did."

In the early afternoon Lusa took a deep breath, picked up the heavy box of vaccine vials she'd bought from the vet, and went down to face her goats. After some weeks of worry over poor eating and lethargy, Lusa had figured out that she had worms in the herd—which according to Mr. Walker was no surprise, given their motley origins. His advice was to worm the whole herd at once with DSZ, which he vowed wouldn't hurt her pregnant mothers, and while she was at it, to stick every last one of them with a shot of seven-way vaccine. Lusa was daunted, but Little Rickie had promised to come up and help. He claimed there was no sense letting all those years of 4-H go to waste.

Lusa found the goats easy to manage most of the time, much easier to herd than cattle once she got the first ones going where she wanted them. She already had them corralled into the small calf pasture by the time Rickie showed up for the rodeo. The idea was to let them through the gate into the bigger field one at a time. Rickie could wrestle each victim down as it came through, then shove the worm pill down its gullet and sit on its head while Lusa sat on the rear end and gave the shot. Simple enough in theory, but it took her a full hour to do the first five animals. Lusa felt like a torturer. The poor things struggled and bleated so, it was hard for her to keep her eyes open and aim for muscle when she jabbed in the hypodermic. Once she accidentally hit bone and cried out as loudly as the goat did.

"I'm a scientist," she said aloud to slow down her fluttering heart. "I've dissected live frogs and sacrificed rabbits. I can do this."

She kept hoping Rickie would volunteer to take over the needle, but he seemed as scared of it as she was. And she didn't think she'd be any better at *his* task, forcing the huge worm pill down the hatch, which he seemed to manage comfortably.

"You should see what you have to do to get a *cow* to take a pill," he told her when she remarked on his skill. "Man. Slobber all the way up to your armpit." She watched him push the white tablet deep into the doe's mouth, then clamp her lips closed and wobble her head from side to side. He was gentle and competent with animals, as Cole had been. That'd been one of the first things she loved about Cole, beyond his physical person.

The second hour went better, and by the time they reached number forty or so Lusa was getting almost handy with the needle. Mr. Walker had showed her how to give the thigh muscle three or four stout punches with her fist before poking in the needle on the last one. When a shot was delivered this way, the animal tended to lie perfectly still.

Rickie was impressed with this technique, once she got it working. "He's a smarter old guy than he looks, I guess. Mr. Walker."

"Yeah, he's that," Lusa said, keeping her eyes on the brown pelt of this girl's flank. The hard part was getting the plunger pushed all the way down and then extracting the needle without getting poked if the goat began to kick. When she was out and clear, Lusa gave the nod, and she and Rick jumped off at the same time, allowing the doe to scramble to her feet. With an offended little toss of her triangular head, she ran with a slight limp toward the middle of the pasture, where her friends had already put the humiliation behind them and were munching thistles in vaccinated, amnesiac bliss.

"Did you know he was Jewel's father-in-law? Old Mr. Walker?"

Rickie thought about it. "*Ex*-father-in-law. I don't think that's a real big thing on the family tree. I don't think he's said boo to Aunt Jewel since his outlaw son ran off. And he didn't say much before, from what I hear."

"No, I guess not," Lusa said, looking over her newly medicated herd with some satisfaction. She was about to turn back to her work when a quick, pale movement up at the top of the field snagged her eye.

"My God," she said. "Look at that."

They both watched as the animal froze, then lowered its body close to the ground and walked slowly along the fence back into the woods.

"That wasn't a fox, was it?" she asked.

"Nope."

"What was it, then?"

"Coyote."

"Are you sure? Have you ever seen one before?"

"Nope," Rickie said.

"Me either. But I could swear I heard some a couple of nights ago. It was amazing, like singing. Dog singing."

"That's what that bastard was, then. Got to be. You want me to go home and get my rifle? I could get up there after it right now."

"No." She put her hand on his forearm. "Do me a favor. Don't turn into your uncles."

He looked at her. "Do you know what those things eat?"

"Not really. I imagine it could kill a goat, or a kid, at least. But it didn't look that big. Don't you think it's more likely to kill a rabbit or something?"

"You're going to wait around and find out?"

She nodded. "I think I am. Yeah."

"You're crazy."

"Maybe. We'll see." She stood for a while longer, staring into the edge of the woods where it had vanished. Then she turned back to the goats in her paddock. "OK, let's get this over with. How many have we got to go?"

Rickie moved reluctantly to the gate, preparing to let in another goat. He counted heads. "A dozen, maybe. We're near 'bout done."

"Good, because I'm near 'bout dead," she said, moving up quickly behind the doe to help shove down with all her weight on its haunches. Once they had it down, Lusa pushed the sweat and unruly hair out of her eyes with the back of one hand before filling the next syringe.

He watched. "Want to swap heads and tails? My part's way easier than yours."

Now he asks, she thought. "No, you're working twice as hard as I am," Lusa said, steeling her sore biceps for the next punch and poke. "I'm just a wimp."

He waited respectfully while the needle went in, then spoke. "No way, you're doing great. I've never seen a woman sit on so many animals in one day."

At Lusa's nod they got up and let the doe saunter off. "Know what I'm dying for?"

"A cold beer?" he asked.

"A *bath*. Pew!" She sniffed her forearms and made a face. "These girls don't smell pretty."

"They don't," Rickie agreed. "And they are the *girls*."

By the time they'd finished all the does and the buck, which they saved for last, Lusa could hardly tolerate the smell of her own body. She turned on the hose bib by the barn for Rickie and walked around to get the big square bar of soap that was down below in the milking parlor. Her mind drifted back to the coyote. It had been so beautiful and strange, almost ghostly. Like a little golden dog, but much wilder in its bearing. If she could find just one other person in this county who didn't feel the need to shoot a coyote on sight, that would be something. Then she'd have a friend.

When she came back around the corner of the barn she walked straight into a spray of cold water that caused her to shriek. A direct hit by Rickie.

"I'm going to kill you," she said, laughing, wiping her eyes.

"It feels good," he said, running the water over his head.

"OK, then, here. You go first." She tossed him the soap and they took turns lathering themselves up and hosing each other down, enjoying a gleeful, chaste, slightly hysterical bath in their clothes. Some of the goats came over and put their noses through the fence to watch this peculiar human rite.

"I can't get over their *eyes*," Lusa said as Rickie turned off the hose. She bent over and shook her head like a wet dog, sending water drops flying into the golden light of late afternoon.

"Who, the goats?" He'd thought to strip off his dark-red T-shirt before hosing down, to keep it dry, and now he used it as a towel to dry his face. Lusa wondered if the display of his body was as ingenuous as it seemed. He was seventeen. It was hard to say.

"They have those weird pupils," she said. "Little slits, like a cat's, only sideways instead of up and down."

He rubbed his head violently with the shirt. "Yep. Funny eyes." He combed his dark hair back on the sides with his hands. "Kindly like they're from another planet."

Lusa studied the faces of her girls at the fence. "Kind of cute, though. Don't you think? They grow on you."

"Oh, boy, she's getting sentimental about goats." He tossed Lusa his shirt. "You need to get out more."

She dried her face and arms with the frankly male-scented shirt, suddenly recalling Rickie's description of her dancing through the pasture waving a buck-scented rag in front of the does. This world was one big sexual circus, or so it seemed to the deprived. She balled up his shirt and threw it back. "For this I owe you big-time, Rick. If I'd known how hard today was going to be, I might have chickened out, but you stuck with me to the bitter end. Can I write you a check for some gas money, for your trouble?"

"No, ma'am, you don't owe me a thing," he said, polite as a schoolboy. "Neighbors and family don't take money."

"Well, your neighbor and aunt thanks you kindly. I don't have the cold beer you're thirsty for, but I could give you some lemonade or iced tea before you go home."

"Sweet tea would hit the spot," he said.

A bird called loudly from up in her fallow pasture behind the house—a dramatic "Wow-*wheet!*" in a voice as powerful and self-important as an opera singer's.

"I'll swan, listen to that," Rickie said, struck motionless where he stood toweling his shoulders. "That was a bobwhite."

"Yeah?"

"You don't hardly hear them anymore. I don't think I've heard one since I was a little kid."

"Well, that's good," Lusa said, impressed that Rickie had noticed a bird, had even declared its name. "Welcome back, Mr. Bob White. I can always use another man on the place." She picked up the box of empty glass vials and walked slowly to the house, feeling the extent of exhaustion not only in her arms but also in her thighs and lower back. She was getting acquainted with these sensations in her body, to the point where she almost enjoyed the tingling, achy release of lactic acid in her muscles. It was the closest thing to sex in her life, she thought, and gave in to a sad little laugh.

When she came back outside with the cold jar of tea and a glass, Rickie had put on his shirt and was sitting on the lawn, barefoot among the dandelions with his long legs stretched straight out in front of him. He'd taken off his shoes and for some reason set them on top of the cab of his pickup truck.

"Here you go," she said, collapsing on the grass beside him, but facing him, to hand him the jar and glass. She'd considered changing out of her wet clothes, but the contrast of cool dampness and warm sun felt wonderful on her limbs. She probably looked like a drowned rat, but she didn't care. She felt a friendly intimacy with Rickie after their long afternoon of sitting on goats together. She stretched her legs beside his, in the opposite direction, so her feet were next to his hipbones. Sitting this way gave her a childhood feeling, as if they were on a seesaw together, or inside an invisible fort. He poured a glass of tea, handed it to her, then turned up the jar and drained it in one long, awe-inspiring draft. Watching his Adam's apple bob made her think of all those huge pills going down all those goat gullets. Teenaged boys were just a loose aggregation of appetites.

He produced a pack of smokes from somewhere—he must have gotten them out of his truck while she was inside, Lusa guessed, since he was entirely wet and they were not. He tipped the pack at her, but she held up her hand.

"You stay away from me, you devil. I've kicked that nasty habit."

He lit up, nodding enthusiastically. "'At's good. I should, too." He snapped his wrist to extinguish the match. "I was thinking about what you said, that you didn't care if you saw thirty or not. Thing is, I really do. I figure it all gets better after high school."

"It does," Lusa said. "Trust me. Barring a few rocks in the road, it's all uphill from high school." She thought about this, surprised by the truth of it. "I can vouch for that. Even depressed and widowed and a long way from home, I like my life right now better than I liked it in high school."

"Is that so?"

"I think so."

"You like the country, then. You like farming. You were meant for it."

"I guess that's true. It's weird, though. I was born into such a different life, with these scholarly parents, and I did the best I could with it. I raised caterpillars in shoeboxes and I studied bugs and agriculture in school for as many years as they'll let you. And then one day Cole Widener walked into my little house and blew the roof off, and here I am."

Rickie nodded, brushing a fly away from his eyebrow. She had her back to the low-slung sun, but he was looking into it. His skin was the color of caramelized sugar against his red shirt, and his dark eyes glowed in the slanted light. She picked a dandelion and smoothed its furry yellow face. White sap bled from its stem onto her fingers. She tossed it away. "I was mad at him for dying and leaving me here, at first. Pissed off like you wouldn't believe. But now I'm starting to think he wasn't supposed to be my whole life, he was just this doorway to *me*. I'm so grateful to him for that."

Rickie smoked in silence, squinting into the distance. Lusa didn't mind whether he spoke or not, or whether he even understood. Rickie would just let her talk, anytime, about anything. It made him seem older than he was.

"Did I tell you my parents are coming to visit?" she asked brightly. "Right before classes start in the fall, when my dad has a week off."

He looked at her. "That's good. You don't see much of your folks, do you?"

"I really don't. It's like a state occasion; my mother doesn't travel very well since she had her stroke. She gets confused. But Dad says she's doing better—she's started on a new medicine, and she's walking better. If she can do the stairs, I'm going to try to talk him into leaving her here for a while. For a real visit. I miss my mother."

He nodded absently. He had no earthly understanding of what it would feel like, Lusa realized, to be anything but completely surrounded and smothered by family.

They heard the bobwhite again, declaring his name from the hillside. Lusa heard it not so much as "Bob White" but more like a confident "All *right*," with a rising inflection at the end, as if this were just the beginning of a long sentence he meant to say. She loved that he was there on her fallow pasture: he was not himself her property but rather a sort of tenant, depending on her for continued goodwill. In all her troubles she had never yet stopped to consider her new position: landholder. Not just a mortage holder, not just burdened, but also blessed with a piece of the world's trust. The condition forbidden to her zayda's people for more than a thousand years.

After a decent interval, long enough to permit a change of subject, Rickie asked, "You're not worried about that coyote?"

"Am I?" She drank half her glass of tea before answering. "You'll just think this is crazy, but no, I'm not. I mean *maybe*, at the worst, it could get one kid, and that wouldn't break me. I can't see killing a thing that beautiful just on suspicion. I'll go with innocent until proven guilty."

"You may change your tune when you see it running off into the woods with that poor little kid squalling bloody murder."

Lusa smiled, struck by his language. "Listen, can I tell you a story? In Palestine, where my people came from, about a million years ago, they had this tradition of sacrificing goats. To God, theoretically, but I think probably they ate them after the ceremony." She set her glass down, twisting it into the grass. "So, here's the thing. They'd always let one goat escape and run off into the desert. The scapegoat. It was supposed to be carrying off all their sins and mistakes from that year."

Rickie looked amused. "And the moral of the story is what?"

She laughed. "I'm not sure. What do you think?"

"It's OK to let one get away?"

"Yeah, something like that. I'm not such a perfect farmer that I can kill a coyote for the one kid it might take from me. There are ten other ways I could lose a goat through my own stupidity. And I'm not about to kill *myself*. So. Does that make sense?"

He nodded thoughtfully. "If you say it does, I reckon it does." He went quiet, smiling to himself, admiring something off in the distance behind her back. Lusa hoped it was the butterflies in her weed patch down below the yard, though she knew enough of young men's minds to know that wasn't likely. She bent her knees, took hold of her clammy feet, and pulled off her shoes, realizing suddenly that wet sneakers were a wretched proposition. That would explain his sneakers on top of his truck.

"You've got pretty feet," he observed.

She stretched her legs out straight again and looked at her water-wrinkled toes, then up at him. "Oh, boy. You should get out more."

He laughed. "Yeah, well. I have a confession to make. I think you look pretty sitting on the rear end of a goat, too. I've had the biggest crush on you all summer."

Lusa bit her lips to keep from smiling. "I kind of gathered that."

"I know. You think it's stupid."

"What's stupid?"

He reached over and brushed the damp hair out of her eyes, softly grazing the side of her face with his knuckles. "This. Me thinking about you this way. You don't know how much I think about it, either."

"I think I may," she said. "It's not stupid. It scares me, though."

He kept his hand against the side of her neck and said quietly, "I wouldn't hurt you for anything," and Lusa was terrified, feeling suddenly every nerve ending in her breasts and her lips. It would be so easy to invite him into the house, upstairs, to the huge, soft bed in which his grandparents had probably conceived his mother. How comforting it would be to be taken away from her solitary self and held against his solid, lovely body. His hands would become Cole's. Just for an hour the starvation that dogged her through every night and day could feast on real sensation instead of memory. Real taste, real touch, the pressure of skin on nipple and tongue. She shivered.

"I can't even talk about this."

"Why not?" he asked, dropping his hand to her knees. He ran his fingers down the inseam of her wet jeans from knee to hem, then clasped his whole hand gently around her bare ankle. She remembered, with acute pain, the sense of small, compact perfection she'd known inside her husband's large-limbed embrace. She looked at his hand on her ankle, then back at his face, trying to forge pain into anger.

"Do I really have to tell you why not?"

He held her eye. "Tell me you don't want me to make love to you."

"God," she gasped, turning her head to the side with her speechless mouth open wide, scarcely able to breathe. Where had he learned to talk like that, the movies? She shook her head slowly from side to side, unable to keep her open mouth from smiling because of his face, his earnest determination to have her. She remembered how that felt, obsessive desire. Oh, God, those days in her Euclid apartment. There was no engine on earth whose power compared with the want of one body for another.

"That's not a fair question," she said finally. "I would want you to, yes, if that were possible. I think I'd like it a lot. That's the truth, may lightning strike me dead, but now you know. Does it make anything better?"

"To me it does. *Damn!*" He grinned a crooked smile she'd never seen except on the face of Cole Widener, in bed. "To me it's sweet. It's like getting an A on a test."

She took his hand from her ankle, kissed his knuckles briskly like a mother repairing a child's hurt, then let the hand drop into the grass. "OK, good. You made the grade. Can we move on to another subject now?"

"Like what? Like throwing a mattress in the back of my truck and heading for the river tonight?"

"You're incorrigible."

"Which means what, exactly?"

"Which means you're seventeen going on eighteen and you've got hormones between your ears."

"I might be that," he said. "I might be a lot of fun, too. You'll never know till you try."

She sat with her arms tightly crossed, wishing she had bothered to change her clothes. "Drowned rat" was not the impression she was making in this wet shirt, evidently. He would be so *appreciative,* she thought miserably. It would be so easy to startle him with pleasures he'd remember for the rest of his life. But then again, maybe not, if he'd already set his standards by the magazines under his bed. Boys never knew what they lost on those magazine girlfriends.

"I'll never know, then," she said, feeling a change in herself, a permanent shift onto safer ground. "I'm not denying it would be fun, maybe even more than fun. But it's completely out of the question, and if it comes up again I'll have to stop being your friend. I'm sorry I confessed I was attracted to you. You should just try to forget that."

He looked at her with a neutral expression and nodded slowly. "Right," he said. "Fat chance."

"Look. Don't take this the wrong way, Rickie, I like you for *you,* but also sometimes you remind me of Cole in ways that make me lose my bearings. But you're *not* Cole. You're my nephew. We're relatives."

"We're not blood kin," he argued.

"But we're family, and you know it. *And,* you're a minor. Just technically, for another few months maybe, but you are. I'm pretty sure what you're proposing would be a crime. Committed by me, against you. If they have capital punishment in this state, your mother and your aunts would probably see that I got the chair."

He closed his eyes and said nothing. He seemed chastened, finally, by all of it: her tone, her words, the truth. Lusa felt both relieved and sad.

"I'm sorry to be so blunt," she said. "I don't think of you as a child. You know that, right? If we were both two years older and you were somebody I'd just met, I'd probably go out with you."

He lit another cigarette and gave his full attention to the business of smoking and staring off into the distance. At length he said, "I'll be sure to remind you of that two years from now when you're burning heavy with some guy around here."

Lusa worked a small stone out of the ground and tossed it past her feet. "I can't even picture that, you know? From where I stand, it looks like a real dry county."

"Well, you're not the Lone Ranger. All the girls at my school are hot to get pregnant and married so they can play house, but they seem like little girls. After I graduate I want to *do* something, like hitchhike to Florida and get a job on a fishing boat or something, you know? See what those palm-tree islands look like. And these girls with their big hair are all down at Kmart looking at the baby shoes going, 'Aren't these *cute?*' They're like cheerleaders for boringness."

Lusa laughed. "And you and me, we're different, right? Two noble souls cast together in dubious circumstances till we can find somebody halfway appropriate to go out with."

He nodded, grinning that damned lopsided grin. "That sounds about right."

"Frankly, your prospects are better than mine. By the time my goats up here drop their kids, I predict you'll have met the girl of your dreams, and I'll be toast."

"Don't bet on it."

"I'll dance at your wedding, Rick. I'm betting on it."

"I didn't get to dance at yours," he said. "You didn't invite me."

"Next time I will," she said. "I promise. That was a big mistake, you know? Don't ever elope. The relatives never forgive you."

"Relatives," he agreed. "What a pain."

"Thank you." She looked at him then, hit by a sudden inspiration. "You know what we need to do, you and me? We need to go dancing. Do you like to dance?"

He nodded. "Yeah. As a matter of fact, I do."

"That's *exactly* what we need to do. Is there someplace around here where they have music on a Saturday night?"

"Oh, sure, there's the college bar over in Franklin, Skid Row. Or we could drive over to Leesport. Cotton-Eye Joe's, they get good country bands in there." He was taking this proposal seriously.

"Do you think we'd scandalize the family if we went out dancing?"

"*Oh* yeah. My mom and aunts think dancing's basically just the warm-up act. Aunt Mary Edna gives this lecture in Sunday school about how dancing always leads to sexual intercourse."

"Well, she's right, that's probably true for most animals. Insects do that, birds do, even some mammals. But we've got great big brains, you and me. I think we could distinguish a courtship ritual from the act itself. Don't you?"

Rickie fell backward on the ground and lay there for some time with his cigarette sticking up like a chimney. Eventually he removed it so he could speak. "You know what drives me crazy about you, Lusa? Half the time I don't know what in the hell you're discussing."

She looked down at him, her beautiful nephew in the grass. "Drives you crazy and that's a bad thing? Or a good thing?"

He thought about it. "It doesn't have to be good or bad. It's just you. My favorite aunt, Miss Lusa Landowski."

"Wow. You actually know my name. And here I am just about to change it."

"Yeah? To what?"

"Widener."

Rickie raised his dark eyebrows and looked at her from his prone position. "*Really*. What for?"

"For Cole, the kids, all of you. The family. I don't know." She shrugged, feeling a little embarrassed. "It just seems like the thing to do. So this farm will stay where it is on our little map of the world. It's an animal thing, I guess. Marking a territory."

"Huh," he said.

"So, let's go dancing, OK? Absolutely no funny business, we'll just dance till we drop, shake hands, and say good night. I need the exercise. You free this Saturday?"

"I am free as a bird this Saturday," he said, still flat on his back, smiling grandly at the sky.

"Good. Because you know, I'm going to be a mother pretty soon. I'd better get out and paint the town red a time or two while I've still got the chance."

Rickie sat up and stubbed out his cigarette pensively in the grass. "That's really nice that you're taking those kids. I mean, *nice,* hell—it's more than that."

Lusa shrugged. "I'm doing it for me as much as for them."

"Well, my mom and Aunt Mary Edna think it's like this gift from God, that you're doing it. They said you're a saint."

"Oh, come on."

"No, I swear to God that's what they said. I heard 'em say it."

"Wow," she said. "What a trip. From devil-worshiper to saint in one short summer."

{28}

Old Chestnuts

his world was full of perils, thought Garnett, and Nannie Rawley was as trusting as a child. She didn't even realize this man was up to no good. Hanging on to her like a cocklebur, but fifty times more dangerous. Garnett had heard of things as strange as a younger man's buttering up some pitiful, sweet old woman and marrying her for her money. Now, on that score Nannie was safe, because she probably didn't have two dimes to rub together until harvest season was done and her crop sold, but she did have the best-producing orchard in five counties, and no living descendants, and everybody around here knew it. There was no telling what this sneaky snake had on his mind.

Garnett couldn't swear he knew, either, but he knew this much: for two days now, every time he'd happened to catch a glimpse of Nannie out in her garden, there he'd been, leaning on the fence. He hadn't even lifted a finger to help her carry her bushel baskets of squash and corn into the house. If that fellow set foot inside her house, Garnett was prepared to call up Timmy Boyer on the telephone and get him over here. He would have to. She didn't know enough to protect herself.

He finished folding the shirts he'd washed yesterday in the washing machine and dried in the dryer. He held the last one up by the peaks of its shoulders and stared at it. It looked as wrinkled and worn as he felt himself. Ellen had had some way of getting them to come out nice and smooth, even without the ironing board. On cool winter mornings before he went to school she'd hand him a shirt to put on that felt as warm as a wife's embrace, and he'd carry that little extra measure of affection on his shoulders all day long. No matter what affronts of youthful insolence he had to face in his day, he'd still have that: he was a man taken care of by a woman.

He piled the folded shirts into a stack as neatly as he could, put the balled-together socks on top, and carried the whole thing upstairs. He paused by the window at the landing, balancing the folded clothes on one hand and drawing the sheer curtain aside with the other.

Almighty stars, there he still was, like a wolf waiting for the lamb. She was not even anywhere in sight. What kind of nerve would it take to just stand there waiting for her like that, with his elbows up on the fence? Garnett squinted hard, trying to bring the details of the man's appearance into focus. By gosh, he wasn't even that good-looking. On the portly side, if the truth be told. Portly, going to lumpy. Garnett felt so irritated he dropped a pair of socks. Never mind, he'd pick them up later. He peered as far as he could into the shadows of Nannie's backyard, but she didn't seem to be around there, either.

Well, then, he thought suddenly, wildly—this was his chance. He could go over there this minute and give that fellow his walking papers. That garden fence was not ten feet from Garnett's line, and he had as much right as anybody to chase off no-goods and vagrants from the neighborhood.

Garnett went on up to the bedroom first, to put his shirts in the bureau drawer. Yes, by gosh, he thought, he was going to do it. He briefly considered fetching his shotgun but then decided against it. He hadn't fired a gun in many a year, since the days when he could claim a better eye and a steadier hand, though he was sure he could still shoot in a pinch, if he had to. The thought gave him courage. Maybe just holding the shotgun would steady him. He wouldn't load it; there wasn't any need. He would just carry it out there with him, to give him the air of a man who meant business.

He walked around to the closet on Ellen's side of the bed, where he tended to keep things he never planned on needing again. The door had gone off its frame a little and scraped the floor as he dragged it open. He batted at the darkness like a blind man, trying to find the pull string to switch the light on, and nearly jumped out of his shirt when something big plummeted down off the shelf, bouncing off his shoulder as it fell. Ellen's old round hatbox. It landed on its side, and out rolled Ellen's navy-blue church hat on its brim, describing a small half-circle on the floor before sitting down flat beside the bed.

"Ellen," he said aloud, staring at the hat.

The hat, of course, made no reply. It merely sat there, flat on its proper little brim, adorned with its little bunch of artificial cherries. If it could have folded its hands in its lap, it would have.

"Well, don't scare me like that, woman. I'm doing the best I can."

He grabbed his shotgun with both hands and hurried out of the bedroom, reaching around behind him to pull the door shut. She didn't need to see this.

"Man, state your business," Garnett called out from the clump of wild cherries in the fencerow, a hundred feet from where the fellow still stood. He gave no sign of having seen or heard Garnett—ha!—who still had it in him to be stealthy as a good deer hunter. The thought gave him some satisfaction, and perhaps a little daring.

He cleared his throat, since his last words had come out sounding a little wobbly, and called out again. "Hello there!"

Nothing.

"I said, hello. I'm Garnett Walker, I own this land here, and I'd like to know your business, if you don't mind."

The man didn't speak, did not so much as turn his head. Garnett had never seen such a display of rudeness. Even the boy who drove the UPS truck would nod a reluctant hello when pressed.

Garnett squinted. This man looked so slack he could be dead. He didn't look young, though. Young people, Garnett had observed, often gave the impression of having too little gumption to hold up their heads. But this fellow didn't even seem to *have* a head. He was hunkered down with his arms crossed in front of him on the fence and an old, dusty-looking fedora pulled down over his ears. His whole body leaned against his arms in an unnatural way, like a pole leaning against a fence. Everything about him appeared unnatural, in fact, from the way his arms in the blue work shirt bent in curves, as if his elbows were rubber instead of hinges, to the trunklike aspect of his big lumpy legs in those jeans. Garnett got the strangest feeling, as if he'd turned up in somebody else's dream wearing no clothes. He felt a blush creep down the front of his neck, though there was no one here to witness it. Thanks be to the Lord for that, no witnesses. He set his gun down gently on its butt end, with its bore against the trunk of the cherry, and stepped through the gate, a few paces onto Nannie's side, to get a better look at the face.

But of course there was no face. There was just a stuffed pillowcase with a hat on it, stuck down into a stuffed shirt and pants. Garnett recalled the locust rail and crossbeam Nannie had been nailing together in her garage. He nearly fell to his knees. For the last two days he'd been burning up with suspicion and ire and jealousy. Yes, even that. He'd been jealous of a scarecrow.

He turned to leave before things got worse.

"Garnett Walker!" she cried, coming around the corner of her house in a hurry.

He sighed. Between Garnett and Nannie, things always did get worse. He should know that by now. He should just give in. There was no paddling upstream against this river. "Hello, Miss Rawley."

She stopped short, with her hands on her hips. She was wearing a skirt, probably getting ready to go to the market. She always prettied herself up a little for market day, in her calico skirt and her braids. She looked quizzical as a little bird, with her head cocked to the side. "I thought I heard somebody over here calling me," she said.

Garnett looked at his hands. Empty. "I was coming over to see if you needed help. Any help loading up your truck for the Amish market. I know how it is for you this time of year. When the winesaps start to come in."

He could have laughed, for how surprised she looked.

"With winesaps," he added emphatically, "when it rains, it pours."

She shook her head. "Well, will wonders never cease."

"I've lived next door to an orchard for the better part of eighty years," he prattled on, sounding foolish even to himself. "I have eyes. I can see it's enough work to break a donkey's back."

She looked at him sideways. "Are you angling for another pie?"

"Now, look here, I don't think that's fair. Just because I've offered to help you out, you don't have to act like the sky's falling. It's not the first time."

"No," she said. "You gave me the shingles, too. Those were a godsend."

"I think it would be fair to say I've been a good neighbor lately."

"You have," she agreed. "You'll have to forgive me if it all takes a while to sink in. I'm just blessed off my rocker these days. I've come into an embarrassment of riches."

He wondered what that could possibly mean, and whether it

was polite to ask. "I didn't know you had relatives anywhere," he tried. "To inherit from."

She laughed, laying her hands flat on the front of her skirt "That's just what I've done," she said, "I've inherited a relative. Two of them, in fact."

Garnett became a little confused, thinking briefly of the man hanging around on the fence, who of course was no man at all, with no interest in anyone's inheritance. He waited for Nannie to explain—which she always did, if you waited long enough.

"Deanna Wolfe," she said simply. "She's coming to live with me."

Garnett thought about this. "Ray Dean's girl?" he asked, feeling briefly, nonsensically jealous of the young Ray Dean Wolfe, who'd courted Nannie for more years than most people now stayed married. Nannie had been so happy in those days, you could hear her singing on any day but a rainy one. But Ray Dean Wolfe was buried in the cemetery now.

"That's right, his girl Deanna. She's like a daughter to me. You knew that."

"I thought she'd gone to live up in the mountains here somewhere, working for the government."

"She did. She's been up there in a cabin living all by herself for two years. But now she's taking a leave from her job and coming back down. And here's the part you have to sit down for: she's going to have a baby."

"Well, that is a shock." He squinted up toward the mountains. "How did that happen, do you think?"

"I don't know, and I don't care. I don't care if the daddy's a mountain lion, I'm going to have a grandbaby!"

Garnett shook his head, clucking his tongue. Nannie looked like the cat that'd swallowed the canary. Women and grandbabies, there was nothing on this earth to beat it. Like Ellen fretting on her deathbed over that child of Shel's. And now there were two of them, a boy and the girl. That Lexington gal with her goats had called him up on the telephone, plumb out of the blue, and announced that she wanted to bring those kids over to see his farm. They wanted to see the chestnut trees. His *trees*.

"I've got grandchildren, too," he told Nannie.

"You always did," she said. "You're just too high-handed to bother learning their names."

"The girl's name is Crystal, and the boy's Lowell. They're coming over here on Saturday." How Garnett had plucked those names from the mossy crevices of his memory, even he would never know. "I was thinking I might be able to teach them how to bag flowers and make crosses," he added. "On my chestnut trees. To help me keep it all going."

To his great satisfaction, Nannie looked stunned. "How did *that* happen?" she asked finally.

"Well, I don't think a mountain lion had much to do with it."

She stood looking at Garnett with her mouth open. If she wasn't careful, he thought, she'd get a bee in there. Then her eye caught on something behind him, and she frowned. "What's that over yonder leaning on the tree in the fencerow?"

He turned and looked. "Oh. That's my shotgun."

"I see. And might I ask what it's doing over there?"

Garnett studied it. "Not very much. Just leaning up against the tree, it looks to me like."

"All right, how did it get there, then?"

"It came out to have words with this fellow who's been leaning up against your fence for the last couple of days."

She laughed. "Oh, this is Buddy. I don't believe you've met."

"Well, Buddy gave us a little bit of a worry."

She narrowed her eyes at Garnett. "Is that right?"

"I'm afraid so."

"And you came over to make sure I was all right, is that what you're telling me? You came over here with your shotgun to protect me from my scarecrow?"

"I had to," Garnett said, spreading his hands, throwing himself on her mercy. "I didn't care for the way Buddy was looking at you in your short pants."

Now Nannie looked more than stunned; she looked lightning-struck. She stared at him until a smile broke out and spread over her face like the sun coming out after a storm. She walked to him with her arms out like a sleepwalker's, put those arms around his waist, and hugged him tightly with her head resting against his chest. It took him a minute and a half before he thought to put his arms around her shoulders and keep them there. He felt as stiff as old Buddy—as if he, too, had nothing inside his shirt and pants but newspaper and straw. But then, by and by, his limbs relaxed. And she just stayed there like a calm little bird inside the circle of his arms. It was astonishing. Holding her this way felt like a hard day's rest. It felt like the main thing he'd been needing to do.

"Mr. Walker. Garnett. Will wonders never cease," she said once again, and to be certain they did not, Garnett held her there. She turned her face up and looked at him. "And here I'm finally going to have a grandbaby in my house, and you're going to have *two*. You've always got to have the last word, don't you?"

"Now, Nannie. You're a difficult woman."

She laid the side of her face against his frail old heart, where the pink shell of her ear could capture whatever song it had left.

"Garnett. You're a sanctimonious old fart."

{29}

Predators

The roar of rain, pounding rain on the cabin's tin roof, was loud enough to drive a mind to madness. It occurred to Deanna that if she screamed, she probably wouldn't hear herself. She opened her mouth and tried it. She was right.

She sat on the bed, hugging her knees to her chest. Trying not to think of it as the bed, she'd pulled up the blankets and propped pillows against the wall to make it into a couch or something— someplace to get comfortable that wasn't *bed*. Inside this white roar she felt as cabin-fevered and trapped as she'd been in the dark of last winter. She plucked at a hole in the toe of her sock, picked up a book, put it down again. For hours she'd tried to read, but the noise had reached a point of drowning out all hope of concentration. She covered her ears with her hands for some relief, and listened to the different roar created by her cupped hands. A throbbing whoosh, the sea in a seashell—she remembered hearing it for the first time on a beach. She and Dad and Nannie had gone to Virginia Beach two summers in a row. A hundred and ten years ago, and a hundred and nine.

It wasn't the ocean, of course, but the tide of her own circulation pulsing inside her, sound carried through bone to her eardrums. Deanna shut her eyes and listened harder, trying to hear some small difference now that her heart was pumping her blood through an extra set of arteries. She'd been craving some proof, but the change so far seemed to inhabit her body only ethereally, like a thought or a magic charm. For now she would have to live with magic.

When she dropped her hands from her ears, the rain seemed even louder. Flashes of lightning brightened the window in an irregular but steady way, like fireworks. The thunder she couldn't hear, but its vibrations reached her through the floor, shuddering up the legs of the iron bed. She considered climbing under the blankets and covering her head with the pillows, but that would be *bed,* alone, and the awful trembling would still reach her. There was no escape, and this storm was growing closer. It was only four o'clock in the afternoon, but the sky was dark as dusk, and darkening deeper by the minute. An hour ago Deanna had decided she'd never seen a storm like this in these mountains in all her life. And that was an hour ago.

Surprised, she remembered her radio. It offered no practical assistance, but it would be company. She jumped up and crossed to the desk to retrieve the little radio from the bottom drawer. She turned it on, held it next to her ear, heard nothing. She studied the thing, located the dial that controlled the volume, and turned it all the way up, but still not a crackle. Batteries, she thought: they'd go dead over time just sitting around. She ransacked the drawer for more batteries, knowing perfectly well she always forgot to put these on her list. Finally she scavenged the ones from her little flashlight, the spare she kept on the shelf by the door.

Lightning hit then, so close to the cabin that she could actually hear its crack above the rain's roar. The sound and light were simultaneous; that was *here*. Probably one of the tall poplars on the hill above the cabin. Just what she needed now, a tree falling on her. Her fingers trembled as she turned over the radio and pried open its back to fish out the old batteries and pop in new ones. "Plus, minus," she said aloud, lining up the poles, her voice completely inaudible to her ears. Even that was terrifying, like a darkness so dark it looked the same with eyes open or shut. She'd had moments of panic in that kind of darkness, wondering whether she'd gone blind, and now it occurred to her that this might be what deafness was like. People assumed it was silence, but maybe it was this, a solid white roar.

She tried the radio again. If she held the little holes against one ear and covered the other, she could hear sounds. Just static at first. It was a tedious business to adjust the tuning, listen, and adjust again, trying to find the Knoxville station, but at last she heard a faint, tinny music of a type she couldn't categorize. She waited awhile to let her ear adjust to this kind of sound. It had been a long time since she'd heard anything other than bird music. Music was something she'd have to relearn, she decided, like learning to speak again after a stroke. There were so many things to bewilder her lying ahead. Electricity, with all those little noises it made inside a house. And people, too, with all the noises *they* made. Labor and childbirth would be the least of her worries.

She tried to think about Nannie. No worries there; she knew how that would be. To take her mind from this frightening high isolation, she pictured herself within the genuine shelter of Nannie Rawley's place, the kindness of that leafy orchard. Longing for comfort and rest, she forced her thoughts through the rooms of Nannie's house, out into the familiar trees and even up into the long grass of Nannie's wilding field, where she'd first learned about the connection between sex and God's Creation.

She'd been half listening to the tinny music for longer than she realized when a different, louder sound brought her attention back to the radio: the long, discordant drone of a weather-service warning. She shifted on the bed and listened as hard as she could for what came next. Tornado watch. *Oga* County, *Ing* County, names she couldn't make sense of—Bin, Din, Fin, *Hinman,* that was it: Logan and Hinman counties, heading northwest. She dropped the radio to her lap. This was it, then, a real end-of-summer hellbender, the tail of the season's first hurricane coming this way. She sent out one small, final hope for Eddie Bondo, the last she would ever allow herself: that he'd had time to get out of these mountains before this storm came down.

She got up and walked around the room, trying to find spots where the reception improved. She discovered it was better in the doorway, even better out on the porch. The roar on the roof wasn't as bad out there, either. She stayed close in under the eave to avoid getting drenched and settled cautiously into the old green chair with her head held stiffly, just so, like a patient in a neck brace, to keep the sound of human speech in her ear. She'd gone two years without news but now couldn't bear another minute without it. It was music now, though. Yes, that was right, that was how they did it: "Emergency, urgent, all life must stop!" and then back to the commercials and corny love songs. The world was coming back to her. She put the radio on her lap and shut it off to save the batteries, which she might need later. Then jumped up and went inside to make sure she had candles where she could find them and the kerosene lamp trimmed and ready to light. Why? She stopped herself, trying to reason a way out of this panic. It was going to be dark, storm or no storm, like every night of the year. Why did she suddenly need four candles laid out side by side with matches at the ready? She wished she could laugh at herself; it would be so much better than this bleak knot of panic in her stomach. What had changed, when she used to be so fearless? But she knew what had changed. This was what it cost to commit oneself to the living. There was so much to lose. She went back outside to the green chair and put the radio to her ear again, leaned her head back, tried to listen. Still music. She turned off the radio, then leaned forward, opened her mouth, and screamed a long, fulfilling howl she could hear pretty well:

"DAMN YOU, EDDIE BONDO!"

Why today, of all the days there were? Did he have a built-in barometer that told him when the weather ahead was getting stormy? She put her arms around herself and leaned back, letting herself be embraced by this dear old broken-down chair. Today or tomorrow or yesterday, it was all the same, she had to believe that was true. She had weathered storms on her own before and could weather this one. She considerately retracted the damnation. Truly, she had needed for him to go before the air got any denser between them. Her secret was getting hard to keep, and keep it she must, there had never been any question about that. Better for this child, better for everybody, that he not know what he'd left behind—and so he never would. She would tell people in Egg Fork, because they sure would ask, that the father of her child was a coyote.

Deanna smiled. She really would. And Nannie would stand by her story.

He'd left with his mind unchanged. If anything hurt Deanna, it was that she'd made no dent, had never altered his heart to make room in it for a coyote.

She'd gone out this morning before dawn for one of her restless walks and had come home at last to the startling absence she'd been waiting for. His pack, his hat, his gun, everything gone this time, she knew in an instant. He'd touched nothing of hers, had left the cabin exactly as it had been three months ago—yet it seemed it must have enlarged, to hold such significant emptiness.

It was several hours later when she opened her field notebook and found his note inside, her only memento of Eddie Bondo—or so he would always believe. A farewell with just enough sting to let her know she needn't wait for his return. On the empty page she'd marked with this date, he had recorded his own observation:

It's hard for a man to admit he has met his match. E.B.

She'd wondered for most of the day whether he meant her, Deanna, or the untouchable coyotes. Which one of them had been too much for Eddie Bondo?

Finally she decided it didn't matter. She tore the page out of her book so she wouldn't have to see it again, then ripped it into tiny pieces that she piled in a corner of her sock drawer for the mice to use when they lined their winter nests. Only then, closing the drawer, did she understand. In his young man's way, he was offering up his leaving as a gift. *Meeting his match* was a considerable concession. He was leaving them both alone, Deanna and the coyotes. No harm would come to anything on this mountain because of him.

A fierce crack of lightning shot her eyes through with a momentary electric blindness. "Oh God, oh God," she sang, withdrawing further into her chair, blinking the rain-blurred landscape back into focus. That was close. That was fifty feet away, or less. She could smell its aftermath in the ionized air. Now it was time to pray that there would be something left of this mountain after the storm passed over. She turned the radio back on and listened. It wasn't music now; it was the names of counties being repeated over and over. They'd gone to full-time emergency mode, listing counties, all of which she knew well. Franklin, Zebulon. The eye of the storm was here. She flipped the radio over and eviscerated it, slipping the batteries into her pocket. Better to save them for her flashlight. She would have laughed at herself if she could. If ever there was a piece of news she did not need a radio to receive, this was it. The eye of the storm was here.

She got up and tried to look through the sheet of water that flowed over the eave like a translucent shower curtain. She walked to the end of the porch and found she could see better out the gable end, where less water came off the roof. The rain seemed a little less dense now. An hour ago the air had been so solidly full of water it looked as if fish could jump the stream banks and swim into the treetops. She'd never seen rain like that. There was less of it now, but an ominous wind was rising. While she watched, in the space of just a few minutes, the rain died back drastically and the lightning seemed to have moved past the ridge top, but a wind came howling like the cold breath of some approaching beast. It blew the rain horizontal, straight into her face. Now frightened to her bones, she went inside and put on her boots and raincoat, and walked a few more circles around the room while she was at it. Every instinct told her to make a run for it, but there was nowhere to go. She felt vulnerable and trapped in the cabin. Standing on the porch seemed a little better, but once outside again, she was shocked by a wind that blew her backward against the cabin wall so hard she felt the humps of its logs against her back. The cold wind hurt her teeth and her eyes. She held both hands over her face and looked out through the small space between them, transfixed by the impossible menace of this storm dancing on her forest. The solid trees she'd believed in were bending unbelievably, breaking and losing limbs. Trunks cracked like gunshots, one after another. Up where the forest met the sky she watched the poplars' black silhouettes perform a slow, ghostly tango with the wind. They moved in synchrony, all the way around the top of the ridge surrounding the hollow. *There is no safety here,* they seemed to be saying, and her panic rose into pure, dry nausea. The trees were falling. This forest was the one thing she'd always been sure of, and it was ripping apart like a haystack. Any of these massive trunks could crush her between one heartbeat and the next. She turned her face against the wall of the cabin, unaware that she was holding her braid in her teeth and both hands protectively over her abdomen. Unaware that she would never again be herself alone—that *solitude* was the faultiest of human presumptions. She knew only that she was standing with her back to the storm in a sheer blind panic, trying to think what to do.

It was dark as night now, but she could make out the alternating dark and light stripes of the horizontal logs and the pale chink-mortar in between. She counted logs, starting at the bottom, to give herself a task she might be able to complete. Surprisingly, she'd never counted the logs before. Eleven, there were in this wall, an odd number. That meant either twelve or ten in the end walls. She ran her eye down the knobby length of one to its end, where all the logs of this wall articulated with those of the next, like fingers of a person's clasped hands. She attached her terrified gaze to that corner, a stack of twenty-one stout tree trunks neatly interlocked.

Shelter, was what dawned on her as she stared. This was the very principle of genuine shelter, these twenty-one interlocked logs. No single falling oak or poplar could ever crush this cabin. This cabin was made of fallen trees. She closed her eyes, pressed her forehead to the rounded trunk of an old, quiet chestnut, and prepared to wait out the storm.

When the rain and thunder died and the wind had gone quiet, coyotes began to howl from the ridge top. With voices that rose and broke and trembled with clean, astonished joy, they raised up their long blue harmony against the dark sky. Not a single voice in the darkness, but two: a mated pair in the new world, having the last laugh.

{30}

Moth Love

The males of the giant Saturniid moths have imperfect, closed mouths and cannot feed. Their adult lives, poignantly brief, are devoted fully to the pursuits of locating and coupling with a mate.

That was the passage she'd been thinking of vaguely for a long time before finding it last night, paging with desperate distraction in the middle of the storm through the same book she'd been reading on the night of Cole's death. It was under the bed; the book hadn't moved at all. Lusa wasn't even sure why she'd wanted to read it again, but when she came across that passage she recognized something in it that explained her life.

People outside the family had begun to ask about her plans. It had happened just lately. Some change in the weather or in Lusa herself had signaled to them that it was now safe to speak, and they always said the same thing: It was a shame about Cole, and had she made up her mind what she meant to do now?

There was no *shame* about it, she wanted to tell them. She imagined quoting that passage from Darwin at them, explaining that there was room in this world even for certain beings who could not eat or speak, whose only purpose was to find and call out the other side of their kind. She had been called here. There was no plan to speak of.

Of course, she said no such thing. It was always in bright, normal places like the cereal aisle at the Kroger's or in Little Brothers' Hardware that people asked her about her plans, and so she always said only this: "I've made up my mind to finish what I started."

And this was what she had started: in the absence of Cole, in the house where he'd grown up, she was learning to cohabit with the whole of his life. It was Cole who'd broken out the top rail of the banister as a rambunctious child, Cole who'd built the dry sink in the pantry for his mother the first year he took shop in school. He'd planted every one of the lilacs in the yard, though that seemed impossible because they were thirty feet tall now. His father had made him plant them for his mother the summer he was nine, as reparation for cursing in front of her. Lusa was making progress toward understanding. Cole was not to be a husband for whom one cooked, with whom one sat down to meals. He would be a second childhood to carry alongside her own, the child becoming the man for all the years that had led up to their meeting. She could coax stories about Cole even from people outside the family: women in town, strangers, Mr. Walker. Country people seemed to have many unwritten codes about death, more of them than city people, and one was that after a given amount of time you could speak freely of the dead man again. You could tell tales on him, even laugh at his mild expense, as if he had rejoined your ranks. It seemed to Lusa that all these scattered accounts were really parts of one long story, the history of a family that had stayed on its land. And that story was hers now as well.

In the afternoon she'd learned she was going to get a dollar eighty a pound for her goats, if everything went according to plan. It was a price unheard of in the county, apparently, for any animal. She considered this now, happily taking a minute to let her success sink in while she rested on her ladder in the darkness and rubbed the tired muscles in the back of her neck. This was like winning the blue ribbon. By her wits she had made something succeed here, where there seemed to be no hope. It didn't even matter that no one would ever properly admire her canny ingenuity. Nobody would realize that the major holidays of three of the world's major religions coincided in the week she sold her goats, like stars aligning for a spectacular horoscope. Only a religious mongrel like Lusa could have seen it coming and hitched her fortunes to it. Probably the real facts of her coup would be transformed into the sort of wild rumor that ran barefoot through Oda Black's and the hardware store, and that nobody believed: Lusa had a cousin with connections to rich Italian gangsters. Lusa had illegally gotten her goats sold to the king of Egypt. In a place like this, some secrets kept themselves, out of a failure to stand up to the competing rumors.

She knew her goat success wasn't any kind of permanent answer; there was no cure-all for the predicament known as farming. She'd have to be resourceful for the rest of her life. At Southern States she'd noticed the native bluestem grasses the government was now paying people to plant in place of fescue, and had been shocked to see what the seed went for. Twenty-eight dollars a pound. That seed had to be grown somewhere; a *grass farm,* imagine the gossip that would generate. Next year she might raise no goats at all, depending on the calendar, though many other people surely would, after they heard what she got for hers. And they would discover they couldn't give their goat meat away. Lusa was beginning to see how she would live out her life in Zebulon County. She was going to be a woman men talked about.

This morning after her terrible night Lusa had awakened feeling shucked out and changed altogether, shaken but sound. As if she'd passed through some door into a place where she could walk surely on the ground of her life. The storm had washed the world clean and snuffed out the electricity in the whole county. Here, it shattered the windows on the north side of the house and rattled every ghost out of the rafters, from both sides of the family. She'd spent the night saying prayers in the languages she knew, feeling sure some kind of end was near, before finally falling asleep curled up on Cole's side of the bed with Charles Darwin in her arms and a candle burning on the night table.

And awoke resurrected. She walked out into the yard, astonished by the downed catalpa branches everywhere and the twinkling constellations of broken glass. Those windows had been the antique, wavy glass original to this house. It was amazing. After all the years this place had known, something new could still happen.

In the first confident act of her new life, she called up Little Rickie and hired him to be her part-time assistant farm manager. Over the phone they agreed on ten dollars an hour (the rule of neighbors and family notwithstanding) and a starting date as soon as he could get the parts from Dink Little to fix the baler. He would mow her hay and help her get it in the barn, then take on the task of clearing the multiflora roses out of any field edges her goats couldn't reach. She would not let him spray any weed killer. They'd argued about it briefly, but she'd won, because this wasn't a marital feud as it had been with Cole. It was a condition of employment. Rickie could clear with the bush hog and a hand scythe or not at all, and he was not to touch the woods, not to hunt squirrel or deer or coyote or ginseng. It would be Rickie's job, too, to find tactful ways of keeping the other men in the family from hunting up in the hollow. This was still the Widener farm, but the woods were no longer the Widener woods, Lusa explained. They were nobody's.

The yard she could take care of herself. He'd offered, but she'd said she wanted to do it. She'd awakened today with a deep desire to put the place in order. Not just to drag the downed branches out of the yard, but to cut back the brambles she'd allowed to creep in over the course of the summer. She couldn't explain why, but she felt closed in and needed to strike out, to take up her Weed Eater and pruners like weapons against the encroachment. She'd been working at it fiercely all day, taking a break only briefly in the afternoon, when the call came from her cousin in New York. Then she'd gone right back to it and continued working long into the evening, with the mountain's breath on the back of her neck and moth wings looping circles in the porch light.

She knew, from Rickie and Crystal, that the family had begun to talk about how hard she worked with her hands. They seemed to respect her use of tools. Earlier in the day she'd showed Rickie how to use a sharpened spade instead of Roundup to cut out the field-apple saplings planted by accident in the lawn. After he left, she'd taken a pruning saw to the creeper vines that were trailing up the sides of the house and over into the boxwoods, getting into everything, the way creeper vines did. Then she ripped out every climbing vine from the row of old lilacs so they could bloom again.

Now, in the gathering darkness, she turned finally to tearing out the honeysuckle that had overgrown the garage. There was enough moon reflected off the white clapboards that she could see what she needed to see. It was only honeysuckle, an invasive exotic, nothing sacred. She saw it now for what it was, an introduced garden vine coiling itself tightly around all the green places where humans and wilder creatures conceded to share their lives.

She ripped the vine down from the walls in long strands, letting them fall in coils like rope on the ground at the foot of her ladder. Wherever she ripped the long tendrils from the flank of the building, dark tracks of root hairs remained in place, trailing upward like faint lines of animal tracks traveling silently uphill. Or like long, curving spines left standing after their bodies were stripped suddenly away. She worked steadily in the cool night, tearing herself free, knowing this honeysuckle would persist beyond anything she could ever devise or imagine. It would be back here again, as soon as next summer.

{ **31** }

She paused at the top of the field, inhaling the faint scent of honeysuckle. It seemed odd for someone to be out down there, this late at night. She kept up her pace, walking quickly through the field at the forest's edge, where the moon found the long, silver part in the grass that had led hundreds of other animals along this field edge ahead of her. She was following a trail she couldn't be sure of, and she was used to being sure. But there was no threat here. She lowered her nose and picked up speed, skirting the top of the long field that lined this whole valley, ducking easily through the barbed wires of fences, one after another. She never strayed far out into those fiercely open places, with their dumb clots of moonlit animals, but was careful instead to keep to the edge of the woods with its reassuring scents of leaf mold and rotted fruit. She loved the air after a hard rain, and a solo expedition on which her body was free to run in a gait too fast for companionship. She could stop in the path wherever she needed to take time with a tempting cluster of blackberries or the fascinating news contained in a scent that hadn't been here yesterday.

She was growing a little uneasy, though, this far down the mountain. She had never been able to reconcile herself to the cacophony of sensations that hung in the air around these farms: the restless bickering of hounds penned behind the houses, howling across one valley to another, and the whine of the perilous freeway in the distance, and above all the sharp, outlandish scents of human enterprise. Now, here, where this row of fields turned back up into the next long hollow, there was gasoline wafting up from the road, and something else, a crop dust of some kind that burned her nose, drowning out even the memorable pungency of pregnant livestock in the field below.

She had reached the place where the trail descended into a field of wild apple trees, and she hesitated there. She wouldn't have minded nosing through the hummocks of tall grass and briars for a few sweet, sun-softened apples. That whole field and the orchard below it had a welcoming scent, a noticeable absence of chemical burn in the air, that always made it attractive to birds and field mice, just as surely as it was drawing her right now. But she felt restless and distracted to be this far from her sister and the children. She turned uphill, back toward safer ground where she could disappear inside slicks and shadows if she needed to. The rest of them would be coming up onto the ridge from the next valley over. The easiest way to find them from here would be to follow the crest of this ridge straight up and call for them when she got closer.

She skirted a steep, rocky bank that was fetid with damp moss and hoarded little muddy pools along its base—a good place to let the little ones nose around for crayfish in the daylight, but not now—and then she climbed into the older, more familiar woods. Here was a nutty-scented clearing where years of acorns and hickory nuts had been left buried under the soil by the squirrels that particularly favored this place, for reasons she couldn't fathom.

She'd had meals of squirrel here before, many times, but now it was dark, and they were nervous things, reluctant to leave shelter after a storm like that one. Still, she could hear the much bolder, needly nocturnal banter of flying squirrels high up in the hickory. She crossed back into the woods and then stopped again to put her nose against a giant, ragged old stump that had a garden of acid-scented fungus sprouting permanently from its base. Usually this stump smelled of cat. But she found he had not been here lately.

She paused several more times as she climbed the ridge, once picking up the scent she'd followed for a while earlier tonight but then had lost again, because a rain like that erased nearly everything. It was a male, and particularly interesting because he wasn't part of her clan; he was no one they knew. Another family had been coming down from the north, they knew that; they'd heard them sing at night and known them to be nearby, though never right here before. She paused again, sniffing, but that trail wasn't going to reveal itself to her now, no matter how hard she tried to find it. And on this sweet, damp night at the beginning of the world, that was fine with her. She could be a patient tracker. By the time cold weather came on hard, and then began to soften into mating season, they would all know each other's whereabouts.

She stopped to listen, briefly, for the sound of anything here that might be unexpected. Nothing. It was a still, good night full of customary things. Flying squirrels in every oak within hearing distance; a skunk halfway down the mountainside; a group of turkeys roosting closer by, in the tangled branches of a huge oak that had fallen in the storm; and up ahead somewhere, one of the little owls that barked when the moon was half dark. She trotted quickly on up the ridge, leaving behind the delicate, sinuous trail of her footprints and her own particular scent.

If someone in this forest had been watching her—a man with a gun, for instance, hiding inside a copse of leafy beech trees—he would have noticed how quickly she moved up the path, attending the ground ahead of her feet, so preoccupied with her solitary search that she appeared unaware of his presence. He might have watched her for a long time, until he believed himself and this other restless life in his sight to be the only two creatures left here in this forest of dripping leaves, breathing in some separate atmosphere that was somehow more rarefied and important than the world of air silently exhaled by the leaves all around them.

But he would have been wrong. Solitude is a human presumption. Every quiet step is thunder to beetle life underfoot, a tug of impalpable thread on the web pulling mate to mate and predator to prey, a beginning or an end. Every choice is a world made new for the chosen.